"LIBBY."

Despairing eyes peered at Matt, and a single tear tracked down her cheek.

He had to clear his throat before he could speak. "Tell me about it. I'll help you any way I can."

A desolate smile claimed Libby's lips. "Nobody can help me." She trembled, her shoulders shaking with silent sobs. "Just hold me."

She turned into Matt's comforting arms and laid her cheek against his bare chest, listening to the steady rhythm of his heart. She'd thought she could live with murder on her conscience, but the remorse and guilt wouldn't remain buried.

Matt believed in right and wrong, black and white. If he learned her secret, she would no longer have his friendship. And she needed his quiet strength more than she had ever needed anything before.

Libby raised her head and found his lips a scant few inches from hers. Thunder pounded in her ears, and at the hungry look in Matt's eyes, her fingers curled into the dark hair of his virile chest

WINTER HEARTS

MAUREEN McKADE

AVON BOOKS ◆ NEW YORK

WINTER HEARTS is an original publication of Avon Books. This work has never before appeared in book form. This work is a novel. Any similarity to actual persons or events is purely coincidental.

AVON BOOKS
A division of
The Hearst Corporation
1350 Avenue of the Americas
New York, New York 10019

Copyright © 1997 by Maureen Webster
Inside cover author photo by Bezy Photography
Published by arrangement with the author
Library of Congress Catalog Card Number: 96-96433
ISBN: 0-380-78871-3

First Avon Books Printing: January 1997

AVON TRADEMARK REG. U.S. PAT. OFF. AND IN OTHER COUNTRIES, MARCA REGISTRADA, HECHO EN U.S.A.

Printed in the U.S.A.

RA   10 9 8 7 6 5 4 3 2 1

Chapter 1

❦

Montana Territory
November, 1870

Sheriff Matthew Brandon propped his shoulder against a wooden post. Through the misty rain, his vigilant eyes focused on a young boy oblivious to his scrutiny. Ragged overalls hung on the kid's slight frame, and despite the cold weather, no shoes covered his filthy feet. Dirt streaked his face, but his chin thrust forward like a bulldog's. Furtively, the youngster glanced about and grabbed an apple from the fruit barrel in front of Pearson's Mercantile.

Matt's lips curved downward and he shook his head. Four long strides placed him behind the youngster, and his gloved hand settled on a bony shoulder. "I don't think that apple belongs to you, Dylan."

A cocky grin replaced the surprise on the child's thin face. "What apple, Sheriff?"

Matt was tempted to shake the stuffing out of the urchin. "That apple in your pocket."

Dylan's arrogant smile faltered. "Old man Pearson ain't gonna miss one stupid apple."

"It don't matter if it's one apple or a hundred dollars; stealing is stealing. Put it back."

Muttering, Dylan did as he was ordered.

1

"Now let's go have a chat with your ma."

The boy's face paled. "You can't. Ma's sleeping and she don't like to be woke up."

Matt shrugged. "Maybe you'll learn you can't be taking things that don't belong to you."

Dylan twisted like a trout on a line, but the sheriff's grip was unyielding. "Please, don't tell my ma! She'll beat the livin' daylights out of me."

Matt sighed and considered. "Tell you what. You go on over and sweep the jail out for me, and I won't tell her. How about it?"

"You promise?"

The desperation on his face roughened Matt's voice. "This time, but if you ever try a fool stunt like that again, I will."

"I won't. I promise, Sheriff."

Matt nodded and released the boy.

"I'll head on over to the jail right now and start sweeping." Dylan loped away under the protection of the eaves slanted over the boardwalk.

Matt shook his head and ducked into the store. A cowbell clanged his entrance. Cinnamon, leather, and other indefinable odors tickled his nostrils. Bags of flour and salt and sugar, as well as bolts of fabric and spools of thread, offered a familiar picture. As his boot heels clicked across the plank floor, he pointedly ignored the temptation to check out the new revolvers.

"What can I do for you, Sheriff?"

Matt's gaze settled on a jar of candy that sat on the oak counter. "How about a handful of that taffy?"

Pearson's head bobbed on his scrawny neck. "Anything else I can get you today?"

Matt pointed to a row of leather shoes. "Do you think a pair of them would fit Dylan?"

The shopkeeper's brow furrowed. "You talking about Sadie's young'un?"

"Yep."

Pearson shook his head. "Don't see why you're worried about him. His ma is one of the richest people in town, with her owning the only sporting house in the county."

Matt ground his teeth. "And she don't spend any more on that kid than she has to. You got a pair of shoes or not?"

Pearson's lips drew into a thin line and his nostrils flared. Brushing his hands on a white apron, he stalked around the counter. "No need to get your hackles up, Sheriff. I was just wondering, is all."

The store owner pressed a bony finger to his chin and examined the shoes. He picked out a pair. "These would probably work."

"Put 'em on my bill."

"Sure will, Sheriff." He jabbed his wire spectacles up on his peaked nose. "You hear anything about the new schoolmarm yet?"

"I hear she's coming in any day now."

Pearson stuffed the purchases in a sack. "Wonder what she looks like."

"Why? Your wife ain't been dead but less than a few months."

"Gets lonely at night, if you know what I mean." Pearson elbowed the sheriff.

Matt swallowed his disgust and shrugged. "Get yourself a dog if you want company. It'd be a lot less trouble."

"I suppose with that scar, women don't even give you the time of day, huh?"

A smile lifted the corners of Matt's stiff lips. "Makes for a lot less grief that way. See you later, Pearson."

The cowbell jangled behind Matt and he paused on the boardwalk. Reflectively, he traced the scar that extended from his hairline down the left side of his face, stopping an inch shy of his jaw. The mercantile owner was right: women didn't exactly trip over themselves to get to him.

"Whoa, you ornery, no-good, mealy-mouthed sons of Lucifer!" The stage handler sawed back on the leather reins.

Matt glanced out of the sheltered overhang and grinned. He lowered the brim of his hat and tugged the ankle-length duster tightly about him, then stepped out into the falling rain, and into the mud.

A grizzled man jumped down from the driver's box.

"Howdy, Hiram," Matt greeted.

Hiram drew an arm across his face and grimaced at the lawman. "Don't know how you put up with this dang weather. Seems to me Deer Creek's always wet 'nuff to drown a duck or cold 'nuff to freeze a mule's balls."

Matt chuckled. "Kind of grows on a person, I guess. Besides, this time of year I'm just glad it ain't snow."

"Well, iffen you ask me, it ain't no place to live less'n you're a fish." The jehu reached up and opened the coach's door. "This here is Deer Creek, ma'am."

A graceful hand encased in a soft kidskin glove accepted Hiram's assistance. A shapely ankle, followed by a flurry of starched skirts, came into view, and Matt's eyebrows raised a notch. His gaze traveled upward from the pleasant sight and collided with wary eyes as green and dewy as a mountain valley in the spring.

Her practical black shoes sank deep into the mud, and in two quick steps, the slender woman joined Matt on the boardwalk.

With his thumb and forefinger, Matt lowered the brim of his hat to conceal his scar, and cocked his head. "Welcome to Deer Creek, ma'am."

Her shuttered gaze flickered over the star on his chest and back to his face. "Thank you, Sheriff. Could you tell me where I may rent a room?"

He scowled at her brusque manner. "I suppose I could."

Lines of tight control etched her features. "Well?"

"Lenore Potts runs a boardinghouse just down the street."

"Thank you." Her glance flitted down the muddy boardwalk.

Matt studied the drab clothing that failed to disguise her shapely figure. "You aiming to stick around?"

She blinked as if surprised he was still there. "Yes, I am. I'm the new schoolteacher."

"You're Libby O'Hanlon?"

"What's so surprising about that?"

"I figured she'd be a slip of a thing with a squeaky voice."

"I'm sorry to have disappointed you," she said, not sounding at all contrite. She brushed an errant auburn curl from her forehead.

Matt smiled self-consciously. "Oh, I ain't disappointed, ma'am. I'm just sorry the kids are going to lose another teacher."

Elizabeth took a quick step back. "I don't understand. I'm not going anywhere."

Her voice was edged with tension, and Matt noticed a haunted expression had crept into her eyes. He frowned. "I just meant that women are scarce in these parts, ma'am. That's why we ain't been able to keep a teacher more than a month."

Her shoulders squared, fire replacing the shadows in her eyes. "I have no intention of ever marrying, Sheriff."

Matt nodded. "I sure hope so, for them kids' sake. They need to be learned reading and writing."

"They need to be *taught* reading and writing," she corrected.

Matt's face warmed. "That's what I said."

"Now, how do I get to Mrs. Potts's establishment?"

"Go down the street about a block. Boardinghouse is on your right, surrounded by a white fence. You can't miss it."

She smoothed the wrinkled traveling jacket over her hips. "Thank you," she said with a strained voice, then turned to Hiram. "Could you have someone bring my trunk over to the boardinghouse?"

"Yes, ma'am," he replied.

Matt's gaze followed her slow progress across the muddy street. When she was safely across, he unconsciously let out the breath caught in his lungs.

"Is she the new schoolteacher?"

Matt shifted his attention to the reed-thin man who had joined him. "Sure is. Miss Libby O'Hanlon."

Dr. Elias Clapper filled a chipped pipe with tobacco from a worn black pouch and sparked a match against a fingernail. He puffed on the stem until a steady stream of smoke created a blue cloud above them. "I give her a month, tops."

Matt scratched his three-day whisker growth. "She says she ain't planning on getting married."

"That's what they all say."

"I got a feeling she means it."

Pale blue eyes twinkled below bushy iron-gray brows. "Sounds like she made quite an impression on you, Matt."

"Yeah, like a porcupine makes when you sit on it," Matt growled.

Eli tamped the tobacco down in the pipe's bowl. "Seems to me you had the perfect opportunity to be the first in line."

Matt shook his head. "I told you, Eli, ain't a woman like her going to look twice at a man like me."

"You worry too much about that damned scar."

"It ain't just that. Hell, she's a teacher. I can barely write my name, and I can't read more'n but a few words."

Eli shrugged. "Ask her to tutor you. That's a good way to get to know her."

"Nope. I ain't a complete fool. I seen how she looked at me."

"Maybe you only saw what you expected to see." Eli pointed at the bag in Matt's hand. "What do you have there?"

"Nothing much," he replied evasively.

Eli peeked in the sack and his eyes narrowed. "Those shoes look a bit small for you."

"They ain't for me." Matt sighed like a preacher caught in a whorehouse. "They're for Dylan. He's running around barefoot and it's nearly winter. He's going to catch his death if he don't start dressing warmer."

They strolled down the boardwalk.

"That mother of his isn't worth two bits," Eli commented. "Sleeping all day and then working all night. It isn't the right way to be raising a child."

"She should've never kept Dylan," Matt said. "She should've found a family who could raise him proper-like. The way he's headed, I'm gonna end up throwing him in jail some day."

"Maybe not. Seems to me you've taken a personal interest in his welfare. Your own son would've been about Dylan's age, wouldn't he?"

Matt ignored the question and paused in front of the jailhouse. "Are you going to eat at Lenore's tonight?"

Eli opened his mouth as if to pursue the subject of Matt's son, but shrugged instead. "As long as nothing comes up. Why don't you come on over, too?"

Despite Miss O'Hanlon's chilly reserve, her auburn hair and jade eyes tempted him. "We'll see."

Matt nodded to Eli and stepped into the brick building. He noted the dusty air and waved a hand in front of his face. "How're you doing, Dylan?"

The boy sneezed and rubbed his nose. "Don't you ever clean in here, Sheriff?"

"Don't see no need to." Matt tossed his battered hat and the package on the pile of papers and food-encrusted tin plates that covered his desk. The chair creaked beneath his weight. "I know right where everything is."

"Really?" Skepticism dripped from the single word.

Matt combed his fingers through his shaggy brown hair. "Yep. You see, I figure it doesn't matter if it's clean or not, as long as a man can find what he wants. And I ain't lost nothing yet."

Dylan leaned against the handle of the broom. "So you found the wanted poster on that man who was at my ma's place the other night?"

Matt shifted in his chair. "That wasn't important. I know where the important stuff is."

The boy grinned insolently. "Then you found the telegram you got last week from the marshal in Helena? You said that was important."

Matt squirmed a little more. "Well, no, I didn't find that neither."

Dylan shoved coal-black bangs out of his eyes. "Then why don't you clean your office?"

Leave it to a kid to use logic. "Maybe I like it this way."

"Don't seem right that you can use that excuse and I can't."

"When you get as old as me, you won't have to clean your room either."

Dylan snorted. "I ain't ever going to get as old as you."

Matt aimed an index finger at the boy. "You keep getting into trouble, and you ain't even going to get out of knee pants."

"I don't ever wear sissy knee pants," Dylan shot back indignantly.

The sheriff hid a grin behind his hand and glanced about the room. "Looks like you done a mighty good job sweeping the place out."

"I worked real hard. You aren't going to tell my ma about the apple, right?"

"I promised, didn't I? And because you did such a good job, I got a couple things for you." Matt fished in the cloth sack and withdrew the shoes.

Dylan stared at the black leather shoes and his mouth fell open. He shook his head. "I can't take these, Sheriff."

"Sure you can. You earned them."

"Ma won't like it. She don't like me taking hand-outs."

"You tell her that you worked an honest-to-goodness job and earned them, and if she don't believe you, send her on over to me. Go ahead, try 'em on."

After a moment's hesitation, Dylan accepted the shoes from Matt's outstretched hand. He plopped himself down on the freshly swept floor, tugged them on, and wiggled his toes. "They're a little big."

"If your feet was as big as your mouth, they'd fit just fine." Matt handed Dylan the last item in the bag. "I figured you might like some candy, too."

Dylan's bright blue eyes widened. "Taffy! That's my favorite."

Matt leaned back in his chair and steepled his fingers. "I thought so. It was my favorite, too."

The boy thrust one at Matt. "Want a piece?"

Matt shook his head but stopped in midmotion. He nodded and winked. "Why not? Nothing says I can't like taffy anymore just because I'm grown up."

They chewed with open mouths, grinning at each other like two conspirators.

Dylan swallowed the chunk of candy. "I don't think you're so mean."

Matt blinked. "What do you mean?"

"Everybody says that you're mean as a skunk without a peter."

Matt pressed his lips together and smothered a chuckle.

"They say that nobody would dare cross a man that looks as mean as you," Dylan continued, seemingly unaware of Matt's mirth.

"As long as folks don't break the law, I don't care what they think of me."

"Folks say you got that scar in a duel fighting over a woman." Dylan stared at Matt, his expression asking for a denial.

A muscle twitched in Matt's jaw. "Folks is wrong. I got it in the war."

Dylan's eyes glowed. "You fought against them dirty Rebs?"

"I *was* a 'dirty Reb.'"

The boy's adam's apple bobbed. "I didn't mean nothin'."

"That's all right, Dylan. I came up here after the war to get away from all that, so I guess I ain't a Reb anymore." He straightened in his chair. "Don't you think it's about time you headed home? Your ma's probably looking for you."

Dylan's expression told Matt he'd rather face a nest of rattlesnakes than confront his mother. He sighed in resignation. "I s'pect you're right."

He clomped to the door and paused, glancing down at the new shoes. "I sure hope I grow into them fast."

Matt joined the boy at the door and settled a hand on his shoulder. "I reckon you'll grow into them faster'n you can say Texas two-step. Remember what I told you—if your ma don't like you having them shoes, have her come talk to me."

"I'll come back tomorrow to sweep again." He paused as if he realized he sounded too eager. "I mean, I do owe you for the shoes and all."

"Sounds good, partner. Hurry on home so you don't get soaked."

Dylan shuffled out and went down the boardwalk, then stopped and turned to look at Matt. With his threadbare overalls and forlorn gaze, Dylan looked like a lost puppy. After a few moments, he shrugged and shambled away.

Matt leaned a forearm against the doorjamb and hooked his thumb in the well-worn holster around his denim-clad hips. His gaze searched the gun-metal gray horizon, but the mountains were hidden by layers of snow-bloated clouds. He hated these dreary days when his only companions were memories.

Maybe he should take his own advice and get a dog.

Libby O'Hanlon scampered across the street, her breath wisping in the cool air. She paused in front of the boardinghouse and shifted the portmanteau from one gloved hand to the other. A chilly wind whipped under her layers of petticoats, and she shivered with cold. And fear. When she'd spotted the sheriff's badge, it was as if a fist had closed around her lungs, suffocating her. The last few months of running and hiding like a hunted animal would have been for nothing if he had recognized her. But he hadn't. She was still safe. For now.

Taking a deep, shaky breath, Libby rapped her knuckles against the door.

Footsteps crossed a wooden floor. The door swung open, and a woman as stout as a whiskey barrel confronted her.

"I'm looking for a room," Libby stated.

The woman's round face split with a welcoming smile and she ushered Libby inside. "You've come to the right place. Goodness gracious, you're chilled to the bone. We'd best get you warmed up before you catch your death. I tell you, this weather up here is about as predictable as one of them French soufflés. I mean, you just never know what to expect when you open the door. But then, that's what's so exciting about living here. Kind of a change from that boring routine of city living, don't you think?"

Libby nodded, though her head swirled with Gatling-gun chatter. "Yes, I suppose. Are you Mrs. Potts?"

The woman flattened a sausage-fingered hand to her ample bosom. "My goodness, I haven't even introduced myself, have I? Lenore Potts is my name, and you'd best call me Lenore if you know what's good for you." The twinkle in the older woman's eyes belied her threat.

"I'm Libby O'Hanlon."

"The new schoolteacher! Why, blessed be the day. I swear, we've gone through two teachers since September. Just can't keep a one. There's a shortage of good women hereabouts, and the men just gather around them like bees to honey as soon as they arrive. Next thing you know, they up and marry, leaving the children behind." She paused for a breath. "And look at you, pretty as a button. One gander at you and the menfolk are going to trip over themselves to see who can propose first."

Libby stiffened. "As I told your sheriff, I have no plans of marrying, so you can rest assured the children will receive an education."

"You met Sheriff Brandon? Hope you weren't scared off by that horrible scar. A lot of folks think he's no better than the outlaws in his jail, but you can't go by looks, that's what I say. Why I knew a fella once, as handsome as the day was long, but underneath them good looks he was rottener than month-old apple pie. Beauty's only skin deep, and that's the truth of it. Not that the sheriff is ugly; no sirree, because he's a fine-looking specimen as men go. Shoot, once you get to know him a little better, you won't even notice that little scar. And I'll tell you a secret; if I was a few years younger, I'd set my hat for him myself. But don't you go telling Eli."

Libby's head spun. "Excuse me, Mrs. Potts, but—"

"Now what did I tell you? My name is Lenore." The older woman smiled apologetically. "I been doing it again, haven't I? Eli keeps telling me I should do more listening than talking, but it just doesn't seem to sink in. I guess I been talking for so long, it's near impossible to change now. And here you are, tired and wet and wanting a room to lie down and get some rest. Come along, honey, and I'll show you which one you can have."

Lenore led Libby up a wooden staircase and to the first room at the top of the stairs. She swung the door open. "I hope it'll do."

Libby stepped inside. A fire burned low in the hearth, warding off the chill of the damp day. A round, braided rug covered a portion of the shiny hardwood floor. A tan ceramic pitcher and basin painted with whirls of intertwined flowers sat on an oak stand. Situated in the far corner, below one of the two windows, was a feather bed, topped by a patchwork quilt. A Boston rocker with a seat cushion stood next to the bed, and Libby envisioned many quiet evenings in the chair.

Her attention returned to the landlady. "It's lovely, Lenore. It reminds me of the room I had as a young girl."

Lenore smiled broadly and her eyes nearly disappeared into folds of skin. "I thought you might like it. Why don't you get out of those wet clothes while I put water on for your bath. You look like you just spent the better part of a week in a stagecoach."

Libby smiled for the first time since she'd arrived in Deer Creek. "I have. And a bath sounds heavenly."

"Have you eaten anything today?"

"I had some soup and bread at the last stage stop."

"If you get hungry before supper, you just come on

down to the kitchen. There's always something for hungry folks to chew on." Lenore turned and faced Libby again. "By the way, supper is at six. Breakfast is served at seven, and lunch at noon. The cost of the room includes all three meals."

"That sounds just fine. Thank you."

The door closed behind Lenore.

Libby sank onto the bed and closed her eyes, grateful there was no motion involved. After five days of continuous travel by stagecoach, her muscles were stiff and sore. The roads from North Platte were alternately muddy and frozen, and she was told she'd been lucky they hadn't run into any blizzards on the route. However, Libby's only concern was that she'd arrived without discovery.

When she'd descended the stage and seen the lawman, Libby had been certain she'd run out of luck. Fortunately, there'd been no recognition in the sheriff's rough-hewn face. In fact, she thought she'd detected a note of admiration in his gruff manner.

She crossed the floor, sinking to her knees in front of the hearth. Pulling the sodden hat off her head, Libby regarded the plumed creation in her hand a moment. The feather drooped, and the small brim had lost its stiffness. She wrinkled her nose, then tossed the hat into the fireplace. The hungry fire devoured it with a flare of orange.

Staring at the hypnotic flames, she wished her tattered past could be as easily discarded as the ruined hat. She closed her eyes, remembering the day that had changed her life forever.

Elizabeth's heart thumped against her breast, and her breath hissed through parted lips. Her gaze darted frantically about the room, but there was no escape.

Dear God, don't let him come in here.

But the knob slowly turned, and the heavy

mahogany door creaked open. An ominous black silhouette filled the opening.

"Come out, bitch! I know you're in here." The man's voice rumbled across Elizabeth's eardrums.

She bit her lower lip and tasted blood. Fear slithered down her back like a twisting snake, and she held back the scream that slid across her tongue.

A string of slurred curses erupted. "Where the hell are you? If I have to come looking for you, you're going to regret it!"

A match scraped and flared in the darkness. Elizabeth curled into a tighter ball to escape the traitorous glare of the lamp's yellow light, her head pounding.

"Where are you, slut?"

The man's voice was closer. A polished black boot brushed her skirt. His cloying cologne curled in Elizabeth's throat, and her breath lodged someplace between her lungs and mouth.

Fingers like a vise jerked her to her feet, and she clenched her teeth in pain.

"You can't escape me, Elizabeth. Remember the last time you tried?"

Her breath exploded as she kicked his shin. He dropped her like a boiling pot.

"Bitch!" He backhanded her.

Elizabeth's calf struck a chair, sending her sprawling on the Aubusson rug. Before she could regain her breath, the man hauled her to her feet.

"Please, Harrison, no. I didn't mean to do it!" she gasped. The side of her face throbbed, and she knew his palm print was etched in red on her cheek.

Harrison Thompson's gray eyes darkened. His breath was sour, like beer left in the sun. "You were displaying your breasts to the men!"

"I wasn't! I swear it, Harrison. I was only helping."

Harrison's hand tightened around Elizabeth's neck. "A lady leaves her blouse buttoned up completely. Only she-bitches in heat act like you did."

"It was warm and it was only one button! I didn't do anything wrong." Elizabeth's fingers wound around her husband's forearms. "He was hurt and the cut had to be sutured."

"How many times have I told you to stay away from the men? Your place is here, not out there. You are my wife, and as such, you will not work like a common tramp."

"You knew I was a doctor when you married me. You said I could continue to practice medicine. You promised!"

A vein throbbed in Harrison's neck and his bloated face reddened. "That was four years ago! You are no longer an idealistic girl. You are the lady of this house, and I expect you to act like it. I'll punish you if you don't behave as your station demands."

The rage faded as his lewd gaze roamed over the slope of her chest. With one hand, he cupped a breast and his cruel fingers twisted the nipple.

Elizabeth blinked back tears and stifled a cry. "No, Harrison! Please, don't—"

"Don't what, my lovely little slut? I thought all whores liked it rough." He slid his hand from her bust to her bodice. He jerked the blouse's material aside, sending tiny pearl buttons dancing across the marble floor.

Harrison gripped both her wrists in one hand and raised them high above her head. Each shaky breath Elizabeth drew pressed her bosom against the thin camisole, and his glacial eyes lit with *lust. With his other hand, he rent her skirt from waist to hem and tossed it aside.*

"You know what I want you to do, Elizabeth."

"No! No more, Harrison. I won't do it!"

"You will, bitch, or I'll kill you!"

The insanity in her husband's eyes convinced Elizabeth he spoke the truth. She nodded. "All right. I'll take them off, but you have to let go of my wrists."

Gauging her sincerity, Harrison slowly released her hands. He took a step back, and she removed her stockings. Elizabeth's hands trembled and her cheek stung where he had slapped her. As Harrison rubbed the bulge in his trousers, she knew he pictured her naked bottom reddened by his palm.

She hated him seeing her like this, trembling and fearful of his power. She hated the way he stared at her, like a snake hypnotizing its victim.

She hated him.

Harrison's gaze traveled up Elizabeth's slender figure. She raised her camisole and his breath quickened. She wondered if her back, still scarred by a whipping months ago, intensified his perverse pleasure. Sweat oozed out of his pores, a few droplets gaining enough momentum to roll down his face.

His leer scorched her, but Elizabeth forced herself to move slowly. She had to remain calm and not give in to the hysteria that battered her self-control. Only one thought remained constant in the frenzied stream of fear and rage: she would not allow him to rape her again. She vowed he would never again vent his anger with a beating, then slake his lust with her unwilling body.

Elizabeth's frantic gaze settled on the fireplace poker. She inched toward it and leaned over as if to lower her drawers. Reaching forward, she clutched the cold metal. She tightened her grasp on the weapon, its weight giving her confidence. It was her only chance.

"Hurry up, Elizabeth. I won't wait forever!"

Her palm grew slippery around the iron and the room shimmered. She swallowed the sickness, blinking to bring the room back in focus.

A hand clamped her shoulder and spun her about.

"What the hell?" Harrison demanded.

With strength fueled by terror, Elizabeth swung the iron poker. The rod struck Harrison's head with a dull thud. He crumpled to the floor.

The poker slipped from Elizabeth's hand, her fingers tingling from the force of the blow. Shock left her weightless, as if a stranger occupied her body, and her mind floated above the gruesome scene. Below Harrison's head, a scarlet stain seeped across the white floor like a macabre meandering river.

Dear God, I've killed him! She hadn't meant to. She had only wanted to stop him.

Her gaze skittered about the huge parlor. The servants had long since gone to bed. What would she do? What could she do? She would be hung if she stayed.

Shock gave way to desperation. Keeping her eyes averted from her husband's still body, Elizabeth ran.

A knock sounded on the door, startling her. Her heart hammering against her ribs, she called out with a shaky voice, "Who's there?"

"Mrs. Potts sent me up with the tub, ma'am."

Libby's shoulders sagged in relief and despair. Would she ever know peace again?

* * *

After her bath, Libby descended the stairs with hesitant footsteps. As her stomach rumbled, she unerringly followed the smell of cooking food. "Can I help you with anything?"

Lenore whirled around and clapped a hand to her stained apron bodice. "My goodness, you took a couple years off my life, honey."

"I'm sorry. I thought I'd see if I could help."

The robust woman placed a huge bowl mounded with mashed potatoes in Libby's grasp. "Take this on into the dining room and put it on the table. I'll get the meat and join you in a minute."

Libby balanced the heavy dish in her hands and used her hip to open the swinging door between the kitchen and dining room. Three men pushed back their chairs and stood. Libby froze.

Lenore entered the room with a platter of roast beef and rescued her. "Miss Libby O'Hanlon, this is George Johnson, Virgil Tanner, and Dr. Elias Clapper. Gentlemen, this is Deer Creek's new schoolteacher."

Appearing as somber as his black broadcloth suit, Johnson held a chair for Libby. "Won't you sit down, Miss O'Hanlon?"

"Th-thank you, Mr. Johnson." Libby set the bowl of potatoes on the table and accepted the seat beside him.

Lenore sat at the head of the table, with Dr. Clapper to her right.

The men's gazes scorched Libby and panic threatened her precarious composure. She wrapped her trembling hands together, hiding them in her lap.

Johnson tucked his cloth napkin into his shirt collar. "What do you think of our fine town so far, Miss O'Hanlon?"

"I—" Libby's voice cracked and she cleared her throat. "I really haven't been here long enough to form an opinion."

"Surely you must have a first impression."

Libby raised her head and forced her momentary alarm to recede.

"It's wet and it's cold," she replied curtly. *With enough mud to make a hog think he'd died and gone to heaven.*

Johnson frowned and his lips drew together.

"At least she's honest," Dr. Clapper interjected. Kindly blue eyes studied Libby. "Arriving this time of year must be a shock if you're not used to Montana winters."

Libby forced her hand to remain steady as she spooned green beans onto her plate. "Actually, I'm not unfamiliar with cold winters. It's just that the dampness is a little strange."

"So where are you from, Miss O'Hanlon?" Tanner asked.

"Ohio."

"What brings you this far north?"

Once again, Lenore rescued Libby. "Would you let the poor girl eat? She hasn't had a decent meal in days. Go ahead, honey, dig right in. These lummoxes can hold off with all their fool questions until you've filled your belly."

"I am a bit hungry," Libby admitted.

She picked a golden brown biscuit from the towering plate and spread pale butter across the surface. The first bite melted in her mouth. Libby closed her eyes in ecstasy and savored the delicate flavor. It seemed like forever since she'd eaten a homemade meal. Eating hot food fresh from the kitchen and sitting at a table with others was an experience she hadn't realized she'd missed.

She swallowed the flaky morsel, and opened her eyes. The sheriff's broad shoulders filled the doorway. The biscuit settled like a rock in the pit of her stomach.

"Hope I ain't too late for some of that fine cooking of yours, Lenore," he said.

"Howdy, Matt. You just pull up a chair over there by Libby, and I'll grab you a plate and a cup of coffee." Lenore bustled into the kitchen.

From beneath lowered lashes Libby observed the sheriff, who appeared as rumpled as he had earlier. His tawny hair was plastered to his forehead and a hat line encircled his crown. The sleeves on his wrinkled tan shirt were rolled up to his elbows, exposing an undershirt that covered his sinewy forearms.

Despite her efforts to remain aloof, Libby allowed her gaze to travel down his powerful chest and trim waist. A holster, held in place by a rawhide strip tied around a muscled thigh, accented his lean hips. Her examination moved upward to his weathered face, planed with well-defined contours and angles. An uncertain look softened the stony visage.

Matt settled on the vacant chair next to her. "Evening, Miss O'Hanlon," he greeted with a tentative smile.

With a dry lump in her throat, Libby bobbed her head.

Lenore returned and set a plate and a cup of steaming coffee in front of the sheriff. "You dig right in, Matt. There's more'n enough for everyone."

"Thanks, Lenore. Looks mighty good, as usual."

Libby's appetite fled with the arrival of the lawman. She sipped her coffee and nervously tucked a few loose strands of hair into her chignon, concentrating on the talk that swirled around her.

"Glad to see you made it, Matt," Eli said. "Must've gotten your work caught up, eh?"

"Something like that." Matt's hooded gaze moved to Tanner. "How's that ranch of yours doing, Virgil?"

"Not bad, considering winter's coming. The almanac says it's going to be a tough one," the leather-faced rancher replied.

"How many head of cattle do you have, Mr. Tanner?" Libby asked.

"About four hundred. Plan to have a thousand in five years. Maybe you'd like to take a ride out to the ranch with me sometime. The buildings are just getting started, but in no time it'll be something to see."

"Oh, no thank you, Mr. Tanner. I'm sure my teaching responsibilities will take most of my time."

"If you're interested, Miss O'Hanlon, I could escort you about town and give you a tour of the bank. I'm a clerk there," Johnson spoke up.

"That's very kind of you, Mr. Johnson, but as I said, I believe I'll be much too busy for such things."

Libby took another bite of her biscuit and glanced over to find the sheriff studying her. Despite the warning in her head to look away, Libby's gaze didn't waver. She searched his eyes, expecting to see what she'd seen in Harrison's. However, there was no hungry lust, only a wariness which reflected her own.

"Libby tells me she's not interested in getting hitched," Lenore said. "Why, when I was her age, I was married and had a couple young'uns swinging from my apron strings. But I suppose times are a'changing. A woman can be a teacher or a nurse and don't have to get married if she's a mind."

"She could even run her own boardinghouse," Eli commented with a quirked eyebrow.

"You know I've worked too long to give all this up, Eli. I'm not about to get hitched again." Lenore looked at Libby. "Eli's been coming around for a couple years now. Keeps thinking he's going to wear me down, but I like being independent."

Libby nodded. "I value my independence, too."

Johnson dabbed at his face with his napkin. "But a woman was made to be a wife and have children. It says so in the Bible."

"Seems to me a lot of them women in the Bible weren't married neither," Matt said. "Look at Martha. She lived with her brother and took care of him." He aimed his fork at Johnson. "Nothing says a woman has to get married if she don't want to."

Libby's eyebrows arched. "I'm perfectly capable of defending my position, Sheriff."

"I didn't mean to insult you, Miss O'Hanlon. I was only saying what I think."

Heat suffused her cheeks. "I'm sorry. It's just that I'm not accustomed to men agreeing with my sentiments."

"I always figured a person's got the right to choose their own life. Fact is, I respect you and Lenore for doing what you do."

"Thank you," Libby replied after a moment of surprise. Though she knew she should ignore him, she studied Matt through lowered lashes. She tried to see his scar, but he kept his head at an angle. It occurred to her that he did it purposely, to hide the disfigurement from prying eyes. She glanced away, ashamed by her morbid curiosity.

"Could you pass me the beans, ma'am?" Matt asked Libby.

She handed the china bowl to him. As he turned to accept it, Libby spied the mark on the side of his face. The jagged white slash followed the edge of his hairline, ending at the curve of his jaw. She imagined the pain he must have endured when he received the wound, and her stomach clenched.

"Did Jack Windler's murderer ever get caught?" Virgil Tanner asked Matt.

"Yep," he replied. "I got a telegram from the sheriff in Corrine telling me he had Rosen in custody. Seems Rosen killed another man down there."

"Do you figure he'll be hung?" Tanner asked.

"More'n likely, though it's a mite late. He should've

been hung a few weeks ago, before he killed anyone else. Murderers are about the lowest kind of vermin there is."

A piece of roast stuck in Libby's throat, and she choked. A hand pounded her back, dislodging the chunk. She swallowed and the meat slid downward.

"Are you all right, Miss O'Hanlon?" Matt asked.

Libby dabbed her tearing eyes with her napkin. "I think so," she said hoarsely.

Matt returned to his chair. "You'd best chew that meat a little better," he suggested roughly.

Libby nodded, though no amount of chewing would have helped. If the sheriff knew she was a killer, he wouldn't have been so quick to act. A rope or a piece of Lenore's roast beef: it wouldn't have mattered to him how she atoned for her crime.

"Is everybody ready for dessert?" Lenore asked.

"As long as it's your apple pie," Eli replied with a wink.

Playfully, Lenore slapped his shoulder. "If it was up to you, it would always be apple pie. But, then, it's my own fault for spoiling you. Come along and help me, Libby."

Libby pushed back her chair and stood, surprised when the sheriff also rose. She had assumed by his appearance that he had few manners. Harrison had been a handsome man, and courteous, but she'd later learned of the evil hidden beneath the thin veneer of propriety.

Libby shivered with remembered fear. She glanced up to catch the sheriff's steady gaze upon her, and straightened her spine. She followed Lenore into the kitchen, the hair prickling at the back of her neck.

"Could you get the plates? They're in there." Lenore pointed to Libby's right.

"Of course." She opened the cupboard door and retrieved six plates. She set them beside the pie tins on the kitchen table.

"Are you feeling all right, honey? You look a bit peaked," Lenore commented, slicing a pie into fourths.

"I'm fine, Lenore."

"Maybe choking like you did scared you some. I was eating this steak one time, and next thing you know I couldn't breathe. My late husband, Willard, God rest his soul, up and squeezes my waist real tight. Now I tell you, that meat just went flying across the room." She shuddered. "I'll always remember what it was like not to be able to get any air into my lungs."

Libby smiled. "It was a bit scary, but I'm all right now."

"Did I tell you Mayor Beidler and his wife are coming by to meet you this evening?"

Libby's breath caught in her throat. "No, you didn't."

"Adelaide Beidler will want to check you out. She personally inspects all the new teachers. Fact is, she'll be wanting to see your papers, too."

The dessert plate slipped from Libby's hand. Shards of china and pieces of apple pie spattered across the kitchen floor.

What papers?

Chapter 2

Matt burst into the kitchen and glanced between the two women. Libby knelt beside the mess she'd made.

"Everything all right in here?" he asked.

"Fine," Lenore assured him. "Libby just dropped a plate. I don't think that's a lawbreaking offense, so you can go back in there with the other menfolk."

"I'm sorry, Lenore," Libby whispered.

Matt stepped toward Libby. "You're white as a sheet, Miss O'Hanlon. Are you feeling sickly?"

Two spots of color appeared in her cheeks. "I'll be fine, Sheriff."

Matt scowled and angled his head to hide the scar from Libby's view. "I didn't mean nothing, Miss O'Hanlon. It's just that you don't look too good."

Her gaze remained averted from his. "Thank you for your concern, Sheriff. Perhaps I am feeling a bit out of sorts. After I get this cleaned up, I think I'll go lie down."

"I'll take care of this, honey. You just go on up to your room," Lenore volunteered.

"I'll help her," Matt interjected. "You go and take that pie out afore you got a rebellion on your hands."

Lenore glanced between Matt and Libby. She nodded and scuttled out of the kitchen.

Matt squatted down beside Libby. She inched away, obviously revolted by his disfigurement. He cursed the scar. She was so close he could smell lilacs in her securely bound hair. She wore a plain brown skirt with a dull yellow blouse, but Matt recognized the womanly curves beneath the unflattering clothing.

As he picked up a piece of broken china, his fingers brushed Libby's sleeve. Her mouth parted slightly and the tip of her pink tongue brushed her lower lip. Matt concentrated on the morsels of apple pie littered across the floor. He noticed an apple slice stuck to Libby's stocking-clad ankle, and he reached for it.

Libby flinched and her hand lashed out, grazing Matt's arm, but he barely noticed it. He stared at Libby. She hunched her shoulders and scooted away from him like a crayfish darting under a rock. Her freckles stood in stark contrast across her pale cheeks, and her eyes resembled those of a caged animal.

"I'm sorry, Miss O'Hanlon," he said gently. She remained immobile. "Miss O'Hanlon. Libby?" Why didn't she answer him? Was she that sickened by his scar? Or was her reaction caused by something else? During the war, he'd seen empty gazes in men who'd witnessed horrors too terrible for their minds to comprehend. But accidently touching her ankle wasn't so horrible, was it?

She blinked and recognition seeped back into her expression. She scrambled to her feet. "How dare you!"

Matt blinked at the abrupt transformation. He pushed himself up. "I was just helping you clean up this mess."

"By touching my—my ankle? I'd hardly call that helping. It was more like taking advantage of a helpless woman."

Matt snorted. "Helpless! You're about as helpless as a she-grizzly protecting her young. And I got news for you, lady, you ain't that sightly that a man's going to lose his head over you. There was a piece of pie on your ankle."

"Oh."

At her subdued reply, Matt regretted his sharp retort, but he couldn't apologize. He didn't dare let her know he had wanted to remove the pins that bound her hair, and explore the curves beneath her proper clothing.

He gritted his teeth against the vision his imagination created. "I think we got it about cleaned up."

"Thank you, Sheriff. I'll take care of the rest."

"You're welcome, Miss O'Hanlon." He paused, still puzzled by her strange behavior. "Are you sure you're all right?"

Libby fingered the broken china, and her gaze skittered from the floor to the cupboards behind Matt. "Just fine, Sheriff. Why don't you go on into the dining room and join the others?"

"Ain't you coming in for pie?"

The corners of her lips quirked upward. "I think we just cleaned up my piece. But that doesn't mean you have to miss out on yours."

The tilt of her stubborn chin was softened by the bare hint of a smile. Her green eyes twinkled. He stared at her full, sensual lips, then quickly looked away, wondering if he appeared as foolish as he felt.

He splayed a hand through his collar-length hair and listened to the voices from the dining room, then scowled. "Sounds like the mayor and his wife are here."

Libby frowned. It appeared she was about to ask him a question, but she remained silent. She studied the door leading to the dining room with a troubled gaze.

"Have you met the Beidlers yet?" Matt asked.

"No." Libby dropped the dish fragments in a round

barrel. "And I don't believe I'll meet them this evening either. Good night, Sheriff."

Libby whirled around and slipped through the door that opened into the front hallway. Pausing in the doorway, she faced Matt one more time. "Thanks for your help, Sheriff. And your concern."

Puzzled, Matt stared after Libby. He prided himself on his ability to size up a person in one measuring glance, but he couldn't figure her and that worried him. One moment she seemed scared of her own shadow, and the next she acted like a tomcat defending his territory. It made little sense, and Matt didn't like mysteries in his town. Not even one as beautiful as Miss Libby O'Hanlon.

Libby tiptoed up the stairs and into her room. She closed the door with a quiet click, breathing a sigh of relief. She'd escaped. She'd expected to be questioned about her teaching credentials, though she hadn't figured it would be the first day she arrived in town.

Libby settled into the Boston rocker and wrapped her arms around her waist. What was she going to do? The only certificate she had was her medical degree, and nobody must know about that. She had no doubt Harrison's housekeeper had given the lawmen a detailed description of her, including her skills as a doctor. It was even possible Sheriff Brandon had a paper on her in his office. Libby shook her head. No; if he had recognized her, he would have arrested her.

She could lie. She could tell the mayor and his wife she'd lost her papers on the long stage trip. She had traveled many miles, and it wasn't impossible to lose one bag in that distance.

Another lie, another foot deeper into the pit of deceptions. But it was either lie or be hung for killing her husband, and Libby had no desire to walk through the fires of hell any earlier than she had to.

She had to keep her distance from the sheriff. He

would undoubtedly receive information on her, and despite his coarse speech, she suspected a shrewd mind lay beneath the unpolished surface. She had glimpsed the intelligence in his somber eyes and it made her uncomfortable. Her first impression of him had been that of a backwoodsman lacking common courtesy. He hadn't even removed his hat when she'd stepped out of the stagecoach. Yet this evening he'd been a gentleman, and there had been traces of kindness in his demeanor.

Until he'd touched her ankle.

Remembered fear rippled across her skin. Libby stood and paced. Perhaps the contact had been an innocent gesture, but the terror it unleashed reminded Libby how much Harrison had stolen from her. At the top of that long list was trust.

She paused in front of the fireplace and bent down to toss another log into the orange flames. Sparks popped, and glowing cinders erupted. Libby sank to her knees in front of the blaze, holding her trembling hands out to the warmth. As she stared at them they blurred, replaced by the image of Matt's tanned fingers and blunt, clean nails. The calluses on his palms told Libby he was a man who had lived a hard life. Yet she suspected those same hands could gentle a colt or soothe a child's pain. Or tenderly make love to a woman.

She closed her eyes but found no respite from the sensual image. She remembered the tangy smell of leather and horses that seemed as much a part of him as his quiet strength. The intensity in his amber eyes both attracted and repelled her. She had never met a man so full of contradictions.

Her eyes flew open. What was she doing? He represented the law, and she was a murderer. She was also a highly educated woman, while the sheriff had probably never seen the inside of a classroom. As long as she used her brains, she could keep one step ahead of Sheriff Matthew Brandon.

However, if she allowed her traitorous emotions to participate in the battle of wits, Libby wasn't so certain she could maintain her advantage.

Lenore waved a wooden spoon at Libby. "Now, you dress warm. These Montana winters are pretty rough on folks who aren't used to them."

Libby tied the strings of her fur-lined hat under her chin. "I'll be fine, Lenore. I'm not exactly a shrinking violet."

Lenore brushed a hand across her forehead and left a streak of white flour. "Fiddlesticks! You should be glad you can look most men in the eye." She chuckled. "Shoot, I wish I could stare down a few of them galoots myself, but God didn't see fit to give me more'n he had to. Of course, He did give me a tad extra around the middle."

Libby smiled and fitted the last button on her long coat through its hole. "You're right, Lenore. I may as well look at the bright side. Well, I'd best go over to the schoolhouse and acquaint myself with the primers. Thank you for telling the mayor and his wife I was feeling poorly last night."

Lenore returned to mixing her batter. "That was nothing. Serves Adelaide right for bothering you the first night you're in town. I swear, that woman doesn't have the sense God gave a jackass. She wanted to go up and see you, but Matt told her in no uncertain terms you weren't to be disturbed."

"The sheriff said that?"

"Don't look so surprised. He's actually a pretty nice fella underneath all the gruffness. Reminds me of a dog we once had. Had half an ear tore off and he limped something awful, but he was the most good-natured and loyal creature on God's green earth."

"What happened to him?"

"Killed by a bear saving my son Samuel's life." Lenore dabbed at her eyes with the corner of her apron. "The sheriff's a lot the same way. He wouldn't think twice about jumping into a fray to save a person's life, even if it meant sacrificing his own."

Libby thought of his eyes alit with compassion. The image discomforted her and she blinked the picture away. "Did Mrs. Beidler say anything else?"

"Yep. She said she'd be seeing you soon. Then she gives me this look like I'm supposed to pass on her majesty's message." Lenore sniffed. "As if I don't have anything better to do than play messenger for Queen Adelaide."

Libby grinned wryly. "I can't wait to meet her." *And this time I'll be ready for her.*

Lenore laughed. "Don't let her bother you. She's all hot air."

"I won't. I'll see you at noon."

Libby lifted a hand in farewell and slipped out into the pristine white snow that obligingly camouflaged the dingy mud. She squinted against the bright sparkle, filling her lungs with the crisp air. Her footsteps lightened.

Today she began a new life away from the perversities of Harrison Thompson. It was time to set the past behind her. Her sole regret was that she could no longer practice medicine. An ache panged in her chest, casting a shadow across her heart. She had wanted to be a doctor since she was five years old, when she'd first accompanied her father on his daily calls. Her father and Corey had engendered in her the confidence she'd needed to endure the taunts by her male classmates and the cold disdain from her professors. Her idealism had vanished, but her dream had persevered. Graduation day had been bittersweet. She had attained a lifelong dream, but her beloved father and brother hadn't been there to share her joy. They'd died before knowing her triumph, but their legacy remained with her. She'd graduated with honors and never doubted her abilities.

Until Harrison had stripped away her self-assurance. She hated what he'd done to her; but after the first few beatings, she'd surrendered her body. Her heart and mind were hers, though, and she'd guarded her precious memories zealously.

The log schoolhouse lay at the edge of Deer Creek, separated from the rest of the town by a copse of birch trees. The secluded location appeared frosty and inhospitable, but Libby envisioned laughing children playing tag in the meadow beside the school. She climbed the stairs into the building. Inside, the air was bitterly cold, colder than outside. Libby made the black potbellied stove in the center of the classroom her first destination.

Twenty minutes later warmth seeped into the room, dissipating the chilliness. Libby removed her hat and tossed it on the desk. After exploring the desk-crammed room, she discovered back quarters containing a bed, a smaller stove, and evidence that her predecessors had lived there.

"You the new schoolmarm?"

Libby's head jerked up and her hand flew to her thundering heart. Standing inside the doorway was a boy about seven years old, with ebony hair and the bluest eyes she'd ever seen.

She lowered her hand. "Yes, I am. Are you one of my students?"

The boy slid his hands into faded overall pockets. "Naw. I don't go to school."

"Why not?"

"Because it's stupid."

Libby placed her hands on her hips. "Oh, so you've learned all there is to know. I'm surprised no one has asked you to teach the other children."

"I know the important stuff, and who'd want to be a dumb teacher anyhow?"

"I would. I'm Miss O'Hanlon. What's your name?"

"Dylan."

"That's a nice name for a handsome young man." Libby noted his ragged jacket and the bony wrists, which extended beyond the end of the sleeves. Newspaper peeped out of holes in his shoes, and his raven hair hung past his collar, obviously a stranger to a comb. No gloves covered his hands and the air had reddened his cheeks.

"Would you like to help me?" Libby asked.

Dylan shrugged and dragged his sleeve across his runny nose. "Not really. I just come over to see what you looked like."

Libby squelched a smile. "Do I pass your inspection?"

"You'll do. But then I don't like no teachers."

"I don't like *any* teachers."

"If you don't like teachers either, then why are you here?"

Libby smothered her laughter. "No, I mean it's *any* teachers, not *no* teachers. I was correcting your grammar."

Dylan scowled. "There's nothing wrong with the way I talk. The sheriff talks the same way and it don't bother him none."

Libby's lips drew together. "Maybe I should have a talk with him. I would like it if you'd come to school, Dylan."

His brilliant eyes revealed none of his thoughts. "My ma says it don't matter if I learn or not. She says I ain't going to amount to anything anyhow."

Libby's mouth gaped. What kind of mother would tell her child something so hurtful? "Maybe I could speak to her."

Panic appeared in Dylan's eyes, though his voice

didn't reflect it. "Naw. It don't matter. I'd best get going."

Before Libby could stop him, the boy was gone.

Though she'd had little contact with children, Libby recognized Dylan's loneliness. Certain he wanted to attend school; Libby suspected fear prevented him from doing so. Once she was organized, she would find Dylan's parents and seek their aid in getting him to attend.

Libby walked back into the classroom and settled into the chair behind the desk. She'd never taught before, but it couldn't be any more difficult than suturing a cut. The pile of lesson books occupied her attention the remainder of the morning.

Matt paused on the boardwalk and squinted across the dirty street. He scowled, sorry that the early snowfall hadn't remained untouched. The morning traffic of buckboards and horses' hooves had ruined its perfection. He wished winter would stop playing hide-and-seek with autumn and gain a foothold in the valley. Though he had come from Texas, Matt preferred the wintry Montana weather to the dusty grit of summer and the muddy quagmires of spring. The arctic cold also tended to weed out the troublemakers, sending them to a warmer climate and into another lawman's jurisdiction.

A movement at the corner of his eye caught his attention. Carrying a wicker basket, George Johnson shuffled across the main road. The clerk passed the bank, piquing Matt's curiosity. He followed the thin man's progress until he surmised where Johnson was headed.

Matt stepped off the dry planks and moved across his path. "Afternoon, George. Kind of cold for a picnic, ain't it?"

"I'm taking Miss O'Hanlon a lunch. Lenore didn't

want her to go hungry and I volunteered my services," he explained.

"Aren't you supposed to be back to work by one? It's already a few minutes after. I tell you what; I'm going to do you a favor. I'll take this on over to Miss O'Hanlon. That way you won't get in trouble with Mr. Pinkney."

"Mr. Pinkney will understand."

Matt rubbed his jaw with a gloved hand. "I recall Ira Wesley said the same thing, and he ended up getting fired."

Johnson swallowed. "Well, if it's no bother, Sheriff."

"Not at all." Matt grasped the basket's handle. "You head back to the bank and maybe Mr. Pinkney won't notice that you're late."

"Thanks, Sheriff. I appreciate it." After one last wistful glance toward the schoolhouse, Johnson hurried off.

Matt frowned. It appeared George had set his sights on Miss O'Hanlon. It shouldn't matter to him if he wanted to try his luck. However, the thought of her bright bloom fading beneath George's pallid shadow didn't set well. He told himself it was only because George wasn't the right man for her. It wasn't because he had any designs on her himself.

The north wind gusted through the breaks in the birch trees, and Matt raised the collar of his long drover coat. Pale gray smoke wafted out of the chimney, confirming Miss O'Hanlon's presence.

He shifted the basket from one gloved hand to the other. The tantalizing smell of fried chicken drifted to his nose, and despite having eaten lunch less than an hour ago, his mouth watered. Lenore's fried chicken would tempt Satan himself. Of course, the same could be said for Miss Libby O'Hanlon.

As Matt approached the building, his apprehension

grew. He questioned his impetuous ambush of Johnson and wondered why he'd appointed himself Miss
O'Hanlon's protector. He'd rather face the James
gang single-handedly than tangle with her again. She
had the uncanny ability to arouse his anger as well as
his passion, with frustration the ultimate winner.

Matt squared his shoulders, then climbed the steps
and opened the door. The scene at the front of the
room froze him in the doorway. Libby's head tilted to
the side, her verdant green eyes drawing him like a
cool lake on a blazing day. Tendrils of burnished hair
escaped the bun at the back of her neck and framed a
fine-boned face brushed with thoughtfulness. Long
tapered fingers held a pencil that lightly tapped an
uneven rhythm on the desktop. A coat engulfed her
figure, but his memory filled in the blanks.

Hot desire sprang unbidden, startling Matt with its
potency. He scowled and reminded himself of the
ugly scar that repulsed all women, including Libby.
Besides, they were from two different worlds.

"Good morning, Sheriff."

Libby's warm greeting nearly undid Matt's resolve.
"Actually, it's afternoon, Miss O'Hanlon," he
drawled.

Libby opened the brooch watch pinned to her
blouse and jumped to her feet. "It's after one o'clock!
Lenore must be furious with me."

Matt sauntered to the desk and set the wicker box
on it. "Nope. She sent over this basket."

Libby inhaled the aroma of chicken and biscuits
and smiled. "I think you've gone above and beyond
the call of duty, Sheriff. Have you eaten yet?"

"Yep."

Libby peeked in the basket. "Lenore sent more than
I could possibly eat. If you have some room left,
you're more than welcome to share."

Matt smiled crookedly. He hadn't expected such a

friendly welcome, but he wasn't about to look a gift horse in the mouth. "I always got room for Lenore's fried chicken."

Libby cleared away the books and set out the food Lenore had sent. As Matt lowered himself to the bench in front of the desk, Libby sank back into her chair.

She lifted a chicken leg from the pile of meat and began to eat heartily. "You're right. Lenore could give me a few pointers on frying chicken."

Matt picked out a thigh piece. "I'll bet you can fry chicken pretty good yourself."

She chuckled. "If you'd ever tasted my chicken, you wouldn't say that. My father always insisted that I should've been a boy, and my brother should've been a girl. Corey could fry up a chicken nearly as good as Lenore."

"Corey was your brother?"

Libby nodded. "He was a couple years older than me."

"Was?"

Her bright expression faded. "He was killed in the war."

Matt glimpsed the pain in her eyes and placed a comforting hand on her forearm. Her muscles jerked beneath his touch and she flinched, drawing away from his grasp. Matt cursed silently. How could he have forgotten?

"I'm sorry. A lot of good men died on both sides of the war," Matt murmured.

Libby remained silent, as if gathering her composure. "Corey was a doctor like my father. He had just graduated from college when he joined the Union army," she finally said. "Did you fight in the war, too?"

Matt nodded but couldn't bring himself to tell her he was on the opposing side.

"You were with the Confederacy, weren't you?"

Her perceptiveness disturbed him. "That's right."

She uncannily guessed his unspoken question. "Your Texas accent. I've heard a few of them in my time."

"It doesn't bother you?"

A sad smile touched Libby's lips and she shook her head. "No. I've always thought it best to forget the past and move ahead. If more folks would do that, there wouldn't be so much animosity in this country."

Matt tipped his head slightly. "Ani-what?"

"Animosity. Bad feelings."

He nodded in agreement. "Half the saloon fights I break up are started by men arguing about the war. You'd think they'd have better things to do than fight about something that's been over for five years."

"It's going to take a lot longer than five years to erase the hatred brought on."

"I ain't never heard anyone say it in so many words before, but you're right." He glanced at the books and papers set to one side of the desk. "You got everything you need to be teaching?"

"I think so. I've been getting some lesson plans organized. Perhaps I can begin classes in a couple days. I already had a visitor this morning. A boy named Dylan."

Matt's gaze flickered to Libby, wondering what Dylan had told her about himself. "I hope he wasn't a bother."

"Not at all. I felt sorry for him. He wore a jacket two sizes too small, and his shoes—"

The door swung open, interrupting her.

Libby gaped at the new arrival. A deep purple cape covered the woman's buxom figure, and a matching hat with an outrageous display of green, yellow, and orange feathers topped her head. Libby snapped her mouth shut and stood. "May I help you?"

"You can if you're Miss O'Hanlon."

"I'm Libby O'Hanlon."

The woman's assessing gaze roamed across Libby. "You're not exactly as I imagined."

Libby's temper rose a notch. "And you're exactly as I'd pictured." She stepped around her desk. "Mrs. Beidler, I presume."

Mrs. Beidler's righteous expression faltered, but she regained it quickly. "You presume correctly, Miss O'Hanlon." She glanced at Matt's face and a visible shudder passed through her considerable figure. "I see you've met our sheriff."

Libby flared at the derision in her voice, and anger burned brighter when Matt tugged the brim of his hat lower. "He was kind enough to bring me a lunch since I missed my own. I've been busy getting organized for classes."

"I'd best head back to town," Matt announced.

"I'll take the basket back when I go." Although Libby had enjoyed his visit, she didn't want him to hear the lies she'd have to tell Mrs. Beidler. She smiled warmly at Matt. "Thank you, Sheriff."

He nodded and strode out of the schoolhouse.

Without him, the room loomed larger and the visitor's presence more threatening.

Mrs. Beidler settled a stern gaze on Libby. "A word of warning. This is a small town and there are few secrets. It would be best if you would remember you are a teacher and comport yourself appropriately. It would not be advisable to be found with the sheriff again without a chaperone. Especially since he is a man who is little more than a ruffian himself."

Libby bristled. "I have found Sheriff Brandon to be kind and helpful, and he has not once acted in an improper manner. And I see no reason why he should be referred to as a 'ruffian' when anyone can see he takes his job seriously."

Mrs. Beidler sniffed, her chest puffing out like a robin's. "I see you have much to learn about life on this despicable frontier. But the reason I braved this miserable weather is to see that all your credentials are in order."

Libby squared her shoulders. "I'm afraid that's impossible."

"What do you mean?"

"I mean you cannot see my credentials. During the trip from Nebraska, I lost the bag containing my papers. I'm sorry, but all I can tell you is that I am qualified to teach, and I believe you will not be disappointed in my abilities." Libby trembled inwardly but kept her expression firm.

Mrs. Beidler's feathers quivered. "That is entirely unacceptable."

Libby clasped her hands and raised her chin. "As you realize, there are many frontier towns looking for teachers. I chose Deer Creek because I believed it would be a community I could call home. However, if you cannot take me at my word, I shall have to leave. I will have no trouble securing another position."

Carefully, Libby closed the open book on her desk.

Mrs. Beidler's mouth gaped. "You cannot be serious, Miss O'Hanlon."

"I'm perfectly serious, Mrs. Beidler." Libby buttoned her coat.

"B-but, you have a contract."

"I haven't signed it."

Mrs. Beidler opened and closed her mouth like a young bird begging for a worm. "Perhaps I was a bit hasty. I am not an unreasonable person, and I would be willing to compromise."

Libby crossed her arms and narrowed her eyes. "And what is this compromise?"

"If you will write the school you graduated from and get a letter of recommendation, you may teach while we are waiting for their reply."

Libby tapped her chin with an index finger and pretended to ponder the concession. Sweat rolled down Mrs. Beidler's plum-colored face, and smug satisfaction tempted Libby to smile. "Yes, that would be acceptable," she finally replied. "Now, was there anything else?"

"That will be sufficient for now," Mrs. Beidler said in a clipped voice. She turned in a kaleidoscope of colors and strutted out the door.

Libby sank onto a desk, her trembling knees no longer able to keep her upright. She finally understood the attraction of a high-stakes poker game. She had laid everything on the table and had won with a single bluff.

But the game wasn't over.

She'd used her mother's maiden name to hide her identity, and the certificate would expose her deception. She'd have to continue the charade and tell Mrs. Peacock Beidler she'd mailed a letter. With any luck, Libby could bluster through the remainder of the school term. When spring arrived and classes were dismissed for the summer, she would move on. It would be too dangerous to remain in Deer Creek any longer.

The remainder of the week flew by as Libby prepared for school and tried to forget the chain of events that brought her to Deer Creek. During the day, primers and lesson plans kept the memories at bay, but the interminable nights tested her sanity. The abuses she'd suffered at Harrison's hands, and the image of his still figure on the white floor, haunted her in the darkest hours. She found solace at the schoolhouse and met many of her students and their parents, who ventured there to learn when school would begin. Without guidance, and unable to tell anyone she'd never taught before, Libby gave herself a few extra days to prepare.

Saturday brought angry gray clouds and a blustery north wind. By midmorning, large snowflakes churned down from the overcast sky, signaling the onslaught of winter.

Despite the nasty weather, Lenore and Libby traipsed over to the mercantile. Libby closed the door behind her, the chilly air swirling around her ankles. She paused to lower her hood and brushed at the snowflakes gathered on her shoulders.

"Good afternoon, Mrs. Potts," Pearson greeted. His gaze raked Libby. "And you must be Miss O'Hanlon. I was wondering when I'd get to meet you."

Lenore introduced Libby to the storekeeper.

"Nice to meet you, Mr. Pearson." Libby offered her hand.

After a moment's hesitation, Pearson shook it.

The weak handshake seemed to last forever, and Libby cringed inwardly. She drew out of his grasp, grateful for the gloves she wore.

Lenore rummaged through bolts of cloth piled on a counter. "Libby and me came to see if you got any new dry goods."

Pearson drew his gaze away from Libby. "A couple freight wagons come in the other day. Had a few new pieces on 'em. I s'pect it won't be long before the wagons won't be able to get through at all."

"You mean we'll be cut off for the rest of the winter with no supplies and no mail?" Libby asked. She held her breath expectantly.

Lenore nodded. "Happens every year, honey. Those who can't get used to it aren't here anymore, but the rest of us know we got to squirrel away for the long winter ahead."

Libby breathed a silent amen to her answered prayer. Without regular mail delivery, she could keep Mrs. Beidler at bay for a lot longer.

"I hope you aren't like some women who can't take the solitary winters, Miss O'Hanlon. I knew a woman who went plumb crazy after three months of being cooped up in a cabin. Killed her husband and children, then killed herself. But they were miles from anywhere. At least we got each other here in town." Pearson's wolfish grin sent a shiver up Libby's spine.

"I've always enjoyed being alone, so I don't think winter will prove to be a great hardship, Mr. Pearson," Libby replied coolly. *And it'll be a cold day in hell before I ask you to keep me warm, you dirty old buzzard.*

She joined Lenore, who picked up a bolt of shiny emerald-green material. She held it under Libby's chin. "My goodness, this would make a beautiful dress for you, with that auburn hair and those lovely eyes. We can make it a bit daring across your bosom, but add some lace to soften it. Then add a bustle, the likes you're used to in the big city. Why, you would be the belle of the ball, looking like a fairy-tale princess."

Libby laughed. "What ball?"

"There's a dance at the schoolhouse Christmas Eve. It isn't exactly a ball, but everybody comes out in their brightest holiday colors. Most folks here are separated from their families, and this dance kind of pulls everyone together. Deer Creek is like one big, happy family that one night of the year. And the children will be expected to have a little program, a reenactment of the first Christmas night. It's tradition."

"I suppose the minister takes care of that."

Lenore glanced at Libby and shook her head. "Why no, the schoolteacher has always taken care of the children's program. You should've seen it last year. Little Micah Sattler tripped on his robe and fell right on top of baby Jesus. Lucky thing, Jesus was a doll. Of course it was Alice's doll, and she threw the darndest fit when Micah broke its leg. But Levi, Micah's older brother, he found a piece of string and tied the leg back on so Alice quit crying and the program went on."

Libby smiled weakly. "I don't know how I can top that."

Lenore squeezed her arm. "You'll do fine. It seems overwhelming now, since you're starting school the week of Thanksgiving. But you'll get to know the children right fast. It'll be fun."

"Fun, of course," Libby mumbled. She could deliver a baby without flinching, but the thought of directing a group of children in a play brought a cold sweat to her brow. *What have I gotten myself into?*

They spent a few more minutes looking at the material, but Libby's mind wasn't on a new dress. She picked out a brush, a woolen scarf, and a pair of sheepskin gloves. After paying Pearson, they trudged back to the boardinghouse as the snow continued to fall.

Through dusk's twilight, Dylan peeked around the corner of the jailhouse. He breathed a sigh of relief when he didn't see the sheriff. Dashing into the office, he stood by the hot stove. He held his bare hands out to the warmth, closing his eyes as feeling returned and imaginary needles riddled his fingers. He wiggled his toes, and the newspaper poking out of the holes in his shoes moved with them.

He sank into a wooden chair and propped his chin in a palm. Why wouldn't his ma buy him a new coat or gloves? He knew she had the money. He had seen it in a wooden box she kept hidden in her room. Dylan had imagined taking from her hoard, but fear always stopped him. If she caught him, she'd beat him within an inch of his life. He had sneaked an extra biscuit one night at supper, and she had gotten out the belt. He winced, remembering the bite of the leather on his bare back and legs. In a mirror he'd seen the welts it left. But he'd never told anyone, because she'd threatened to make the next punishment even worse if he did.

"So there you are. I been wondering what you've been up to the last few days."

At the sound of the sheriff's voice, Dylan's head jerked up. He leapt to his feet. "I got to get going."

He ran for the door, but Matt caught him by his pitifully thin arm. "Where's the fire?"

"Ma will be looking for me."

"She's more'n likely getting ready for her customers. Why don't you and me go get something to eat at the hotel?" Matt's gaze swept across Dylan's chapped cheeks and down to his feet. "Where are your new shoes?"

Dylan buried his chin in the collar of his coat. "Ma didn't want me wearing them for everyday. She said I'd ruin them."

Matt squatted down in front of the boy and raised his chin. "Where are your new shoes, Dylan?"

The boy blinked. Moisture gleamed in his blue eyes. "Ma took'em back to old man Pearson. I think she took the money for them." He grabbed hold of Matt's arm. "These shoes are okay. At least I ain't barefoot."

Matt studied Dylan's frightened eyes, and as furious as he was with the boy's mother, he was more concerned with Dylan's fear. "Don't worry, partner. I ain't mad at you. It's just that your ma shouldn't have taken those shoes. I bought them for you, and she didn't have any right taking them back to Pearson. Do you understand what I'm saying?"

Dylan nodded. "I didn't want her to take them, but she slapped me; said I was no better than a beggar. She said I didn't need the new shoes, but she could use the money she got back for them."

Matt's teeth clenched. He placed his hands on the boy's shoulders. "She was wrong, Dylan. I know she's your ma, but that don't mean she's always right. I'm going to have a talk with her."

"No!" Dylan hollered. "If you go see her, she's going to be mad at me."

Matt worked the muscle of his jaw. "I'm going to make sure she's mad at me and not you."

"You don't understand."

"What don't I understand?"

Dylan lowered his head. "I can't tell you."

"She beats you, don't she?"

Dylan's eyes widened and he shook his head. "No, she don't."

Rage filled Matt and his hands trembled. "Stay here, Dylan. I'll be back in a little while."

"What're you going to do?"

The terror in Dylan's expression tripped Matt's heart. "Don't worry. Everything will be all right. I promise." He straightened and rubbed his jaw. "The jail could use another good sweeping. You stay here and clean this place up, then when I come back we'll go out and have a steak dinner. How does that sound?"

The worry in Dylan's face receded slightly and he nodded. "As long as I can have my own steak."

"You got it."

Half-heartedly, the boy took hold of the broom handle, then Matt laid a hand on his head. "I won't be gone long."

Matt strode out into the swirling snow and arrived at Sadie's sporting house a few minutes later. Red lanterns on either side of the door told visitors what to expect, and Sadie had built her business on pleasing customers. He opened the door and stepped inside.

"Well, well, if it isn't the high and mighty Sheriff Brandon," a husky female voice spoke. "I'm surprised you lowered yourself enough to come inside."

Matt pressed his hat back from his forehead and met Sadie Rivers's bloodshot gaze. His glance swept across the glittery red dress that barely contained her prominent breasts. The hem touched her knees and black stockings covered her skinny legs. The suggestive clothing should have excited him, but it didn't. He looked away to the large entry and beyond to the parlor room, where a huge chandelier hung suspended from the ceiling by a heavy chain. Gaudy purple paper lined with velvety gold covered the walls, and Victorian lamps with tasseled shades added to the hollow illusion of glamour. Yellow drapes with frayed orange draw-cords prevented curious eyes from viewing the bawdy activities.

Matt's attention returned to Sadie. "This ain't a social visit. I want my money back."

Sadie blinked, revealing bright blue eye shadow and eyelashes thickened by black powder. "I don't recall taking any money from you, Sheriff."

"You took a pair of shoes that didn't belong to you."

"What belongs to my son belongs to me."

Matt placed himself directly in front of the madam. "I gave *him* the shoes, not you. I want either the shoes or the money back right now."

Sadie's red-rimmed eyes narrowed. "Come into my office where we can continue this conversation in private."

Matt followed her through the garish parlor, where three scantily clad women eyed him suspiciously. The girls had been lured from neighboring farms and taught the art of selling their bodies. The life aged them far beyond their years. Matt ground his teeth and tallied another mark against Sadie.

Inside the office, she closed the door and settled into the crushed-velvet chair behind the rosewood desk. She leaned back like a queen about to hold court. "What I do with my son is no concern of yours, Sheriff."

"It is when you take things from him that you

didn't buy. I got them shoes for Dylan. If you don't start taking better care of your son, he's going to get pneumonia, or worse."

Sadie tossed back frizzy hair, bleached almost white. "You got no right sticking your nose in where it don't belong. I'll do as I please, and I won't have you or anybody else telling me how to take care of him."

"I'm the law in this town, and if you ain't a fit mother, I can take Dylan away from you. And believe me, I'm damned close to doing that now."

Sadie leaned forward in the chair, her breasts nearly spilling out of the plunging décolletage. "No one takes what's mine! No one! Do you understand, Sheriff?"

Matt nodded and narrowed his eyes. "I understand more'n you know. If you so much as touch that boy again, I'm coming to take him. Do *you* understand?"

Sadie's cold eyes blazed. "Just because you're the law in this town don't mean you're right. I have a lot of influence around here. I know men who'll take care of a problem for the price of a bottle of whiskey."

Matt planted his knuckles on the desktop and leaned forward until only a few inches separated him from the woman's painted face. "Is that a threat?"

Sadie jumped to her feet and stalked around the desk. "No, a promise! You keep away from me and my son, Brandon."

"Give me the shoes or the money now."

"And if I don't?"

Matt kept his fists close to his sides, afraid he would forget Sadie was a woman. "I'll have a little talk with Mrs. Beidler. I'm sure she'd like to know where her husband spends his evenings. Who knows, maybe she'd stir folks up enough they'd run you out of town. But before she did, I'd throw you in jail for stealing."

Rage glittered in the madam's eyes, but a moment later her expression softened and she sidled close to

Matt. Her hand trailed up his thigh. "How about if you and me go on upstairs and I'll pay you back in trade? I could do things you can't even imagine."

Her fingers curled around him.

Matt recoiled. "You couldn't pay me enough to sleep with you."

Sadie's complexion blanched beneath her caked makeup, and her nostrils flared. She jerked open the top drawer of her desk and withdrew a few coins. She threw them at Matt. "Here's your money. Now get out."

Matt smiled without warmth and tucked the money in his pocket. "By the way, if you happen to think about him, Dylan is staying with me tonight."

"You got no right!"

He shrugged innocently. "I asked a friend to stay the night and he agreed."

"Get the hell out of here!"

Matt wrapped his gloved hand around the doorknob and turned back to Sadie. "If I hear that you laid a hand on that boy, I'll be back, and next time I won't be so friendly."

As he crossed the street, Matt grinned in satisfaction. He'd made an enemy of Sadie Rivers, but he had no doubt he could handle her. She wouldn't harm Dylan and risk being thrown in jail. It wasn't that she cared about Dylan, but her business would suffer if she was behind bars.

The air was fresh and Matt breathed deeply to dispel the stink of cheap perfume trapped in his lungs. He remembered Sadie's hand upon his leg and shuddered, trying to shake off the memory. If he and Sadie Rivers were the last two people on earth, the human race would die out.

Matt strode into the evening, his open coat flapping about his legs. The wind coaxed a few flakes out of the dark sky to settle on the earth. He spied the first star of the night and without pause made a wish, then grimaced at his own folly. Twinkling stars and wishes-come-true were for children, not men who no longer believed in miracles.

He rounded a corner and collided with a soft body. Instinctively, Matt grabbed the cloaked figure and steadied her. Wide eyes stared back at him, and he was reminded of a deer poised for flight. He immediately removed his hands from Libby's arms. "Pardon me, Miss O'Hanlon, but ain't it kind of late for you to be out?"

Libby straightened so quickly her hood slipped from her head. Her cheeks flushed. "Ah, well, Sheriff, I couldn't sleep and decided a walk might help."

"This probably ain't the best place for you to be walking."

Matt's height shadowed Libby, and she found her gaze captured by his broad shoulders. Her perusal moved lower to the patch of skin at the base of his neck, then down to his chest, settling on his belt buckle.

What am I doing gaping like an adolescent girl? She ordered herself to look into his fathomless eyes. "I guess I wasn't watching where I was going."

Matt's hooded eyes twinkled. "I'm just as much to blame. Maybe I'd best escort you back to Lenore's so you don't get lost again." His expression sobered. "You shouldn't be out this late on a Saturday night. There are a lot of ranch hands in town, and most of them ain't seen a women in some time. No telling what they might do."

Libby's embarrassment faded and indignation filled the void. "I thought you said men didn't find me very 'sightly.' "

Matt glanced down at his boots. "Some men don't care what you look like as long as you're a female."

Bewildered hurt laced through Libby. "Why should

she care if Matt didn't find her attractive? She should be relieved—but she wasn't. "Thank you, but I can find my own way back."

She turned and, holding her shoulders stiffly erect, marched away. Matt fell in step beside her.

"I said you needn't put yourself out, Sheriff," Libby reiterated in a taut voice.

"No problem, Miss O'Hanlon. I was headed that way anyhow."

Despite his quietly assuring words, Matt was a formidable man, and Libby's defenses remained in place. Her elbow brushed his arm, and through her coat a tingle spread upward. The night's cold disappeared, replaced by a warmth from within. Her gaze slid down Matt's profile, and she tried to muster disapproval of his whiskers and unruly hair. However, the heat only spread to her stomach and lower. She ached to touch his thick hair, to see if it slipped through her fingers like the whisper of silk. Her traitorous mind wondered how his lips would feel on hers. Would they be warm and gentle, or harsh and demanding? Libby's stomach fluttered and her breathing intensified.

"We can slow down if you'd like," Matt said.

"What?"

"This ain't a race. We can slow down some so you ain't breathing like a lathered horse."

"Oh, no, that's all right. I'm fine." Mortified, Libby concentrated on the pinch of her left shoe, the small hole in her glove, the tie-down of Matt's holster on his muscular thigh.

Ignore his anatomy!

Libby began to count to one hundred. At nine, she wondered if he had dimples when he smiled. At twenty-two, she wondered how his whiskers would feel against her cheek if he kissed her. At thirty-nine, she wondered how his hard body would fit against hers. At forty-five, she gave up counting.

"Sorry I ran out on you when that strutting pea-hen came to the school the other day," Matt said.

Libby forced the sensual musings aside and brought the present into focus. "After talking to her, I don't blame you. I only wish I could've run out, too."

Matt chuckled. "The Beidlers figure they're royalty here. Heard tell he come from a rich family back east. Married Adelaide and was expecting to live a soft life. But they lost everything in the war, so they up and moved west. Ended up settling here in Deer Creek."

"Must've been difficult for them to adjust, after having had everything," Libby said softly.

"You sound like you know how they feel."

Startled by his accurate observation, Libby laughed nervously. "No. I have a good imagination."

"So, are you all ready for school to start?"

"As ready as I'll ever be."

"If I didn't know better, I'd say you never taught before."

The hair on Libby's neck prickled. "What makes you say that?"

Matt shrugged. "Just a feeling. *Have* you taught before?"

Libby's gaze fixed on a twinkling star in the evening sky. "Of course. I'm not some young girl recently out of the classroom."

They stopped in front of Lenore's gate.

"Thank you, Sheriff. I appreciate you escorting me home, though I don't think it was necessary."

Matt touched the brim of his hat and nodded. "My pleasure, Miss O'Hanlon."

She slipped into the house. His gut told him she hadn't answered truthfully, but why would she lie? Libby O'Hanlon wielded pride like a warrior carried a shield, and she might view her inexperience as a sign of weakness.

His gaze probed the rooming house one last time. He would keep a close eye on Deer Creek's new schoolteacher in the event she needed assistance. Recalling flashing green eyes, and the sway of her nicely rounded derriere beneath the drab skirt, Matt smiled. Compared to breaking up saloon brawls and throwing overly zealous drunks in jail, watching her would be paradise.

Chapter 3

Libby's eyes flashed open and she pressed a hand to her mouth to stifle a scream. Her heart pounded in her chest, and her nightgown was tangled around her like a mummy's wrappings. Bits and pieces of the nightmare drifted in her mind, becoming more elusive as consciousness replaced sleep. But the desperation remained, reminding Libby she was a prisoner to the past.

She sat up, her back against the pillow. Hazy visions of Harrison and a scarlet belt raised to strike her lingered. Matt had been there, too. He'd attempted to stop Harrison, and the leather strap became a fireplace poker used to strike him. The blood flowing on the marble floor was no longer Harrison's, but Matt's.

A rapid knock on the door roused her from the chilling vision. "Libby, honey, are you awake? It's after seven."

Lenore's announcement chased away the terror-filled scenes. Today was the first day of school and she would be late.

"Oh, no!" Libby threw back her covers and leapt to the floor, disregarding the cold wood beneath her feet. "I'll be down in five minutes."

She splashed cool water from the ceramic basin on

her face and quickly dressed in a navy skirt, white blouse, and dark blue sweater. A black ribbon at her neck completed the somber outfit. Libby whisked a tortoise-shell hairbrush through her auburn tresses and created a snug coil at the back of her neck. She examined her reflection in the mirror above the dresser and pinched her cheeks, giving color to her pale face.

Grabbing her bag of books and the long caped coat, she hurried out of the room. She flew down the stairs and into the dining room, where she met the stares of George Johnson and Virgil Tanner.

"Uh . . . , good morning. Excuse me, but I'm in a bit of a hurry this morning." Libby rushed into the kitchen, nearly bowling over Lenore. "I don't have time to eat."

Lenore firmly steered Libby to a stool beside a high table. "You sit down and eat some oatmeal. You don't need your stomach telling you and the whole class that you haven't eaten anything. Those kids are going to see how much they can get away with, and you're going to have to lay down the law right fast." Lenore snorted. "And fact is, a person works better if they have a good rib-sticking breakfast. That oatmeal is guaranteed to stick to anything. Why, I even used it to put up wallpaper one time. Worked darn good, too."

Despite her anxiety, Libby laughed. "That wall must've had an interesting texture."

Lenore's cheeks dimpled and her blue eyes twinkled. "Willard didn't mind. He swore that was all my oatmeal was good for anyways."

Libby surreptitiously wiggled her spoon free of the sticky mass. She had to agree with the late Willard Potts.

Lenore wrapped a sandwich in brown paper. "Put this in your bag so you have something to nibble on over lunch."

"You didn't have to do that."

Lenore waved a hand. "Pshaw, someone's got to watch out for you. Why, last night I thought you were going to come right through the floor with that pacing. Don't worry, you'll do just fine."

Libby didn't explain her sleeplessness was more complicated than worry over teaching. How could she tell Lenore about the unladylike thoughts she'd harbored when Matt had escorted her home Saturday evening? How could she face Lenore if she told her about the sensual images that kept her tossing most of the night? How could she confess her fascination with Matt Brandon when she didn't even understand it? "I hope I didn't keep you awake."

"Don't worry about that, dear. I can sleep through anything. One time, I even slept through one of them funnel clouds. Guess it was quite a thing to see. Blew John Randall's prize bull right out of the barn and landed him in the middle of Abe Landy's heifers. Abe sure had a passel of calves that year. Sure wish I would've seen that tornado." She sighed heavily. "Anyhow, I was just worried about you."

Unexpected moisture filled Libby's eyes and she clasped Lenore's pudgy hand. "Thank you, but I'll be fine. I'm a survivor."

"I knew that the first time I laid eyes on you. You and the sheriff are like two peas in a pod that way. Both of you have that same sad expression when you think no one's looking, but I seen it. Everyone has to put up with a measure of hurt in their lives, but sometimes God gives some folks an extra measure. But then He gives them friends to ease the burden, too."

Uncomfortable with the topic, Libby valiantly finished her oatmeal and slipped off the stool. "I'd best get over to the school. The children are going to have to keep their wraps on until I have the fire going well. I was hoping to make a better first impression than showing up late and making them sit in a cold room."

Lenore patted Libby's arm. "It'll be fine. You'll see."

Wishing she had some of Lenore's optimism, Libby bid her farewell.

Fresh snow glittered like a field of diamonds. No clouds littered the cerulean sky, but sun dogs ringed the yellow orb. Her footsteps crunched across the still street, her breath leaving a white vapor trail behind her.

The familiar path seemed longer than usual, and Libby cursed the long wool skirt that impeded her progress. Apprehension grew with every step. As the school came into view, the butterflies in her stomach became circling vultures. She hurried inside and shoved the door shut behind her. A wave of heat and the comforting smell of woodsmoke greeted her.

Who'd made the fire? The empty room shared no secrets. She checked the woodbox and found it overflowing, just as she'd left it, yet someone had obviously filled the stove. Whoever had done the good deed had also ensured she wouldn't run out of fuel.

Before she could ponder the mystery further, the door opened and admitted a pretty blond girl with cherry cheeks and shining blue eyes.

"Good morning," Libby greeted. "I'm your teacher, Miss O'Hanlon. What's your name?"

"Jennifer Olson, but you can call me Jenny." A perfect smile brought dimples to her cheeks.

Libby returned the friendly expression. "Why don't you find a place to sit while I get ready?"

"Thank you, Miss O'Hanlon."

Jenny's polite manners brought a glow to Libby's mood. If all her students were as courteous, teaching would be easier than she'd expected.

A whoosh of cool air announced another arrival. A

tall towheaded boy stood with the door open, allowing the cold in and the warmth out.

"Could you please close the door?" Libby called out.

He shrugged. "I suppose I could."

He remained where he was, an insolent grin on his adolescent face.

"Close the door now." Impatience sharpened Libby's tone.

"Come on Jacob, do like Miss O'Hanlon says. It's getting cold in here," Jenny added.

"Already the teacher's pet?" Jacob retorted.

"That's enough, Jacob. Do as I said and sit down," Libby ordered.

He heaved a tremendous sigh and did as ordered. He slumped in a seat and stared at her.

"What's your full name?"

Crossing his arms over his chest, he tipped his head. "Jacob Olson."

"He's my brother," Jenny admitted in an embarrassed voice.

Libby nodded and wondered which one was adopted.

By eight o'clock, the room hummed with excited whispers. Libby wrote her name on the blackboard and the students quieted. She rubbed her damp palms on her skirt furtively and hoped no one noticed her hands trembled. "Good morning, and welcome back to school."

"Sit down and have some buttermilk and cookies. You look like you could use some cheering up," Lenore greeted Libby.

Libby heaved an exhausted sigh. She dropped her bag on the floor and removed her coat. "That sounds wonderful."

"How many students showed up?"

"Twenty-three, but it felt like one hundred and twenty-three."

"I only had seven of my own, but I can tell you they aren't always the little joys from heaven the preacher says they are. They can be downright devils when they got a mind to be contrary."

Libby nodded and dipped a cookie in the glass of milk. "Seth Billings and Jacob Olson had a mind to be contrary all day. No matter what I said or did, they had an impudent reply. And that Mary Sue Beidler figures she's the queen of the classroom since her mother is queen of Deer Creek."

Lenore clucked her tongue. "And she's the spitting image of Adelaide, too. I hope you didn't let those scalawags get away with sassing you."

Boot heels echoed on the wood floor and the kitchen door swung open. The sheriff appeared, and Dylan poked his head around Matt's waist. "Afternoon, ladies. I thought Lenore might have a couple cookies to spare."

"You know darn well that Monday is cookie day. No need to act so innocent," Lenore scolded with a twinkle in her eyes.

"Guilty as charged." Matt winked at Libby.

Libby laughed at his unrepentant expression.

Lenore turned to Dylan. "You hop on to that stool next to Miss O'Hanlon and I'll get a plate of cookies just for you."

"Thanks, Mrs. Potts." Dylan scrambled up beside Libby.

Matt removed his hat, keeping the scarred side of his face averted. He hitched himself up on a stool so he and Dylan flanked her.

Matt's arm brushed hers and Libby's skin tingled. His jacket radiated the cold, fresh scent of winter and wood smoke. A clean shirt and bandanna replaced the wrinkled worn clothing of the previous days. However, the change she found the most appealing was the disappearance of his whisker growth. "You shaved."

He grinned crookedly and awareness curled in the pit of her stomach. "I had my yearly trip to the bath and barber."

Lenore set a plate of cookies and a large glass of milk in front of Dylan. "He knew you'd be here, so he got all gussied up."

Matt's freshly shaven face reddened and Libby's cheeks grew warm, though not with embarrassment. To cover her discomfiture, she turned to the boy. "I didn't see you in school today, Dylan."

He shrugged. "My ma had some chores for me to do. 'Sides, I told you I don't like school."

He lifted the glass to his lips and emptied the contents in a few gulps. A white mustache remained above his upper lip, and he dragged his worn coat sleeve across his mouth.

"But you'd get to play with children your own age," Libby argued.

A whole cookie disappeared into his mouth, and it was a full minute before he could answer. "Naw. I like to play by myself."

Libby glanced at Matt and he shook his head in warning, his expression telling her she didn't know all the facts. She drew her eyebrows together in question and again Matt gestured a negative reply. Her attention returned to Dylan. "I'd like you to come to school."

He stopped chewing and his sober eyes studied her with an intensity beyond his seven years. "Why would you want me there? I'm a—" he stumbled, "a trouble-maker. My ma says so."

Lenore laid a hand on the boy's shoulder. "Your ma doesn't mean it, dear. How could anyone as sweet as you be a troublemaker?"

Dylan's face flushed and he fidgeted. "The kids'll

laugh at me. I ain't never been to school before. They'll call me dummy and . . . well, other things."

Moisture gathered in Libby's eyes, and she clasped her hands in her lap to keep from hugging the boy. "Some children can be cruel, Dylan, but not all of them are like that. And I'll be there to help you."

Dylan's eyes sparkled, but the light vanished a moment later and he shook his head. "I better not. Ma won't like it."

Matt cleared his throat. "How did your first day of school go, Miss O'Hanlon?"

Libby frowned and studied the child a moment before answering him. "I was telling Lenore I've got a couple of boys whose mouths are bigger than their feet."

Dylan stifled a giggle.

"Them the two I saw chopping wood out back after school?" Matt asked. "The Olson boy and Hank Billings' oldest?"

"Those are the ones. I thought some physical labor outside might make them a bit more inclined to keep quiet inside."

Lenore withdrew a sheet of cookies from the oven. "You're probably going to need a horsewhip for those two. I think they were the ones who drove Miss Kingsley and Miss Vanderhoff to marry so fast. Spare the rod, spoil the child, that's what I say, and that's what happened with them two boys. Their folks were so tickled when they were born, they gave them anything they wanted."

"They're just plain mean," Dylan said with a full mouth, scattering a few damp cookie crumbs across the table.

Lenore refilled Matt's coffee cup. "That could be, too. I seen it happen. A boy from a good, God-fearing family turned like a rabid dog, became a thief and murderer. His poor folks, they didn't know what they done wrong, and I told them sometimes it happens and it isn't anybody's fault. The boy ended up in a hangman's noose and I can't say I was sorry."

"She's right, Dylan," Matt said. "It don't matter who your folks are or where you come from. What matters is which trail you follow."

Libby listened to the conversation and wondered about Dylan's background. "Where do you live, Dylan?"

Matt interrupted his reply. "I'll bet if you asked Mrs. Potts real nice, she'd get you another glass of milk. Miss O'Hanlon, there's something I'd like to show you."

His enigmatic expression confused Libby. He led her into the sitting room, where a crackling fire burned brightly in the hearth.

"What is it you need to show me, Sheriff?" Libby kept her voice cool, though Matt's nearness had her more than a little heated.

He closed the door. "There's something you need to know about Dylan. He ain't exactly like the other kids."

Libby remembered his threadbare clothing and her tone softened. "He shouldn't be ashamed that his family doesn't have much money. He can't help that."

"His ma is the richest person in town."

"I don't understand."

"Dylan lives in a . . ." Matt's rugged face reddened. "His ma is a madam."

Libby's forehead furrowed and she repeated impatiently, "I don't understand."

He took a deep breath. "Dylan lives in a whorehouse, and his ma owns it and the girls inside."

Libby's cheeks burned. "You mean, she's a—a soiled dove?"

"More like a dirty buzzard."

"B-but why does he wear rags if his mother has so much money?"

Anger clouded Matt's visage and his eyes blazed.

"Because she's a selfish shrew who figures Dylan's more trouble than he's worth."

Righteous fury flooded Libby. "What about his father? Doesn't he have any say in the matter?"

"Nobody knows who his father is. Sadie drifted into town a few years ago with Dylan and bought the house where she runs her business."

"Then we've got to take Dylan away from her. He can stay with me until we find him a proper home, a place where he won't be mistreated."

"You'd do that for a boy you hardly know?"

"No child deserves that kind of treatment, and I'd be just as bad as his mother if I did nothing."

Matt studied her indignant posture and resolute expression. If a child she barely knew could evoke such a passionate response, how would she respond to the man she loved?

He gently took her hand and noted with relief she didn't recoil from the touch. "We can't take Dylan away without evidence. But Sadie's used a strap on Dylan more than once. I seen the scars on his back. I told her if she does it again, I'm taking him away from her. I don't know if I can keep him away, but I'm going to try my damnedest."

Libby's eloquent eyes bespoke her concern for Dylan, and Matt's grasp tightened.

"If anybody can do it, you can," she said softly, squeezing his hand in return.

Her gaze captured Matt, suspending him in bittersweet agony. No fear showed in her trusting eyes.

The grandfather clock's pendulum ticked with each arc. Sounds from the kitchen faded into oblivion, and Libby's gentle breathing became the center of Matt's universe. Her fingers remained in his hands, but misgivings assaulted him.

He would disappoint her, replace the trust in her eyes with disillusionment. It had happened before. It would happen again. She believed he could make everything right, but he was no hero. If she knew how he'd come to live in Deer Creek, disenchantment would supplant her blind faith.

He stepped back, and for a second Matt thought he saw disappointment in her wide eyes, but he dismissed the impression. "I'll try to make sure Sadie don't hurt him anymore. That boy's been through enough."

"Do you think you can get him to school?"

"I'll try, but I think he's right. The kids are going to be mighty rough on him. They can be real mean when they don't know otherwise."

"What about the teachers before me? Didn't they try to get Dylan to come to school?"

"They never figured he was worth the bother," Matt replied bitterly. "You're the first teacher I seen who cares enough to try."

Libby's hands balled into fists. "That makes me so angry I could spit tacks! Dylan has no say in who his parents are, and people shouldn't expect him to be held accountable for their mistakes."

"I'll get him there tomorrow. If it don't work, what're you going to do?"

"I don't know yet, but I'll figure something out. I won't let Dylan miss out on an education simply because no one, including his spiteful mother, cares."

Matt smiled gently. "You and me care, and we'll make sure he gets what he needs."

"Thank you, Sheriff."

"Call me Matt."

Libby tipped her head. "Is it acceptable for the spinster teacher to call the sheriff by his first name?"

"Only if she lets him call her by her given name."

"Fair enough, Matt." An impish grin touched Libby's lush lips. "Besides, who cares what Mrs. Beidler and her flock of busybodies think anyway?"

"I suppose we should get back to the kitchen before Lenore and Dylan wonder where we got off to." He opened the door and ushered Libby ahead of him.

As they entered the kitchen, Matt asked, "You about filled up there, Dylan?"

"He'd better be," Lenore said. "He's eaten nearly every cookie that came out of the oven."

"I ain't ate that many," Dylan defended.

"I haven't eaten that many," Libby corrected.

He groaned. "There ain't anything wrong with ain't, is there, Sheriff?"

"It ain't proper," Matt said firmly, then realized his mistake. "I mean, it isn't proper."

He glanced at Libby and, to his surprise, met a soft smile. A sheepish grin twitched his lips. "Maybe some learning wouldn't hurt me neither."

"You're always welcome to come to school," Libby said.

He shook his head. "A mite late for that, I'd say."

"It's never too late to learn, Matt. That reminds me—I have a bit of a mystery for you. I overslept this morning, and when I got to school the stove was already fired up. Do you have any idea who would've done that? I'd like to thank him."

Dylan pointed at Matt. "The sheriff and me got it going. He was kinda worried when you didn't show up, so we started the fire for you. He said we could surprise you on your first day of teaching."

Matt shifted from one worn brown boot to the other. "Anyone ever tell you you got a big mouth, Dylan?" he growled. He slanted a glance at Libby. "It wasn't anything. We were up and making rounds when I noticed the chimney wasn't smoking, so I figured we'd help you out."

"You did and I thank you both. It was very thoughtful." Libby's warm gaze clothed Matt and Dylan with gratitude.

To cover his embarrassment, Matt turned to the

boy. "C'mon, Dylan, we've used up our welcome here. Lenore ai—isn't going to give us any cookies next time if we eat her whole batch today."

Matt closed the top button of Dylan's jacket and helped him with his scarf, all the while aware of Libby's contemplation. He straightened and realized he'd forgotten about his scar, forcing Libby to endure the sight of his disfigured face for most of the visit. He tossed on his hat and angled the brim downward. His lips thinned, angry with himself.

"Thank Mrs. Potts for the milk and cookies," Matt said stiffly to Dylan.

The boy dutifully did as he was told, then said goodbye to both women.

"You come back anytime, and bring that stubborn sheriff with you. There's always room for a couple more at the dinner table," Lenore said. She handed Dylan a cloth sack and whispered, "There's a few oatmeal cookies in there for a snack later."

Matt touched two fingers to his hat. "Thanks for the cookies, Lenore. They were right tasty. Good evening."

"Good night, Dylan. Good night, Matt," Libby said.

He risked a look at Libby's face, risked seeing the disgust over his blatantly exposed scar. However, only concern showed, as if she noticed his curtness and was puzzled by it. Either she was adept at hiding her feelings, or the puckered tissue truly didn't bother her.

He forced himself to relax. "Good night, Libby, and tomorrow I'll do like we talked about."

"Thank you."

He placed a hand on Dylan's shoulder and steered him out the back door.

"What was that all about?" Lenore asked curiously. "What's this Matt's going to do tomorrow?"

"Just a little favor." Libby grabbed her long-abandoned bag and coat. "I'd best run upstairs and get some homework done before supper."

"What's that girl up to?" Lenore spoke aloud in the empty kitchen. Her frown was replaced by a sly smile. "So they're calling each other Libby and Matt now. Well, things are right on schedule. It's been years since Deer Creek's had a Christmas wedding."

Dylan kicked at a frozen dung heap and grinned when a turd flew across the street.

"You ought not to do that," Matt scolded. "Don't go ruining them good shoes right off. Your ma wasn't too keen on you getting them the way it was."

Dylan frowned and stuck the hand not holding the bag of cookies into his overall pocket. "Ma ain't too keen on anything I do."

"Was she glad to see you yesterday after I brung you home?"

"I guess. She didn't say much."

"What'd she do?"

Dylan's fingers curled into his palm. He shrugged, not wanting the sheriff to see his fear. Only crybabies got scared. "She didn't hit me or nothing like that, but she was plenty mad. She said I was getting too big for my britches."

"Them overalls are getting a mite short on you," Matt teased. "Maybe we should go on over to Pearson's and see if he's got any clothes your size."

Dylan glanced at the sheriff, certain he was still funning him, but the man looked serious. "What'll Ma say?"

Matt shrugged. "When I take you home, I'll have a talk with her. Fact is, I'm going to ask her if you can go to school tomorrow. How would you like that?"

Excitement woven with uncertainty threaded through Dylan. "I don't know. What if the kids laugh at me?"

"You ought not to be worried about them. Why, I'll

bet you're smarter'n most of them already. You just need to catch up on your numbers and letters and then you're going to leave them behind."

"You really think so?"

"I wouldn't have said so if I didn't." Matt drew an imaginary *X* on his chest. Cross my heart."

Dylan weakened, torn between apprehension and eagerness. "Would you go with me?"

"I'll pick you up at your ma's and we'll walk over together."

"Then you'll stay for a time?" He gazed at the sheriff hopefully.

"If you want me to, I will."

"It won't be so scary knowing you're there, too."

Matt hunkered down beside him and laid his hands on Dylan's shoulders. "You don't ever have to be scared of anything. I'll always be here to help you."

Dylan blinked back unwanted tears. Nobody had ever looked out for him before. He glanced down at the boardwalk patched with ice and snow, and scrubbed his eyes with a fist. "I ain't ever scared," he mumbled.

"I know that, son. But everybody gets a little worried some time or another."

Dylan's gaze shot to Matt. "Even you?"

Matt smiled crookedly. "Especially me."

"What do you worry about?"

The sheriff straightened and they continued walking down the boardwalk. "About you and what your ma does to you when she's mad."

Dylan's shoulders drew back. "I don't cry." Bitterness crept into his young voice. "I think she likes it when I cry, so I stopped. She don't hit me so much anymore."

"I want you to tell me if she ever hits you again."

The sheriff's low voice sounded angry and a shiver chased up Dylan's arms. He studied Matt's grim face and knew the fury wasn't directed at him. He sighed in relief. "You going to talk to her tonight about me going to school?"

Matt nodded. "Yep, but first we're going to buy you some new clothes."

Steered into Pearson's Mercantile, Dylan paused inside the door. He barely registered the sound of the cowbell's clang. He inhaled deeply of the store's rich aromas: coffee beans, leather harnesses, and vinegar. Colors jumbled into a blur and he tried to separate them, but only succeeded in getting dizzy.

"Evening, Sheriff," Pearson greeted. He sent Dylan a glare and his eyes narrowed.

Dylan drew closer to Matt and eyed the storekeeper suspiciously.

"Evening. You got any of them ready-made clothes here that would fit Dylan?"

"Still trying to make a silk purse out of a hog's ear, I see," Pearson remarked with an arched eyebrow.

Matt's arm tightened around Dylan's shoulders. "You got any or not?"

"I'll check." Pearson shuffled to the pile of clothing.

"What'd he mean by trying to make a purse out of a pig's ear?" Dylan whispered to Matt.

"He didn't mean nothing by it. He was just being a busybody."

Pearson poked around for a few minutes and returned with a pair of brown trousers and a matching wool plaid shirt. "These should about fit him."

"Got a place he can try them on?" Matt asked.

"He can go into the storage room there, but make sure he don't take anything."

"Go on, Dylan. See if they fit." Matt handed Dylan the clothing and gave him a gentle shove in the right direction.

Dylan thrust the bag of cookies Lenore had given him into Matt's hands and clutched the stiff material. He hurried into a room nearly bursting with supplies. It took him a few minutes to remove his old overalls and wriggle into the new outfit. His fingers fumbled with the pants opening and he left his shirttails hang. He'd never worn anything besides overalls before. He pushed aside the curtain.

"Those don't look too bad," Matt said. "Tuck the shirt in, see how it looks."

Dylan shoved the tails into the waistband, revealing the misaligned buttons at the front of his pants.

"I couldn't get them right," he mumbled.

Matt smiled. "As long as they fit, don't worry about them now. Tomorrow morning I'll help if you need a hand. Put your overalls back on."

Dylan nodded. A few minutes later he emerged and joined Matt.

"If you want my opinion, I think it's a big mistake, putting him in——" Pearson began.

"Keep your opinions to yourself," Matt interrupted. "Let's go, Dylan."

"What about my clothes?" Dylan asked.

"They're already taken care of. Put'em in this here bag."

Matt opened a sack and Dylan noticed a few items already in it. "What else did you get?"

"Socks and long underwear. Winter's coming." He handed Dylan a pair of mittens. "You'll need these, too."

Tentatively, Dylan touched the soft leather. He grinned at the sheriff and pulled them on his cold-roughened hands. He placed his trousers and shirt on top of the underwear, then took the package from Matt.

"Good night, Pearson," Matt said.

"Night, Sheriff."

Darkness enveloped the town, though pools of light spilled out of a few buildings along the main street. They strolled away from the mercantile and, with the sheriff beside him, security teemed through Dylan. However, when they turned down the street leading to the brightly lit house, dread weighted his hunched shoulders. He dragged his feet, postponing the moment he'd have to face his mother.

"It'll be all right, Dylan. I'm with you."

Matt's firm voice bolstered his flagging courage. He clutched the precious clothing closer to his chest and went around to the back door where he and Matt entered the kitchen.

"There you are! Miz Sadie was wonderin' what happened to you," the dark maid scolded.

"Me and the sheriff went over to Mrs. Potts and had some cookies," Dylan replied defiantly.

"What do you got in that there bag?"

"It ain't no concern of yours," Matt answered. "Where's Sadie?"

The woman scowled. "She's gettin' dressed for business."

The kitchen door swung open and nose-tickling perfume heralded the entrance of Dylan's mother. The maid bobbed her head at Sadie and left.

"It's about time you get home. I suppose you been hanging around with your good friend Sheriff Brandon," Sadie remarked.

Dylan cringed at her caustic voice. No matter how often he heard the tone, he still cowered with terror, expecting a slap or worse.

"I want to talk to you, Sadie," Matt said.

Sadie leaned against the table, her hips thrust forward beneath the turquoise and silver dress. "I'm listening."

Matt handed Dylan his bag of cookies. "Go on upstairs."

Dylan glanced from his mother to Matt and nodded. He used his back to push open the door and slipped out of the kitchen. In the other room, he laid an ear against the wall and listened to the exchange.

"What is it now?" Sadie asked.

"I'm taking Dylan to school tomorrow morning," the sheriff stated.

Dylan inhaled sharply and waited for his mother to explode. He didn't remain in suspense for long.

"Damn you, Brandon! I got things around the house for him to do. Who the hell am I going to get to fill the wood boxes and carry water and do all the other things he does around here?"

"Hire someone. Dylan ain't a slave, he's your son! He deserves an education, and you got no right treating him like he's a nobody."

Sadie's high-pitched laughter rang, and Dylan ground his teeth. "What've you been doing? Filling his head with the great things he could do if he went to school? He's a bastard, Brandon! Bastards don't become bankers or ranchers or politicians."

"Do they become whores?"

A loud slap sounded and Dylan cringed. He knew exactly what it felt like. He bit his lower lip, drawing blood.

"My life isn't any of your goddamn business, Brandon! Just like my son isn't any of your business."

"I made him my business. You ain't going to turn him into a thief or a killer. He don't deserve that. He's a good boy. You're so blinded by bitterness, you can't even see that. Hell, I've seen dogs treated better than you treat your own son, your own flesh and blood."

"I never wanted him. He was a goddamn mistake. When his father found out I was pregnant, he didn't want anything more to do with me. He left me in a little godforsaken one-horse town. I begged for food until I had the brat. Tried to get rid of him, but nobody'd take him. If he'd turned up missing, they'd have known I did something to him. I had to keep him, and I'm not about to let him forget it. He owes me, Brandon, and he's going to pay me back for as long as he lives."

Dylan slumped to the floor, and the bag of cookies crunched below him. A single tear rolled down his cheek and he swiped at it with an angry hand. He'd always believed that his mother loved him deep down and she just didn't know how to show it. But now he knew. She truly hated him.

"As long as I'm here, you're going to treat that little boy like a human being. And that means he goes to school like any other kid. I'll be here at eight to get him."

The door slammed and Dylan straightened. He ran up the back stairs to his tiny room. He hid his new clothes under the bed and threw himself on the narrow mattress. He swallowed back tears.

Heels clicked up the stairs and paused by his door. The knob turned and his mother's shadow filled the opening. "School isn't going to change anything. You're still going to be a good-for-nothing bastard."

She stalked toward him and stopped beside his bed. She loomed above him like a circling vulture. "You ain't worth nothing to anybody, including the sheriff. He feels sorry for you, thinks it's his Christian duty to help. Pretty soon he's going to forget all about you, just like a bug he stepped on. And then there's only going to be me again. You remember that."

"No he won't! He ain't going to forget about me. Him and Miss O'Hanlon, they said they'd help me."

"So that's the bitch's name. I saw her last week. Thinks she's too good for the likes of us. It won't matter that she said she'd help. She'll change her mind when she finds out what you're really like. She'll see you're more trouble than you're worth, and she'll beat the hell out of you just like I got to do."

"She's not like that!"

Sadie smacked Dylan's cheek, the sound ringing in the confines of the sparse room. "Don't sass me! After the customers leave, I want you to fill the wood boxes and clean up the parlor."

She strode to the door and paused before leaving. "You tell the sheriff I hit you and I'll do worse next time."

Staccato footsteps faded to silence. Only the tinny sound of the player piano and the laughter of the girls drifted into his cell. Dylan's hand crept to his hot cheek, but his eyes remained dry and he studied his sterile surroundings as if seeing them for the first time. A rickety dresser that held only another pair of thready overalls and a couple pairs of underwear, gray from too many washings, stood in the corner. No framed pictures or knickknacks garnished his room.

He reached under his pillow and withdrew a stuffed dog, the tail missing and nearly bald from too many hugs. One of the black button eyes hung from a piece of thread. Dylan wrapped his arms around the worn animal. "Someday I'll have a real dog and he'll follow me everywhere I go, so I won't ever have to be afraid again. And he won't care that I'm a bastard."

Chapter 4

Libby arrived at the schoolhouse early the next morning, making up for her tardiness the day before. Using the wood Jacob and Seth had split during their punishment, she built a fire in the stove. The room's temperature rose steadily, and when the first student arrived, Libby removed her coat.

Twenty-three children trooped in, taking the seats they'd been assigned yesterday. The youngest were arranged across the front row and the oldest in the back, with the middle desks filled by those in between. Libby glanced at the watch pinned to her bodice: eight-fifteen, time to begin. Where were Matt and Dylan?

She stalled, straightening the books on her desk. Eight-sixteen. She wiped the blackboard free of chalk dust. Eight-nineteen. She couldn't put it off any longer. She opened her mouth to begin, and abruptly closed it as the door whisked open.

Matt and Dylan entered and stamped their boots free of snow. Dylan appeared frightened to death, but Matt blocked his escape. Her heart went out to the boy.

"I'm glad to see you could make it, Dylan. Hang your coat and come sit right up front beside Jenny. Sheriff, if you'd like to observe for a little while, you can make yourself comfortable at the back of the classroom." Libby's gaze sent Matt a silent request to sit between Seth and Jacob.

Matt removed his jacket, revealing a freshly laundered tan shirt with a black vest buttoned up over it. A brown bandanna filled the vee at his neck and worn leather chaps clung to his thighs, framing muscular hips. Libby's heart quickened at the masculine sight.

Dylan eased himself into a seat between Jenny Olson and Paul Billings, Seth's younger brother. Dylan's shirt and pants appeared stiff with newness, and his shoes had no paper sticking out of them. His midnight-colored hair lay flat, obviously slicked down with bay rum. Knowing his mother wouldn't have been so extravagant, Libby recognized Matt's contribution. He obviously cared for the boy, and that concern severed a link in the chain of distrust that bound Libby's heart.

Dylan's eyes appeared enormous in his unusually pale complexion, making Libby yearn to comfort him. He seemed so terrified and alone.

Matt had taken her hint and sat between the two older boys. Hatless, Matt averted his head so she wouldn't see the scar, and she longed to tell him she didn't care. With or without the scar, he was one of the most decent men she'd ever met.

"Elvina, please pass out the primers to the oldest group, and Teresa, please give everyone in your section an arithmetic book," Libby said. She handed a stack of books to each of the two girls.

"I'd like the older children to open their primers to page fifty-six," Libby announced. "Read the story and we'll discuss it after I've finished with the others. The middle group, turn to page fifteen. On your slates, do the first ten problems and we'll correct them in a little bit. The rest of you, we're going to have a lesson with letters and sounds."

Matt's thoughtful gaze followed Libby. She picked up a piece of chalk and wrote *a, e, i, o,* and *u* on the large blackboard at the front of the room. As she turned to face the children, her dark wool skirt swirled about her legs. Libby rubbed her hands across her hips and a white chalk mark smudged a slender thigh. She pointed at the letters she'd written. "Can anyone tell me what these are?"

Jenny raised her hand.

"Yes, Jenny?"

Matt leaned back in the too-small chair and crossed his ankles. He folded his arms over his chest and tried to listen to Jenny's answer. He sent sidelong glances at Seth and Jacob, and frowned when he saw the page numbers their books were opened to.

"Miss O'Hanlon said page fifty-six, not eighty-three," he growled.

Startled, the boys flipped to the assigned story and silently began to read. Matt studied the book over Seth's shoulder. He moved his lips, trying to formulate the words by picking out the few letters he recognized. After a few minutes he gave up, frustrated by his inability to understand something a fifteen-year-old could. He glanced up to find Libby's probing gaze upon him. He tried to tell himself that she didn't know what he'd been doing, but it didn't work. Libby was far too perceptive.

His right hand balled into a fist. How could he expect someone like Libby to be attracted to a man who couldn't even read a simple primer? The only emotion he should expect from her was pity. Yet he recalled seeing something different in her eyes as they'd talked in Lenore's parlor. Had he imagined the glow in her cheeks and the pressure of her hands on his fingers? Matt shook his head inwardly. The threads of passion had been there, as surely as his own heartbeat had threatened to thunder out of his chest. What if she *was* attracted to him? A shiver traveled his spine, terrified she might be and equally frightened she wasn't.

He shoved the unnerving thoughts aside and looked at Dylan. A smile tugged at his lips. Little Jenny Olson helped him, correcting a letter he'd written in chalk. They bent over their slates, her light blond hair contrasting with Dylan's dark coloring.

The rest of the children worked quietly, an occasional whisper breaking the silence. Libby strolled around the classroom, her sharp scrutiny missing little. She answered questions in a kind but authoritative voice, and Matt's respect for her jumped another notch. She passed by him and touched his shoulder in a gesture of gratitude. The innocent brush of her hand pierced him with a stab of desire as powerful as a steel blade. As she walked away, he watched the gentle sway of her skirt. Her own scent wafted in her wake, and Matt savored Libby's sweetness. Visions of her lying in bed, with only lilacs and unbound auburn hair clothing her, reeled his senses. His fingers ached to explore the curves and crevices that lay beneath her staid wardrobe. He imagined her calling his name as he brought her over the pinnacle of passion.

"Do it!"

The hoarse whisper snapped Matt out of his erotic reverie.

Jacob leaned back in his chair and spoke behind Matt. "Go ahead, Seth, do it."

Matt's gaze shifted to Seth, sighting a slingshot made of a Y-shaped branch. Before Matt could stop him, Seth released the elastic band and a white projectile flew across the room, splatting on the blackboard a few inches from Libby. Her face turned to the white spot beside her, and she planted her hands on her hips. Her thunderous gaze searched the room.

Seth tucked the weapon into his back pocket.

"Give me that," Matt ordered.

Seth folded his arms over his chest. "Give you what?"

Matt extricated himself from his seat and grabbed him by the shoulders. He hauled the boy out of the classroom into the cool but sunny morning. "Give me that slingshot or I'll take it, and you ain't going to like how I do it."

With a trembling hand, Seth handed him the dangerous toy. "What're you going to do with it?"

"I don't aim to shoot any spitballs at Miss O'Hanlon. Fact is, I think I'm going to keep it in case anybody else starts acting up." Matt gazed at the slingshot. "Yep, this looks to be a mighty good one, too. I could probably knock off a smart-mouth boy at fifty feet with this."

"But I spent three days working to get it right," Seth whined.

"The school ain't no place for you to be fooling with something like this. What if Miss O'Hanlon had turned and you got her in the eye? You could've hurt her or one of the kids. Did you even think about that?"

"I was just having some fun. School's boring."

"It may seem boring now, but you're going to appreciate it later on when you write a letter or read a newspaper. You should be glad you got another teacher so fast."

Seth shrugged. "I s'pose."

Matt released the boy. "After school, you're going to clean the blackboards and fill the wood box for Miss O'Hanlon. You understand?"

He nodded without enthusiasm.

"Go back in there and apologize," Matt said.

Seth opened his mouth as if to protest but instead pursed his lips.

Matt propelled him up the stairs and back into the

classroom. Silence descended and everyone turned to stare.

"Seth has something he'd like to say," Matt announced.

Libby's fingers intertwined and she rested her hands in front of her. "Yes?"

Seth stared at the floor and shifted his feet. "I'm sorry."

"For what?" Libby asked.

"For, uh, shooting the spitball at the blackboard."

Giggles erupted and Seth's face reddened.

"Quiet down, children." Libby waited until silence resumed. "Thank you, Seth, and I assume you won't be shooting any more spitballs in the classroom."

Seth nodded. He slipped into his chair and glared at Jacob.

"Sorry about the interruption, Miss O'Hanlon," Matt apologized. "I'd best get back to work. Thanks for letting me sit in for a time."

"You're welcome, Sheriff. Come back whenever you'd like," Libby replied with a smile.

Matt caught Dylan's gaze and winked. He set his hat on his head and threw his coat over an arm. With one last nod at Libby, he left the classroom.

He strode across the school yard, squinting against the dazzling sun reflected off the snow. He had enjoyed observing Libby teaching, had enjoyed it too much. She was easy on the eyes, but more than that, there was a quality about her that drew him like a bee to honeysuckle. The proud tilt of her chin, and stubborn eyes the color of mountain grass in the summer beckoned him, tempting him to forget the past. However, his wife and son weren't easily dismissed from his thoughts. Their faces haunted his dreams and stole his peace of mind.

Gunshots brought Matt's head up sharply. Two men were backing out of the bank. As they turned to mount their horses, Matt saw masks covering the lower half of their faces. With a smooth motion, he withdrew his revolver and raised it to fire, but their galloping horses took them out of range. Matt holstered his Colt as he ran down the street, then jumped up the stairs to the boardwalk and into the bank.

Chaos reigned inside.

"Sheriff!"

Matt turned at the sound of his name. "What happened, George?"

"Mr. Pinkney's been shot," Johnson replied, his voice pitched high with terror.

Matt pushed past him and squatted down beside the bank owner. Blood stained Pinkney's arm and Matt tore the sleeve open, looking past the splash of crimson. "He's all right. It's just a graze. Have Eli get it bandaged up." He glanced over and saw a woman's body on the floor. With the bright red coat and yellow hat, there was no doubt who it was. "Is Mrs. Beidler all right?"

A man dressed like a farmer nodded. "She fainted."

"Anyone got some smelling salts?" Matt asked.

"Throw a bucket of water on her. That'll wake her right up," the sodbuster suggested.

Matt envisioned Adelaide Beidler's yellow feathers plastered across her face, and a smile tempted his lips. He placed a hand over his mouth to rub away the smirk and he straightened. "Can anyone tell me what happened?"

George Johnson stepped forward and mopped his sweating brow. "Two men came in and stepped up to my window. They both pull out their guns, and one of them tells me he wants all the money in the drawers back here. We weren't about to argue. I stuffed the money in a bag for him. Right then Mr. Pinkney comes out of his office and sees what's happening. He tried to get out the back door, but one of the men shot him."

"You recognize either of the robbers?"

George shook his head.

"Anybody else recognize either of the men?" Matt asked.

Heads shook a negative reply.

Eli pressed through the growing crowd and stooped down beside Pinkney. He opened his black bag and, with a sharp scissors, cut away his sleeve. He glanced at Matt. "I heard the commotion and figured I might be needed."

Matt nodded. "You figured right. How's Pinkney?"

"It's nothing serious. You going after them by yourself?"

"I ain't got a choice," Matt answered with a shrug.

"Get a few others to ride with you."

"There's only two of them. I can handle it."

Eli sighed. "You and that damned pride. I've seen enough of your blood the last few years."

Matt strode out of the bank, aware of Eli's muttering behind his back. He'd made a few mistakes in his time and he wasn't proud of them, but they'd happened and he couldn't change things. Matt often wondered if Eli still saw him as the half-dead drunkard he'd found in the alley four years ago.

He detoured to his office and retrieved his Spencer rifle and extra ammunition. Grabbing his bedroll and saddlebag, he headed to the livery. Puffy gray clouds had moved in from the northwest. He smelled a hint of snow in the air, but his long-legged stride didn't falter.

Excitement coursed through him. He would find the two men and bring them in to face the judge. In his town, lawbreakers didn't escape the hand of justice. To Matt, the law was the only thing in the world that was truly black and white, right and wrong. There were no shades of gray involved.

His chestnut gelding neighed a greeting and Matt swept a hand across the horse's neck. Alamo had saved Matt's life more than once during the war and had come all the way from Texas with him.

"We got us a couple bad hombres to catch, partner." Matt tightened the saddle cinch beneath the horse's belly.

Alamo snorted.

Matt rubbed the velvety nose affectionately. "Yeah, I know there's some snow coming, but I got a job to do. These folks hired me to take care of problems like this, and I ain't going to let them down."

Coaxing the metal bit into the horse's mouth, he fitted the bridle on. He stuffed his duster in the blankets, tied the bedroll behind the saddle, then led Alamo out of the stable and mounted agily. By habit, he angled the brim of his hat lower on the left side of his face. He glanced in the direction of the schoolhouse but could see only a thread of smoke rising amidst the trees. The overpowering urge to tell Libby goodbye surprised him. Getting away for a time would help him to sort out his conflicting emotions. With a determined oath, he urged Alamo in the opposite direction.

The students scrambled for their lunch buckets, then jostled one another as they sat in small groups and ate. Libby noticed no one asked Dylan to join them and he remained in his seat, his face buried in a book. After a moment's hesitation, she dug in her bag and her fingers closed around the sandwiches Lenore had made that morning. Probing a little deeper, she found a sack of cookies.

Libby lowered herself into the desk beside Dylan. "Are you hungry?"

Dylan's eyes widened when he spied the food and he began to nod, but stopped himself. "Naw."

Libby unwrapped the brown paper. "That's too bad, because I was hoping you'd help me eat my lunch. You see, Mrs. Potts thinks I need fattening up, so she sent all this food with me."

The smell of roast beef surrounded them and the boy's gaze fastened on her lunch. "If you're sure you ain't—I mean, aren't—going to eat it all."

"I'm sure." She handed Dylan the other package. "And we have cookies for dessert, too."

Dylan took a monstrous bite. "As long as you're sure," he mumbled.

"What did you have for breakfast this morning?" Libby asked, hoping she sounded merely curious.

"Nothing. Didn't have no supper last night neither. I ate the oatmeal cookies Mrs. Potts gave me."

"Why didn't you have supper?"

"Ma was feeling poorly," he said with a note of defensiveness.

"I tell you what. If your ma is feeling poorly again, you come on over to Mrs. Potts and eat with us. Would you like that?" Libby held her breath, hoping her fury hadn't spilled out in her tone.

"Can the sheriff come, too?"

"You can bring him if you'd like." Much as Libby hated to admit it, she looked forward to seeing Matt across the supper table again.

A shy smile graced the boy's thin face. "Then I'd like to."

Libby nibbled a cookie and gave the remaining ones to Dylan, who wolfed them down. She smiled gently and touched the boy's shoulder. Dylan jerked beneath her hand and her lips curved downward. "Did I hurt you?"

Dylan blinked and his dark eyelashes swept across his cheeks. "No."

Libby's frown grew. "Did someone else hurt you?"

He shrugged and picked up his book.

She lifted the primer from his hands and asked softly, "Did your mother hurt you last night?"

"No."

She recognized the lie of omission, for she had often used it herself. Was Dylan also lying to himself? Was he telling himself that his mother wouldn't beat him again? Did he truly believe tomorrow would make everything better? Overwhelming empathy for the boy filled Libby. His pain became hers, and tears threatened behind closed eyelids.

A small hand settled on her arm. "What's wrong, Miss O'Hanlon?"

Libby opened moisture-laden eyes to Dylan's concerned expression. She shook her head and smiled with quivering lips. "Nothing time won't heal. I know what you're feeling, Dylan. If you ever want to talk to anybody, or if you need help with anything, you can come to me."

Dylan nodded, and trusting eyes accepted the offer.

Gently, Libby touched Dylan's cheek and stood. She moved to the front of the classroom and clapped her hands together. "Time to get back to work."

The afternoon sped by uneventfully. By three o'clock, sullen gray clouds pillowed the sky and feathered the air with snowflakes. Before Libby allowed the children out of the schoolhouse, she checked each one for buttoned coats and tightly bound scarves.

She tugged Dylan's cap over his ears and tied the wool scarf around his neck. The familiar smell of bay rum wafted up, and visions of Matt awkwardly helping Dylan dress brought a painful lump to her throat. She swallowed. "Would you like me to walk you home?"

Dylan shook his head. "I'm going to see the sheriff."

"Have him take you home. You shouldn't be out in this weather by yourself."

"I like the snow. It makes everything all clean and white, like it's covered with sugar."

Libby smiled. "All right, but you be careful."

"Bye, Miss O'Hanlon."

"Goodbye, Dylan." The boy loped into the swirling snow and disappeared.

She turned from the door to find Seth and Jacob still in the classroom. "You boys should get going before the weather worsens."

Seth kicked at the puncheon floor with a booted toe. "The sheriff said I had to stay and clean your blackboards and fill the wood box before I left."

Libby stifled a chuckle at the boy's obvious discomfort. "Since Jacob was just as guilty as you, I think both of you should take care of the blackboard and wood box."

Jacob's lips curled into a scowl. "I'll bring in the wood."

Libby worked on the following day's lessons until Seth and Jacob finished. She glanced out the window and a curtain of white greeted her. "Now get on home before your parents start worrying."

"Good night, Miss O'Hanlon," Seth said and received a poke in the ribs from Jacob.

Libby ignored Jacob's surliness and smiled sweetly at Seth. "Good night, Seth. Good night, Jacob."

Their arguing voices faded behind the closed door. Intent on reaching the boardinghouse before a full-blown blizzard descended upon the town, Libby tossed her long coat on. She turned down the damper on the stove and blew out the lantern.

Somber clouds darkened the day and Libby used the faint lights of town to guide her home. Crunching across the snow, she thought about Dylan. The familiar fear she'd glimpsed in his enormous eyes brought black memories tumbling out of the hidden recesses in her mind. She understood Dylan's terror and confusion, and her stomach cramped with her remembered torment. She recalled the trapped helplessness when the sadistic blows were delivered, and the pain of leather rending skin. And all the horrible acts were executed by someone who was supposed to love you.

By the time she arrived at the house, snowflakes covered her head and shoulders and clung to her eyelashes. Pots and pans clattered in the kitchen, and Lenore's off-key singing met Libby's ears. A need to be alone with her tortured recollections sent Libby up to her room.

After removing her damp coat and shoes, she pulled the Boston rocker close to the fireplace. She added another log to the flames, then tucked her feet beneath her on the chair and wrapped her arms around her waist. How many times had she told herself not to anger Harrison, to walk softly, and speak only when spoken to? If she did these things then he wouldn't beat her. So much pain, so much self-recrimination, so much loss. She had believed it was her fault, that Harrison was only punishing her for her misdeeds. After killing him, she'd spent days alone thinking, wondering what had turned Harrison into the monster he'd become. He'd been raised in a wealthy home and wanted for nothing. The man she'd fallen in love with had been thoughtful, courteous, and treated her with respect. Only after the wedding had he revealed the beast beneath the gentleman's attire. The four years they'd been together, he had chipped away her soul, leaving only a shell of a woman. Despair had controlled the hands that swung the iron poker.

Would Dylan's mother someday push the boy too far? Would Dylan someday reach the end of his tolerance just as she had? Would Dylan someday kill his own mother? She couldn't allow him to ruin his life as she had destroyed hers. Before she left in the spring, she would ensure Dylan was free of his mother's insanity. Matt would help. He cared about the boy, and maybe he knew of a family who would adopt him.

Branded a murderer, Libby's future lay as barren as the Montana winter. And as a doctor, Libby had violated the highest decree: preservation of life—and she would bear that burden on her conscience forever.

Lenore passed the mashed potatoes to Libby. "Have some more potatoes and gravy. You need more meat on your ribs if you're going to survive a Montana winter."

Libby smiled and handed Virgil Tanner the bowl. "I've already eaten two helpings."

Tanner spooned the remainder of the potatoes onto his plate and poured some smooth brown gravy over the mound. "Lenore's right, Miss O'Hanlon. You're just getting a taste of winter. It's going to get a whole lot worse before it gets better."

"He's right, honey. Why, the temperature's fallen thirty degrees if it's fallen a notch."

Libby accepted the remark without comment. "Where's Mr. Johnson? He didn't have to work late in this storm, did he?"

"You didn't hear, did you?" Lenore asked. Libby shook her head. "The bank was robbed shortly before noon. I'm sure George had to get an accurate account of what was stolen for old Pinkney. I swear, if Pinkney so much as loses a nickel, he turns the bank upside down looking for it."

"Was anyone hurt?" Libby asked.

Eli's arrival interrupted Lenore's reply. "Pinkney was shot, but nothing serious," he answered. "You got any food for a tired old sawbones, or has Virgil cleaned you out?"

Lenore pressed him into a chair. "I always got extra. You sit yourself down and I'll fill a plate for you."

"Were the men caught?" Libby asked Eli after Lenore bustled into the kitchen.

He shook his head. "Matt went after them."

"Did he get them?"

"He's not back yet."

Libby's heart flipflopped. "You mean he's somewhere out in the blizzard?"

Eli nodded, concern furrowing his brow.

"Shouldn't someone go out looking for him?"

"Then we'd have more than one person missing. We can only hope Matt found some shelter out of the storm."

"And if he didn't?"

"You can't think that way, Miss O'Hanlon. Matt's damned resourceful. He'll be fine."

"Then why are you worried?"

"A doctor always worries. It comes with the job." He smiled, but Libby noted the gesture didn't touch his eyes.

Her hunger fled. Alone in the snowstorm, Matt had little chance of surviving the cold if he didn't find sanctuary from the bone-chilling north wind. He could become disoriented and lose his way home. In Nebraska, she had seen her share of frozen livestock that had died within twenty feet of shelter. The vision of Matt's unseeing eyes and frost-covered face brought terror to her heart.

Lenore set a plate in front of the doctor. "Here you go, Eli. Eat up."

Libby pushed back her chair and stood. "If you'll excuse me, I think I'll go up to my room. I've got schoolwork to do."

"You come on down to the parlor in an hour and have some bread pudding with rum sauce," Lenore invited.

Libby managed a weak smile. "I'll be down."

Helplessness loomed over her like a vulture, and she forced herself to stroll calmly to her room. She closed the door and leaned against its welcome solidness. A week ago, she'd considered Matt Brandon an illiterate lout. Now the thought of him alone in the middle of a blizzard twisted her stomach into knots. What if he didn't return? Dylan would be devastated, and Libby wasn't so sure her own heart would be unaffected.

Chapter 5

$\sim\!\!\text{---}\!\!\text{---}\!\!\infty\!\!\infty\!\!\text{---}\!\!\text{---}\!\!\sim$

The parlor was warm, almost hot, and Libby suspected Lenore had added extra fuel for Eli's arthritis. He sat comfortably on the sofa beside Lenore, who mended one of his shirts. If Libby hadn't known better, she would've thought they were a long-married couple.

Libby managed to eat a small portion of the bread pudding. Her gaze traveled to the window, and she wondered for the hundredth time if Matt had found shelter from the storm. She picked up a needlepoint project she'd begun to pass the time during her weeks of hiding in hotel rooms. Holding the needle with accustomed deftness, she stitched a tight line.

"You hold that needle like you're a surgeon," Eli commented.

Libby nearly dropped the pillowcase. "Why do you say that?"

"The way you concentrate on those tiny stitches, like you're stitching up a vein or artery."

Libby swallowed. One of her professors in college had made the same observation. She laughed with more breath than sound. "I've heard of women doctors, but I can't imagine myself as one."

Eli pulled the pipe from his mouth and studied the stem. "I don't know why not."

Eli's comment surprised her and reminded her of her father. Neither man held the common belief that females were too delicate to be doctors. Homesickness welled within her, and moisture clouded her gaze. She wished she could confide in Eli as she'd done with her father.

Libby concentrated on her needlework to make the tears disappear. After a couple of stitches her mind wandered once more to Matt, and the material lay forgotten in her lap.

"What's got you woolgathering?" Lenore asked.

"I was thinking about the sheriff, wondering how he was," Libby answered honestly.

"I'm a mite worried myself. He's too stubborn for his own good, that's what I say. Why, when Eli first found him half-frozen and more dead than alive, I figured for sure he was headed for the pearly gates, but he pulled through. I always thought it was the whiskey in him—pickled pretty good, he was."

"Are you talking about Matt?"

Lenore nodded vehemently. "He never touches strong spirits now, only coffee. He's afraid he'll get a taste for the whiskey again."

Libby allowed the new information to sink in. "Did he start drinking after he got the scar?"

"A couple years afterward, but I think the scar had something to do with the it," Eli replied.

"What do you mean?"

"Miss O'Hanlon, there's one thing you should know about Matt Brandon. He's a proud man, and that pride was his downfall a few years back. I hope he's got more sense now. Although, in all the years I been healing folks, I've found pride is like a chronic disease—keeps coming back when a person least expects it."

Libby wondered if pride made Matt so self-conscious of the scar. She had seen far worse on others, and they hadn't seemed as worried as Matt. Why was he so ashamed of the disfigurement?

"Don't you worry. He'll be back in time for Thanksgiving. There's nothing that can keep him from my turkey and dressing," Lenore assured.

Only freezing to death. Libby chastised herself for being so pessimistic, but the fear wouldn't vanish. "Thanksgiving is still two days away. He'll be back before then, won't he?"

Eli shrugged. "Depends on how far he has to track the thieves. Matt's done this before and he's always come back. There's no reason this time should be any different."

Libby nodded and commanded her lips to form a tailored smile. "I'm sure you're right. I'd best turn in."

"Good night, dear," Lenore said.

Eli echoed her sentiments, and Libby returned to her room. Since the fire had burned down to embers, cool air nipped her cheeks. She added more wood and listened to the popping and crackling. The comforting sound should have soothed her, but the underlying fear refused to be consoled.

Matt rubbed his gloved hands together and held them over the tiny fire. "Never thought the day would come when I wished I was back in Texas."

His voice sounded unusually loud in the tight confines of the dim cave, and Alamo's ears pricked forward. The wind wailed in the night, and a stray breeze sent glowing sparks shooting upward to disappear in the blackness. Matt shivered, tugging his collar up to cover the back of his neck. His fingers were clumsy, the cold causing them to alternately tingle and grow numb. He stuck his hands under his arms to warm them.

Matt glanced at the patient horse. Alamo stood between him and the cave's entrance, blocking some of the frigid gusts. Matt had smelled the snow long before the sky clouded over, but he'd thought he'd be able to catch the two thieves prior to the storm hitting. But Mother Nature had her own ideas, and he'd been lucky to find the cut in the sandstone hills.

He didn't doubt his survival skills, but the loss of the two robbers angered him. The snow would obliterate any sign of the men unless he stumbled upon their bodies. He didn't hold much hope for that outcome. He'd memorized the horses' tracks, and if luck rode his shoulders, he might spot the cracked shoe print in the snow or mud someday.

Hell, I'm grasping at straws. What would everybody, including Libby, think of a lawman who couldn't even protect his own town? His shoulders slumped as exhaustion stole across him. Ten years ago he'd had a wife, a son, and a small ranch; now all he had was a gun, a horse, and his badge. Not a hell of a lot to show for thirty-eight years. If he froze to death, he'd leave no legacy behind, nothing to mark his passage on this earth.

The thought terrified him.

The wind rattled the windows and flung ice crystals against the glass. The morning sun lay hidden by the blowing snow, and Libby debated whether she should go to school or not.

"The children won't come in on a day like this, so you don't have to worry," Lenore stated, pouring batter on a hot griddle.

Libby sipped coffee from a steaming mug. "But what if someone does show up?"

"You're thinking of Sadie's boy, aren't you?"

"I'm worried about him, Lenore. If he shows up and I'm not there, he might think I abandoned him."

"He's a bright boy. He won't go over in weather like this."

"He is smart, isn't he? I wish his mother wouldn't

fight us every step of the way. Just because she's a . . ." Libby glanced around, "soiled dove doesn't mean she has to ruin her son's life."

"I worry about him, too, but you got to remember he does belong to Sadie. I knew a woman one time who loved her children, but she'd have fits and beat them black-and-blue. She didn't know what she was doing, and afterward she'd cry and carry on, sorry for what she'd done. Maybe Sadie's like that."

"That's no excuse, Lenore. Children shouldn't have to fear their own parents. It's just not natural."

"Sounds like you know from experience." Lenore's sharp blue eyes peered at her.

Libby lowered her gaze. "My mother died when I was a baby. My father and older brother raised me, but they never laid a hand on me. If the truth were known, they spoiled me rotten."

Lenore slid another golden flapjack on to Libby's plate. "Well, I think they done a fine job, and you aren't a bit spoiled. Eat up."

Libby spread pale butter over the pancake and added a few drops of sorghum. "After I'm done eating, I'm going over to the school, Lenore. If the weather improves a few of the children might show up, and I should be there since there won't be classes tomorrow."

Lenore sighed and aimed a wooden spoon at Libby. "You shouldn't be going out in this weather, but I can tell you got your mind made up. My Willard was the same way. Once he got something in his head, dynamite couldn't get it out. One time he decides we need a new privy and he's going to make it with bricks. We were the laughingstocks of the county until a storm came through and that privy was the only thing left standing. After that, folks always said they wanted their places built like Willard's brick outhouse."

Laughter convulsed Libby. "You made that up!"

"Are you calling me a liar? Because if you are, I'm

going to have to throw you out of my kitchen." Lenore's wink belied her threat.

Libby smiled and shook her head. "I would never call you a liar. However, I would say you had a gift for storytelling."

"My pa, now, he could tell a good story. I remember many a night listening to him spinning some yarn." Lenore's gaze turned inward. "I can still see him sitting under the old oak tree, pipe in his mouth and wearing patched overalls. Ma called him lazy and no-good, but I'll always remember how safe I felt listening to that deep voice of his."

"Is he still alive?"

"He died about twenty years ago. Consumption got him. Ma died a few months later. We always figured a broken heart took her, because no matter how much she complained about Pa, she loved him."

Libby nodded. She would never know that kind of love. When she had killed Harrison, she had forfeited her own chance at happiness. The threat of the law someday finding her would haunt her forever.

She finished the flapjack, though she didn't taste the last few bites.

Libby forged through the dense drifts, glad she'd worn her trousers beneath the heavy skirt. She arrived at the building out of breath and sweating beneath her warm clothing. Thankful that Seth and Jacob had filled the wood box, Libby started a fire in the black potbellied stove. She thawed her fingers and took a shovel to create a path from the school to the outhouse and to the woodpile. After bringing a couple of armloads of wood in, Libby sat down and caught her breath.

She'd only been in the chair a minute when the door opened and Dylan entered.

"Good morning," Libby greeted, surprised and

concerned to see him. "I wasn't sure if anyone would come to school today."

"I seen it worse than this," Dylan remarked. "Last year there was a drift bigger than me. I tried walking over it, but I fell in and the sheriff had to pull me out."

"Don't try that now. The sheriff isn't here."

With red hands, Dylan fumbled with his coat buttons.

Libby knelt down to help him.

"You think the sheriff is all right?" Dylan asked quietly.

"He'll be just fine. The sheriff can take care of himself." Libby wished she felt as confident as she sounded.

Dylan sighed. "That's what I thought, but Ma said nobody could survive that storm last night."

"Is your mother still feeling poorly?" Libby removed Dylan's threadbare scarf from around his neck.

Dylan shrugged. "She's okay, I guess."

"Did she hurt you?"

"Naw." He pressed his right cheek to his shoulder and a haunted expression touched his somber eyes.

Libby frowned and tilted her head to view the side of his face. A faint blue and purple swelling shadowed the area below his eye. She swallowed, but the fury refused to abate. "Did she do that to you?"

Dylan's chin jutted forward. "I ran into a door."

He wasn't ready to confide in her yet. "Go ahead and sit down."

She moved to her desk and studied the vulnerable boy. His shirt was wrinkled and his dark hair mussed. Obviously he'd dressed himself for school.

When no other children arrived by nine o'clock, Libby moved her chair closer to the stove. "It looks like it's just you and me. Bring your desk over here so we won't get so cold."

Anxiously, Dylan dragged the wooden seat up beside Libby. "You mean you're just going to teach me today?"

Libby nodded. "Is that all right?"

A toothy grin gave his answer.

"Why don't we start with some new letters," she suggested.

Flakes of snow sifted in through a crack in a corner of the room, but Libby kept the stove filled to keep them toasty warm. Lunchtime showed little change in the weather, and Libby split her generous meal with Dylan. During the afternoon she gave him a lesson in arithmetic, and the boy caught on to addition and subtraction quickly.

The wind and snow diminished in the afternoon, and by four o'clock, they could see Deer Creek.

"Would you like to clean the blackboard for me, Dylan?" Libby asked.

A smile lit up his face and he nodded eagerly.

"You think the sheriff is back?" Dylan asked after the board was spotless.

"I don't know. What do you say we walk over to the jail and find out?"

A few minutes later they bustled down the main street and into the sheriff's office. The room was cold, and there was no sign anybody had been there in the past twenty-four hours.

"It doesn't look like he's back yet," Libby stated. A haphazard pile of papers in the center of the messy desk drew her attention. "What are those?"

"Wanted posters," Dylan answered. "The sheriff looks through them most every day."

Libby shifted uncomfortably. "Has he gotten any new ones lately?"

"He gets 'em all the time."

She inched closer to the scarred desk. "Do you think he'd mind if you and I looked at them?"

Dylan grinned. "Naw. Maybe we can catch us an outlaw."

"Maybe," Libby said weakly. She removed a dirty tin plate from the chair and lowered herself into the scuffed seat. Her buttocks shifted across the slight ridge in the middle of the worn cushion. Obviously Matt had spent many hours sitting there, and the padding had molded to his shape. Libby closed her eyes, slowly rubbing her hands over the chair's arms, and envisioning Matt behind the desk. The faint smell of bay rum tickled her nostrils and her eyelids lifted, but Matt wasn't there. Disappointment replaced her tantalizingly wicked thoughts.

Dylan propped an elbow on the desktop. Tentatively, Libby reached for the stack and studied the first outlaw. Weasly eyes under bushy eyebrows peered at her, and a scruffy beard lent the picture a villainous overtone. She shivered.

"What'd he do?" Dylan asked.

"It says he's robbed two trains and shot a passenger."

Dylan screwed up his face and studied the number across the top of the paper. "One thousand dollars." His sparkling gaze found Libby. "If we got him, we'd get one thousand dollars. That's a lot of money, isn't it?"

"It sure is. Who taught you how to read numbers?"

"The sheriff. He teached me while we looked at the wanted posters."

"He 'taught' me."

Dylan frowned. "That's what I said."

Fondly, Libby smiled at the boy, imagining Matt painstakingly showing Dylan each number and explaining what the zeroes meant. "What would you do with a thousand dollars?"

"I'd get me a dog and a horse and a gun."

"What would you do with a gun?"

"I'd practice with it until I could draw as fast as the

sheriff, then I'd leave this old town and never come back."

"Wouldn't the sheriff be lonely without you? I know I'd miss you."

Dylan scrunched up his face and thought for a moment. "You and the sheriff can come with me."

Libby clasped his chapped hand and squeezed gently. "That's very generous of you, Dylan, but you won't solve any problem by running away from it."

The impulsive words were spoken before she could stop herself. *Who am I to be giving advice I can't even follow?*

Dylan shrugged and looked at the next paper. "He looks mean."

Libby read the crimes he'd allegedly committed. "He should. He killed three men."

Dylan's dark eyes saucered. "I bet we'd get a lot of money if we caught him."

"Ten thousand dollars." *What price is on my head?*

They continued leafing through the papers, studying each outlaw's picture and the heinous crimes associated with each man. With every new sheet, Libby held her breath, wondering if her likeness would be next. The pile trickled down until only a few remained.

"I figured you'd be here."

Libby glanced up to see a blond woman with a heavy layer of powder on her face, and eyelashes spiked with black coloring. Frigid blue eyes studied her and a scowl curled the woman's red lips.

"I'm afraid the sheriff isn't here," Libby said.

"I wasn't looking for the sheriff. I was looking for my son and looks like I found him." The woman's throaty voice grated like fingernails on a chalkboard, and Libby clenched her teeth.

She rose from behind the battered desk and stepped around Dylan. "It's nice to meet you, Mrs. Rivers."

She ignored Libby's outstretched hand and sniffed

contemptuously. "It's miss, not missus. You must be the new schoolteacher."

Libby withdrew her hand and intertwined her fingers to cover their trembling. She fought the urge to scratch out the callous eyes. "That's right. Libby O'Hanlon. I've been meaning to talk to you."

Sadie stepped forward on surprisingly tiny black high-heeled boots and grabbed Dylan's arm. "There ain't nothing we need to talk about. He's got chores to do at home."

Libby's fingers curled around Sadie's spangled wrist. "Let go of him."

A flinty gaze clashed with Libby's eyes and moved downward to her unflinching hold. "Take your uppity hands off me! He's my son and you have no right telling me what I can and can't do to him."

Dylan remained Sadie's prisoner, his muscles tense, but he didn't attempt to escape.

"You don't have the right to be working him to death or beating him. A child isn't a possession to do with what you please, but a responsibility to see that he is loved and knows right from wrong," Libby exclaimed.

"I said take your lily white hands off me."

Orneriness kept Libby's grasp about the thin wrist a moment longer. She released it reluctantly. They battered stares like two mountain goats fighting over a piece of a cliff.

"You and the sheriff had best learn you got no business interfering with my son. I won't stop him from coming to school, but you remember this, he isn't going to be nothing but a bastard. No amount of learning can change that."

"He can be whatever he wants to be, Miss Rivers." Libby noticed Dylan's pasty complexion. "I'd like to talk to him for a minute, then I'll bring him home."

"You've talked to him all day. I need him now."

Libby bit her tongue. "Please."

A triumphant sneer thinned Sadie's lips. "Well, since you put it so nice and polite-like." She released Dylan. "I want you home in five minutes."

Dylan nodded, fear clouding his expression.

Sadie glanced about the cluttered office and a cruel smile lit her ruby lips. "I see Sheriff Brandon isn't back yet. I wouldn't be surprised if he's frozen under ten feet of snow. Who says Fate doesn't have a sense of humor?"

Her chilling laughter echoed off the sturdy walls long after the door slammed behind her.

Moisture pooled in Dylan's luminescent eyes. "Is he really dead?"

Libby knelt in front of the boy and wrapped her arms around his shoulders. He jerked back, away from the comforting gesture. Startled, Libby studied the abject fear written in his features. His mother had already left an indelible mark of terror in Dylan, but a thread of trust still twined through the wariness. It wasn't too late. Yet.

"Do you know what tomorrow is, Dylan?" Libby asked softly.

He shrugged.

Libby's heart twisted at the boy's apathy. "It's Thanksgiving, and Mrs. Potts said she's going to cook a huge turkey. There'll be so much food we're going to need help eating it all. We'd really appreciate it if you'd come over and eat with us."

A spark of interest flared in Dylan's dull face. "I don't know if I can get away from my ma."

"I'll come over and get you at noon, and you can spend the rest of the day with Mrs. Potts and me. After we eat, we can play checkers or read or whatever you'd like to do."

Animation brightened his grave countenance. "Ma usually don't wake up until late, so she won't know."

Libby got to her feet. "All right. You be ready to go when I come to get you." She held out her hand, and after a moment's hesitation, Dylan grasped it. Nearly overcome by the simple gesture of trust, Libby blinked to dam the threatening tears.

After a silent trek across the street and down the alley, they arrived at the huge white house. The imposing structure didn't impress Libby, for she'd lived in a far larger home. However, the method by which the house had been paid for disgusted her. Leaving Dylan in such a place, no matter how ostentatious, brought an internal rebellion. At that moment she didn't know who she hated more: Sadie Rivers for raising Dylan in such a place, or herself for abandoning him.

She gazed down into vulnerable blue pools. "I'll be here tomorrow to get you, Dylan. I promise."

He nodded but didn't release her hand. His fathomless stare brought an ache to Libby's chest. She stepped away first.

"Goodbye, Miss O'Hanlon." The tone of his voice reminded Libby of a death knell.

"Good night, Dylan," she managed to choke out.

He entered the back door and Libby turned away. Her breath froze in the air, creating a haze of white that dissipated before the next cloud formed. She blinked back the moisture banking her eyes. How could Dylan's mother treat him like a beast of burden and call him such spiteful names?

She'd been in Deer Creek less than two weeks, and was already entangled in the lives of a mistreated boy and an enigmatic lawman. What was wrong with her? She had her own problems, her own horrible secrets to keep hidden. But no matter how much she wanted to forget Dylan and Matt, she could do so no more easily than she could make her soft heart stop beating.

Libby brushed aside a lone tear. She had forfeited

her chance to be a mother when she'd killed Harrison. She suppressed a sob and pressed her fists into her stomach. She'd sacrificed everything to save her sanity. Had the price been too high?

By nightfall Matt had not yet returned, and Libby's nerves were strung tighter than a piano wire. She'd eaten supper at the unusually quiet table, and as soon as she'd forced down a few mouthfuls, she readied herself for bed. Removing the somber clothing that had become her uniform, she replaced it with a petal-soft, snow white nightgown. Brushing her full auburn hair, she counted the strokes but found her concentration lacking. At what she thought was one hundred whisks through the riotous tendrils, Libby braided the mass into a thick plait extending nearly to her waist.

She added a log to the fireplace and crawled into bed. Her stiff body refused to relax, and the confrontation with Dylan's mother played across her mind. How could a woman treat her own son so deplorably? Matt had no family connections to the boy, yet he cared for him as if Dylan were his own. Libby blinked. *Could he be Matt's child?* Perhaps he and Sadie had known each other during the war, and Dylan had been the result of that "friendship." The possibility seemed slight, especially since Matt had fought for the Confederacy and Dylan's mother had no trace of a southern accent. No, if he were Dylan's father, Matt would do anything short of murder to get the boy away from the heartless woman.

Libby reached for a book on the bed stand. She studied the frayed cover of her favorite dime novel, *Ambush at Chimney Rock*. Perhaps escaping into an imaginary adventure would banish her dismal thoughts for a little while. Libby scanned the first page, but visions of Matt snowbound in the night intruded. Where was he? Had he found a place to escape the brutal wind and heavy snowfall? Or had he fallen into a deep crevice in the side of a mountain, and lay buried alive? She envisioned him trying to dig out of the wintry grave, his strong hands bloody from ice and desperation. Libby attempted to dispel the tormented images, but tendrils of fear wrapped themselves about her chest and squeezed tightly.

She tossed the book aside and threw back her covers. Pulling on her long flannel robe, Libby settled into the rocking chair. Shadows created by the flickering fire danced on the walls. A man's voice from the street hollered an obscenity, and footsteps clomped on the boardwalk below. Faint snores from George Johnson's room floated up through the floorboards. The normal, everyday sounds held no place in the whirling tumult of her mind: Matt was missing, Dylan was all alone, and she was a murderer.

Libby lifted four plates down from a cupboard and carried them into the dining room. A minute later she returned to the kitchen and sniffed appreciatively at the varied aromas, the dominant one being the turkey baking in the oven.

"I hadn't realized Mr. Johnson had relatives living in town," she commented to Lenore.

"He spends every holiday with his sister and her family but doesn't see much of them otherwise. And Virgil, he heads to his brother's place over near Juniper for Thanksgiving and Christmas, as long as there isn't a blizzard brewing. Course, I recall him going there one year with a norther coming. I tried to talk him out of it but you know men. It was like talking to a post—just as dense, if you know what I mean."

Libby grinned. "I know exactly what you mean. My father and brother were the same way."

Lenore stirred the lumpy gravy vigorously, splashing some on top of the stove. "Where do they live?"

Libby's amused smile fled. "Father died about seven years ago and Corey was killed in the war. I don't have any other family."

A plump hand patted Libby's arm. "You got me. You remind me of my girl, Sara." Lenore opened the stove. "Another hour or so and it'll be ready."

Libby's expressive eyes widened at the succulent turkey. "How are four of us going to eat all that?"

Lenore's jolly face creased in a grin. "You haven't seen a seven-year-old boy put away food, have you?"

She shook her head.

Lenore closed the oven door and speared a potato in the boiling pot. "It's a sight to behold. When my Daniel was seven, he couldn't get enough to eat. I would make six pies and set them out to cool, and I swear Daniel would have one eaten and be working on the second before I could catch him. Boys start filling up in the toes and work up. By the time they're full up to the top of their heads, their toes are empty again. Besides, Eli can do some damage to a good meal, too, and when Matt gets here, why, we'll be lucky if we have enough."

"You really think Matt's going to make it back for dinner?" Libby asked hopefully.

"Not a doubt. He's not going to miss out on my corn bread stuffing."

Despite Lenore's optimism, worry for Matt's safety overshadowed the holiday mood. Libby prayed for his return, but didn't expect the supplication to be answered. Too many entreaties had been ignored by God in the past few years. To distract her disheartening thoughts, she asked, "Where are all your children now?"

"Scattered to the four winds. Two died when they were just young'uns. Then I got a couple down in Missouri, another in Kentucky, one settled in Colorado, and one is back east in Philadelphia."

"Do you get to see them at all?"

"Not nearly as much as I'd like. Miss the grandchildren, too. Got eleven of them." She handed Libby a jar. "Here, open this and put some of those pickles in a bowl."

Libby wrapped a corner of her apron around the lid and twisted until the cover turned. Vinegar and pickling spices tickled her nose. Using a fork, she fished into the jar. "So why do you stay here? You could go down to Missouri and be closer to some of them."

Lenore leaned a fleshy hip against a wood counter and shook her head. Gray curls dipped around her face. "I wouldn't want to be a burden to them. Besides, I have a life here. Who would mend Eli's clothes, or cook for you and the others? No, Deer Creek is where I plan to spend the rest of my days and, God willing, that will be a few more years."

"You have everything you want, don't you?" Libby asked softly.

Lenore turned back to the stove. "Nobody ever has everything they want, but some of us get real close. I always say it's no use looking at a glass of milk and saying it's half empty when it's really half full. Now, you'd best go get Dylan before he thinks you forgot him."

"It's still a little early."

"Better early than late, especially with a little shaver like him."

Libby nodded and reached behind her to pull the bow loose at the back of her apron. She tugged it over her head and whisked out of the kitchen.

Five minutes later she arrived at the brothel and knocked softly. She glanced around uneasily and shifted her feet, wondering what Mrs. Beidler would say if she spied her. She held a gloved hand to her mouth to stifle the giggle as she imagined a purple face and throbbing veins on the woman's horse face. The livid violet would match her cape and hat.

The door swung open to reveal Dylan, dressed in the same clothes he'd worn to school the last two days. It appeared they'd been laundered but not pressed.

"Hello, Dylan. Are you ready to go?"

"I got to get my coat," he replied in a whisper.

Libby lowered her voice. "Don't forget gloves and a scarf."

He nodded and scampered through the kitchen, making little noise across the polished floor. A couple of moments later he returned carrying the clothing. He slipped outside and Libby helped him into the outerwear. Once he was fully attired, they set off for the boardinghouse.

"Did the sheriff get back yet?" Dylan asked.

"I don't think so. At least we haven't seen him." At the boy's downcast expression, she added, "But Mrs. Potts thinks he'll be back in time for dinner. She says he's never missed a Thanksgiving meal at her place."

Dylan's vulnerable face brightened. "I hope he is."

"Me too."

With all the businesses closed except for the hotel's cafe, the town appeared deserted. No more flakes had fallen since the daylong blizzard, but heavy drifts remained undisturbed in the alleys. The wooden buildings retained their white mantles, but the boardwalks had been cleared, and the street was a mixture of dirt and snow.

Libby and Dylan entered the boardinghouse and removed their coats. Wonderful aromas of turkey, fresh bread, and warm apple cider washed across them.

"It sure smells good in here," Dylan remarked.

Libby leaned down to whisper in his ear. "Wait until you taste it."

She hung their coats on wooden pegs and turned back to Dylan. With his hands in his pockets and a shuttered expression across his young face, he tried to shield his anxiety, but Libby could see his nervousness.

"Come on into the kitchen. I'll bet Mrs. Potts needs some help." She steered Dylan down the hallway.

"Happy Thanksgiving, Dylan," Lenore greeted the boy. She leaned over to hug him, and after a moment of stiff hesitation, Dylan accepted the embrace without wiggling. "Why don't you and Miss O'Hanlon finish setting the table?"

Looking lost, he glanced at Libby and she nodded encouragingly. "Let's get the silverware."

Though Libby could've completed the task in half the time, she showed Dylan the correct placement of the utensils. Glasses were arranged next, and Dylan filled each one with cold well water. Touching the cornucopia in the middle of the table, he eyed the centerpiece with amazement.

"You did a fine job, Dylan," Libby praised.

She heard the exterior door open and her heart missed a beat. Had Matt returned? The light footsteps gave her answer before she saw Eli enter the dining room.

"Happy Thanksgiving there, Miss O'Hanlon, Dylan. We couldn't have asked for a better day, could we?" Eli asked.

Libby smiled. "Actually, a little warmer might've been nice."

Eli waved a veined hand. "Nonsense. This is balmy compared to Thanksgivings I remember as a kid."

"Don't tell me you grew up at the North Pole?" Libby asked with mock incredulity.

Eli chuckled. "Vermont, though it did feel like the Arctic sometimes."

"Where's the North Pole?" Dylan asked with a frown.

"It's the place Santa Claus lives," Libby answered. "It's always winter there."

"I saw Santa Claus once. He came to the house to visit ma and they went into a room together. When they came out, his beard and red clothes were gone."

Uncomfortable silence filled the room and Libby's mouth gaped. Did Dylan understand what his mother did for a living?

Eli cleared his throat. "I don't think that was the real Santa Claus, son. You see, the real one would never shave his beard."

"Oh. Then I guess I ain't ever seen him."

Libby, who'd regained her composure, corrected him gently. I've *never* seen him. Maybe you'll see him this year."

Dylan shrugged. "Maybe."

Lenore scuttled out of the kitchen, carrying a bowl in each hand. "Eli, you bring in the turkey, then you get to carve it."

"Matt usually does that," Eli said.

"Well, he isn't here yet, so that leaves you."

Everyone made a couple of trips to carry all the bowls and platters into the dining room. Libby imagined she heard the table groan under the overabundance of food. Dylan's eyes widened with wonder at the bountiful sight.

"Lenore, why don't you say grace?" Eli suggested.

Libby caught Dylan's eye and bowed her head. He followed her lead.

"Dear Lord, we want to thank you for bringing us together on this Thanksgiving Day and for being so generous with all your gifts. We ask you to watch over our families wherever they are. And please bring Sheriff Brandon home safe and sound where he belongs. Amen."

Amens echoed from Libby and Eli. Dylan's boyish voice chimed in last.

Eli balanced the carving knife in his hand a moment and shook his head. "This is Matt's job. He should be here doing this." Silence hung over the table for what seemed an eternity. Eli sighed and raised the blade above the turkey. "I suppose—"

Clicking boot heels interrupted him. The door to the dining room swung open, and Matt's familiar figure appeared.

Chapter 6

—————— ∞ ——————

"Sheriff!"

Dylan launched himself up, knocking the chair over behind him. He wound his skinny arms around Matt's waist. "I told my ma you weren't dead. I knew it!"

Matt hunkered down and gathered the boy close to his chest. "A little snow isn't going to get me," he said huskily.

Libby barely restrained herself. She wanted to touch Matt, to prove he was real, not a figment of her tortured imagination. Five days of whisker growth surrounded his pale scar, but to Libby the jagged line enhanced the lean angles and contours of his ruggedly handsome face. His damp tawny hair brushed the top of his collar, and his clothes were clean but wrinkled, as if he'd pulled them out of a drawer and immediately donned them. He appeared tired, with dark circles under his eyes, and empathy slipped past her defenses.

Temptation overcame prudence. Libby pushed back her chair and joined Matt and Dylan. After the hours she'd spent conjuring up the worst scenarios, she craved physical reassurance. She wanted to lay her palm against his windburned cheek, and revel in the essence of bay rum and pine-scented soap.

Matt released the boy and stood. His intense gaze captured Libby and she abandoned discretion.

"Welcome home, Matt." Libby reached up and her arms crept around his neck. She leaned into his open embrace and, cocooned within his arms, relief washed across her. She didn't care that Eli and Lenore witnessed her momentary weakness. All that mattered was Matt's steady heartbeat against her breast.

Though surprised by her affectionate greeting, Matt gladly accepted her warmth and softness. Libby's auburn crown of curls tickled his chin, and lilacs and her own musky scent coiled inside him. Her rounded bosom pressed against his chest and her hips brushed his thighs. Despite his exhaustion, he longed to draw her tight against him. He ached to undo the tiny pearl buttons of her blouse, and slip a hand inside to weigh each breast in his palm.

The sound of a cough broke the amorous spell. As he drew away from Libby, an abyss gaped inside him. Libby's warm reception had filled cracks of loneliness within him he hadn't even realized existed. Unwilling to release the intoxicating sense of belonging, Matt stretched an uncertain hand toward her.

A tug on his sleeve pulled him back to reality. His arm fell to his side and he glanced down at Dylan.

"Mrs. Potts said you'd be here for Thanksgiving dinner, but I wasn't so sure," Dylan admitted with a sheepish expression.

Matt ruffled the boy's hair. "You don't think I'd miss turkey and Mrs. Potts's special stuffing, do you?"

"Or your favorite pumpkin pie," Lenore interjected. "Of course, I had to make apple strudel, too. What's Thanksgiving if you don't have an apple strudel?"

Matt grinned. He had grown accustomed to Lenore's German variations to American holiday meals. "You sure you got enough food, Lenore? I'm so hungry my belly's shaking hands with my backbone."

"Set yourself down. I'll run into the kitchen and get you something to eat with." She bustled through the swinging door.

Matt held Libby's chair for her and she sank onto it. He took the open place beside her.

Dylan sat down and squirmed. "Did you get them, Sheriff?"

"Only one," he replied. "The other one got away with the money."

"Maybe you can get your prisoner to tell you where he might be," Eli suggested.

"He ain't talking much."

Libby's mouth dropped open at his proclamation.

"I had to bring him in slung over his saddle," Matt finished.

"You killed him?" Libby asked, reproach in her voice.

Matt's frowned. "He didn't give me a choice."

Lenore returned to lay a plate and silverware in front of him, and resettled in her chair.

"You recognize the dead one?" Eli asked.

"Yep. He and his brother were in town about a week ago. Said they were passing through." Matt snorted in disgust. "Passing through long enough to check out the bank. I should've figured out what they were doing."

"You're not expected to be a mind reader, Matt," Libby inserted. "I think you did well to bring even one of the men back, considering the weather."

Her gentle assurance surprised him and muted his self-reproach. "Thanks, but it's my job to keep the town safe."

"Good heavens, Matt," Lenore exclaimed. "A body can't expect to be everywhere at once. I swear you're your own worst enemy. Eli, give him the carving knife. Dylan wants to see if this bird tastes as good as it smells, and Libby hasn't eaten enough the last few days to keep a cricket chirping."

Matt glanced at Libby. "Have you been sick?"

Libby shook her head and a flush spread across her cheeks. "I was nervous about teaching in a new town."

"Rubbish. She was worried about you, Sheriff," Lenore stated. "She was up to all hours pacing her room while you were gone. A person couldn't even get a good night's sleep, with the floor creaking like a rusty gate."

Matt studied Libby, whose blush contrasted with the snow-white lace collar of her blouse.

Libby glared at Lenore, then looked at Matt. "Maybe I was a little worried about you, too."

Matt's chest constricted and he swallowed the tightness in his throat. What had he done to earn her concern? "I got to admit I was a little worried myself. I was lucky to find a place to sit out the worst of the blizzard."

To hide his unexpected discomfort, Matt took the carving knife from Eli. After a few deft motions, slices of white turkey breast lay on the platter. Serving bowls overflowing with mashed potatoes and apple stuffing and sweet potatoes began traveling around the table, and they all heaped their plates.

Matt ate quickly and was the first to finish. Leaning back in his chair, he laced his fingers across his satisfied stomach. Contentment teemed through him as he savored Libby's nearness. Dylan's presence across the table also evoked a sense of rightness. A feeling of belonging he hadn't experienced in years swept across him.

"We were beginning to wonder if you'd make it back, Matt," Eli commented.

"I didn't have a doubt," Lenore said. "I told you he'd never miss Thanksgiving dinner. Besides, that little snow was nothing. Back when I was Dylan's age, we had us a real blizzard. It started a couple weeks before Thanksgiving and by the second day, snow had drifted over the entire house. We had to dig a tunnel to the outhouse and barn. We never did know when it quit snowing. We used that dogtrot between the cabin and the barn until some neighbors finally dropped in."

"What happened? Did the tunnel melt?" Libby asked.

Lenore's blue eyes twinkled. "Nope. The Schindlers, who lived seven miles down the old mill road, came visiting—and fell right through the roof, smack dab into the middle of our Thanksgiving dinner. Yep, dropped right in, they did."

Laughter rippled around the table, with Dylan's childish voice rising above them all. Matt enjoyed the sound but sobered when he wondered how often the boy had experienced lighthearted teasing.

Eli pushed back his empty plate and leaned back in his chair as well. "I bet I can top that one. Back when I was first starting out as a doctor, I lived in a small town in Kansas. I was just getting ready to sit down to have Thanksgiving dinner when there's a pounding at the door. Albert Schmidt tells me his wife is going to have her baby, so I grabbed my bag and followed him to his place. I went in, and sure enough, Mrs. Schmidt was screaming something awful. Less than five minutes later, I'm holding a tiny baby boy who's making as much noise as his mother. I figured the worst was past, but the missus was still hollering. Next thing I know, I'm holding a little girl."

"Twins," Lenore commented.

Eli shook his head. "By the time I was done, there were two boys and two girls crying at the top of their healthy little lungs."

"Quadruplets," Libby stated. "I remember reading about a family in Europe where quadruplets were born in every other generation. The doctors had no idea why it happened, except that it involved heredity and was related to something in the cells."

"I didn't realize you were so well versed in biology and anatomy," Eli said with a canted gray eyebrow.

Libby reddened. "I have an interest in many fields, and biology happens to be one of them."

"Which college did you attend?"

"Oh, I didn't go to college. I went to a finishing school back east."

"What's the name of it?" Eli pressed.

"It was a very small school. I'm sure you've never heard of it."

Matt noticed she avoided Eli's gaze and her voice quavered slightly. He narrowed his eyes. "So how did you pick up all that?"

"I read whatever I can get my hands on," she replied.

Ashamed by his inability to read but a few words, Matt retreated behind a cloak of indifference.

"What about you, Libby? Have you any Thanksgiving stories to tell us?" Lenore changed the subject, as if sensing Matt's wounded pride.

"Nothing as exciting as yours and Eli's," she said. Her gaze turned inward. "But I do remember one in particular. I had been away at school and decided to come home to be with my father, since Corey had joined the Union army. It didn't feel like Thanksgiving without him, and it was a quiet meal. Afterward, we went to the parlor to play chess. It was nearly dusk when the front door opened, and there stood Corey! His unit was camped only ten miles away, so his commanding officer let him have the evening off to come home. We got out the leftovers from dinner and this time we had more to celebrate. I'll always remember how Corey looked, so tall and handsome in his uniform."

Silence echoed in the room. Matt reminded himself that Corey was her brother, but unexpected jealousy flared at the idolization that glowed in Libby's freckle-dusted face. He yearned to see that same adoration directed at him.

"Did your brother fight against the sheriff?" Dylan asked innocently.

Libby shook her head. "No. Corey was a doctor, so he didn't fight in battles like the sheriff did."

"Oh," Dylan said, clearly disappointed.

"Miss O'Hanlon's brother worked to save lives, while I only tried to take them," Matt said softly. "It takes a lot more courage to care for the sick and wounded than to kill, Dylan. He was the hero, not men like me."

"That's not true, Dylan," Libby amended. "Men like my brother and the sheriff and thousands of others did what they believed was right. A hero is only a person who does the best he can in a terrible situation."

Dylan didn't appear convinced.

"More turkey, Dylan?" Lenore asked.

He nodded eagerly, and she placed a piece of white meat on his twice-emptied plate.

"Your shirt is going to pop if you're not careful, Dylan," Libby teased.

He glanced down at his belly and shook his head. "Nope, I still got some room, Miss O'Hanlon."

Libby smiled at the boy affectionately and handed him a napkin. "No wonder, half your meal is on your face."

Dylan wrinkled his nose but wiped most of the gravy and cranberry sauce from around his mouth.

Lenore looked at Matt. "Did you want some more stuffing, Sheriff?"

Matt patted his stomach. "If I eat anything more, *my* shirt's going to bust. You fixed a fine spread as usual, Lenore. Thanks."

"It looks like we'll have to hold off on that dessert for a couple hours," Lenore said. "Libby and I'll clear the table and you men can go on into the parlor."

Eli pushed back his chair and stood. "I got a better idea. Why don't we help you clear the table, then we can all go into the parlor?"

Lenore winked at Libby and turned back to Eli. "I'd best take you up on that offer, since you probably won't ask again."

Lenore ordered everyone about like a cavalry drill sergeant as they removed the leftovers and dirty plates. Lenore washed the dishes and Dylan and Eli dried. Meanwhile, Libby and Matt secured the leftovers in jars and carried them outside to the porch. Matt lifted the latch to the root cellar and Libby went down first.

Walking down the dark stairs, she missed a step, and Matt steadied her with a firm hand. "Are you all right, Libby?"

"Fine," she replied. "Thank you."

With only the light from the door illuminating the small room, Matt kept his hold on her arm. The strong grasp both excited and frightened her, and a delicious shiver tingled all the way to the tips of her toes. When they reached the bottom, he released her and his withdrawal left Libby bereft.

They placed the containers on an empty shelf in the cold, damp room. Libby turned to leave, but Matt's muscular body blocked her way.

"Did you really worry about me?" His warm breath cascaded across her cheek.

Libby wanted to lie, but she knew he would detect the deception. She nodded slowly, certain her voice would betray her.

"Nobody's worried about me for a long time," he said softly. He brushed her cheek with the back of his hand.

His wistful tone brought an ache to Libby's heart, even as his touch sent quivers of longing through her. Her legs wobbled and she thought they'd drop her in a heap on the earthen floor. She braced her knees. "Why not?" she asked with a thready voice.

A wry smile tugged at his lips and he shrugged. "Look at me. Why would anyone worry?"

Startled by the self-deprecating question, Libby frowned. "Because you're a good man, Matt."

"You've only known me a couple weeks. How can you be so sure?"

His light caresses scattered her thoughts into disarray, and she fought to bring them back into focus. "I've seen how much you care for Dylan. A man who thinks that much of a boy who isn't even his own has to have some good in him."

"Is that the only reason?" He stepped closer until only a couple of inches separated them.

Without warning, panic lanced through Libby's passion. Remembered helplessness seized her, and her palms grew moist. She backed into the wooden shelves as sour bile rose in her throat. "Isn't that enough?"

Matt frowned. "What's wrong, Libby?"

"Nothing. We'd better get back to the kitchen."

Trembling like an aspen leaf, she attempted to duck under his arm, but Matt caught her. In the darkness, his face blurred and Harrison's drunken leer filled her vision. Terror twisted her stomach into knots, and she buried her face in her hands to escape the grotesque sight. "Get away from me," she cried.

He released her arm. "Sorry."

The contrite voice wasn't Harrison's, and Libby raised her head warily. She blinked and Matt coalesced into view. What happened? Why had she thought Matt was Harrison? A different kind of fear took hold of her: fear for her sanity.

Embarrassed by her strange outburst, Libby couldn't look at him. "I'm sorry. I don't know what came over me."

Matt retreated a couple steps. "I understand. C'mon, let's get out of here."

He moved back to allow her to pass without brushing him, and she gave him a tremulous smile. Libby wished she could confide in Matt, but she couldn't tell him the truth without revealing her crime. The horrible secret must remain buried with Harrison.

They found the kitchen empty and walked down the hallway. Libby noticed Matt kept his distance, and he looked at her as if she'd grown horns and a tail. She didn't blame him. She couldn't even explain what had happened. One moment she'd been experiencing wondrous sensations she'd never known existed; and the next, fear had plummeted her into the past. Married to Harrison, Libby had convinced herself all men were like him, obscene groping creatures who inflicted pain to enhance their pleasure. Although Matt and Harrison were both men, the similarities ended there. She had thought Harrison the most handsome man she'd ever laid eyes on, but she'd learned the devil owned many masks. Matt's granite-carved face could hardly be called beautiful, but the sharp angles and lines added a depth of character Harrison had sorely lacked. In the short two weeks she'd known Matt, Libby recognized the decency rooted deep within him, and that goodness drew her like a clear lake beckons a thirsty man.

Dylan met them at the door of the parlor and dragged them into the warm, cheery room.

"How about poker?" Dylan suggested.

Theatrically, Libby arched an eyebrow at Matt. "Poker? Have you been corrupting this boy? Isn't that against the law?"

Matt turned the scarred side of his face away from Libby. "Don't blame that on me. I figure one of his mother's friends taught him."

Matt's shuttered expression bewildered Libby. The

kind, gentle Matt, who'd touched her like no man had ever done, had disappeared, replaced by the distant sheriff she had first met. He didn't retreat, but his gaze distanced her as skillfully as if he had stepped away.

"We were wondering if you two got lost down there," Lenore commented from her favorite chair.

Libby laughed weakly. "That was my fault. I wanted to see what you had on the shelves."

Eli's gray eyebrows drew together as he tamped the tobacco down in the pipe's bowl, but he didn't comment.

"Maybe the sheriff will teach you how to play checkers," Libby suggested to Dylan.

He turned beseeching eyes to Matt. "Will you?"

As Libby's gaze collided with Matt's, she caught a glimpse through the windows of his soul, but too quickly Matt drew a curtain across them. Her heart constricted at the ragged pain reflected in the rich depths. What burden did he suffer in stoic silence? What could bring such torment to a man so seemingly strong and fearless?

An icy chill slid down her spine. The incident in the cellar reminded her of her precarious situation. She couldn't risk allowing her friendship with Matt to continue. She had nothing to offer but lies, and instinctively, Libby knew Matt was a man who tolerated many things, but never outright deceptions. If he learned the truth, she would only add to his buried grief, and that would hurt her as much as him.

She picked up a book and settled on the sofa, tucking her feet beneath her. Despite her vow to distance herself from Matt, her attention strayed to him and Dylan who sat cross-legged on the floor, a small table between them. Matt showed the boy how to set up the checkerboard and where the pieces went. In a few short games, Dylan mastered the rules and crowed zealously when he claimed Matt's lost pieces.

A knock at the door interrupted them.

"I wonder who that could be," Lenore mused. She pushed herself up and left the room. Low voices sounded, and Lenore returned a few moments later.

"Eli, Stephen Miller's wife is going to have her baby," she announced.

Eli got to his feet and eased the kinks out of his back and legs. "Isn't there a law that says babies can't be born on holidays?"

"Sorry, Eli, but I ain't ever heard of one like that," Matt said. "You want me to ride over with you?"

"No reason to." He leaned over and pecked Lenore on a plump cheek. "Thanks for dinner."

Lenore waved an impatient hand. "You go on now and bring another healthy baby into this world."

"I'll stop by for dessert when I get back to town," Eli said.

"Provided you don't have to deliver four babies," Libby said with a mischievous grin.

"I hear that only happens once in a lifetime." Eli limped out with an arthritic gait.

Lowering her bulk into her chair, Lenore heaved a tremendous sigh. "He's getting too old to be running off any hour of the day or night to take care of sick folks."

"Maybe he could get another doctor to come to Deer Creek," Libby suggested.

Lenore picked up her knitting needles. "He wouldn't think of it. Still figures he's a spring chicken, when he's getting to be an old rooster. Maybe I should just set him down and tell him he's getting too long in the tooth to continue like he's been doing."

Matt moved into a high-backed rocker. "You know that won't set very well with him, Lenore. He's lived in Deer Creek ever since the town raised its first building, and the folks here trust him. You can't be telling him that he ain't good enough to do his job anymore. If you do, you may as well shoot him through the heart."

"I know. It's just that I worry about him." Lenore looked at Libby. "Why don't you read one of those dreadful dime novels to us?"

"Are you sure you want to hear about Texas Jack and his band of cutthroats?" Libby asked with a smile.

"Yeah!" Dylan shouted enthusiastically. He threw himself on the couch next to Libby. The checker game lay forgotten, pieces staggered across the board.

"How about you, Matt?"

"Sure," he said curtly.

Unexpected hurt erased Libby's smile. She opened the book and angled the pages so the kerosene lamp cast a smoky light across the words.

Libby brought the story to life with a voice that rose and fell dramatically, and her small audience breathlessly followed the tale of the infamous outlaw. Lenore's half-finished afghan lay in her lap, and Dylan looked over Libby's arm at the pictures in the book. Matt had tipped his head back against the rocker, his countenance thoughtful.

Half an hour later she finished the tale. Her gaze slid across the room to Matt, and tenderness welled within her. He slept soundly, and his face appeared younger and more vulnerable without his defenses in place. She turned to Dylan, pressed a finger to her lips, and whispered, "Shhh, the sheriff's asleep."

Dylan nodded. "He must be tired."

Lenore pushed out of her sturdy chair and held a hand out to Dylan. "Let's you and me go see if there's anything to eat in the kitchen."

Dylan went along eagerly and they tiptoed out of the room.

Left alone with the slumbering Matt, Libby memorized each ridge and hollow of his rough-hewn face.

His broad chest rose and fell, accented by a soft snore. Muscular legs covered by tan trousers were stretched out in front of him, and his booted feet were crossed at the ankles. Long fingers that ended with clean, blunt nails were intertwined, and his smooth-backed hands lay in his lap. She tried not to think about his light caresses on her cheek, but the hot liquid that pooled in the center of her being mocked her. Compassion, coupled with longing, created a hunger she didn't know how to appease.

Ragged coughing interrupted her heated perusal.

She leaned forward on the settee and waited until Matt regained his breath. "It sounds like you're coming down with the ague."

"It ain't nothing but a chill." Matt stood and stretched.

His brown shirt molded his wide shoulders and lean torso, drawing Libby's appreciative gaze. A pale butter-yellow scarf tied loosely about his neck accented his sun- and wind-darkened skin. His solid body reminded Libby of a sleek lion, deceptively languid but able to spring at a moment's notice.

"Where'd Dylan go?"

"Lenore took him into the kitchen." Libby untangled her legs and rose. "What do you say we go join them for some coffee and pie?"

He tipped his head slightly and motioned for her to precede him. Another spate of coughing from Matt accompanied them and Libby pursed her lips in concern. But she held her tongue, knowing she had to put a halt to her curiosity.

"I suppose you want some of my strudel," Lenore said. "Dylan claims he likes it better than pumpkin pie."

Libby smiled at the apple mixture around Dylan's mouth. "Is there any left?"

"Of course." Lenore sounded insulted. She cut a

hefty piece of the German dish, scooped it onto a plate, and handed the dessert to Libby. "Now what about you, Matt?"

"My usual, Lenore. It ain't Thanksgiving without pumpkin pie."

"That's what you say about Christmas, too," Lenore said.

She divided the pie into fourths and served Matt one of the substantial slices. Libby poured three cups of thick black coffee and refilled Dylan's glass with buttermilk.

Matt put away two pieces of the spicy pumpkin pie and finished his coffee. "I'd best get back to the office. What do you say I walk you home, Dylan?"

Conflicting emotions crossed the boy's face. "Ma'll probably be looking for me."

"Didn't you tell her where you were going?" Matt asked.

Dylan shook his head.

Libby spoke up. "He had to sneak out since his mother never would've approved of him coming here for dinner."

A muscle clenched and unclenched in Matt's grizzled jaw. "Why don't you ask Lenore for another piece of pie, Dylan? I got to talk to Miss O'Hanlon for a minute."

Puzzled, Libby allowed Matt to steer her back into the empty parlor. He closed the door.

Matt paced the area in front of the fireplace. Abruptly, he stopped a few feet from Libby. "Do you know what Sadie's going to do to Dylan when she finds out where he's been?"

Startled by the accusatory tone in his voice, Libby's posture stiffened. "She wouldn't dare hurt him. Besides, I thought you'd be glad I asked him over."

"I would've liked it better if Sadie knew about it."

"I told you, she wouldn't have let him come."

"How can you be so sure?"

Exasperation crept into Libby's tone. "You know what she's like. She doesn't like you or me interfering with her son, and she sure wouldn't have liked him spending the holiday here."

Barely controlled anger sharpened Matt's tone. "And now she's going to take it out of Dylan's hide."

"But you warned her that if she beat Dylan again, you'd take him away."

"If I know about it."

"Surely Dylan would come to you if she hurt him."

"You don't know a damn thing about that little boy, do you? He's lived with these beatings all his life, and even though she's a sorry excuse for a mother, Sadie's the only family he's got. Besides, she threatens him with more of the same if he tells. You know how much courage it took for him to sneak out today and come over here, knowing that he'd probably pay for it tonight?" Matt's forefinger punctuated his words.

Hot tears pricked the back of Libby's eyelids. "I didn't know."

"That's right. You didn't. Now I got to take him home and hope I can put the fear of the devil into Sadie so she won't hit Dylan."

"I'll go with you. I'll explain to her it was my fault."

Cold fury hardened Matt's features. "I think you done enough. I'll take care of it."

He spun on a worn boot heel and threw open the door. His footsteps clicked down the hall with a menacing cadence.

Misery settled upon Libby like a heavy cloak. She had wanted to make Dylan happy, allow him to enjoy a holiday like a normal child. Had that been so wrong? Matt had been right. How could she have been so stupid to think Sadie wouldn't punish Dylan when she learned where he'd been?

She closed her eyes and a tear trickled down her cheek.

"Miss O'Hanlon?"

Her eyelids flickered open and she dashed the moisture away. Shifting from one foot to the other and wearing his too-small coat, Dylan stood in the doorway. A fond smile loosened her stiff features. "Are you going home now?"

Dylan nodded. "The sheriff said I had to thank you."

Thank me for getting you in trouble with your mother. To hide her self-contempt, Libby knelt and tied his scarf snugly about his neck. "No, I want to thank you for sharing yourself with us."

"I don't understand."

"You will someday." Libby leaned forward and gathered him close. Expecting him to resist the embrace, she was surprised when his arms encircled her neck. "Thank you for coming."

She released him and gazed at his sober expression. "If you ever want to come over and see us, just drop in. I can guarantee Mrs. Potts will have the cookie jar full."

"Okay. Goodbye, Miss O'Hanlon."

"Goodbye, Dylan. I'll see you in school tomorrow."

Dylan waved and scurried away. From the kitchen, Matt's low voice and Lenore's vibrant tones flowed into unintelligible static, but the farewells sounded clearly. Silence descended upon the house. Like a dog with his tail tucked between his legs, Libby entered the kitchen.

"I'll wash the dishes if you'd like to go and sit down," Libby volunteered.

Lenore, her hands already submerged in soapy water, shook her head. "You can dry."

Libby plucked a towel from a rack near the warm stove, then lifted a plate out of the rinse water.

The matronly woman remained uncharacteristically silent.

When Libby's conscience shouted so loudly she

could no longer ignore the accusing voice, she spoke. "Do you think Dylan's mother will punish him?"

"Hard to say with someone like her. She's about as predictable as a rabid skunk."

"Matt said I was wrong for going behind her back and helping Dylan sneak out."

Lenore's hands stilled. "Is that what you think?"

"I don't know. I don't think I could've talked her into letting him out, but I wouldn't have been able to enjoy Thanksgiving, knowing Dylan was all alone."

Lenore continued scrubbing. "I knew a preacher once. His sermons lasted no less than three hours. After the first thirty minutes, half the congregation would be snoring and the rest of the folks would be moving around, trying to keep their behinds from going numb. Somebody finally got their nerve up to talk to him. This preacher was plumb shocked. He considered his words to be almighty important and didn't even realize he was losing his flock. Once he took off his blinders, he turned into a mighty fine preacher."

"What are you trying to tell me?" Libby asked.

"You got to look at the situation with wide open eyes. You can't breeze in here and dangle a carrot in front of that boy, then take it away without so much as a by-your-leave. Will you be here six months from now? How about a year? Or ten years? If not, then don't get that boy's hopes up."

Libby's temper flared. "What am I supposed to do? Treat him like a pariah like most everybody else in this town does?"

"Of course not, honey. All I'm saying is be careful. I had no idea that little boy had so many crosses to bear, or I would've had Matt bring him around earlier." She paused. "Dylan's had too many disappointments in his life already. I don't want you to be another one."

* * *

"There ain't no reason for you to talk to my ma," Dylan announced.

Matt paused and glanced at the boy. "I don't want her being mad at you, son. I'm afraid when she finds out where you been, she's going to throw a holy fit."

Dylan pointed to a window on the second story of the ostentatious house and Matt followed his finger.

"That's my ma's room. The curtain's still pulled, so I know she's still in bed," Dylan explained. "She won't even know I been gone."

"How do you know she just didn't forget to open it?"

"I figured it out a long time ago. If they were closed, I was safe."

Matt studied the boy skeptically. "If you're sure. . . ."

Dylan nodded and grinned. "Thanks for bringing me home, Sheriff." His smile fled. "Tell Miss O'Hanlon I didn't mean to make her sad."

"Why do you think she was sad?"

"I could tell. Her eyes were kind of wet and she hugged me real tight before I left." He kicked at the snow. "I don't like to be hugged much, but it was okay."

"You didn't make her sad. I did," Matt admitted.

"Why'd you do that?"

Matt shuffled nervously. How could he explain to Dylan he'd been disappointed by her and had retaliated with sharp words he hadn't meant? "We had a little disagreement, was all. No need for you to worry."

Dylan thought for a moment and nodded. "All right. Is she going to be at school tomorrow?"

Matt pasted on a too-bright smile. "No reason she wouldn't be. You're going to be there, ain't you?"

"If I can get away from Ma, I will."

"Don't you sass your ma or she's going to make it tougher on you," Matt warned.

"I won't," Dylan assured. "I'll see you tomorrow?"

"Count on it. And stay out of trouble."

Dylan loped to the back door and waved at Matt. He entered and disappeared behind the cold walls.

Matt shivered in the afternoon chill as he hurried to the jailhouse. Inside, the bitter air surrounded him and he started a fire in the potbellied stove. As the room warmed, he settled in the comfortable chair. He noticed the stack of wanted posters had been separated into two piles, one large and the other much smaller. Who would've looked at them? Stymied by the mystery, Matt set the papers aside and leaned back. He propped his feet on the desk, crossing them at the ankles. A bout of coughing interrupted his routine of thoughtful contemplation. Once he'd regained his breath, he swallowed and grimaced. His throat felt like it was lined with barbed wire. He set aside his worry that Libby may be right, convincing himself it was nothing more than a cold.

He laid his head against the back of the chair and his thoughts drifted to Libby. He'd made a damned fool of himself, thinking she really cared about him. Her peach velvet cheek had been so soft and her eyes had seemed willing. He'd been stunned by her mercurial transformation. The disgust in her voice and her inability to look him in the eye had told him everything he needed to know. She'd hidden her revulsion well, but the truth couldn't be contained forever. He had believed her different than other women, who judged on appearance rather than substance. She'd even called him a good man.

His tapered fingers traced the jagged scar, and Matt swore. What a fool he'd been.

Libby pondered Lenore's words as she readied herself for bed. When she and Matt had discussed getting Dylan to school, Libby had believed her motives unselfish. She truly wanted the bright boy to receive an education, but had she overlooked the sacrifices Dylan would make? How often had his mother threatened him, even whipped him, since she and Matt had coerced her into allowing Dylan to attend school?

Libby crossed the floor to stare into the street below. A few lanterns illuminated the boardwalk and the saloons had reopened for business. She raised her wistful gaze to the winking stars in the evening sky. If she were free, she would adopt Dylan and ask Dr. Clapper if he would like a partner.

But the fates weren't so forgiving. She'd have to make a clean break when she left town, and that meant no more involvement. Starved for human contact, Libby had allowed her heart to rule her mind. She'd befriended Dylan, thinking she could magically fix his life; but when she moved on, he'd again be left with his cruel mother. Lenore had been right. She'd been blinded by her own loneliness. She'd separate herself from Dylan before it was too late—her conscience couldn't bear another burden. Matt would take care of the boy.

Matt was another complication she hadn't counted on. When she'd learned he didn't have an inkling of her past, she'd set aside her caution. She hadn't counted on the relationship progressing so quickly, but he fascinated her.

Everything about him bespoke of a hard life, but morality and empathy remained. He intrigued her and made her wish she'd met him before she'd learned to distrust the touch of a man. She could no longer indulge her curiosity. She would have to keep her distance from Matt before her interest snowballed into dangerous intimacy and she lowered her guard.

With Harrison, she'd been able to endure by allowing nothing and no one to breach the walls that enclosed her innermost thoughts and memories. She could do it again.

Libby kicked at the bedpost in frustration, and her foot struck the trunk beneath it. She knelt down and snagged the handle of the big suitcase, easing it out. She opened it reverently. Strapped to the inside of the cover was an array of medical tools. Her fingers trembling, Libby touched the shiny surface of one and blinked back the flood of memories that accompanied the feel of the smooth metal. Spying a worn handle, she lifted out a black leather bag. She unclasped the hook and opened it. Reverently, she handled each instrument, remembering the times she'd used them. How could she never again use the tools that had once been an extension of her hands?

Her gaze darted about the small room and claustro-phobia urged flight. Libby breathed deeply to dispel the anxiety. She slowly replaced the items in the trunk and closed the lid, but the damage had been done. By opening Pandora's box, she'd broken the recently healed wound. She thought she'd resigned herself to a life of anonymity, but her dream ran too deeply—and wouldn't allow her to forget a lifelong aspiration forged in love and hard work. She'd leave Deer Creek in the spring and go far enough away to have her own medical practice.

Only five more months, and she would begin her search for the end of the tarnished rainbow.

Five long, lonely months.

Chapter 7

"I'm moving into the back of the school-house."

Libby's announcement the next morning brought Lenore's head up sharply. "What in the world are you talking about?"

Libby wrapped her trembling hands around a steaming mug of coffee. "I've decided to live in the teacher's quarters."

"What brought on this nonsense?"

Libby ignored the question. "It's not that I don't like it here. You've made me feel like a member of the family. It's just that my money is dwindling. If I move over there, I'd be able to save a little."

Lenore's sharp gaze searched Libby's expression. "I got a feeling there's more to it than that."

Libby assumed a mask of innocence. "Why else would I move?"

"Why else indeed?" Lenore's eyes nearly disappeared into folds of skin. "Unless it has something to do with the sheriff."

Libby laughed unconvincingly. "What on earth are you talking about? The sheriff and I are only friends."

Lenore sniffed. "And cows take a flying leap over the moon every night."

Libby continued as if Lenore hadn't spoken. "I'll

clean the room tomorrow and move in on Sunday. I'll pay what I owe you."

Lenore pounded a ball of dough with her fists. "I'm not worried about the money, dear. I'm worried about you."

Libby rose and placed her coffee cup in a large metal pan filled with soapy water. "You needn't worry about me. I can take care of myself."

"I'm going to miss you, honey, but I understand you have to do what you think is right." She stabbed a flour-covered finger at Libby. "But I expect to see you sitting at my supper table at least a twice a week."

A lump as big as the yeasty mixture Lenore kneaded filled Libby's throat. She swallowed. "I will. I won't be that far away. I can visit in the afternoon, after school is dismissed."

"You going to bring Dylan with you?"

"If he wants to come, I will," Libby replied, careful to keep her voice neutral. "I'd better get to school."

"Have a nice day, honey."

Libby's mood matched the gray hues that filled the wide sky. The mountain tops to the west had disappeared into sooty clouds, and heavy air enveloped her. The walk to the schoolhouse seemed to last forever, and Libby's temples throbbed with each footstep. Once inside the small building, she lit a crackling fire in the stove to dispel the damp cold.

Fifteen minutes after she arrived, a bright-eyed Dylan stood in the doorway. Her heart lifted at the sight of him, but she didn't allow the emotion to show on her face. "Good morning," she greeted.

"Hi, Miss O'Hanlon." He removed his coat and scarf and walked to her desk. "Are you still sad?"

Libby frowned. "What makes you think I was sad?"

"Because you hugged me so hard yesterday."

She wished his perception didn't equal Matt's. "I was just happy that you'd been able to spend Thanksgiving with us. Did you have a good time?"

He grinned and nodded. "Yep. I liked Mrs. Potts's apple strudel, even if the sheriff didn't."

A smile tugged at Libby's lips despite her attempts to stifle it. "I did, too. Why don't you go and sit down?"

Dylan nodded and slid into his seat. He opened his McGuffey's reader and thumbed through it.

Libby wanted to ask him if his mother had been angry with him for spending Thanksgiving at Lenore's, but she didn't dare express any more concern than she had already. Lenore's words haunted her, and Libby prayed she wouldn't be another disappointment in Dylan's life.

The children stomped in in groups of two and three, and at eight-fifteen, Libby stood. Placing a dispassionate mask over her features, she called the class to order.

She studied Dylan's behavior throughout the day and tried to discern if he'd been beaten. He didn't appear to be in pain, and he talked and giggled with Jenny. Matt must have succeeded in frightening Sadie enough that she'd not hit her son.

When class recessed, Dylan left with the rest of the children, leaving Libby both saddened and relieved. During the day she'd remained too busy to think of her plight, but in the silence of the desk-filled room, the desolate voice of loneliness reverberated in her mind. She knew she'd made the correct decision to distance herself, but the consequences of her choice would be difficult to bear. A piece of wood popped in the stove, startling her out of her self-pity.

Straightening her shoulders, Libby wove between the desks to the front of the room. A door hinge creaked, and she turned to see a kaleidoscope of colors draped across the rotund shape of Mrs. Beidler. Involuntarily she braced for battle, and sent the mayor's wife a polite nod. "Good afternoon, Mrs. Beidler. What can I do for you?"

"I wish to speak with you on a couple of matters of the utmost concern." The purple feather on her canary yellow hat bobbed with every other word.

Libby clasped her hands across her thighs. "And what are those?"

Mrs. Beidler sashayed to the front of the room, her violet coat flowing behind her like a queen's cloak. She raised an imperious nose. "It's been brought to my attention that you and the sheriff have been spending quite a bit of time together. Alone."

Libby's heart thundered in her chest. "The sheriff has been out of town and I have been here teaching. When could we have spent time together?"

Two pink spots appeared on the older woman's sour face. "You were seen walking with him at an unseemly hour."

Libby raised her eyebrows. "Because he escorted me to the boardinghouse one evening, we're thought to be having a tête-à-tête? The fact is, I had been out walking alone when the sheriff ran into me and suggested I go home. I believe he thought I may have been in danger. Surely you don't condemn a man for doing his job."

"You haven't been here long, so I will tell you about the sheriff. Before he became a lawman, he was a slovenly sot. I remember the few times I saw him, before Doctor Clapper saved him from some of his drinking friends who beat him senseless. Your Sheriff Brandon used to sit in front of the saloon drunk as a skunk and looking as if he'd lived in his clothes for weeks. Why, the smell of him was enough to make a body ill." She shuddered. "That is the type of man Sheriff Brandon is."

Though Mrs. Beidler's accounting of Matt startled her, Libby refused to give the flamboyant woman any satisfaction. "That is the type of man Sheriff Brandon *was*. Everyone is allowed to make mistakes, Mrs.

Beidler, and I believe the Bible says, 'Judge not, lest ye shall be judged'."

Mrs. Beidler drew herself up and thrust her abundant bosom forward. "As a molder of young, impressionable children, you are expected to maintain the highest level of respectability. Be warned that consorting with a man like the sheriff could constitute means for dismissal."

Libby clenched her teeth, holding back her temper by sheer force of will. "I believe you said you had two matters you wished to discuss with me."

"The other involves one of your students. The son of Sadie Rivers, to be precise."

"His name is Dylan."

"The boy should not be allowed to associate with decent, God-fearing children. He's a bad influence upon them. He cannot continue to attend school."

Fury boiled in Libby. "How dare you speak about that little boy as if he's less a person than the other children! Dylan has an intelligent mind, and I will not tell him he's not allowed here anymore. He's got as much right to an education as your Mary Sue."

Mrs. Beidler's face approached crimson. "He's a bastard," she hissed. "He has no right infecting our children with his tainted blood."

Cold anger settled in the pit of Libby's stomach. "He had no choice in his parentage, and I will not have you deny him the privileges other children take for granted. Everyone is equal in the eyes of the Lord."

"I can have you dismissed from your position." Mrs. Beidler's three chins quivered.

"We have a formal agreement. If you break your side of the contract, you will still have to pay what is owed me for five months of teaching."

Libby saw the enraged frustration in the face of her adversary. If Mrs. Beidler were a man, Libby suspected a string of curses would have erupted. Instead, Mrs. Beidler stared at her as if Libby were something on the bottom of her pointy-toed patent-leather shoe.

"I believe in poker it's called put up or shut up," Libby delivered flatly.

"I can see that we have made a grievous mistake in hiring you," Mrs. Beidler said stiffly. "As you have pointed out, we have little choice but to keep you for now. However, if *you* break the agreement, we do not owe you one penny."

Libby crossed her arms. "I have no intention of quitting."

"Not yet."

The sly cunning in Mrs. Beidler's face set off an alarm in Libby's mind. What could she possibly do to make her quit?

"I always have my way, Miss O'Hanlon." With that statement, Mrs. Beidler swung around and marched out the classroom.

Libby collapsed in the chair behind her desk, trembling from head to foot. Her temper had demolished her well-laid plans, but she could not allow Mrs. Beidler to speak so callously about Dylan. The overdressed hussy probably swept aside her skirt hems when she passed him so she wouldn't be contaminated by the disease he supposedly carried. Also, the woman's disrespect she had for Matt shocked Libby. She knew of Matt's drinking problem, since Lenore had spoken of it a few nights ago, but to hear Mrs. Beidler speak so viciously about Matt's past incensed her. It shouldn't matter to Libby what Mrs. Beidler thought of Matt. But it did.

Early Saturday morning, Libby arrived at the schoolhouse with a bucket and rags to clean the living quarters in the back. She wore a threadbare skirt that had been mended in three places, and a faded green scarf bound her flyaway curls. Lenore had lent her a patched coat two sizes too large and forty years out of date, but the wool jacket kept her comfortably warm while she worked.

Libby threw out the old papers scattered about and kept the few cans of food still in the cupboards. Awkwardly, she lifted the mattress off the bed and lugged the cumbersome pad outside to hang it over a tree branch to air out. With a stiff straw broom, she swept the mouse droppings and dirt out the back door and rid the whitewashed walls and corners of cobwebs. With an old brush, she scrubbed the puncheon floor vigorously. By noon, the tiny room had undergone a major overhaul.

Libby placed her hands on her lower back and tried to stretch out the stiffness. Her knees were nearly raw from kneeling on the rough floor, and her fingers looked like shriveled raisins. She hadn't worked so hard since before she'd married Harrison. In their mansion, hired help had taken care of the cleaning and cooking. She'd been nothing but an ornament to grace Harrison's arm during parties and balls. She hadn't enjoyed the submissive role, but would have tolerated it if he had left her alone in private.

The sound of a boot sole on sand granules startled Libby. She turned to see Matt standing in the doorway of the cloakroom. Her heart thumped against her breast, but she didn't know if surprise or the sight of him caused it. One hand went to her scarf and the other smoothed the plaid coat over her patched skirt. She drew her arms to her sides, silently admonishing herself for her vanity even as she wished Matt hadn't seen her in the old tattered clothing.

She injected aloofness into her tone. "Can I help you, Sheriff?"

Matt tipped back his worn brown hat and a lock of tawny hair fell across his creased forehead. The urge to brush it back possessed Libby, and she rolled her fingers into her palms. As his eyes roamed across her, Libby could imagine what he thought of her unflattering outfit. When he returned his gaze to her face, neither approval nor disapproval showed on his impassive features.

He turned his face slightly so his scar was less noticeable. "Lenore told me you were moving in here."

Unable to still her nervous hands, Libby grabbed a brush and scrubbed the surface of the cookstove. "There isn't a law against it, is there?"

"Nope."

Awkward silence grew between them.

"Then why are you here?" Libby demanded. She hoped her voice didn't reveal her agitation.

Impatience shadowed Matt's craggy face. "I just came by to let you know Sadie didn't even know Dylan had gone over to Lenore's for Thanksgiving. She was still sleeping when I took him home."

Momentarily, she closed her eyes in relief. She looked at Matt. "Thank you for telling me."

Matt fidgeted with his gloves and nodded tightly. He touched the brim of his hat. "Afternoon, Miss O'Hanlon."

His footsteps echoed across the wood floor. The door closed behind him, and Libby wilted into one of the ladderback chairs. Only two days had passed since she'd seen him, but the time had seemed endless. His amber eyes and the strength reflected in his angular face brought back a flood of warmth. But it was his dark hands that triggered a confusing mixture of emotions. Matt's gentle caress fluttered across her memory, igniting a spark deep within her. She smothered the flame, forcing herself to remember how quickly tenderness changed to violence. Harrison had taught her well the capricious nature of men.

Libby stood and groaned. She'd pay for her labor with painful muscles, but pride in what she'd completed outweighed the minor aches. A sense of accomplishment she hadn't experienced in years washed across her like the the sun's rays filtering through the mountain peaks. She hoped she stayed long enough to enjoy the fruits of her aches and pains.

For the remainder of the day, Libby added the finishing touches to the school quarters. Lenore gave her bedding and blankets and a few towels, and Libby paid a visit to Pearson's Mercantile with a list of other items she needed. Following the service on Sunday, Libby moved her meager belongings into her new home. Reluctantly, she carried the last of her bags out of the boardinghouse. When Lenore hugged her affectionately, Libby nearly capitulated. And later that evening, in the silence of the schoolhouse, regrets plagued her. But the same determination that kept her sane during her marriage to Harrison strengthened her resolve.

She lay awake the first night, listening to the mice scurrying across the floor and wishing life had dealt her a better hand. However, helpless musings were for Mrs. Harrison Thompson, not Libby O'Hanlon. She squelched the useless thoughts and tried to sleep.

Monday morning brought a nippy room, and Libby scrambled to get a fire going in the stove in the classroom. She dressed in her serviceable navy blue skirt and white blouse with a black sweater. Studying herself in the broken mirror that hung crookedly on a wall, Libby pinched her pale cheeks. Her eyes appeared bloodshot after too little sleep, and she moved as if her feet were mired in mud.

As warmth seeped into the corners of the school, she ate a lonely breakfast at her rickety table. By the time the first student arrived, Libby welcomed the presence of another body to erase the oppressive silence. With some trepidation, she noticed Mary Sue Beidler was absent from her desk, as were a few other students. However, the arrival of Dylan, right before she began lessons, reinforced Libby's resolve. Perhaps the mayor's wife ruled everyone else in town, but she couldn't tell Libby who she could and couldn't teach.

Relieved her second week of teaching was nearly over, Libby allowed her thoughts to wander. She stared out over the children's heads, and for the hundredth time in the last six days wondered how Mrs. Beidler planned on ridding Deer Creek of their outspoken schoolteacher.

"Miss O'Hanlon?"

The voice startled Libby out of her sober thoughts. She glanced up to see Dylan's hand raised. "Yes?"

"I got a question."

A couple snickers from the back row brought a glare from Libby, and Jacob and Seth settled back to their lessons. She stepped over to Dylan and leaned over his desk. "What is it?"

"I don't understand this one."

Libby explained the arithmetic problem, and Dylan's eyes lit with comprehension. She was amazed by the newfound confidence in the boy's attitude, and knew she'd done the right thing standing up to the mayor's wife despite Mary Sue's absence. She wished Mrs. Beidler wouldn't punish her daughter by depriving her of an education.

"Thank you," Dylan said.

"You're welcome."

She straightened and strolled about the room, checking the children's work over their shoulders. However, her gaze drifted to her star pupil more often than not. In the short time he'd attended school, Dylan had gone from an insolent boy to an insatiable student who soaked up information like a sponge.

He grasped concepts quickly, putting him on the same skill level as children who'd attended school much longer. She had no doubt he would surpass them before Christmas.

He would be so easy to love. Pain constricted her heart. He belonged to a woman who didn't even recognize his gifts, and who gave him attention only when she punished him. Libby had thought she could turn off her growing fondness for Dylan, but affection wasn't like a candle flame she could extinguish with a single breath.

When she recessed for the day, Dylan remained behind.

"Can I clean the blackboard, Miss O'Hanlon?"

Libby couldn't resist the boy's genuine enthusiasm for the mundane task, and she smiled warmly. "Thank you. I'd appreciate your help."

Dylan conscientiously wiped the board with a damp rag, making sure he removed all specks of white dust. Twenty minutes later he appeared satisfied with his work. He stood in front of Libby's desk and swiped his forearm across his nose.

Libby reached into a desk drawer for a plain linen handkerchief. "Use this instead of your sleeve."

Dylan accepted the cloth and blew his nose noisily. He handed it back to her.

Libby bit the inside of her cheek to keep from smiling. "No, that's all right. Go ahead and keep it."

He shrugged and balled the material into his pocket. "I'll see if the sheriff wants it."

"Doesn't he have a handkerchief of his own?"

"I don't know, but he was coughing something awful the last time I saw him."

Concern unsettled Libby. "When was that?"

"Guess it was Tuesday after school."

"You haven't seen him since?"

"Nope. I stopped by the jail a few times, but he was

never there. Nobody knew where he was." Worry furrowed the boy's forehead. "Maybe I'd best go see if he's back yet."

Libby fingered her pencil nervously. Her gaze strayed to the patch of cerulean sky through the window. *Where was Matt?* Maybe a visit with Lenore would yield answers to her questions.

She piled her books and papers in the center of her desk. "What do you say we go see if Mrs. Potts has any cookies left in the cookie jar?"

Dylan nodded eagerly. They donned their coats, and after Libby was assured the boy was bundled tightly against the cold, they slipped outside. The bitter cold stuck in Libby's lungs and she couldn't breathe for a few moments. Icicles glittered in the sunlight, casting diamond sparkles along the eaves of many of the wood buildings, but the beauty was lost on Libby. They stopped in front of the boardinghouse and Libby's gaze found the silent jail. With Dylan leading, they entered Lenore's.

"Well, look what the cat dragged in," Lenore exclaimed. She hugged Dylan tight, then did the same to Libby. "Get rid of those coats and light a spell."

"Well, we only—"

"I got chocolate cake," Lenore bribed.

Dylan's jacket flew off and Libby's followed with a bit more decorum.

A few minutes later, Libby forked sweet frosting into her mouth. "It's good."

"Uh-hum," Dylan agreed, chocolate circling his lips.

"Guess I got to make it more often, just to get you to come calling," Lenore said.

Guilt washed across Libby. "I'm sorry I haven't been over. I've been getting used to the new place and all."

"I heard Mrs. Beidler paid you a visit last week."

"How did you know?"

Lenore shrugged her fleshy shoulders. "Not much goes on in this town I don't hear about. Comes from being a gossipy old woman who can't mind her own business. What did Queen Adelaide have to say?"

Dylan giggled behind a hand. "She ain't no queen."

"Isn't a queen," Libby corrected automatically. She turned back to Lenore. "What did you hear?"

"Would you like to look at some pictures, Dylan?" Lenore asked.

He nodded.

"You wash up and I'll tell you where I've got something called a stereoscope."

The boy placed his empty plate and glass in the pan of water and cleaned off his face. He swiped his hands once across the towel and followed Lenore out of the kitchen.

"You know what a stereoscope is?" Lenore asked. Their voices faded to nothing, and Libby ate another forkful of cake but found she could hardly swallow past the dry lump in her throat. Returning a few minutes later, Lenore set a bucket of potatoes on the table. She handed Libby a sharp knife and took one herself. She lowered herself into the chair across from Libby.

"My ma used to say peeling spuds always gave her time to think things out," Lenore said.

Libby picked up an oblong potato. "What is it I should be thinking about?"

"Mrs. Beidler's got her drawers in a knot over little Dylan, don't she?"

Libby tried to pare the entire skin off without breaking it. Round and round she went until she cut too thinly. A long piece fell to the table. "She thinks Dylan will infect the rest of the students."

Lenore snorted. "Blamed fool woman. Doesn't she know a child can't be held accountable for his parents' mistakes?"

"I tried to make her see that, but she got all huffy

and made some remark about forcing me to quit. Can she do that?"

"Adelaide can do just about anything she puts her petty mind to."

Libby's hands fell to the tabletop. "What am I going to do?"

"Have you thought about tutoring Dylan after school, away from the other children?"

"Are you saying I should buckle under to her majesty's demands?" Libby asked, aghast.

"Of course not. What I'm saying is you're a smart gal. There's ways around this problem. You want Dylan to get an education, right?"

Puzzled, Libby nodded.

"Can you teach Dylan after the rest of the kids are gone?" Lenore pressed.

"I suppose I could," Libby admitted. "But it's wrong to separate him."

"I agree, but sometimes in this life we got to make decisions where neither choice is the right one. If you teach Dylan after school, Adelaide won't have reason to make things tough on you, and Dylan can still get an education."

Libby considered Lenore's solution. She hated treating Dylan like he was an outcast, but she had her own future to worry about, too. "How do I explain why he can't come to school anymore?"

"Tell him the truth—or at least most of it. I'll bet you he takes it better than you think he will."

"I don't know, Lenore. I'd be going against everything I believe is right, and I'm not so sure Dylan will understand. He's smart, but he's also sensitive, and I might hurt him so badly he'd revert back to the distrustful little boy he used to be. I've got to give it some thought." Libby paused and swallowed nervously. "Mrs. Beidler had more on her mind than Dylan when she came to see me."

"I didn't hear about anything else."

"She accused me of consorting with Ma—, I mean, the sheriff."

Lenore's eyes twinkled. "I can't imagine how she got such a foolish notion in her head."

Libby glared at the older woman. "There is nothing going on between him and me. Nothing. I haven't even seen him this week."

Lenore's expression sobered. "Not many folks have. Eli went to talk to him the other day, but Matt wasn't around. Found out he was off to the Ballards' ranch to check on a couple missing cows. Yesterday Eli had to go up north to pay house calls to a few of the folks up in that area. Said he wouldn't be back until Sunday night. Awful quiet around here without anybody underfoot."

"You still have Mr. Johnson and Mr. Tanner. Did you say the sheriff made it back from the Ballards'?"

"I didn't say, but I heard tell he did. Virgil saw him when he got back."

"How long ago was that?"

"A couple days ago, I reckon. You aren't worried about him, are you?"

Libby's face warmed under Lenore's scrutiny. "Certainly not. He can take care of himself."

Matt's self-effacing statement echoed in her mind hauntingly. *Nobody's worried about me for a long time.*

Libby finished peeling the potato in her hand and stood. "I'd better get Dylan home."

"Won't you two stay for dinner? I got plenty," Lenore invited.

"How about tomorrow night?"

"You know you're welcome here any time, honey."

Libby walked down to the parlor and found Dylan engrossed in looking through the stereoscope. "Ready to go?"

Dylan bubbled with excitement. "Look at this, Miss O'Hanlon. Mrs. Potts said it was San Francisco. I want to go there someday and see all the ships."

Libby gazed through the eyepieces at the three-dimensional image created by two pictures. The sails of the boats seemed to billow toward her, and she smiled with childlike enthusiasm. She lowered the instrument. "Do you want to be a merchant when you grow up?"

Dylan shook his head. "I want to be a sailor."

"You can be whatever you want to be. Remember that, Dylan."

Libby helped him bundle up, and after she buttoned her coat, they thanked Lenore for the cake. They scurried down the boardwalk against the cutting northwest wind.

Dylan pulled Libby in the direction of the jail. "I want to go see the sheriff."

Libby planted her feet on the wood planks. "I can't. I have to get back to the school."

"Why?" Dylan demanded.

Libby searched her mind for an answer. "Because I have homework to do."

"Teachers don't have homework."

"This one does."

"Do it tomorrow. Please, Miss O'Hanlon?" Dylan coaxed.

One look in Dylan's pleading eyes and Libby's resolve melted. "All right, but just for a few minutes."

Dylan grinned and he led her into the chilly office. His lips thinned to a frown. "He's not here."

His disappointment mirrored Libby's own dashed hopes, but she tried to mask her letdown. "He's probably out hunting down some nasty outlaw like Texas Jack."

The smile Libby hoped to cajole from the boy didn't materialize. Instead, his face darkened.

"What is it?" she asked softly.

"Something's wrong."

The mature voice out of the seven-year-old body startled Libby. "You're letting your imagination run away."

Stubbornly, Dylan shook his head. He grabbed her hand and tugged her out of the office. "Let's go to his cabin."

Libby's feet made the decision before she could think of a plausible excuse. With a growing sense of dread, she followed Dylan. The sheriff's cabin stood closer to the edge of Deer Creek than the schoolhouse at the opposite end of town. A stand of pines kept it hidden from curious eyes, and a tiny frozen creek lay a few hundred feet from the front door.

Without asking Libby's permission, Dylan pounded on the door. "Hey Sheriff, you in there?"

No answer came.

Libby breathed a sigh of relief, though anxiety crowded the other emotion aside. "He isn't home. We'd better get back to town."

Dylan used both his fists on the solid wood. "Sheriff, it's me and Miss O'Hanlon."

The ominous silence remained and Libby grew uncomfortable. A sense of unease surrounded her like a morning mist, curling in her stomach and fanning outward.

Dylan looked up at her and seemed to discern her apprehension. "Let's just go in."

Libby grabbed his arm. "Let me."

Her trembling fingers stretched to the latch as a foreboding voice screamed loudly in her mind. It told her to run far and long and not look back. She ignored the command, cautiously pushing the door inward. Cold, stale air struck her nostrils and fear took substance. Her frantic gaze searched the dim room, and she spied a door leading to a bedroom. "Stay here, Dylan."

"But—"

"No. Wait here." She pressed down on his shoulders, gaining strength from the physical contact.

With a thundering heart, she moved across the room on leaden feet and paused in the doorway. A body lay atop a large bed.

"Oh God," she whispered. Anguish wrenched her insides. Was Matt alive?

She leaned over to touch his shoulder.

Matt rolled over and came up with his revolver in hand, unerringly aimed at Libby. She pressed a hand to her mouth to stifle a yelp of surprise.

"Libby?"

The hoarse tone little resembled the deep timbre of his normal voice.

"I'm here, Matt. What's wrong?"

He lowered his gun but couldn't seem to find the holster strapped to his thigh. Libby took the weapon from him and laid it on the nightstand. A ragged cough shook Matt's frame as Libby knelt beside him. She laid a cool palm against his forehead, flinching at the radiating heat. His breathing rasped loudly in the ominous silence of the cabin.

"So hot . . . tired . . . hard to breathe." The short, fractured statement exhausted him, and he closed his eyes.

Libby's mind raced. He needed a doctor, but Eli was out of town for a couple more days. Two days might be too late. Did she dare expose her medical skills? How would she explain her familiarity with the treatment of pneumonia and the medications needed to care for him?

Matt muttered something unintelligible and thrashed about on the straw mattress. His eyelids lifted and the feverish glint in his eyes stabbed Libby. How could she not use her knowledge to save his life?

"What's wrong with him?"

Dylan stood behind her shoulder, looking small and scared. Libby turned and grabbed his arms.

"Listen to me, Dylan. I need you to run back to my room at the schoolhouse and get something for me. Can you do that?"

Dylan continued to stare at Matt, fear clouding his expression.

Libby shook him gently. "Dylan, did you hear what I said?"

He blinked and nodded.

"In my room and under the bed is a black trunk. Open it up. You'll find a bag just like Dr. Clapper's. Bring it here as quickly as you can. Do you understand?"

His head bobbed and dark bangs fell across his forehead. "I'll get it."

"Don't stop for anything or anyone." Libby released him, and Dylan sent the sheriff one last frightened glance before hurrying away. She turned her attention back to her patient. "Matt, I have to get a fire going in here before you freeze to death."

"Too hot," Matt mumbled.

"That's the fever."

Libby straightened and went to the stove. The empty wood box told her Matt must have kept the fire going until he'd been too sick to bring in more wood. By the time Dylan returned with her medical bag, a blazing fire cast warmth into the chilly room.

Libby put forth her most reassuring bedside manner. "You did well, Dylan. Now I need you to fill the wood box, while I see what I can do for the sheriff."

He nodded and hurried outside.

Libby removed her coat and took a deep breath. Approaching Matt, she rolled up her sleeves. "I have to get your boots and coat off so I can examine you."

A bleary gaze searched her face but Matt didn't speak. Instead, he fumbled with his coat buttons until Libby pushed his hands aside gently and took over the task herself. She helped him to a sitting position and pulled one sleeve free, then the other. Tossing the heavy sheepskin coat on a nearby chair, she moved to his feet. After a few tugs, his worn brown boots lay on the floor.

Libby's fingers touched the warm leather holster around his lean hips, and her heartbeat rivaled Matt's rapid pulse. As her knuckles brushed the front of his trousers, heat suffused her cheeks.

"I'm sorry, Libby," Matt whispered.

"What on earth are you sorry about?" The conversation gave her something to think about besides what lay beneath the gunbelt.

"Being such a bother. I ain't used to bein' sick."

"I can tell," Libby replied dryly.

"Pneumonia?" The single word sounded like a dirge.

"I don't know," Libby answered honestly.

"You're the best I got, with Eli out of town."

A spasm of coughing nearly choked him, and Libby held him in a sitting position until the bout ended. She eased him back. Shock rippled through her at his usually ruddy face that now matched the pillowcase. She sternly set aside her swirling confusion and removed the holster without any further embarrassment.

She opened her black bag and withdrew the stethoscope. She blew across the metal to warm it, then moved his shirt aside to lay the round end above his heart. The springy dark hairs on his chest grazed her fingers. She moved the instrument to listen to his lungs and heard a soft rattle. Matt had guessed correctly, but the illness hadn't progressed as far as she had feared.

Focusing on his condition, Libby reviewed the procedures to break up both the congestion in his lungs and the fever that ravaged his body. She had helped her father care for folks with pneumonia, and she had dealt with her own share of patients with the same. It wasn't inexperience that brought the fear churning in her stomach. It was the knowledge that few people afflicted with pneumonia recovered, which stoked the profound fear that all her years of medical training could prove fruitless in saving Matt's life.

Chapter 8

The hotter-than-hades desert scorched and burned, leaving a trail of bleached bones and hollow-eyed skulls. Sweat no longer dampened Matt's shirt, but his dry tongue swelled and gagged him, and exhaustion overwhelmed him. Breathing seemed to take more energy than he possessed.

He had tracked the Comancheros through hell itself, and victory lay within his grasp. The renegades burst over a cactus-shrouded hill, their shrill screams echoing in his head. The war cries changed to rebel shouts, and cannons blasted from all sides. The Comancheros blurred, becoming blue-coated boys who emanated the stench of death. A soldier wearing the face of a child raised a saber and rushed him. His finger settled on the gun's trigger, but recognition froze the survival instinct.

Dylan.

He couldn't shoot, and he couldn't escape the blade's deadly arc. The sharp-honed edge reflected blinding sunlight, and Rachel appeared at his side, holding a swaddled baby in her arms. She lowered the cloth, revealing a tiny skeleton. Hysterical laughter cackled across her twisted lips and Matt covered his ears, but the demented sound grew louder. The maddened voice changed to shrill obscenities, dripping with venomous hatred. . . .

Coolness feathered across him, and a soothing voice whispered as if through a long black tunnel. From some inner reserve, he found the strength to cough. Pain wracked his body. Gentle hands cradled him, and the same comforting tone washed across him like undulating waves sweeping across grains of sand. Oxygen flushed his lungs, giving him the impetus to continue filling his chest with vital air.

"Matt, can you hear me?"

The disembodied voice took shape and substance. Matt concentrated all his will into lifting anvil-weighted eyelids. Dimness surrounded him, and awareness took a few moments to penetrate his foggy senses.

"Thank heavens, you're awake."

Matt turned to see a pale oval hovering over him. Meadow-green eyes peered at him from an anxious ivory countenance. The angel's name eluded him, dancing at the periphery of his memory. He frowned and searched the clouds in his mind and, like a bolt of lightning, recognition struck him.

"Libby?" He hardly recognized the weak, scratchy voice as his own.

She smiled and nodded. "How are you feeling?"

"Like I been through a battle."

"You've been fighting pneumonia. For a while I thought we were going to lose the war."

"I feel like I did," Matt muttered with a cottony mouth. "Water?"

She moved out of sight, returning a few moments later with a tin cup. A cool hand slid under his neck and raised his head. Greedily, he swallowed the icy water that slipped past his dry lips. All too soon the liquid disappeared and he leaned back against the pillow.

"Do you want more?" Libby asked.

Matt nodded. She repeated the procedure and this time his thirst was slaked. He closed his eyes, exhausted by the simple task of swallowing. He forced himself to open his eyes and remain awake. "How long?"

Libby lowered herself to the edge of the bed, her weight shifting his position slightly. "Two days since Dylan and I found you. I don't know how long you'd been sick before that."

"What day is it?"

"Sunday."

"The last thing I remember is thinking I'd best get to work Thursday morning." He frowned. She had said she and Dylan had found him. "Is Dylan here?"

"He'll be here tomorrow morning to stay with you while I teach."

Another thought struck Matt. "You been here the last couple days?"

She glanced down and smoothed the blanket by his side. "You've been very sick, and I didn't think you should be alone."

"What you're saying is no one else would've stayed with me." Bitterness laced his tone.

Libby's eyes widened in surprise. "I didn't ask anyone."

The rancor evaporated. "Why?"

Her gaze sidled away. "I had to make sure you were taken care of properly."

Matt suspected she hid something from him, but he was too tired to unravel the puzzle. Blessed nothingness beckoned, and he surrendered to sleep's allure.

"Read page thirty-eight."

Matt awakened to Libby's quiet instructions, and the rise and fall of Dylan's young voice followed. He craned his neck and spotted them sitting at his pine table. A kerosene lamp burned brightly, casting shadowy figures on the wall.

"The sheriff's awake," Dylan cried. He scrambled down from his chair and rushed into the bedroom.

Libby followed more sedately and broke the silence with a quiet greeting. "Hello, Matt."

Dylan grinned. "You were snoring so loud the walls were shaking."

"I don't snore," Matt retorted. "What're you doing here?"

"Miss O'Hanlon's teaching me because I stayed with you today and I missed school. I bet you're starving." Dylan finally paused for a breath.

"I am kind of hungry, at that," Matt said. He glanced at Libby. "I hate to be any more bother."

Libby shook her head. "I already have chicken soup on the stove. Dylan can get you a glass of water while I get your supper."

Matt found he had gained enough strength to hold the cup himself, and he drained the contents in a few gulps. Libby returned with a steaming bowl, a napkin draped over her forearm. She stopped by the bed and stood awkwardly.

"Can you feed yourself?" Libby asked.

He raised a trembling hand and shook his head disgustedly. "I don't think so."

"I can do it," Dylan volunteered.

"I have a better idea. You come sit in the chair by the bed and recite your lesson while I help the sheriff," Libby suggested. She perched on the edge of the mattress, apparently ill at ease.

"It doesn't set right with me putting you out, Libby. Whatever you done, it worked and I'm grateful. You and Dylan don't need to be staying with me any-more."

"You could've died, Matt. I'm not going to waltz out of here and leave you to get sick again. Dylan will be here during the days for the rest of the week, and I'll come by after school and make your meals for you," Libby said firmly.

"Eli can come by and check on me, and I can have Dylan bring me something to eat from the café. No need for Dylan to miss school or you to risk your reputation by being here at all hours."

"I think it's a little late to start worrying about that. Open up." Libby thrust a spoon of cooled broth at his mouth.

To escape being jabbed by the utensil, he did as she ordered. The warm liquid slid down his throat, soothing the rawness.

She pressed another spoonful at him, but he blocked the path with his hand. "What do you mean it's a little late to worry about your reputation?" He narrowed his eyes. "Has Mrs. Beidler already been giving you problems about staying here?"

Libby shook her head. "Folks know you're sick, but no one except Lenore knows you have pneumonia. I doubt Mrs. Beidler figured it out unless she's come here to spy on you."

"But people are bound to find out. That's the way with gossip," Matt argued.

"I've been careful, and your place is hidden from town. Besides, what could I have done any differently? Now stop worrying and eat."

Libby cut off any more arguments with the broth-filled spoon. Matt surrendered to her obstinacy and hoped her reputation would remain unsullied. He didn't need her on his already crowded conscience.

While she fed him, he feasted his hungry gaze on her. Though he'd seen little of her in the past week, she'd branded his thoughts and never strayed far from them. His memory had failed to recall the gold threaded through her auburn tresses and the flecks of blue in her green eyes. And he hadn't noticed the tiny cleft in her stubborn chin or the dainty earlobes pinkened by winter's caress. However, his recollection of her rounded breasts and small waist that flared to gently curved hips had lacked nothing but substance. Her nearness played havoc upon his characteristic stolidness, and he shifted uncomfortably.

"Am I hurting you?" Libby asked.

"Not exactly," Matt murmured.

To detract from his increasing discomfort, he concentrated on Dylan's reading. The boy rarely stumbled over a word and when he did, Libby corrected him gently. Dylan's animated face revealed his pleasure at performing for a captive audience, and Matt genuinely enjoyed listening. The boy had bloomed under Libby's tutelage, and an odd mixture of jealousy and pride swirled within him.

"Very good," Libby praised.

Dylan beamed and turned to Matt. "Now I can read all your papers so Dr. Clapper don't have to."

Matt's face burned with humiliation. Dylan hadn't meant to embarrass him in front of Libby, but the sting of his casual remark cut deep. He'd hidden his lack of education from most people, ashamed he couldn't read or write a simple letter. Being a schoolteacher, Libby had far more education than he'd even dreamed of, and now she would see him as he truly was: unlearned and ignorant.

"Maybe the sheriff can sit in on your lessons and he can learn to read just like you have," Libby suggested.

Startled, Matt shot a glance at Libby and expected to see ridicule, but found only a searching look.

"What do you say, Matt?" she asked.

Indecision plagued him.

"C'mon, Sheriff. I can help you, too," Dylan implored.

One look at the boy's earnest expression tipped the scales. He nodded. "Since I'm going to be laid up for a time, I may as well take advantage of my own personal teachers."

Libby smiled and laid a warm hand on his shoulder. "You won't regret it."

Her light touch singed his bare skin, and despite his

weakness, desire heated his blood. He shifted beneath the quilts and another need made itself known.

"I, uh, need to take a walk," he said.

Libby shook her head. "You almost died. You can't just wake up and start walking around."

"It ain't exactly that I want to," Matt muttered.

"Good, because you're not getting out of that bed for a few days."

"I don't think that'd be such a good idea. The call of nature ain't going to wait that long."

Libby's mouth closed and her lips quirked upwards. "You're still not getting up. That's why we have chamberpots."

Unaccustomed to speaking to a woman about his bodily functions and anything related to them, Matt's eyes refused to meet Libby's. "I aim to walk out to the privy, and you ain't going to stop me."

Libby rose from the bed and stepped back. "Be my guest."

Matt narrowed his eyes. She'd given in too easily. "Turn around."

She shrugged and complied with his request.

Throwing back his blankets, Matt swung his underwear-clad legs off the mattress. He pushed himself to a sitting position and the room spun. He closed his eyes, trying to regain his equilibrium, but that only increased the dizziness. Before he lost what little he had in his stomach, he lay back down. The world stopped reeling and he opened his eyes cautiously.

"I warned you," Libby said. Her voice lowered. "If you feel uncomfortable with me helping you, I'll step outside for a few minutes and Dylan will stay with you."

Matt frowned. "I figured you might be embarrassed, being an unmarried woman and all."

Libby shook her head. "My father was ill for some time before he died and I took care of him."

She whispered a few words to Dylan, then donned her coat. The door closed behind her and cold air eddied across the floor.

With Dylan's help, Matt managed to swallow his dignity and gave in to the dictates of his weakened body. Libby returned a few minutes later with snowflakes powdering her hair and face.

"Looks like we may get a few inches of new snow," she commented.

Matt nodded and appreciated her tact in not asking any embarrassing questions. A spate of coughing caught him off guard, and he choked for nearly a full minute before he could catch his breath. Libby appeared beside him, concern creasing her forehead.

"Dylan, could you get me the camphor?" she called.

He brought a small jar to Libby, his worried gaze settling on Matt.

The strength Matt thought he'd regained had disappeared, and he had to concentrate on clasping Dylan's shoulder. "Don't look so down in the mouth, son. The devil ain't ready for me yet." Matt's grip slackened and his arm fell to the bed.

"It's getting late, Dylan. I think you'd better head on home before your mother comes looking for you," Libby suggested softly.

Dylan nodded but kept his attention focused on Matt.

"You heard Miss O'Hanlon. You'd best get going," Matt said with a raspy voice.

The boy turned and put his coat on. "I'll be here in the morning."

Libby smiled and covered his head with a woolen hat, pulling the flaps down over his ears. "I'll be watching for you. Good night."

With a shy wave, Dylan left.

Returning to the bed, Libby picked up the jar of

camphor. She unscrewed the top and dipped her fingers into the mixture. A grimace of distaste crossed her face, her pert nose wrinkling.

"Smells pretty awful, don't it?" Matt asked.

She smiled. "That's why it works."

· Libby's delicate hands whispered across his chest and Matt inhaled sharply. The light touch sent tingles shooting through his body, concentrating in the center of his masculinity. Her smooth motions tickled his chest hairs, and his senses congregated below the sensual massage. The muscles of his stomach tensed, twitching with each downward stroke.

He had to concentrate on something other than the blissful agony that stormed through his unshuttered defenses. He shifted his attention to Libby. An untamed curl had escaped her snug chignon and fallen across her puckered brow, obliterating the image of propriety. The concentration etched in her face appeared incongruent with the mindless task of rubbing in the camphor, but the telltale pink flush in her cheeks hinted at a crack in her businesslike demeanor.

"The camphor will cause you to cough more, but it should also break up the congestion in your lungs," Libby said.

Her matter-of-fact statement riled Matt. "You get that out of a book, too?"

"I told you, my father was a doctor. I used to help him."

He noticed she didn't meet his gaze but continued to massage the ill-smelling medicine across his chest. "Where'd you come from, Libby?"

"I grew up in Ohio."

When she didn't expand, Matt frowned. "How'd you end up in Montana?"

"I saw an ad in the paper for a teacher, so I applied."

"Which paper?"

Libby finished her ministrations and covered his

torso with the blankets. "Why are you asking all these questions?"

"Just curious is all."

Libby crossed the room to the pump, then washed and dried her hands. "I'm going to heat some water and mix some of the camphor with it. Then I'll have you breathe the vapors to open up your lungs even more."

Matt spotted a black medical case on the floor. "What's Eli's bag doing here?"

"That's my father's old bag. I kept it after he died," Libby answered.

"He must've taken good care of it. Looks almost new."

Libby hesitated. "He did."

Libby stood by the stove and stared at the kettle filled with water. With her arms crossed and her back ramrod straight, she appeared ready to go to battle.

"I ain't going to bite you," Matt said.

Libby turned and her wide eyes resembled a startled doe's. It wouldn't have surprised Matt if she had turned tail and run.

"What?" she asked.

"I said I ain't going to bite you. Why don't you sit down and keep me company?"

She shook her head. "The water will be ready in a few minutes."

She acted like a long-tailed cat in a room full of rocking chairs. He tried to remember if he'd done anything to cause the skittishness, but came up empty. He idly traced the scar, noting the scratchy whiskers surrounding the raised line, and grimaced. Not shaving for a few days made the jagged mark stand out in stark contrast to the dark bristles. Any mirror would've told him why she couldn't stand to be near him.

"If you get my razor for me, I can shave," Matt said.

From beside the stove, Libby turned. "You wouldn't be able to hold the razor long enough to finish one side."

"I figured you might not be so jumpy around me if I got rid of the beard."

"What makes you think I'm nervous around you?"

"It's clear you like being here as much as you'd like being caged with a rattlesnake."

Libby strode to Matt's side. "I'm not afraid of you, and I don't mind staying until you're back on your feet."

With a swiftness surprising both of them, Matt's hand latched on to Libby's arm. "Maybe you should."

A spark of terror flashed through her eyes, and she yanked out of his grasp and moved out of reach. Her nostrils flared with every uneven breath she drew, and Matt sensed she fought some inner skirmish for control. He regretted the impulse to frighten her, but he couldn't tolerate her revulsion. He wanted her away from him before he did something stupid, like try to kiss her.

"You wouldn't hurt me, Matt."

The lingering fear in Libby's face belied her firm tone, and anguish lashed like a whip across Matt's soul. Though he'd tried to scare her, a part of him hoped she would see through his ruse. He'd chop off an arm rather than harm her, but she didn't understand he had to protect himself, too.

He glanced at the stove. "The water's boiling."

Libby fixed up her concoction and set the kettle on the small table beside the bed. The fumes drifted over Matt and he wrinkled his nose. "You trying to kill me?"

She handed him a towel. "Put this over your head and the pot, then breathe."

Matt grumbled but obeyed. After the water cooled and the vapors diminished, he removed the towel and leaned back in his bed.

Libby carried the kettle to the door, threw the contents out, and slipped back inside. She busied herself with small chores, and Matt suspected she worked the inconsequential tasks to avoid him.

Her somber skirt contained no bustle to hide the shape of her God-given body, and Matt heartily approved of the style. Unable to do anything but observe, he followed Libby's movements with an admiring gaze. His loins reminded him he hadn't been to Dresper to visit one of the gals at the Lucky Horseshoe in nearly three months. However, the thought of slaking his needs with Charity or Hope didn't appeal to him. Temptation lay buried in the proper attire of Miss Libby O'Hanlon—and despite the pneumonia that robbed him of his strength, one part of him didn't seem to be afflicted with such weakness.

The reason for his pleasant distress approached him.

She lay a cool palm against his forehead and frowned. "I thought your fever broke, but you're feeling warm again. I'll get a cool cloth and we'll see if that brings it down."

That ain't going to bring down what needs to be brought down. Matt closed his eyes and thought of ice-cold streams and bitter north winds. Anything but sweltering summer eyes and a lush behind made to be cupped in the palms of his hands.

A damp cloth settled on his forehead and his eyelids flickered open, capturing her gaze. Her pink tongue slid across her dry lips, and Matt groaned with a growing need to plunder the depths of her sweetness.

"Anybody home?"

Libby withdrew, breaking the spell. "Come in, Dr. Clapper."

Eli entered and brushed the snow off his shoulders. Libby came forward to help him remove his coat.

"I'm glad you got my note," she said.

Eli nodded. "I came straight over when I read it. Took me an extra day at the Justins' to deliver a stubborn little girl. Now, what is this about pneumonia?"

"Matt came down with it last week. Dylan and I found him Friday," Libby explained.

Eli stepped over to Matt. "Should've figured something like this would happen after that beef-brained stunt you pulled, tracking down those robbers in a blizzard. You got more pride than sense, Matt."

"Don't go giving me one of your sermons. Besides, Libby's been lecturing me enough for both of you," Matt said.

Eli snorted. "Fat lot of good they did, too."

He removed his stethoscope from the bag and listened to Matt's heart and chest. He looked at Libby. "What'd you do for him?"

"Kept him warm and spread oil of camphor on his chest. Gave him chicken broth and as much liquids as he wanted," she replied.

Eli sniffed the air and his nose twitched. "Smells like you had him breathing camphor, too."

Libby nodded.

"Seems to be working. Lungs sound pretty good, and his heart's pounding like a smithy's hammer. Fever?"

"I thought it broke last night, but he seems to be a little hot again."

"I'm fine," Matt muttered. "Would you two quit talking like I ain't here?"

Eli cocked his head. "You hear something, Libby?"

She shook her head. "Must've been the wind."

Eli chuckled.

Matt's growl was interrupted by another bout of coughing. After he recovered, he lay back exhausted.

"Get some sleep, Matt. That's the best thing for you now," Eli said.

Much as Matt hated to admit it, he couldn't remain awake any longer, and he drifted off to sleep.

Libby poured coffee and Eli joined her by the table. She traced her cup's handle and rim with a nervous finger.

"He should be all right," Eli stated. "You've done a fine job taking care of him."

"Thank you," Libby said. "My father taught me quite a bit when I went with him to visit sick folks."

"I'm sure he did, but I'm also fairly certain there's a lot of things you know that you aren't admitting to. Take that bag for instance."

Her fingers stilled on the coffee cup, her carefully sewn lies threatening to unravel. Caring for Matt and terrified she'd lose him, Libby hadn't had a good night's sleep for three nights, and tiredness dulled the edge of her fiercely guarded secrets. She glanced at her black medical case. "Like I told Matt, it was my father's."

Eli snorted. "If that bag's more'n five years old, I'll hang up my stethoscope. It's not any of my business where you came from or what you're running from, but I know Lenore and Matt worry about me, and I'm getting to a point where I'm ready to admit I need some help."

"You don't understand," Libby said.

"What's there to understand? You know medicine and I need an assistant. I realize you have an obligation as the schoolteacher here, but I wouldn't be needing you that much to begin with. And maybe if you want, come next spring, you can quit teaching and work with me all the time."

Four years ago Libby had prayed for such an offer to join an established doctor, but none had come, and Harrison had offered her another option. *If only . . .*

Libby shook her head. "I'm not who you think I am."

Eli's wisdom-filled eyes studied her. "I got that

impression when you first arrived, but it's not my place to be judging folks. I seen enough of you to know you got a fine head on your shoulders, and enough natural skill to be a damned fine nurse or even a doctor. I'm sure whatever you did, you had your reasons, and I'm equally certain you did the only thing you could. What do you say to my proposition?"

The barest flicker of hope sparked in Libby's breast, and tears prickled her eyes. To do what she loved and have the support and acceptance of another doctor was more than she could have dreamed. She squelched the last remaining piece of doubt and nodded. "I think I'd like that. I've always had an interest in medicine."

"You got more than an interest. You have a gift, and I hate to see anyone not use the talents the good Lord blessed them with." Eli settled back in his chair and sipped his coffee. "I'd also hate to see you leave Deer Creek. In the month you've been here, you've done a world of good."

"I haven't done anything but get Mrs. Beidler riled," Libby argued.

Eli chuckled. "Does that woman good to finally meet her match. Maybe it'll open her eyes. You've given little Dylan a reason to stay out of trouble, and he about worships the ground you walk on. It's a miracle what a little love and some attention can do for a boy. Same holds true for Matt."

Libby smiled. "I keep him out of trouble?"

"More than you realize. What do you know about him?"

"I know he's honest and compassionate, and he cares for Dylan like he's his own. And I know he used to have a problem with drinking and he doesn't know how to read."

Eli's bushy eyebrows shot upwards. "I'm surprised he told you about his lack of education, with his bull-headed pride."

"Dylan let it slip tonight, but I had already figured it out. We talked Matt into sitting in with Dylan's lessons."

"That's good. He was too stubborn to ask for help and too proud to admit it. No other schoolteacher we had figured out Matt's illiteracy. I think they were too scared to get near him."

"Why on earth were they scared of him?"

Eli chuckled. "That's what I like about you, Libby. You got backbone and you don't even know it."

Libby's face warmed and she wondered if he would've thought the same if he'd known the spineless coward she'd been with Harrison.

The mirth left Eli's face. "You know your reputation is going to suffer, staying here with Matt."

"I know, but I don't see how I could've done things differently."

Eli shrugged and filled a pipe with dark strands of tobacco. "As long as you understand you may become my assistant sooner than you think. Mrs. Beidler won't be real forgiving."

Libby frowned. "Why does she hold so much power in this town? Isn't there anyone who'll stand up against her?"

"There was nobody willing to risk her disapproval until you came. Of course, she didn't sway the menfolk against Matt like she tried. The men in this town respect a man who used to be a Texas Ranger and fought in the war, so they don't pay much mind to Adelaide's haranguing about his drinking." Eli puffed on the lit pipe and aromatic blue smoke circled above them. "She's not a bad woman. Life dealt her a poor hand and she's doing her best to stay in the game."

"You're more understanding than I am, Doctor. The way she talks about Dylan makes me want to throw that overstuffed goose in a stew pot."

"Age has a tendency to mellow a person, Libby. Life doesn't hold as many surprises as it used to, because you've pretty much seen it all." His keen gaze settled on her. "In fact, I doubt you could tell me anything that would shock me."

Libby recognized the invitation to share her troubles, but no matter how much he reminded her of her father, she had no right to burden him with her affairs. She smiled gratefully. "I'll remember that."

Matt mumbled in his sleep, and Libby glanced at the bedroom door. She rose and walked into the room to check his temperature.

Libby returned to the table. "He feels a little warm."

Eli nodded. "I know you said his fever broke yesterday evening, but he'll continue to have a low-grade fever overnight until he's completely shaken the pneumonia." He pushed back his chair and stood. "I'd best head on over to Lenore's and let her know I'm back. You need anything, give me a holler, but something tells me Matt's in good hands."

Libby followed Eli to the door. "Good night, and thanks for coming out."

"You take care of that stubborn jackass—and you have my permission to tie him down if he won't stay in bed," Eli said. "Good night."

Libby dropped the latch into place and leaned against the solid wood. The course of events had forced her to once more become involved in Matt and Dylan's lives. She couldn't have left Matt in the hands of someone who had no medical training, and she couldn't let anyone else see her knowledge in treating him. Only one fortunate result came out of the episode—she had found an excuse to keep Dylan from attending classes: Matt's illness. What excuse would she find for next week?

Doubts assailed her decision to work with Eli, but she firmly stamped them down. To be able to use her medical skills again had been too tempting a proposition to refuse. No one would discover she actually was a doctor if she pretended to know less than she did. And later she would credit Eli for teaching her about medicine, so no one would question her knowledge. The arrangement seemed the perfect solution, and hope once again blossomed. Perhaps Fate had given her a chance to balance out the past injustices.

She rubbed sore, gritty eyes. She needed sleep but doubted she'd get much on the wood floor where she'd slept since staying with Matt. Her gaze strayed to the room where he lay on the large four-poster bed. The lure of resting on a soft mattress didn't even cause a ripple in her conscience. Instead, a shiver of anticipation skittered up her spine. Sorely tempted to sleep on the other side of the bed, she had to talk herself out of such scandalous behavior. She sighed, resigned to another restless night on the cold floor.

Sleep still eluded her a couple hours later, and she welcomed the task of feeding the fire. Dancing orange flames relegated the black night to the corners of the cabin, and heat spilled out to chase the chill away. Tightening her hold on the quilt wrapped around her shoulders, Libby tiptoed into Matt's room. He snored quietly. She laid her hand on his weathered forehead but didn't find a hint of fever. Relieved, she smiled in the darkness.

She smoothed a few stray locks of hair from his temples and her fingers tingled under the silky strands. As she allowed her curious gaze to drink in the strong lines of his ruggedly handsome face, the knot in her stomach grew. With a feathery-light touch she traced the angle of his jaw, pausing a moment on the endearingly familiar scar, and her heart cried for the awful pain he'd endured. She recalled the horror stories her brother had told her of the tent hospitals during the war and the suffering of the men because of the lack of morphine. If Matt had received the injury fighting for the Confederacy, she suspected he'd been one of those who'd had to bear the agony without benefit of an anesthetic. She wondered about the other scars she'd seen when she'd removed his shirt. How violent a life had Matt led?

Libby shivered and pulled her hands into the warmth of her quilt, but she couldn't drag her sight away from Matt. So different than Harrison, yet how could she be sure Matt wouldn't become the beast her husband had? Her heart told her Matt could never hurt a woman, but her mind remembered too clearly how gentleness could turn to cruelty in the blink of an eye. She admired Matt for his goodness and strength and the security he brought to her, even as she feared he'd turn against her if he knew what she'd done. He must never learn her secret, for Libby wouldn't be able to bear his disgust.

Her eyelids drooped and the soft bed beckoned her again. What harm could there be? Wearing her clothes and wrapped in a quilt, she could lie on the blankets beside him. No one would know, and she would awaken before Matt and move back to the floor in the early morning. Too exhausted to fight the temptation, Libby went around the bed and carefully lowered herself to the mattress beside his comforting strength. She sighed blissfully and closed her eyes.

The dim glow of dawn's coral light greeted Matt's bleary gaze. He stared out a frost-rimed window and tried to shake the last vestiges of sleep. Embers glowed in the hearth in the other room, and he debated the lure of the cozy bed and the knowledge he should stoke up the fire. Awareness of warmth on one side of his body made him turn his head. He blinked. He had dreamed of Libby O'Hanlon in his bed, but never believed his wish would come true. She lay curled against his side, her face pressed into his shoulder and her long hair fanned across the pillow. If he believed in heaven, he would've believed her an innocent angel sent down to test his restraint.

A daintily curled hand rested beneath her chin and her eyelashes brushed her rosy cheeks. Full lips were parted slightly, and she snuffled softly with each breath. Matt smiled tenderly, wondering if she knew she snored. A light smattering of freckles on the bridge of her nose spilled outward, dappling her cheeks. Matt's memory of her satiny softness begged for another stolen caress. As his calloused thumb feathered across her features, passion surged through his blood. He hadn't slept a night with a woman since Rachel, and he'd forgotten what it was like to awaken beside soft contours and a beautifully sculpted face.

He frowned. Though he desired her, a primitive protectiveness insinuated itself, and the urge to hold her overruled his virile needs. He didn't want to feel more than simple lust. He had loved a woman once, and she had destroyed his heart with blatant affairs and sadistic taunts about his maimed face. Rachel had had no qualms about informing everyone he was no longer man enough to satisfy her.

He studied the arch of Libby's brows and the perfect earlobe exposed to his hungry perusal. Everything about her drew him like a bear to honey, and he'd probably get stung just as badly. She'd made her revulsion for the damned scar plain enough, but the disgust didn't dull his ardor for her. Why did he torture himself?

Libby sighed and her eyelids fluttered open. Her eyes widened and she attempted to escape, but the quilt effectively kept her prisoner.

"Good morning," Matt said.

"This isn't what you're thinking," Libby said breathlessly.

"And what am I thinking?"

Flustered, Libby rambled. "I don't know, but it's not that. I couldn't sleep on the floor and I was really tired, so I lay on the bed. I planned on waking up before you so you wouldn't think what you're thinking."

Laughter bubbled out of Matt. "Relax, Libby. I wasn't thinking anything." *Liar.*

"Oh." She relaxed. "I'm sorry I snapped at you. I haven't gotten much sleep lately, and I was afraid I'd fall asleep during school if I didn't get some rest."

"Have you been staying here every night since I've been sick?"

Libby nodded. "Dylan couldn't, without getting in trouble, and I didn't trust anyone else."

"Is that the only reason?" Matt asked, his voice intimately low-pitched.

Libby paused long enough to send hope spiraling in Matt. "Why else?"

He propped his head on his hand and gazed down at Libby's flushed face. "Did you know you snore?"

The red in her face deepened to scarlet. "I do not."

Matt grinned mischievously. "I heard it. I also noticed you have very nice earlobes, Miss O'Hanlon." He slowly lowered a hand to her thick tresses and wrapped a fat curl around his finger. "Why do you hide such pretty hair in an ugly bun?"

Libby blinked. "It wouldn't be proper to wear it loose."

"Well, I think it's downright indecent not to. You're a beautiful woman, Libby, and you ought not be ashamed of that." The tempestuous coil slipped off his forefinger, and he traced the slope of her cheek. "Have you ever been kissed?"

He could see the question caught her off guard, but after a moment she nodded. "Once or twice."

"Did you like it?" Matt didn't know why he asked the question, though he truly wanted to hear her answer.

"It was all right."

"Just all right?" He continued to stroke her rosy cheeks, her defiant chin, and her silky neck.

Libby murmured an incoherent reply.

"Do you want to find out if a kiss can be better than 'all right'?" Matt whispered.

Her wide, luminous eyes swathed a path straight to Matt's soul. He wanted to kiss her so badly he trembled with the need, but the wish to soothe her fears dominated. "Don't be afraid. I'd never do anything you don't want me to. I couldn't," he said honestly. He cupped the side of her face in his palm, his thumb making tiny whorls across her flushed cheek. Her breaths grew quicker, more strained, and Matt's heart pounded in his ears. "Are you afraid of me, Libby?"

"No," she murmured.

Matt accepted her acquiescence with a groan of passion. His head lowered to hers, and his lips met her stiff mouth. Gently he kissed her, holding back the urge to plumb the depths of her sweetness. After a few moments of exquisite torture, Libby relaxed. Her pliant lips became a playground for Matt's sensual games, and Libby became an active participant.

His nostrils flared with her womanly scent, and when her mouth opened to invite his plunder, he accepted her timid offer. He craved more of her innocent charms and arched his body against hers. Too many blankets separated them, and Matt blindly reached for the quilt hiding her softness from him. His knuckles grazed her firm breast, and he brushed the plump underside gently, deepening his kiss. Could he trust himself to stop with only a taste of heaven?

Libby pressed against his chest and wrenched her mouth from his. "No, stop!"

Matt stared down into feral eyes. Confusion overtook passion. "What's wrong? Did I hurt you?"

"No. Please don't."

"Don't what? What is it you don't want me to do?"

"Don't ask me. Please."

Her broken sob stabbed his gut, and a tear rolled into her hair to twist the knife even deeper. "I'm sorry. I shouldn't have forced you—"

"You didn't do anything. It's me, not you." Libby wrestled with the quilt, jumped off the bed, and dashed out of the bedroom.

Matt's concern mounted with each second of oppressive silence, and he risked rising. He steadied himself with a palm against the wall and shuffled to the doorway to lean against the wood frame.

Libby knelt in front of the fireplace, jabbing at the embers with a black poker.

"Libby, I'm sorry if . . ."

She froze in the middle of prodding the glowing red coals.

Matt noticed her preoccupation. "What're you doing?"

She dropped the iron rod, scrambled to her feet, and stared at the tool as if it were a writhing snake.

Chapter 9

Weak as a newborn calf, Matt stumbled to Libby's side.

"Libby, what's wrong? What is it?" he asked in a low, urgent voice. He peered into her vacant eyes, and the sensation that someone walked over his grave sent a cold shudder up his spine. He gripped her arms and shook her gently. "Libby!"

Awareness filtered back by degrees, and she blinked as if waking from a deep sleep. Her glassy eyes settled on him and confusion retreated. "What in the world are you doing? You're not supposed to be out of bed."

Matt refused to budge, fear for her strange behavior hardening his tone. "What was *I* doing? What were *you* doing, is a better question. I thought you went loco."

"What do you mean?"

With his free hand, he pointed at the fireplace poker. "You dropped that like it come to life, then stared at it like it was going to jump up and bite you. What happened?"

Her shoulders stiffened beneath his arm. "It was hot."

The words lacked conviction.

Matt's concerned anger ebbed and he studied Libby's pale face. Her frightened eyes appeared tired and drawn, with dark circles beneath them. Gone was the self-assuredness he'd admired, but the vulnerability that replaced it triggered a much deeper response. Protectiveness surged through him, and he swore silently. He wanted to remove the shadows that haunted her face, but he was helpless unless she told him about the specters. "Libby."

Despairing eyes peered at Matt, and he had to clear his throat before he could speak. "Tell me about it. I'll help you any way I can."

A single tear tracked down her cheek. "I can't."

Matt swallowed the hurt. "You don't trust me."

Libby's hands tightened on his arm; anguish glistened in her eyes. "I do trust you, and if I could tell anyone, I'd tell you. But I can't, Matt."

"I want to help."

A desolate smile claimed Libby's lips. "Nobody can help me." She trembled, her shoulders shaking with silent sobs. "Hold me."

She turned into Matt's comforting arms and laid her cheek against his bare chest. The steady rhythm of his heart lent her the will to halt the tears threatening to crack the dam of restraint. Safe in Matt's snug embrace, Libby felt protected and cherished. The heat of his body warmed her, and for the first time since she'd killed Harrison, tranquillity eased her troubled mind. She'd thought she could live with murder on her conscience, but the remorse and guilt would not remain buried.

Matt believed in right and wrong, black and white. He thought her a good person, but if he learned her secret she would no longer have his friendship. And she realized she needed his quiet strength more than she had ever needed anything else before.

She raised her head and found his lips a scant few inches from hers. Thunder pounded in her ears, and the hungry look in Matt's eyes brought a quiver to her knees. Her fingers curled against his virile chest, the dark hairs brushing her knuckles. The realization that he was clad only in the lower half of his long underwear increased her heart's cadence. His musky scent enveloped her, and the evidence of his arousal pressed against her thigh. She repressed the now-familiar panic, daring the dark currents raging within her. She wanted him to kiss her again, and that acknowledgment brought no fear. Libby lifted her hand, tracing Matt's jaw with a light finger as she had done while he'd slept. Tenderly, she paused on the scar, and his body stiffened.

Matt's smoldering gaze disappeared, replaced by a shuttered expression. "I'd best get back to bed. Guess I'm not as strong as I thought."

Mortification filled Libby. "I'm sorry, Matt. You're right. You shouldn't be up."

With his arm around her shoulders, Libby helped him back to his room. He stretched out on his back and she averted her gaze, remembering too well his hard, probing flesh. She covered temptation with the blankets and shame heated her cheeks. What must he think of her? She'd slept beside him and almost begged to be kissed.

"I'll make breakfast," Libby murmured and scurried away.

She couldn't face his disgust at her brazen behavior. In her selfish desire to taste his tantalizing lips, she'd completely forgotten about his weakness. A doctor did not become emotionally involved with a patient—especially when he was a lawman and she a murderer.

Dylan trotted into the cabin as the smell of coffee filled the room and oatmeal bubbled on the stove.

"Good morning," Libby greeted, grateful to have Dylan's presence as a buffer between herself and Matt.

"Morning," he responded and made a beeline for the bedroom.

"Did you wipe your shoes before you went traipsing across the floor?" Libby called.

Dylan shook his head and returned to the rug in front of the door. He carefully scraped the snow from his soles, then hurried to Matt's side. "Morning, Sheriff. You look a lot better."

Matt smiled. "I'm feeling better, partner. Did you have breakfast?"

Dylan shook his head. "Ma's never up when I leave."

"Does she know you're staying with me during the day?"

The boy concentrated on unwinding the scarf from his neck. "Nope. She doesn't care what I do."

Leaning against the doorjamb, Libby frowned. "Doesn't she ever ask where you've been?"

"She don't care," he reiterated.

Libby blinked, and for a split second, she shared a concerned glance with Matt. She pressed back her worry and turned to Dylan. "You must be starved. Take off your coat and come have some oatmeal."

He shrugged out of his jacket and dashed to the table. Libby set a bowl of hot cereal and a plate of biscuits in front of the boy.

"You got any jam?" Dylan asked.

Libby arched an eyebrow. "Excuse me?"

He flushed. "Could I please have some jam?"

"I think I might be able to find some."

She discovered a small crock of strawberry preserves on a cupboard shelf and set the jar in front of Dylan.

"Thank you," he said.

"You're welcome." She called to Matt. "Would you like some strawberry jam on your biscuits, too?"

"Sounds good," he replied.

Libby carried Matt's breakfast on a tray fashioned from a flour-keg cover, and set the meal on the small table beside his bed. She removed her apron. "I think you're strong enough to feed yourself. I have to get to the schoolhouse."

"Aren't you going to eat first?"

Libby couldn't meet his gaze. "I'm running late this morning."

Matt shrugged and reached for his coffee cup. "Suit yourself."

His indifference brought stinging moisture to Libby's eyes. She returned to the table, where Dylan shoveled oatmeal sweetened by sorghum into his mouth.

"The sheriff's doing much better, but he still needs sleep. Rub camphor on his chest once this morning and then once this afternoon," she instructed.

Dylan wrinkled his nose. "That stuff stinks worse than a wet polecat."

Libby smiled. "I know, but if we want the sheriff to get well, we have to use it."

The boy nodded reluctantly.

"Maybe you can read your lessons to him if he doesn't mind," she suggested.

His expression brightened considerably. "Okay."

"Don't forget you have arithmetic problems and your cursive to do, too. When I come back after school, we'll go over what you did and we'll have a lesson in geography."

"Don't worry, Miss O'Hanlon, I'll get my work done." He glanced at the nearly empty wood box and sighed. "I suppose I'd best bring in some wood, too."

She leaned down and hugged Dylan's shoulders. "Thank you."

Libby returned to the cabin after school had been recessed and followed Dylan and Matt's laughter to the bedroom door. They didn't notice her arrival, and she observed their enthusiastic game of checkers. The afternoon sun slanted a golden glow across Dylan's dark head, bent close to Matt's tawny hair. For a precious moment, Libby imagined them her family, and the thought sparked a painful longing. She took a deep breath and forced a stiff smile. "I'm back."

Dylan grinned a welcome. "Hi. I'm beating the sheriff again."

Libby approached them. "How many games have you played?"

Matt glanced up and his expression subtly shifted from boyish enthusiasm to masculine scrutiny. Libby dipped her head, afraid she'd see disgust in his face.

"Eight and he's bested me five of them," he replied.

Dylan jumped Matt's last two kings and Matt raised a wry eyebrow. "Make that six."

Despite her discomfort under Matt's perusal, she smiled fondly at Dylan. "It looks like he's as good a student at checkers as he is with his school lessons. How did the rest of the day go?"

"The sheriff snored like an old bear," Dylan remarked.

"I'm not the only one who snores," Matt said, his twinkling gaze on Libby.

Her face warmed with his teasing, and relief made her light-headed. His morning coolness had evaporated, leaving no disdain in his ruggedly handsome features. "You shaved."

"Dylan helped me," Matt reassured. "You were right. I never would've been able to do it alone."

Libby cocked her head and noticed powdered alum dotting his neck. "It looks like your razor needs some sharpening, or the barber needs more practice."

"I got to hold the razor and everything," Dylan said, excitement lacing his tone. "I can't wait until I get whiskers."

"You've still got a few more years to go. No need to be in such a rush to grow up," Matt said.

"You did very well for the first time," Libby complimented the boy.

Dylan tilted his head and studied Matt. "It was kind of hard and I was kind of scared. I didn't want to give him another cut."

Matt blanched at his casual remark. He didn't want to draw attention to the scar, especially in front of Libby. "Did you show Miss O'Hanlon the work you got done today?"

Dylan hopped down from the bed and hurried to the table. He returned a few moments later with a handful of papers. "I did my 'rithmetic and I showed the sheriff how I write my name."

Libby looked at the top sheet and smiled. "You've done a fine job. We'll look at these closer after we eat. Let's get this cleaned up."

She leaned over Matt and picked up the red and black checkers. The scent of lilac soap and chalk dust wafted across him. He pretended to search for more game pieces, while his hungry gaze roamed over the swell of her breasts and down the inward curve of her waist and the gentle flare of her hips below the staid brown wool skirt.

"I think we got them all," Libby said, and turned to Dylan. "What do you say you help me with supper while the sheriff gets some rest?"

Dylan followed Libby to the kitchen, but his reluctant backward glance told Matt he would've preferred to stay with him. He couldn't blame the boy; peeling potatoes wasn't nearly as exciting as listening to Texas Ranger stories. Though if Matt had a choice, he would've chosen the boring task as long as Libby worked beside him.

Libby closed the school door behind her and tightened the ties of her hood under her chin. She pressed her hands into the deep pockets of her ankle-length gray coat. A sun devil curved around the cold yellow disc in the western horizon, looking like a faint circular rainbow. A few stubborn leaves rustled from bare tree branches, but nothing else stirred across the white barren land.

She shivered, wondering if purgatory resembled the desolate Montana wilderness. A lonely cry sounded overhead, and Libby searched the sky for the brave soul who dared winter's silence. An eagle soared in slow, lazy circles high above the snow-encrusted landscape. The solitary bird's flight kindled a sense of kinship in Libby, and her gaze followed the eagle's progress until her nose grew numb.

Reluctantly, she stepped off the stairs and trudged toward Deer Creek. Her boots crunched through the thin, icy crust of the snow, giving her something to listen to besides the keening song of loneliness in her soul.

Matt grew stronger with each passing day, and by the end of the week, her time with him would be at an end. The realization both relieved and saddened her. She'd grown accustomed to having another person around, and being honest with herself, she liked that person to be Matt.

As she emerged on the main road into town, a wagon passed by. Libby glanced up, recognizing the thin woman on the buckboard as Jenny's mother. Raising her hand in greeting, she smiled. Mrs. Olson turned away, but not before Libby noticed a marked coolness in her expression.

Libby pondered the puzzle and walked down the boardwalk. She noticed the Olson's wagon in front of Pearson's Mercantile and, since she needed coffee anyway, decided to speak to Mrs. Olson to learn if she'd inadvertently insulted her. The cowbell's clang announced her presence and the four people inside turned to stare.

She smiled hesitantly. "Good afternoon."

Only Mr. Pearson acknowledged her greeting. He

came out from behind the counter and rubbed his hands over his apron front. "What can I help you with, Miss O'Hanlon?"

"I need some coffee," she replied.

"Is that all for you today?"

She looked into Pearson's beady eyes. "I'm not sure. I think I'll look around for a few minutes."

"If there's anything I can help you with, just let me know."

Libby ignored his lecherous wink and moved past the row of canned goods and black kettles. She paused beside Mrs. Olson, who appeared engrossed in looking at bolts of cloth. "Good afternoon, Mrs. Olson."

"Miss O'Hanlon," she responded curtly and stepped away from Libby.

She tried a new approach. "Jennifer is a joy in class. She learns so quickly."

Pride flickered in the older woman's eyes. "We are proud of her and would like her to *continue* to attend school."

"Surely you're not going to keep her home, are you?"

"That's up to you."

Libby's mouth gaped at the abrupt dismissal. What had she done to deserve the woman's snub? And why would Jennifer's attendance be dependent upon her? Did Mrs. Beidler's tyranny extend to all the inhabitants of Deer Creek? By the time Libby regained her aplomb, the Olsons and the other woman had left.

"Did you find anything else, Libby?" Pearson asked.

She blinked, startled by his audacity. "My name is Miss O'Hanlon, Mr. Pearson."

His lascivious gaze raked over her. "I'll bet the sheriff doesn't call you Miss O'Hanlon."

"What the sheriff does or doesn't call me is none of your business. How much do I owe you?"

"Forty-five cents."

Libby paid him, ensuring her fingers didn't touch his palm. "Thank you."

He stuffed the coffee can in a sack for her. "Here you go, Miss O'Hanlon. You just let me know if there's anything else you need. Anything at all."

Libby's stomach churned at the blatantly obscene offer. She grabbed the package from him, twirled away, and hurried out of the suffocating store. Outside, she paused, dragging in gulps of fresh wintry air. After regaining her composure, Libby scurried in the direction of Matt's sheltered home.

The buggy in front of the cabin brought a groan to Libby's lips. *What now?* On leaden feet, she nearly entered without knocking. She caught herself and rapped her gloved fist against the wood.

Dylan swung the door open and grinned. He grabbed her hand, pulling her inside. "Guess who's here?"

"Hello, dear," Lenore greeted, and wrapped her arms around Libby.

Briefly, Libby closed her eyes in relief. "What are you doing here?"

Lenore stepped back and planted her hands on her generous hips. "What do you think I'm doing here? I'm being neighborly."

"She brought cookies and bread and soup," Dylan said.

Libby brushed a few crumbs from the front of his flannel shirt. "I can see you haven't been shy about helping yourself to the cookies. I hope you didn't eat so many that your appetite is ruined for supper."

"He could eat a whole barrel of cookies and still put away more than you and me for supper," Lenore remarked. "He's a growing boy."

Libby laughed, knowing she couldn't win a food argument with the chubby woman. She glanced toward the open door of the bedroom. "Has Eli examined Matt?"

Lenore nodded. "They're just chewing the fat now. Why don't you and me go warm up the soup?"

"I'm going in with the men," Dylan said, and disappeared into the bedroom.

Steam from the coffee swirled upward to thaw Libby's cheeks and nose. She sipped the hot liquid, which soothed her throat. Lenore sat across the table from her.

"Eli tells me you've been spending the nights here since Matt sickened," Lenore said.

Libby narrowed her eyes. "That's right."

After a few moments of uncharacteristic silence, Lenore threw her hands in the air. "No reason for me to be beating around the bush. There's talk, Libby."

A fist to her stomach couldn't have taken away Libby's breath faster. "What kind of talk?"

"About you spending so much time here with Matt. Mind you, no one but Eli and I know about you staying the nights, but it's bound to get out, the way peoples' mouths flap and all."

"Why can't everyone just mind their own business?" Libby demanded. "My God, Lenore, Matt could've died and no one would've known."

Lenore patted her hand. "There, there dear. I didn't mean to get you all riled up, but I want you to know what you're up against."

Libby stood to pace.

"I should've realized it, the way Mrs. Olson treated me at the store. You'd think I was a leper the way she acted. And Mr. Pearson . . ." She shuddered with disgust.

"Mrs. Beidler's bound and determined to get you fired. Why don't you just quit, honey? Eli'll take you on right away, and you won't have to worry about the old busybodies who got nothing better to do than liven up the boring winter at the expense of innocent folks like yourself."

Libby shook her head. "I can't, Lenore. If I quit, she'll think she won, and I refuse to give her the satisfaction. Besides, Dylan needs to attend school and if I leave, he won't be allowed in the classroom."

"I thought you'd decided to tutor him after school?"

"I can't do that. It would kill him if he couldn't come to school any more. I know he'll still be teased, but he needs to be around others his own age and play like a normal boy."

Lenore sighed. "You've got a mighty tough battle ahead of you, and you've got two strikes against you already."

"I haven't been a real strong person in the past, Lenore, but this time I promise I will hold to what I believe is right, and damn the consequences." She paused as the terrible memories battered her conscience. "If I don't, I'll have nothing left."

"Well, can't say I'm surprised, and I want you to know you got me in your corner. It's time folks peeped out of their self-righteous shells and got smacked by a little compassion." She laid her palms against the tabletop and stood. "I'd best get Eli and head back to town."

"Aren't you staying for supper?"

"I'd like nothing better, but I got folks to feed at the boardinghouse." She studied Libby a moment. "Hold your head up and don't let those gossipmongers get to you, honey."

Libby closed the door behind them, but Lenore's words hung in the cabin like the wispy smoke from the kerosene lamps. All Libby had wanted was a nice, quiet town where she could remain anonymous as the prim and proper schoolmarm.

Fate had fooled her.

Again.

"Go ahead, Matt. Sound it out," Libby said.

He stifled his irritation at her pragmatic tone and read the word on the slate. "Dog."

"Good."

After three days of lessons, he'd graduated to one-syllable words. Matt didn't feel like he'd accomplished a major feat, but Libby was pleased with his progress.

Pleased.

The teacher was pleased with her student.

Matt ground his teeth. She treated him like one of the children, and maintained the same remote reticence. Since the morning they'd shared a kiss, Libby had retreated both physically and emotionally. Although she continued to doctor him, that too was done with a detached air.

"Matt."

Libby's impatient voice cut into his thoughts. "What?"

"If you don't want me to tutor you, say so," she said. "It's not as if I'm forcing you to do this."

Matt's imposed bedrest and Libby's constant nearness of the past week made him testy. "No? Then why did you use Dylan to get me to agree to these lessons?"

"I didn't use him. Dylan wants you to be able to read and write, too."

Exasperation colored Libby's face, and remorse flashed through Matt. "I'm sorry. It's just that I'm blamed tired of laying in this bed. I ain't used to doing nothing."

Libby sighed and set the slate aside. "I know. I think you've graduated to getting up and dressed tomorrow."

"Tomorrow's Saturday, ain't it?"

"Isn't it?" Libby corrected. "And yes, it is. I'll come by if you'd like me to."

"You're not staying the night?"

She shook her head. "You're well enough to take care of yourself now."

"What about Dylan? Will he be over tomorrow?"

"I doubt anyone could keep him away. It's apparent you're his hero."

"Where'd you get a fool idea like that?"

"Dylan thinks you can do no wrong." Her eyes twinkled. "He probably thinks you can walk on water, too."

Matt smiled absently. "Has his ma left him alone since I been sick?"

"I think so. I've been watching him pretty closely, and he doesn't act like he's hurting. I don't want to ask him straight out if she's hit him, though."

Matt nodded thoughtfully. "Good idea. He can clam up faster'n a politician in a bawdy house."

Libby laughed softly.

Her amusement warmed Matt, and a familiar shaft of desire furrowed through him. "Where'd Dylan take off to?"

"Lenore baked a pie for you and Dylan went to get it," she replied.

"You and Dylan are going to eat supper here, aren't you?"

Libby nodded. "There's corn bread baking in the oven, and I'd better get to frying the chicken."

"You've spoiled me," Matt said. "I don't know how I'm going to eat my own cooking again."

"I'm sure you'll manage."

"Nothing says you can't come over whenever you'd like and make a meal for us."

Libby stood and wiped her hands on her apron. "I don't think that would be a wise idea."

"It won't be any different than what you've been doing."

"There's a world of difference, Matt. You've recovered from pneumonia, so there's no reason for me to come here any longer. There's folks who would say I had no business being here at all."

"Has there been talk?" Matt demanded.

She shrugged and studied the pathetically plain curtain covering the window. "You know how people can be."

Matt stroked his scar. Yes, he knew how people could be. "I'm sorry you got mixed up with me, Libby. If you hadn't, they wouldn't have anything to talk about, and your reputation wouldn't be hurt."

She planted her hands on her hips. "Dang my reputation. The alternative would've been to let you die of pneumonia, and nothing is worth more than a life." She paused and glanced at Matt. "Did Eli tell you he offered me a job?" Surprised, he shook his head. "He thinks I would make a good assistant, after seeing how I cared for you."

"What about your teaching?"

"After the term ends in the spring, I'll start working for Dr. Clapper."

Elation caught him unaware. "So you'll be staying?"

"I suppose so." The ghosts returned to shadow her face.

"You don't sound excited about it."

"No, I am. I've always had an interest in medicine, and I'm honored that Dr. Clapper thinks I'm good enough to help him."

Was the memory of her father the source of her haunting sadness? "You must've learned quite a bit working with your pa."

"I did. I wish you could've met him, Matt. You would have liked him."

He smiled wryly. "I doubt he would've liked me, being a Reb, and your brother being a Blue Belly."

"That wouldn't have made any difference to him.

He could read a man like a book and could always tell what kind of person he was. He would know what I know, that you're a good man, Matt."

A good man? Matt cursed to himself, knowing that if she could read his mind, she wouldn't think he was such a good man. During the long nights, he'd listened to her toss restlessly on the floor in front of the fireplace and imagined her sleeping beside him as she had the one night. However, his imagination didn't stop at their impassioned kisses, and Matt had grown hard with the tantalizing images. If Libby knew of his lustful urges, what would she think of him?

He thought again of her flowering response to his caresses that morning. Hadn't she been a willing participant after she'd overcome her initial shyness? But what of her peculiar behavior in front of the fireplace, after she'd escaped his embrace?

He patted the mattress next to his hip and tilted his head so she couldn't see his disfigurement. "Sit down, Libby."

"I should get supper on."

"It'll wait a couple minutes."

After a moment of indecision, Libby lowered herself beside him, but her rigid back revealed her unease.

Matt lifted her flowing curls over her shoulder. "I'm glad you've started wearing your hair down. It makes you look younger, not so serious."

She kept her spine as stiff as a plank and tried to ignore the flare of desire sparked by his softly spoken words.

"I don't even know how old you are," he said gently.

"Twenty-six," she replied to the unasked question.

He gathered a handful of her thick tresses and smelled deeply of the fresh scent. "Twenty-six and she thinks kisses are just 'all right.' Seems to me we were interrupted last time we were testing that theory."

"Please, don't." Libby's lower lip trembled, though she couldn't have moved away if she'd tried.

Matt's brow creased. "I told you that you didn't have to be afraid of me. Don't you believe me?"

His thumb caressed her cheek.

Libby shuddered. Could she trust him? Her heart cried yes, but her instincts screamed no. With his light touches, he enticed her to leave her fears behind and allow the lava that pooled in her stomach to spread to her limbs. She heard a soft moan and recognized the sound as her own.

She gazed into his smoldering eyes, and the heat threatened to consume what remained of her soul. His fingers brushed her neck, then followed the slope downward. Below her blouse her skin tingled in his trail, and the knotted tension grew. She shifted on the bed and her breast slid into Matt's cupped palm. Through the material he flicked her nipple, shocking Libby with the wondrous sensation.

"Kiss me, Libby," Matt whispered hoarsely.

Instinctively heeding the sensual command, her mouth descended to his—and flames threatened to erupt. Dizzy from his skillful virtuoso across her lips, Libby allowed the heart-stopping music to press the fear into a far corner of her mind. She placed a tentative hand on his solid chest, where springy curls tickled her fingers. Matt groaned beneath her hesitant exploration. Delighting in her power over him, she grew bolder in her tactile survey of his torso. His increased breathing told her he was as affected as she by the mutual caresses.

Her shirtwaist opened beneath Matt's skillful fingers, and his hand slipped inside her blouse. She inhaled sharply. The feather-light brushes skimmed over the swell of her breast, only her sheer camisole preventing his complete invasion. She'd never known such sweet ecstasy existed.

"You smell so fresh, like a crisp winter morning," Matt murmured against her neck.

His wispy breath fanned desire's flames and Libby thought she'd melt in the turbulent inferno. Cool air brought a moment of lucidity, and alarm found a niche in the moment of sanity.

She rolled away from Matt, yanking her blouse closed over her heaving bosom. Ashamed by her body's betrayal, Libby refused to look at Matt. With shaking fingers she attempted to put the buttons through their holes, but ended up misaligning them and starting over.

Matt studied her with frustration marring his rugged face. "I won't apologize for what I did, because I think you wanted it, too."

He thinks I'm wanton, and I haven't done anything to prove him wrong. Harrison was right. I'm not a proper lady.

On her wedding night, Harrison had punished her for her body's desires, telling her a wife was not supposed to enjoy the act of mating. After that, he'd beaten her for imaginary transgressions and had never taken her until she'd been "disciplined."

Would Matt turn on her and accuse her of being no better than Dylan's mother? Would he take it upon himself to chastise her? Would his pleasure-giving hands turn into instruments of pain?

She finished straightening her blouse, turned to face Matt, and raised her chin. "I'm sorry if I led you to believe something that wasn't true. I promise you, it won't happen again."

She marched to the kitchen with purposeful strides and concentrated on frying the chicken. She refused to think about her unseemly behavior, but vowed again to keep her distance from Matt. She couldn't trust him before, and now she couldn't trust herself.

"I wish you'd tell me what's bothering you."

Matt's beseeching voice startled Libby and her hand flew to her heart. She glared at him. "Don't you ever sneak up on me again."

Libby was grateful he'd pulled on a pair of pants and a shirt, so she could maintain her ire. Clad only in his underwear, she would have recalled too well the feel of his sinewy chest beneath her fingers.

He leaned against the wood box and crossed his arms in a deceptively relaxed pose. "I want to know what's going on."

Libby's heart pounded in her breast. "I don't know what you're talking about."

"One moment you're hotter'n a two-bit pistol, and the next you're colder'n an icehouse in January."

Libby's palm flashed toward Matt's cheek, but he caught her wrist.

"How dare you," Libby hissed. "I resent being spoken to like I'm no better than a—a whore."

"A whore? What in tarnation are you talking about? I've never thought of you that way." Indignant fury peppered his words.

Libby jerked her arm out of Matt's grasp. She fought back with the only weapon she had. "No? Yet I assume you had no intention of marriage if I had let you . . ."

Matt broke his gaze, and Libby tasted the bitterness of her costly victory. For the first time, she thanked the blind fear Harrison had left as his legacy. If she had allowed Matt the liberties he'd clearly wanted, he would have learned she'd been married—and that would have precipitated more lies.

Her stomach roiled and she bit her tongue to keep the bile from rising. No matter how hard she tried to maintain aloofness, her body betrayed her. Being a doctor, she'd been prepared for her wedding night. She had even anticipated the moment of consummation. Harrison had come to their bedroom while she still wore her wedding dress. She'd asked him to leave while she changed into her nightgown, and she could still hear his sadistic laughter when he'd refused.

You're my wife now and I may do as I please with you. Remove your clothes, Elizabeth.

Libby had trembled beneath his heated gaze and did as he commanded. She'd stood naked in the center of the bedroom while Harrison walked around her, examining her as critically as he would a priceless painting or a prize bull. He stroked her back, her breasts, her hips, and the juncture of her thighs. Libby's body reacted to his gentle caresses. Lulled by his seemingly tender touches, she whimpered and reached for him. And he'd slapped her. Hard. She'd always remember the coppery taste of her own blood and the beating that followed.

The scenario had been repeated numerous times throughout the four years of the hellish marriage. She thought Harrison had destroyed her ability to take pleasure in anything related to the marital act. However, in a month's time, Matt Brandon had effectively drawn out her sinful urges with a single kiss.

She had bungled every plan she'd made for her new life in Deer Creek. She'd allowed the town's sheriff to caress her, after swearing never to allow another man to touch her. She'd accepted an offer from the doctor, after deciding she could never practice medicine again. And she'd become involved with Dylan and Lenore and her students, after hardening her heart against all emotional entanglements.

She'd even failed as a doctor. She had killed a man after she'd sworn to uphold the sanctity of life.

Would she forever be destined to fail?

Chapter 10

S he had to get back to her solitary cell at the schoolhouse. Exhaustion disheartened her, and she needed peace and quiet to regain her confidence and place her priorities back in their proper order.

Libby used a fork to turn over the chicken in the skillet, focusing her gaze on the task. "As soon as we've eaten supper, I'll be leaving." She took a deep breath and turned to Matt. "I'll continue to help you learn to read and write only if you promise not to touch me again."

She tried not to squirm under his scrutiny.

"What are you afraid of?" he asked quietly.

That you'll hate me if you learn who I really am.

"Nothing," she replied.

"Everyone's afraid of something."

Libby took the offensive. "What are you afraid of?"

He shrugged. "More than I care to admit."

Stubborn green eyes parried with somber amber ones. Dylan barged in and their battle of wills ended without a victor.

"Mrs. Potts made an apple pie for us," he announced exuberantly.

Despite her frustration with Matt and her own emotions, Libby smiled. "Why don't you and the sheriff wash up, then we can all eat at the table."

Dylan's excited chatter made the uncomfortable meal bearable, and Libby focused her attention on him rather than Matt's formidable presence. Dylan helped Libby with the dishes while Matt sat at the table, silent and watchful.

After the last piece of silverware was placed in its proper drawer, Libby faced Matt reluctantly. "I'd like to examine you one more time and make sure your lungs are clearing up."

Opening her black medical bag, Libby pulled out her stethoscope. She slid the circular part under Matt's shirt, against his warm chest. The dark crisp hairs tickled her fingertips and the tingle traveled up her arm and spiraled in her stomach. Noticing his quick intake of breath, she determinedly ignored her own response. She concentrated on the increased heartbeat of her patient and the almost inaudible rasp in his lungs.

Libby placed the stethoscope back in her bag. "Everything sounds fine. If your fever should return and breathing becomes more difficult, send someone for Dr. Clapper. I'm going to leave you the rest of the camphor, and I want you to use it once a day until it's gone. You're going to feel tired for another week or two, so get plenty of rest."

"Whatever you say, Doc," Matt said.

Libby's eyes widened and her mouth went dry, but his belated wink told her he'd been joking. She swallowed nervously. "Would you like me to walk you home, Dylan?"

He nodded. "Okay. I'll see you tomorrow, Sheriff."

"You'd better," Matt responded. "When would you like me at the schoolhouse, Libby?"

"Have you decided to agree to my terms?" she asked.

"I can abide by your rules. Can you?" he dared with a honey-smooth voice.

"What rules?" Dylan asked curiously.

Libby glanced at Dylan and her face warmed. "It's a grown-up game, sweetheart." She ignored her tripping heartbeat and looked at Matt. "Do you promise?"

Matt drew an imaginary X on his chest. "Cross my heart."

She nodded. "How about Monday evening, about six?"

"Sounds fine."

Libby donned her long woolen coat. Matt's large hands fumbled with Dylan's jacket buttons, and the endearing sight warmed Libby.

"Bye, Sheriff," Dylan said.

"Goodbye, partner. Good night, Libby."

She nodded stiffly. The cold evening air took Libby's breath away and swept under her layers of skirts, sending a shiver racing up her spine. Dusk had fallen and Dylan led the way across the dim trail back to town. Libby sensed Matt followed their progress with his hooded eyes.

"The sheriff isn't going to die, is he?" Dylan asked.

Libby blinked, startled by the question. "No, he's going to be fine. You don't have to worry about him."

A long wisp of vapor told Libby the boy sighed heavily. "Good. I was scared he'd leave, too."

They reached the edge of town.

"Who left you, Dylan?" Libby asked.

"This man who played cards where Ma used to work. She didn't like him, but he was nice to me and taught me how to write my name and how to work with numbers. He called it knowing the odds, but I just called it memorizing the cards and which ones had been played."

So that's where he'd learned poker. "What happened to him?"

Dylan shrugged his thin shoulders. "He got conniption."

Libby thought for a moment. "You mean consumption?"

"Yeah. What's consumption?"

"It's a disease that stops the lungs from working. The sheriff wasn't as sick as your other friend was."

"I don't ever want you or the sheriff to get that sick."

Libby's hand tightened on Dylan's.

As they passed Pearson's Mercantile, a burly body bumped Libby. The violet-coated woman turned, and the stuffed sparrow in her brightly colored hat nearly lost its perch. "Excuse me," Mrs. Beidler said. "Oh, it's you, Miss O'Hanlon."

Instinctively, Libby shielded Dylan from her view. "Good evening, Mrs. Beidler."

The woman peered down her pointed nose. "Who's that with you there?"

Libby raised her chin. "One of my students."

Mrs. Beidler examined the boy closer. "That's Sadie Rivers's whelp. I thought he no longer attended classes."

"I had to take care of the sheriff," Dylan spoke up.

"It was only a temporary arrangement," Libby said. "I tutored Dylan in the evenings." She sent Dylan a reassuring smile. "Why don't you go on ahead and I'll catch up to you."

He left reluctantly.

"So he will be returning to school Monday?" Mrs. Beidler asked.

Libby returned her attention to the other woman. "That's right. Nobody has the right to deny a child an education, and I will not allow you to dictate to me who I can and cannot teach in my classroom. I truly hope you will send Mary Sue to school on Monday, but if you don't, the blame will lie with you, not myself." Libby leaned closer to her formidable opponent. "I realize you have an image to uphold, Mrs.

Beidler, but you cannot use an innocent boy as a pawn to maintain your appearance of propriety."

The older woman's nostrils flared. "You have no idea what it's like for me in this backward frontier town, do you? I used to be a Linden, of the Boston Lindens."

Libby gaped.

Mrs. Beidler lifted her chin and her lips thinned with smug satisfaction. "I see you've heard of us. I grew up in a mansion on Beacon Hill where I wanted for nothing, and when I married Abraham, my life was all I had dreamed it would be." Virulence spilled into her tone. "Then the war broke out."

Libby recalled how Mrs. Beidler's father had been accused of aiding the Confederacy, and the resulting scandal that destroyed the Linden shipping empire. "I'm sorry."

Mrs. Beidler's eyes spat fire. "I don't want your sympathy. I had enough of that from our so-called friends. Abraham and I were forced to leave Boston, and we settled here in the middle of nowhere."

Understanding softened Libby's tone. "And that's why you hate Sheriff Brandon, isn't it? He fought on the same side that ruined your family."

Mrs. Beidler stiffened her back. "We've strayed from our original discussion. If you allow that boy to attend school, I shall see to it you never teach again."

"I wish I could change your mind. You're so blinded by bitterness, you won't listen to me. The only thing that'll help you is to let go of the past, Mrs. Beidler." Libby turned to leave, but paused. "I still feel sorry for you—but not because you lost so much. Because you refuse to see what you have here in Deer Creek. Good night."

Libby strode away from the motionless woman and, a block later, came upon Dylan waiting for her.

"Why is she always so mean to me?" Dylan asked.

"It's not just you, sweetheart. She's angry at the world. Don't let her bother you," Libby reassured.

They arrived at their destination a few minutes later. The red lanterns on either side of the door told visitors the establishment was open for business, and they went around to the back door.

As ribald laughter from within the elaborate house filtered outside, Libby pursed her lips. "I wish I didn't have to leave you here, Dylan."

"It's all right, Miss O'Hanlon. Ma hasn't hit me for a couple weeks." Dylan bit his lower lip, realizing what he'd admitted. "I mean, it ain't so bad. She is my ma."

Libby breathed a sigh of relief. Though she hadn't seen any sign of abuse on Dylan, his unintentional confirmation eased her worry.

"It *isn't* so bad," she correctly gently, and squatted down so her gaze was even with Dylan's. "And she's very lucky to have a son like you. If I had a boy, I'd want him to be just like you."

"Even if I'm bad sometimes?"

"I'll tell you a secret. I wasn't always good when I was your age either. I seem to recall a few times when I pulled some pranks that weren't very nice, but my family still loved me. And if you did some bad things, I'd still love you. Why, I'll bet the sheriff even got into all sorts of mischief when he was your age."

"Really?" Dylan's huge eyes reflected amazement.

Libby smiled. "Why don't you ask him tomorrow?"

"Okay." He glanced at the door and somberness claimed his pale face. "I'd best go before Ma gets mad."

"Remember what I said. You're always welcome to come visit me."

Dylan nodded. "I know. Night, Miss O'Hanlon."

"Good night, Dylan."

He slipped inside and disappeared behind the stark walls. Feeling like she'd abandoned Dylan, Libby stood and reluctantly headed in the direction of the schoolhouse. She paused in front of Dr. Clapper's dark office and imagined her name below his: Dr. Libby O'Hanlon. Certainty flowed through her like a mountain stream, and deep in her heart, she knew she'd made the right decision.

She'd been granted a second chance in Deer Creek, and she vowed to follow the advice she'd given Mrs. Beidler. What she could have here would far outweigh the losses she'd suffered.

Dylan dragged his sleeve across his forehead and yawned wide. Friday nights were the second busiest night of the week. He hated them. Men who acted all-fired important during the day turned into stupid fools with the women who worked for his ma. They bragged and laughed and touched the girls' legs under their dresses. After that, they'd go upstairs and come back down a little while later.

He sighed and carried in the last load of wood for the evening. He wound his way through the noisy couples in the large parlor. Nobody paid any attention to him as Dylan set the logs in the wood box and knelt in front of the brick fireplace to add more fuel. The loud voices rose and fell, interspersed by laughter that didn't sound real. He usually didn't pay much mind to what anyone said, but he heard the teacher's name and strained to find the source.

He spied his mother and Mr. Pearson sitting close on the purple couch, the old storekeeper's hand rubbing her leg under her skirt. Dylan leaned toward them to hear their conversation.

"She thinks she's so much better than the rest of us, but Libby O'Hanlon just doesn't do it honest like we do," his mother said.

Pearson nodded. "Personally I got nothing against the sheriff, but I can't figure how he steered a woman like her off the straight and narrow."

"Because she's no better than the likes of me. Who knows, maybe when Brandon gets tired of poking her she'll come work here, then you'll get your chance at her." She rubbed his crotch and licked her lips. "Got yourself all excited thinking about her, don't you?"

Dylan frowned. He didn't understand what they meant, but he did know they were being disrespectful to Miss O'Hanlon. Indignation gave him the courage to approach the sofa where they sat touching each other.

"Miss O'Hanlon is a nice lady," Dylan defended.

His mother glared at him. "What're you doing in here? You're supposed to be cleaning the kitchen."

"I done that already." Dylan's stomach twisted with fear, but righteous anger spurred him on. "The sheriff and Miss O'Hanlon haven't done anything wrong. He was sick and she stayed with him to make him better."

"I bet I know how she made him feel better, too," Pearson said with a wink.

Dylan stamped a foot. "She didn't do anything bad."

His mother lurched to her feet and grabbed his ear. He struggled to escape, but her taloned fingers twisted the tender flesh and Dylan clenched his lips together against a cry of pain. She dragged him into the kitchen and released him.

Her eyes blazed. "What the hell do you think you're doing? I told you a hundred times never to interrupt me when I'm working. Get to your room and stay there. I'll take care of you later."

She stomped out of the kitchen and didn't look back.

Trembling with fear, Dylan stared after her. What did she mean? How would she take care of him later? She hadn't hit him for a long time, and he wanted to believe she'd finally decided to stop beating him. But she'd been awful mad.

He shivered anew and trudged up to his tiny cell. He threw himself on the narrow mattress. The low rumble of voices from downstairs surrounded him. In the next room, springs creaked and bedposts rapped the wall in a steady cadence. Dylan wondered what the men and women did behind the closed doors. None of the ladies bothered to answer him when he'd asked. He'd peeked in one time, and the couple had been wrestling on the bed. The sight had confused him further.

Someone hollered and the noises in the bedroom ceased. Dylan stuck his hand under his pillow and withdrew his secret friend. If his ma knew about the stuffed dog, she'd throw it away. She never liked anything he did. He snuggled the tattered animal.

He'd tried hard to do everything right and not make his mother mad the last couple weeks. He'd hoped maybe then she would start to like him a little bit and not hit him. All he wanted was a mother like all the other kids had, one who tucked him in bed at night and made him a lunch to take to school.

With no one to witness his momentary weakness, two tears coursed down his cheeks.

Early the next morning, silence awakened him. Rubbing his eyes, he sat up. The rising sun cast a coral glow and Dylan smiled. He liked the way dawn's rosy color splashed over the room's drabness. He could pretend he lived in a real home and had bright wallpaper and cozy rugs to walk on on cold mornings.

Dylan sighed. The dream disappeared with the harsh light of day, and he slipped out of bed. He removed the clothes he'd slept in and threw on a heavy shirt and a pair of threadbare but clean overalls.

"Where do you think you're going?"

Dylan's startled gaze shot to his mother, who stood in the doorway. Stringy strands of hair hung haphazardly around her smeared face, and her red-rimmed eyes glowered at him. Fear shimmied through Dylan. "N-nowhere."

She smiled heartlessly and stepped closer. "Before I get some sleep, I figured to take care of some unfinished business."

Dylan wished she would disappear, but her sinister figure remained. "W-what do you mean?"

"Last night you bothered me while I was working. You know what happens when you break the rules."

"I thought you weren't going to hit me anymore," he said.

"You have to be punished."

Dylan stared into his mother's menacing eyes and he shivered. Maybe if he explained, she wouldn't hurt him. "You and Mr. Pearson were making up bad things about Miss O'Hanlon and the sheriff."

Her hand lashed out almost faster than Dylan's gaze could follow, and stinging pain confirmed the blow. He bit the inside of his cheek and the bitter taste of blood filled his mouth.

"It don't matter what we were saying. I don't ever want you to interfere with me and one of my customers again." Stale liquor breath washed across his face and Dylan's stomach lurched.

She slapped him again. The force sent Dylan stumbling back, and he cracked his head on the corner of the metal bed. Involuntary tears sprang to his eyes and his mother's face swirled in front of him.

"Let me tell you something, you little bastard. Sweet Miss O'Hanlon isn't as nice as you think. She and your precious sheriff have been making fun of you, telling you how much they care when they really don't give a damn for anything except their ownselves," she stated through clenched teeth.

Dylan blinked back moisture and his chin trembled, but he didn't cry.

"The wood boxes need filling and the parlor has to

be cleaned. Get down there and get to work. I'm going to sleep," Sadie said.

Her robe swung around her legs and she left him lying on the floor.

A low buzz sounded in Dylan's ears. He staggered drunkenly to his feet and plopped onto his pallet, the ceiling spinning above him. He blinked and the whirling stopped. The left side of his face throbbed, and he touched the stinging warmth with a cautious hand.

Dylan wasn't certain what his mother and the mean storekeeper meant, but he knew enough to realize they weren't being nice. He couldn't let the dirty lies about the sheriff and Miss O'Hanlon continue. He liked them even better than the man who'd played cards and taught him how to write his name.

"Dylan?" a soft voice called from the doorway.

He sat up and winced. "Becky?"

A girl eight or nine years older than Dylan tiptoed to his side. "Are you all right?"

"Yeah."

"You're bleeding."

Dylan glanced at the scarlet circle on the pillow. He checked the back of his head, and his fingers found matted hair.

Becky took his hand. "Come on. Let's go to the kitchen and we'll get you cleaned up."

"What about my ma?"

"She went to her room."

Dylan balked. "Won't she be mad at you for helping me?"

"It'll be our secret."

She held out her hand, and Dylan allowed her to lead him down the back stairs. She motioned to a chair, where he sat down. Becky wet a cloth and blotted the blood from the injury. "It won't stop bleeding."

Dylan blinked back a wave of dizziness. "It'll stop. It always does."

"Maybe you'd best go see the doctor. Sadie'll sleep until this evening."

Dylan's head throbbed, and his queasy stomach threatened to lose its meager contents. "I'll be okay. You can go."

Becky laid a hand on his shoulder. "If you need me, I'll be in my room."

Dylan nodded, regretting the motion immediately. The room tilted, and he pressed a hand to his mouth. He didn't see Becky leave, but she was gone when the world righted itself.

Saturday morning Libby entered the boarding-house, where welcome warmth washed across her like a summer breeze. She continued to the kitchen, smiling at the typical scene before her. Lenore vigorously beat a mixture in a large blue china bowl and a mouth-watering scent wafted from the oven.

"It's high time you came calling," Lenore greeted. "Light and have a cup of coffee."

Libby removed her coat and gloves and hitched herself up on a stool. Lenore handed her a steaming cup. "Thank you. And thanks so much for the apple pie last night. Between Dylan and Matt, they finished it off."

Lenore returned to stirring. "I hope you grabbed a piece for yourself before those boys ate it all."

"I managed to get one, and it was delicious," Libby assured.

"I don't think I told you how happy I am to hear you'll be helping Eli with his doctoring. He tells me you have a gift not many folks can claim. Said you took right good care of Matt, and did as good as he could've done."

"I don't think it's as much a gift, as experience with

my father. I was just glad I could help." Libby traced circles on the table with one finger. "I wonder how long it'll take for the fine, upstanding folks of Deer Creek to fire me and get a new teacher."

"They don't know you spent the nights with Matt."

"It's just a matter of time."

Lenore shrugged. "So you'd start working with Eli earlier than you'd planned. I never figured you for a teacher anyhow. Too much starch in your drawers. The teachers I know wouldn't think of upsetting the apple cart. Too worried about their positions."

"When I came here, I was worried about making a good impression. Now it seems everything I've done has been wrong."

"Fiddlesticks. You've done a fine job. You got to understand folks around here . . ."

The door to the kitchen swung open to reveal George Johnson. His skittery gaze caught Libby, and his watery eyes widened behind his spectacles.

"Hello, Mr. Johnson," Libby said.

"Miss O'Hanlon." His greeting was as cold as the north pole.

"Did you want something, George, or are you going to stare at Miss O'Hanlon like she's a two-headed calf?" Lenore asked.

George's ascetic face reddened. "I wanted to tell you I'll be late for lunch."

"I'll keep a plate warm for you."

"Thank you. Good day." Without another glance at Libby, he strode out.

"Mr. Johnson must've heard the rumors, too," Libby remarked dryly.

"Fools, all of them," Lenore muttered.

"They may be, but even if I went to work with Eli, I'd have to live with those fools."

"You aren't thinking about hightailing it out of town, are you?"

"I don't want to."

"You haven't done a blessed thing wrong, but if you leave everyone will be convinced you did."

Libby thought about her behavior at Matt's, and wondered if Lenore would say the same if she knew what had happened. Her conscience squirmed with the lie of omission. "I didn't tell you everything."

Lenore poured the batter into a rectangular pan. "What is it you didn't tell me?"

Libby's tongue stuck to the roof of her mouth. "W-we kissed." *And more.*

"Matt's a fine looking specimen of man. If I was thirty years younger, I'd set my bonnet for him myself. I'll bet he could show a woman a fine time in bed, too."

Aghast, Libby's mouth dropped open. "A good woman doesn't think about such things, much less discuss them."

"And who told you such a ridiculous thing?"

"It's not ridiculous. That's how to tell a good woman from a bad one."

"Then you're looking at a bad woman. Willard and me had seven children, but it wasn't just children that kept us together. I know I complain about my Willard, but truth be told, he knew how to pleasure me."

Shocked embarrassment suffused Libby. "Lenore!"

The older woman wiped her flour-covered hands on her apron and withdrew three pies from the oven. She set them in the pie pantry, then turned to Libby. "You said your ma died when you were born, so I figure you haven't had a woman to tell you how it is in the marriage bed."

Black memories poured into Libby's mind. She didn't need anyone telling her what happened between a married couple. She had spent the last three months trying to forget. "I know more than you think. My father was a doctor."

"You know what goes in where, and you know

where babies come from, but there's a whole lot in between you don't know."

Libby wanted to crawl into a hole and hide. She knew exactly what lay in between, and she didn't want to remember the accompanying humiliation. "Please, Lenore, I don't want to hear about it."

"It's high time you did. I know you've been told by everyone that it's a woman's duty to lie beneath her man." She glanced at Libby and chuckled. "When you love each other, there's a heap more to it than that. You find the right man, and he can make you feel all tingly in the center of your female parts. No reason to be embarrassed, honey. That's the way it was meant to be."

Despite her distaste for the subject, Libby remembered how Matt's touches had produced a pool of warm honey inside her. The sensation he created in her made her wonder if she was only a step away from heaven. But the years of suffering Harrison's pain-inflicting perversions made it difficult to accept Lenore's words so readily. "Isn't it wrong for a lady to express her"—Libby stumbled—"to express her pleasure?"

"Whoever told you that nonsense never knew how to love. What's good for the goose is good for the gander, I say."

"But what about when a man lies with a woman who isn't his wife? The woman is branded a harlot and the man moves on."

"Not all the time. Take me and Eli for instance. You don't think I keep him around just for conversation, do you?"

Libby stared, shocked. "You mean you and Eli . . ."

Lenore's eyes twinkled mischievously. "Just because we're not spring chickens doesn't mean we can't kick up our heels once in a while."

"Don't people know?"

Lenore shrugged. "I'm sure most do, but nobody

talks about it. Why, I'll bet half the married men in this town pay Sadie's house a call at least once a month. Nobody talks about that either."

Libby forgot her embarrassment and assimilated the new information. "So why does Mrs. Beidler worry about my virtue?"

"Because you're the teacher and young children look up to you. I figure what people don't know won't hurt them."

Libby's eyes narrowed. "If I didn't know better, I'd think you were trying to get Matt and me together. You aren't, are you?"

"I don't see anything wrong with a little match-making."

"It would never work. Fire and water don't mix."

"Who says you're fire and water? By that blush on your face, I'd say more like fire and kerosene."

"There are things you don't know about me, Lenore. I can't afford to get involved."

"Since you accepted Eli's offer, you'll be staying in Deer Creek for a time, right?"

Suspicion brought a frown to Libby's face. "That's right."

"Did I ever tell you about Esther Rostenberger?"

Libby shook her head and prepared herself for another of Lenore's parables.

"Esther was the reverend's daughter. Pretty young thing. More importantly, she had a fine mind. Her father taught her to read, and he wasn't one of those preachers who only let her read the Bible. She read everything and anything she could get her hands on. Her father raised her to be independent and she surely was that. Swore she didn't need a man to boss her around and that the world would be a better place if women ran it. One day a rancher rode into town and caught sight of Esther. He decided then and there to make her his wife, only he didn't have a clue as to how contrary she'd be. He never gave up, and he courted her for five years—until he wore her down and she finally said yes. Heard tell they had ten children in as many years, and she was one of the first women in Wyoming to vote."

"And the point?" Libby prodded.

"Independence is a two-edged sword, and if you aren't careful, you're liable to cut your own throat with it."

"You're making this difficult for me."

Lenore chuckled. "Good. I'd like to see you and Matt with a passel of young'uns. Maybe you'd even let me and Eli be their grandparents."

"Sometimes things aren't that easy."

"Sure they are. You're the one making things so blamed muddled. Forget about everything else and think about Matt. The answer will come clear enough."

A spark of hope flared in Libby's heart. Lenore had a way of uncomplicating things. What if Libby allowed Matt further liberties? Could it be as pleasurable as Lenore said? Would she take a step into heaven, or would she stumble back into the pits of hell she'd so recently escaped?

The ember in her chest fizzled and died. The uncontrollable panic that threatened to choke her when his caresses became too heated would never allow her to learn the answer.

"I can tell you're thinking on it," Lenore said. "That's a good sign."

Libby smiled weakly. "Maybe not."

Lenore poured herself a cup of coffee and settled herself on a chair across from Libby. "So tell me what you have planned for your program on Christmas Eve."

The two women visited for nearly an hour, then Libby returned to her tiny room at the schoolhouse.

After Lenore's companionship, the silence seemed oppressive. Firmly, Libby set the loneliness aside, fired up the small stove, and put a battered tin coffeepot on to brew.

She scraped the frost off a window and peered outside. Bare trees shivered in the brisk northwest wind and a gray mass of clouds marched toward the town. She suspected they'd have another couple inches of new snow by evening. She'd been lucky the weather had remained clear while she'd cared for Matt.

Matt. The thought of his lean body and craggy face brought a wealth of emotions vying for attention. She tried to ignore the clamoring in her soul, but her body refused to obey the commands. She'd become a master of control with Harrison, but the memory of Matt's kiss turned her into a quagmire of passion.

The smell of fresh coffee lured her back to the stove, and armed with a cup of the hot, bitter liquid, she forced herself to work on lesson preparations for the following week.

Half an hour later, the door opened. She squinted through the dim light of the room at the slight figure. "Dylan, what are you doing here? I thought you'd be with the sheriff today."

Dylan shrugged and made no move to approach Libby. "Naw. I figured he'd probably be sleeping."

Libby frowned. "I doubt he'd sleep all day. He was hoping you'd visit him."

"I seen him all week."

Libby studied the young boy, noting he remained by the door. "Since you're here, why don't you come over to the stove and warm up?"

Dylan shook his head. "I'll stay here."

Libby stood, came around the desk, and walked toward Dylan. He shrank under her gaze, raising the scarf higher around his face. She stopped in front of

him and knelt down. Libby lowered the cloth. An
angry red puffiness covered his left cheek, and vicious
black and purple swelling nearly closed his eye. Horror rose in her throat. "Dylan, what happened?"

"I fell down."

The obvious lie startled Libby. "Tell me the truth,
sweetheart."

Dylan thrust his chin forward and stared at Libby.
He remained stubbornly silent.

Libby straightened and took his chapped hand in
hers. "Where are your mittens?"

"Guess I lost 'em."

His insolence challenged Libby to call him a liar,
but she only grew more concerned. This defiant boy
resembled more the urchin who first visited her rather
than the excited student he'd become. She led him
back to her quarters, pressed him into a wobbly chair
by the table, and removed his scarf. The extent of his
injury took her breath away and empathy filled her.

"I'll get something to take the swelling down," she
said.

Libby grabbed a clean dishcloth and slipped outside. She snatched a few handfuls of snow, returned to
Dylan, and knelt beside him. Carefully, she pressed
the cold compress to his bruised cheek.

Dylan jerked away. "Ow!"

"I'm sorry, honey. Why don't you hold it so I don't
hurt you?"

Without comment, Dylan did as she suggested. He
swung his feet back and forth a few inches above the
floor and stared at the tabletop.

Libby looked down at him and frowned. His hair
lay matted against the back of his head, and she
probed the swollen area with skilled efficiency. Blood
continued to ooze out of the gash. Dylan yelped.

Libby leaned back to study him. "What happened?"

He shrugged.

Frustration laced through Libby. "I'm afraid I'll have to stitch it."

Dylan's eyes widened with fear. "You mean with a needle?"

"If I don't, the cut will keep bleeding and you'll be a very sick boy. I promise I'll be careful."

She prepared a needle and catgut and set the black medical bag on the table beside Dylan. She squatted down. "I'm not going to lie and say it won't hurt, but I'll try to do it quickly."

He nodded. The reddish purple mark contrasted sharply with his powder white complexion.

She stood behind him and brushed his hair away from the injury. After soaking a clean white square of cloth with carbolic acid, she pressed it against the wound gently. "I'll tell you a secret if you promise not to tell anyone."

"I promise."

"I've done this a lot of times. You relax and try not to move, and I'll be done before you know it."

"Okay."

Libby removed the material from the cut and took a deep breath to ease the fluttering wings in her stomach. "I'm going to start now." She eased the needle through the first flap of skin.

Dylan jerked and yelped. "Ow!"

Libby froze and pressed a hand to his shoulder. "I'm sorry. I need to do this to stop the bleeding."

"It hurts."

His plaintive cry stabbed Libby's heart and moisture clouded her vision. "I'll hurry, sweetheart."

She steadied her nerves and wove the needle in and out to draw the sides of the gash together. Dylan remained motionless except for a few flinches. Sweat slid down Libby's forehead, the task seeming to take forever. She finished with a quick knot.

Her hands trembled. She knelt in front of Dylan

and gently brushed away the two tear trails with her thumbs. "You did fine, Dylan."

"You're done?" he asked hesitantly.

Libby nodded.

He drew his forearm across his nose. "I tried not to cry."

Libby's insides caved in and she embraced him. His downy hair tickled her nose. "I'm proud of you, Dylan. I know grown men who aren't half as brave as you."

She released him and stood.

Dylan glanced at the bloody needle and her open bag on the table. "You have stuff like Dr. Clapper's. Are you a doctor, too?"

Chapter 11

***

Libby straightened her mess. "What would you think if I were?"

"I'd like it, because if I got sick, I could come to you."

She hated lying, but she didn't have a choice. "Even though I'm not a doctor, you can still come to me and I'll take care of you."

"Like you done for the sheriff?"

"That's right." She placed her bag under the bed and perched on the edge of a seat next to him. "Do you have any dizziness, or feel sick?"

He paused a moment and nodded. "Not so much anymore, but this morning after Ma, I mean, after I fell down, I felt kind of sick."

Libby trembled with barely suppressed rage and struggled to control her anger. How could a woman commit such an atrocity against her own son? She intertwined her trembling fingers and laid them in her lap. She had to remain calm and figure out what to do next. "Dylan."

He glanced at her with suspicious eyes.

She leaned forward. "Your mother did this, didn't she?"

Stony silence.

"When I was about your age, I got in a fight at

school. This boy was making fun of a younger girl because she couldn't read very well, and I told him to stop it. He ignored me and pushed my friend down and tore her dress. I got so mad that I struck him, and he hit me back. When I went home that night my father asked me how I got the black eye, and I was scared to tell him. You see, I was afraid I would get in trouble because I threw the first punch. When I finally admitted what happened, he said I had a right to be mad, and though he didn't like me fighting in school, he was proud of me. I had stood up for someone else. He went to talk to the teacher about the bully, and after that, we never had any problems with him. Maybe if you tell me who did this, I can help so it doesn't happen again."

Silence filled the room. Dylan seemed to ponder her words for a few minutes. Finally, his gaze lifted. "Why would the sheriff poke you?"

The inference took a moment to penetrate Libby's mind, then humiliation and wrath blazed brightly. She swallowed. "Where did you hear that?"

"My ma was talking about you and the sheriff, and how you could come work for her when the sheriff got tired of poking you."

Libby's face suffused with heat. She forced a calmness she didn't possess. "What she said wasn't very nice, Dylan. I would never work for your mother."

"I knew that. I told her and that mean Mr. Pearson to stop telling lies about you and the sheriff."

"You defended us and she hit you, didn't she?"

"Not right away," Dylan admitted. "This morning she came to my room and said she had to punish me."

Agonized empathy stole Libby's breath, and tears filled her eyes. "You're a very brave boy to go against your mother," she whispered.

He shook his head. "I'm not very brave. I was scared."

Libby recognized the effort it took for Dylan to admit his fear. She clasped his hand, roughened by countless chores. "Only a fool wouldn't have been scared. I'm glad you told me."

Disbelief crossed his vulnerable features. "You're glad I was scared?"

"I'm proud of you for admitting it. I care for you, and I hate seeing you hurt like this."

Dylan stared at her a moment, then his face crumbled. "I don't want to go back."

Moisture stung Libby's eyes. "You don't have to. You can stay here with me."

He threw his arms around her, and she held him tight against her shoulder.

She knew what Dylan had endured at his crazed mother's hands, and she understood his helplessness. Libby'd had no one to help her escape, and desperation had made her a murderer. However, she could save Dylan. "Everything will be all right. I promise."

A soft lump beneath his jacket pressed against Libby's chest, and she released him.

She nudged the odd shape. "What's in there?"

A red flush crossed Dylan's face and he reached into his coat to pull out an old, ragged stuffed animal. "It's my dog. The man who taught me cards gave him to me before he went away."

Libby looked at the frayed toy and wondered how many nights Dylan had cried himself to sleep with his only friend tucked in his arms. A lump filled her throat, and a full minute passed before she could speak again. "He won't bite me if I pet him, will he?"

Dylan giggled and Libby smiled at the wonderful sound.

"He's not alive," he said. "But someday I'm going to have a real dog and he'll be only mine, but I'll make sure he never bites you."

Libby scratched the toy between its sagging ears. "What do you say all three of us have some lunch?"

He nodded eagerly.

An hour later, Libby put the last of the dried dishes away and glanced at Dylan. His eyelids drooped heavily and tenderness swelled within her. She picked up his scruffy dog. "He looks tired. Why don't you take him and lie down on my bed?"

Dylan blinked and nodded. "Okay."

He lay down on top of the covers with the stuffed animal under his chin, and Libby spread a blanket over them. "You can sleep if you'd like."

She gently brushed back his hair and kissed his forehead.

He gave her a drowsy smile and closed his eyes.

As Libby studied the small figure, her hands curled into fists. She vowed no one would beat him again. She would keep that oath no matter what the cost.

Realization struck like a lightning bolt, and Libby pressed her knuckles to her lips. Dylan's soulful blue eyes and trusting smile had burrowed deep into her soul. She could no longer deny it: she'd lost her heart to the young boy.

Matt buckled his gunbelt across his hips and checked the revolver's cylinder, a habit he'd picked up while serving as a Texas Ranger. The ritual had saved his life during his time with the Rangers, as well as in the war between the states. He reached for his drover coat and shrugged it on. Then, with a tug on his battered hat brim, he left the warmth of his cabin.

The stars and moon remained obscured by the clouds and a few white flakes continued to drift down. Matt breathed in the fresh scent and pain exploded in his chest. He coughed, his eyes tearing, and he leaned against the porch post until the burning receded.

He couldn't abide sitting around any longer. Besides, Saturday nights tended to be unruly, with cowboys blowing off steam from a week of tending stock and mending fences. Trouble was often averted by his presence, and Matt's sense of duty overruled Libby's order to get plenty of rest.

Instead of saddling his buckskin gelding, he walked the short distance to Deer Creek and checked his office. A few more papers littered his desk, but nothing appeared vitally important. He continued down the boardwalk and followed the tinny sound of a piano.

The off-key notes led him to the Golden Slipper, a favorite place for rowdy men to have a few drinks, play some poker, and converse with something other than a horse. A smoky haze greeted Matt. A path opened and some of the men shook his hand, welcoming him back. He leaned against the bar, placing a booted foot on the brass rung.

The bartender set a cup of coffee on the pocked wood surface. "Good to see you up and around, Sheriff."

Matt sipped the hot liquid. "Evening, Albert. I see the coffee hasn't improved."

Albert shook his bald head. "Coffee ain't our specialty." He leaned close. "I got a couple bottles of the good stuff, if you're interested."

He stared into Albert's pale eyes. "You know I don't drink."

"It don't seem natural for a man not to ever touch liquor."

Matt shrugged. "It doesn't matter to me what you think. Been quiet around here?"

"More or less. Rosco Weller tried to start a fight last night." He leaned over the counter and hefted a double-barreled shotgun. "One look at old Bessie and he decided he didn't want to fight that bad."

"I don't want you shooting anyone."

Albert appeared hurt but set the weapon back in its proper place. "Now, Sheriff, you know what a peaceable man I am. Glad to see you back on your feet. But

I suppose it wasn't too bad to be in bed, when you got a woman to share it with." He elbowed Matt.

He stiffened. "What the hell do you mean?"

"Everyone knows about you and the school-teacher."

"What does everyone know?" Matt asked in a deadly calm voice.

Albert stepped back. "Well, that she took care of you while you were sick."

Matt grabbed Albert's stained apron front and jerked him halfway across the bar. "That's right, she did. And that's all she done."

Albert raised his hands in surrender. "Whatever you say, Sheriff."

"If you hear anyone else sullying Miss O'Hanlon's name, I expect you to set them right. Do I make myself clear?" The red-faced bartender nodded and Matt released him. "Thanks for the coffee."

He strode to the door and left the cacophony behind. A few minutes later, Matt entered a smaller saloon. Fewer people and no dance partners made the Plug Nickel's atmosphere tamer. He joined Eli at his usual table.

"You shouldn't be up yet," Eli scolded. "Didn't Libby tell you to rest?"

Matt shrugged. "It's Saturday night."

"What's that got to do with anything?"

"Most of my business comes on Saturday nights."

"In other words, you know better than Libby what's best for you."

He glared at Eli. "You're being ornerier than usual. Did Lenore finally come to her senses and throw you out?"

Eli snorted. "You need a wife to shorten that fuse of yours."

"Not a wife, just a willing woman."

"She's got you going, doesn't she?"

"I don't know what you mean."

Eli shrugged. "Suit yourself. If you want to make yourself miserable, who am I to take away your fun?"

The bartender delivered coffee in a chipped cup to their table and returned to his place behind the plank-and-barrel bar. Companionable silence surrounded the two men.

Matt removed his hat and tossed it in the center of the rough-hewn table. He leaned back and threaded his fingers across his waist. "What am I going to do?"

"Is that a real question, or just a piece of rhetoric?"

Matt ignored the remark. "Albert, over at the Golden Slipper, told me there's been rumors about me and Libby."

"You didn't expect any?"

Matt shifted uncomfortably on his chair. "I figured she knew what she was doing."

Eli arched a gray eyebrow. "So none of it is your fault?"

"I didn't ask her to stay with me."

"Did you expect her to abandon you like your wife did?"

"Leave Rachel out of this." Cold fury laced the brittle words and he glared stonily at Eli.

The doctor tamped the tobacco down in his pipe calmly. "It matters if Rachel's ghost is holding you back from doing right by Libby."

"Have you ever thought that maybe Libby doesn't want anything to do with a sorry son-of-a-bitch like me?"

"If that were true, she wouldn't have nursed you."

Matt pounded his fist on the table, sloshing coffee on the surface. "Don't! I been to hell a few times in my life already. I ain't going back." He slammed back in his chair, rubbed his jaw, and fought the urge to flee. He didn't know if he wanted to run from Libby or from himself. Whiskey beckoned, promising to rid him of the newfound confusion. He was tempted to let the cheap liquor numb him against the onslaught of crushing memories.

"Plenty of men came back from the war minus an arm or leg, and their wives didn't cuckold them," Eli said. "Rachel probably used your scar as an excuse to continue what she'd been doing all the while you were gone."

Matt stared past Eli and thought back to the day he'd returned from the war. He'd spent three months in a Confederate hospital, recovering from the saber injury and a bullet to his shoulder. The trip back to Texas took nearly the same length of time, and he'd arrived without warning. He'd grown pale and haggard under the hardships he'd suffered, and his appearance had shocked Rachel. He no longer resembled the man Rachel had married, and she never again allowed him to touch her. Instead, her contempt for him had burgeoned—until she'd thrown her indiscreet affairs in his face, accusing him of being less than a man and unable to satisfy her.

The venomous words wounded Matt critically, and he remained her husband in name only, while his beautiful and once beloved Rachel allowed every other male in the county to bed her.

"Libby's not Rachel," Eli said, uncannily guessing Matt's thoughts.

Matt tried to picture his dainty wife's whitish gold hair and china blue eyes, but the willowy woman in his mind had auburn curls and freckle-flecked cheeks. The vision brought an ache to his chest. Libby possessed a strength of character he had never witnessed in Rachel. Libby's concern and tenderheartedness extended to those less fortunate than her, yet the softer emotions were tempered with stubborn determination. While she'd cared for him, he'd seen both sides. He'd also discovered a gold mine of passion beneath her reticent facade, and he wanted to excavate the depths of that treasure.

Would he strike it rich, or would he find fool's gold?

Night crept into the schoolhouse and Libby raised the wick of her kerosene lamp. Pale yellow light illuminated her sparse quarters, relegating the darkness to the corners.

"Supper was real good, Miss O'Hanlon," Dylan remarked.

Libby took the damp towel from him and hung it near the stove. "Thank you. I don't often get to cook for anyone but myself. The water is nearly warm enough."

Dylan scowled. "Why do I need a stupid bath?"

Libby crossed her arms. "Because you're staying with me, and I don't like dirty little boys."

"Ain't nothing wrong with a little dirt."

Instead of correcting the ornery boy, Libby narrowed her eyes.

Dylan squirmed under her stare. "Well, there isn't."

"A little dirt isn't bad, but I'm afraid you have more than a little. You aren't scared of a bath, are you?"

"I'm not scared of anything."

"Good. I expect you to be stripped down by the time I have the tub filled."

"Then you got to promise you ain't going to watch me."

"I promise."

Libby turned away and rolled up her sleeves. The mutters behind her, followed by the nearly inaudible sound of clothing being removed, brought a smile to her lips.

Five minutes and a few feeble protests later, Dylan lowered himself into the warm water. "Okay, you can turn around now."

Libby swung around and noticed the washcloth

Dylan held in place. She fought a smile and handed him a block of lye soap. "Scrub."

Dylan stared at the lump in her palm like it was a squashed frog. He glanced up at Libby, sighed a surrender, and took the bar. "Do I have to wash my hair, too?"

Libby shook her head. "Not with those stitches in there."

He grinned widely.

Libby busied herself with tasks in the classroom, and fifteen minutes later Dylan appeared in the doorway. The clean trousers and shirt she'd loaned him hung on his small frame.

"I never knew a woman who wore pants before," Dylan commented.

"I used to wear them when I went riding or when I had work to do outside," Libby said. "I think it's about time you went to bed, young man."

"But I slept all day."

"How about if you lie in bed and I read to you? I've got a new dime novel," Libby bribed.

Indecision resolved into a reluctant nod. "But you got to read the whole thing."

"But I *have* to read the whole book," Libby corrected. "And I suppose that's only fair if you stay awake."

"I'm not a kid," he said, lower lip thrust forward.

"Even grown-ups get tired," Libby said.

Dylan lay on his side in Libby's cot with the covers tucked around him. Libby moved a chair next to him. "Do you think your mother will come looking for you tonight?"

"I don't know," he mumbled. "I don't want to think about it."

Libby brushed a fine strand of black hair back over his ear. "I know you don't, honey. Did you tell anyone you were coming here?"

He moved his head back and forth on the pillow.

Relief tugged at Libby, but a part of her mind warned her the confrontation was only delayed. Sadie wouldn't accept Dylan's desertion without a fight. Libby needed Matt's support, but the hour was too late to find him. She'd have to tell him tomorrow.

Now she had a promise to keep. She opened the book and her voice filled the quiet of the temporary sanctuary.

"Thanks," Matt said to the bartender. He carried the two cups of coffee back to the table he shared with Eli and resumed his seat. He scanned the room. Nothing appeared amiss, and Matt's vigilance relaxed. "I should be over at the Slipper. That's where trouble usually blows up."

"They survived last week without you. I'm sure they'll survive one more night," Eli said. "Same goes for Sadie's place."

"You seen Dylan lately? I thought he was going to come over to my cabin today, but he never showed up."

Eli shook his head. "I was out at the Bronsen's this morning and I didn't see hide nor hair of him this afternoon. I wonder what he's up to."

Matt frowned. Dylan said his mother hadn't touched him for a couple weeks. What if her temper had snapped and she'd made up for lost beatings? Unease grated his nerves.

"Doctor Clapper?" One of the cowhands from the Circle T stood by their table.

"What is it?" Eli asked the weaving man.

"It's Jonas. He's moanin' something awful, and he got his arms wrapped around his gut. I think he's dyin'."

Eli stood. "Where's he at?"

"Back by the privy."

Eli looked at Matt and sighed. "Probably too much whiskey. I'll see you."

Matt tipped his head in reply. Eli and the Circle T wrangler moved out of the saloon. Disquiet grew in Matt. Dylan wouldn't disappear unless something was wrong. He shoved out of his chair and followed in Eli's wake.

A few minutes later he entered the red-light house. Deep voices and high-pitched laughter met his ears, and he grimaced.

A tiny blonde wearing only a chemise and panta-lettes greeted him with a Southern accent. "What a nice surprise, Sheriff."

Matt eyed the scantily clad girl and frowned disap-provingly. "Your folks know you're here, Becky?"

Becky's lips thinned and her coquettishness disap-peared, as did her drawl. "They don't care. One less mouth to feed. You want to talk to Sadie?"

"Not if I can help it. I'm looking for Dylan. Have you seen him?"

Her black-powdered eyelashes swept downward. "Not since this morning."

She turned away, but Matt caught her arm. "Where is he?"

Becky glanced over her shoulder nervously. "I don't know."

"Tell me."

"I said I didn't know."

"You know something you're not telling me." Matt tightened his hold on her.

Becky sent another anxious look toward the parlor. She lowered her voice conspiratorially. "This morning—"

"Get back to work, Rebecca."

The girl's face blanched at Sadie's command. She twisted out of Matt's grasp and ran into the gaudily decorated room.

Sadie held a cheroot in her tobacco-stained fingers. "Accosting my ladies? I wouldn't have thought you'd be so randy after a week with Miss Prissy O'Hanlon. Shame on you, Sheriff."

Red dots of rage danced in Matt's vision and he crushed his hat brim in his hand to keep from slapping the smug expression from her painted face. "I'm looking for Dylan. Where is he?"

"Good question. He didn't show up this evening. I figured he was with you."

He didn't believe her. "Where's his room?"

Sadie's expression dropped its haughty mask and Matt noticed a flicker of apprehension. Cold contempt blanketed her expression once more. "You have no right going up there."

Matt stepped closer to Sadie. "I got every right. Nobody's seen him all day, and I'm thinking maybe you had something to do with it."

"He's my son."

He arched a disbelieving eyebrow. "That's never stopped you before."

"Get out."

"Not until I check his room." Matt pushed past her and took two steps at a time up the staircase.

Sadie followed, yelling obscenities at his back. Matt ignored her and the silent, gawking customers in the parlor. He opened doors indiscriminately, interrupting a couple involved in a vigorous tussle in one bedroom.

"Pardon me, Mayor," Matt said.

At the end of the hall, Matt almost missed a room built into a corner alcove. He entered the tiny storage space and immediately knew he'd found what he was looking for.

Sadie grabbed his arm. "Get out or I'll have you thrown out."

Hot anger erupted in Matt. "My prisoners have better quarters than this. How the hell can you treat

Dylan like he's no better than a slave? He's your own damn son!"

She released his arm and her blue eyes blazed insanely. "That's right, he's my *damn* son! I damned him when he was born, and I swore he'd live to regret the day he ruined my life."

"He didn't ruin your life. You did that to yourself!"

Matt's gaze fell on the bed, and he leaned over to pluck the pillow from the thin pallet. A brownish red stain colored the rough material, and he heaved the straw-filled square against the wall. With trembling fingers, he clutched Sadie's arms and shook her like a rag doll. "What did you do to him?"

"I didn't kill him, though I wish I would've." Virulent hatred vibrated through her words.

Matt let go and stepped back. "When I find him, I'm keeping him with me. You aren't ever going to touch him again."

Matt spun on his heel and stomped out of the stark bedroom. Fear for Dylan's safety thrummed through him. In her madness, Sadie could've done anything to him. Matt turned a deaf ear to Sadie's rantings and passed the milling people at the bottom of the stairs without acknowledging their presence. Most of them had to have known what she did to Dylan, but no one had protected him. Matt's stomach churned with revulsion and he continued out the door.

"Sheriff!"

Matt paused in the middle of the street and Becky joined him.

"What is it?" he demanded.

Becky shivered and wrapped her skinny arms around her waist. "This morning I saw Sadie go into Dylan's room. I hid around the corner and I saw her hit him real hard a couple times. I think he hit the back of his head against something sharp, because he was bleeding pretty bad."

"How bad?"

She shook her head. "I don't know. I told him to go to see the doctor, but I don't know if he did or not."

"Eli was out of town this morning and he said he hadn't seen Dylan." He glared at Becky. "Why didn't you try to stop her?"

Moisture spiked her eyelashes. "I got no other place to go, Sheriff."

Sympathy slipped past his fury. "Look, I can help you go far away from here and start a new life."

She shook her head. "I'm a whore, Sheriff, and there ain't nothing else I can do. But just because I'm a whore don't mean I like Sadie hitting Dylan. He reminds me of my little brother."

"Do you know where he went?" Matt asked gently.

"No, but I think he left before lunch."

Matt touched her cheek with a gloved hand. "Thanks, Becky. You'd best get back in before you freeze."

"I hope you find him and keep him far away from Sadie." Becky dragged a hand across her eyes, smearing the black powder, and hurried back to the house. Matt set aside his pity for the girl and concentrated on his search for Dylan. Where would he have gone?

He crossed the street to Lenore's house and knocked on the whitewashed door. A few moments later, Lenore appeared in the doorway.

She pulled him inside. "Matt, what in the world are you doing out at this hour? Lord almighty, you could catch your death again if you aren't careful."

"Is Dylan here?"

Lenore blinked at the abrupt question. "No. He's missing?"

Matt nodded. "Nobody's seen him since before noon."

"Have you checked the schoolhouse?"

"Not yet."

She shoved him back into the wintry night. "Then

get going. If he's not there, find Eli and he'll help you search."

"Thanks."

Matt's boot heels echoed crisply on the frozen boardwalk, and his breath wisped a vaporous cloud. His main concern was to find Dylan, but the prospect of seeing Libby sidetracked his thoughts. Her absence in the cabin the night before hadn't dulled his passion for her. Dreams of her in his bed haunted him while he lay awake. The same images followed him in slumber. The memory of her ripe fullness filling his palms and the sweetness of her kisses taunted him. Even while he worried about Dylan, his mind swirled with visions of Libby.

A lantern glowed dimly from a window of the looming schoolhouse, and Matt's step faltered. Matt Brandon, veteran of the Texas Rangers and the War between the States, feared a woman. If the threat weren't so real, he would've laughed. Libby had coaxed feelings out of him he thought he'd buried forever. Squaring his shoulders, he walked the last hundred feet and entered the classroom like he was confronting a Comanche raiding party.

Libby's eyes widened. "Matt, what are you doing here?"

Matt's breath caught in his throat and his heart hammered against his ribs. The lantern on the desktop wove golden strands through her hair, and her intelligent eyes glowed with the brilliance of a mountain meadow in the spring. A mousy brown shawl covered her upper body, but Matt's memory needed little encouragement to recall the fullness of her breasts and the curve of her slender waist.

He removed his hat and angled his head so his scar remained hidden in the shadows. "Dylan's missing."

Libby stood and crooked her finger. "Come here."

Puzzled, he joined her. She led him to the doorway

of her quarters and pointed at the bed. Matt's eyes adjusted to the darkness, and he recognized Dylan. He heaved a sigh of relief.

"I thought Sadie hurt him," Matt said in a low voice.

Libby's voice, a mere whisper away from him, replied, "She did."

Matt followed her back into the classroom.

Libby leaned against the solid desk and crossed her arms. Worry webbed her forehead. "He showed up here this morning with contusions on his face."

"You mean bruises?"

Libby nodded. "He also had a lump and a bad cut on the back of his head. I finally got him to admit his mother had beaten him again."

"I saw blood on his pillow and thought Sadie had . . ."

"No, she didn't kill him this time." She stared at Matt with the ferocity of a lioness protecting her cub. "I won't let you take him back."

Surprised by the determination in her voice, Matt blinked. "I don't aim to let her near him again."

Her body relaxed and she sighed. "Thank you. I was so afraid Sadie might show up tonight and force me to give him to her."

She reached over and opened a desk drawer, revealing a double-barreled derringer. "I didn't plan on letting her take him."

He raised his hand to touch her but dropped his arm to his side. "You should've come to me, Libby. I don't want that boy hurt any more than you do."

"You're not completely recovered yet."

Matt sensed she wasn't totally honest with him. "You still don't trust me."

Libby's unwavering gaze met his. "I trust you, Matt."

Instinctively he knew she spoke the truth, and the

knowledge buoyed him. His fear for Dylan appeased, Matt's attention focused on the woman before him.

The lantern lent her a golden red halo and shadowed each contour of her upturned face. Her firm jaw curved to a delicate but stubborn chin. The peach glow from the lantern brushed the hollow between her neck and shoulder, and Matt wanted to press his lips against the tantalizing valley.

"What're we going to do about Sadie?" Libby asked.

We. Her faith blanketed him in warmth. "Don't worry. I can handle her."

Eyes flecked with gold dust met his gaze. The air between them sizzled. He feathered the back of his hand across her velvety cheek, and her eyelashes fluttered under the sensual invasion.

She wrapped her fingers around his wrist. "Sadie could be dangerous."

His danger didn't come from Sadie. Libby held the power to harm him as nobody else could. He should step away before she recognized the weapon she possessed, but his feet refused to obey. "I'll protect you and Dylan. I promise."

Her grip tensed. "Who'll protect you?"

His throat tightened. Nobody but Libby would've thought of his well-being. Her concern was only another reason he needed to protect himself.

"I can take care of myself." The words came out harsher than Matt intended.

A sad smile and a mysterious glimmer in her eyes unnerved him. Why didn't she flee at his gruff tone? Couldn't she see he was no good for her? He wasn't the man she thought he was. Her confidence in him was lethal. He couldn't run from her any more than he could leave Dylan with Sadie.

"Thank you," he whispered, close to her ear.

She shivered. "Matt, we can't."

"We can't what?"

"We're fire and water."

"No, you're the flame and I'm the kindling."

He continued his assault and nibbled her perfect earlobe, inhaling the unique scent of Libby, lilacs, and chalk dust. "You even smell beautiful."

With a whimper, she released his hand. He continued his exploration, skimming his knuckles along her jaw and down her creamy neck. Libby closed her eyes, her heartbeat pulsing under his tender pilgrimage.

Desperation seared him and white hot desire spiraled through his veins. He didn't know where want began and need took over, but he recognized the all-consuming desire to bury himself in her welcoming heat.

Matt dropped his hat on the desk and slid his fingers up Libby's slender arms. He lifted the shawl from her rigid shoulders and the wrap joined his Stetson. He glided his hands down her back, lingered a moment, and tentatively followed the curve of her deliciously rounded bottom.

Libby moaned and pressed her body against his burning arousal, eliciting a groan from Matt. His loins pulsed, and exquisite pain mixed with pleasure clouded his agitated senses.

Her yearning gaze met his, and Libby's tongue swept over her luscious red lips. Unable to resist the invitation, he lowered his head, meeting her soft mouth with tender assurance. He coaxed her to lower her defenses and her lips opened to receive him. Matt drank of her honeyed ambrosia, forgetting everything but the banquet she offered.

Libby's arms encircled Matt's neck and drew him closer. She threaded her fingers through his hair, and her tongue played hide and seek with his. Her uninhibited action surprised and delighted him.

She moved against him in rhythmic abandon. Heavenly agony filled Matt, and he withdrew before he lost all control. Confusion and disappointment shone in Libby's eyes, undermining Matt's attempt to rein in his stampeding emotions. Hunger gnawed at his gut and Libby's responsiveness prompted his return to her willing embrace. He met her fragrant breath, and once again Matt fed his fervent appetite. Needing to taste more than her sweet lips, he planted light kisses on her dappled cheeks, not missing a single freckle in his tender quest. He trailed kisses down her ivory neck, savoring her satiny skin. He skimmed his hands up her sides, settling below her breasts and cupping their fullness.

Libby's hips were braced against the desk. She arched her back, and her bosom strained against her blouse. With trembling fingers, Matt opened the buttons and his palm swept over her thin chemise. Her nipples pebbled in reply. She moaned deep in her throat, and Matt echoed her keening sigh. He tugged the white ribbon, liberating her milky whiteness. Deliberately, he lowered Libby's garments, and she drew her arms out of the sleeves. Matt's greedy gaze drank in two perfect globes with a small rosy circle on each peak. The tempting morsels beckoned him, and he lowered his head. His tongue laved one succulent mound, then moved to the other and back again. He pressed his surging hardness against Libby and she whimpered her own need, tightening the coil in Matt's stomach.

He inched the hem of her skirt upward, his hand skimming over her black cotton stockings. The practical hose couldn't disguise the smooth curve of her calves, and the blood surged in his veins. He caressed her dimpled knee while his lips continued to suckle her coral-tipped crests.

"Matt." Breathy rapture textured Libby's voice. Her fingers laced behind his head and drew him closer.

Matt explored her lithe legs and encountered the

opening of her drawers. He invaded the slit with a gentle hand. He stroked her silky inner thighs, and the scent of her excitement wafted upward. Her response increased his hunger, and his fingers crept toward the source of her heat.

She feathered her fingertips across his face, followed the scar's path, and hesitated.

Matt stiffened, and reality cleared away the fog of desire. He pulled back, suppressing his body's longing with a powerful shudder. He'd been a fool to think his disfigurement could be set aside like an old hat.

He lifted his gaze and forgot to breathe. Libby stared at him with wide, luminescent eyes; her breasts lay like ripe fruit ready for harvest. Strands of auburn hair framed her anguish-filled face. He swallowed and took a deep breath. If he lived to be a hundred, he'd never forget the soul-stirring vision before him.

Libby deserved better than a man who couldn't even please his own wife.

With a vicious oath, he nabbed his Stetson and pivoted away from the bewitching picture that would forever be etched in his memory, then fled.

Chapter 12

〜ᗡᗡ〜

Shock flooded Libby, and she tugged her chemise and blouse over her nakedness. Buttoning her shirtwaist with trembling fingers, she fought threatening tears. The center of her femininity throbbed with unfulfilled frustration, and Libby understood a part of what Lenore had told her. She ached to have Matt complete what he'd begun, and dispel the last remnant of mindless fear Harrison had instilled.

She stood on shaky legs and wrapped her discarded shawl around her shoulders. Why had he left her? His desire had been evident.

Libby struggled with conflicting thoughts. She'd tasted the heady flavor of passion Lenore described, but Harrison's painful lessons lurked, casting doubt on her newfound appetite. Perhaps she'd been too eager, and Matt had been disgusted by her willingness. Or were her feelings a natural part of being a woman? Matt had seemed to enjoy her participation in the sensual journey, until he'd abruptly stepped away. There had been no revulsion in Matt's smoky eyes when he left. Instead, she'd recognized a need as deep as her own . . . and something else.

Libby frowned. What had caused him to pull back? Her face burned with remembered pleasure at his caresses. She'd wanted to please him, too, and her fingertips had traced his handsome face. She'd paused on the old injury, and her heart had swelled with an empathy so strong the emotion had taken her breath away. The next moment Matt had moved away, leaving a cold void where his strong, hard body had been. What had she done?

The answer came with a gasp. The scar. He always angled his head in such a way to keep the mark hidden, and every time she'd touched the jagged line, he'd retreated behind a mask of coldness.

Libby's gift as a caregiver had been evident even as a child, when she'd assisted those weaker than she. She prided herself on being a healer and often sensed the pain people couldn't, or wouldn't, admit, yet she hadn't realized the true extent of Matt's scar. She'd seen only the external mark, not the deep festerings on his soul.

Since the moment she descended the stagecoach in Deer Creek, her predominant concern to hide her past had repressed her natural sensitivity. However, the innate compassion refused to be buried, and she'd journeyed out of the black void. Dylan, Lenore, Eli, and Matt had unknowingly given Dr. Elizabeth O'Hanlon back her identity.

Libby paced the length of the schoolhouse. She owed Matt the greatest debt, for teaching her that not all men were like Harrison. And she knew how she would repay him—she'd tell him he didn't have to be self-conscious about his scar.

No, he wouldn't believe her. She'd have to show him. A smile nudged her lips. She knew exactly how she would accomplish her task.

Sunday morning, Libby entered the small church with Dylan clutching her hand. She sensed the congregation's curious gazes upon them but refused to give anyone the satisfaction of seeing her anxiety. They joined Lenore and Eli in a middle pew.

Lenore patted Libby's gloved hand and whispered, "Good to see you, honey."

Libby smiled gratefully.

The service began with a hymn, and ended an hour later with another song. People filed out and visited in small groups. Lenore, Eli, Libby, and Dylan lagged behind the others.

Dylan heaved a sigh of relief. "Do we have to do this every Sunday?"

Libby nodded. "You'll get used to it."

He wrinkled his nose, but didn't argue.

"You and Dylan are coming over for Sunday dinner," Lenore said.

Her statement left no room for argument.

"What do you think, Dylan? Would you like to go over to Mrs. Potts'?"

A crooked grin appeared on his bruised face. "Do you have pie?"

"Dylan," Libby chided.

Lenore took his hand. "I always have pie for handsome young men."

Libby and Eli followed them out of the building.

"Did you stitch him up?" Eli asked in a low voice.

Libby nodded, and rage as cold as the winter day brought a tremor to her voice. "When Sadie hit him, he must've fallen back and bumped his head."

"By the looks of it, you done a fine job."

"Thank you."

"I suppose your father taught you how to suture?" Eli asked curiously.

Defensiveness replaced the remnants of anger. "Yes, he did."

"He was a good teacher."

What would Eli do if he learned she held a medical degree? Would he patronize her, like most of the other male doctors she'd known? Or would he treat her as an equal? She sidled a gaze at the gray-haired doctor and suspected he would grant her the courtesy afforded a fellow practitioner.

They paused outside at the bottom of the stairs. As Reverend Sonder turned to greet them, his smile lost its benevolence. "Mrs. Potts, Dr. Clapper. Always glad to see you at worship."

"A wonderful sermon on forgiveness, Reverend," Lenore said. "Maybe next week's could be on the evils of gossip."

The preacher pursed his colorless lips.

"You remember Miss O'Hanlon, the schoolteacher, don't you?" Lenore went on.

"Miss O'Hanlon," he said stiffly.

"The young man with her is Dylan Rivers."

"I recognize him."

Libby's temper soared and her hands clenched into fists.

"Eli, would you mind taking Dylan on over to the house?" Lenore suggested.

"Sure. C'mon young fellah, maybe we can find a few cookies hidden in the kitchen," Eli said.

Dylan glanced at Libby and she forced a smile. "Go on. We'll be along in a few minutes."

The boy nodded, though he seemed to sense the tension among the adults.

Eli and Dylan crunched across the snow to the boardinghouse.

Libby turned to Reverend Sonder. "I don't care how you treat me, but that boy has done nothing to deserve your condemnation."

The cleric opened his mouth to reply, but Lenore beat him.

"Do you remember the parable of the good Samaritan?" she asked the white-collared man.

"Of course," he replied tersely.

"Let me tell you about Deer Creek's good Samaritan," Lenore began. "Miss O'Hanlon took it upon herself to care for Dylan after his mother nearly beat him to death. Before she came here, nobody else in this town, including you, did much of anything for that innocent lamb. We were so caught up in our self-righteousness that we refused to see what was happening in front of our noses. May heaven forgive us."

A scarlet flush spread across Reverend Sonder's round face. "Mrs. Potts—"

Lenore continued without acknowledging him. "It took someone like Miss O'Hanlon to open our eyes to his plight. I say you'd best start living what you preach, Reverend—or we're going to have to look for a new shepherd for our flock."

Lenore put her hand through the crook of Libby's arm. "Come along, dear. We should get back to the house before Eli and Dylan eat everything in sight."

Once out of earshot of the preacher, Libby giggled. "I thought he was going to have a fit."

"Humph! Would serve the old hypocrite right for acting like he's better than everybody else. I'll bet Mrs. Beidler bent his ear about you and Matt and Dylan."

Libby sobered. "We can control Mrs. Beidler's tongue about as easily as we can the weather."

"I don't know who's worse, Adelaide or Sadie. Both of them hurting a boy guilty only of being born on the wrong side of the blanket, and that not even his fault. It's a crying shame."

Libby grimaced. "Yesterday he came over to the schoolhouse shortly after I got back from visiting with you. His mother must have hit him two or three times. She could've killed him, Lenore."

"There, there, honey. Everything'll work out fine. I can keep Dylan at my place. I've got more than enough room."

Maternal protectiveness surged in Libby. "I want to keep him with me."

"For how long?"

"I want to adopt him."

Lenore didn't seem surprised. "The judge may not let you. They're shortsighted on things like unmarried females keeping kids that aren't their own."

"I don't care what the court says, I'm not letting him go back to Sadie and that—that whorehouse. He's suffered enough."

"Mrs. Beidler isn't going to like you having the county's most notorious madam's son with you."

Libby shrugged. "She was going to find some excuse to fire me anyhow. At least this is a worthwhile reason."

"Then you and Dylan would have to move into the boardinghouse. What a shame." Lenore's triumphant smile belied her words.

"After all the work I've done on the Christmas pageant, I hope I can finish this week with the children. The party is Saturday night."

Lenore nodded distractedly. "Christmas Eve. Why doesn't Dylan stay with me through this week? You can tell Adelaide you're going to quit at the Christmas shindig, then you can move back in the boardinghouse and be with Dylan."

Libby pondered the proposition. "The teacher's quarters *are* awfully small, and as long as Dylan's with you, I'll know he's safe."

Lenore squeezed Libby's arm. "It's settled then. That reminds me, I've got something to show you after dinner."

"What?"

"You'll see." The glimmer in Lenore's merry eyes puzzled Libby.

Crossing the threshold into the house, Libby was assailed by the mouth-watering aroma of a pot roast. After removing her warm coat and hanging it on a hook in the hallway, she and Lenore walked to the kitchen.

Dylan and Eli sat by the table, the cookie jar between them.

Libby placed the lid on the crock. "You'd better save some room for dinner."

Lenore tied an apron around her waist and handed Libby another pinafore. "Put this on so you don't get your good clothes mussed."

Libby did as Lenore said, and jumped in to help with the meal.

"Eli, Dylan. Make yourselves useful and set the table. Remember to put down a place for Matt, too," Lenore called out.

"The sheriff's coming?" Dylan asked Eli excitedly.

They went through the door and Libby didn't hear Eli's reply. Her knees wobbled. "Matt's going to be here?"

Lenore opened a jar of green beans and poured them into a kettle. "He's always here for Sunday dinner."

Libby added more flour to the bubbling gravy. "Dylan will be happy to see him."

Lenore chuckled. "I reckon he won't be the only one."

"I'm not sure happy is the word I'd use."

Lenore dropped a dollop of butter on the vegetables. "Anxious?"

"A little."

They worked in companionable silence for a few minutes.

"There aren't many men around like him, Libby. You'd be a fool to push him away," Lenore stated.

Libby stilled her stirring and she recalled how she'd done the opposite the night before. "I know."

"Well, at least you're thinking on it." Lenore scrutinized her. "Matt came over to the schoolhouse looking for Dylan last night, didn't he?"

"That's right." Libby concentrated on a lump in the creamy mixture.

Lenore slapped her thigh and crowed. "I told you he knew how to treat a woman, didn't I?"

"We didn't do anything," Libby retorted. The heat in her face didn't come from the stove top.

"If you're embarrassed, you don't have to tell me a thing. I can read that glow in your cheeks."

Libby refused to be baited. "How did Matt get his scar?"

Lenore sobered. "Eli said the war."

"He's sensitive about it, isn't he?"

"If I've told him once, I've told him a hundred times, he worries about it too much. Granted, it isn't very pretty—"

"Pretty is for women," Libby interrupted. "I don't see anything wrong with the way he looks."

"Then tell him." Lenore clucked her tongue. "Sometimes men can be as dense as bread pudding."

"If I simply told him his scar didn't bother me, he'd never believe me. I've got a plan."

"I hope your idea works. If it doesn't, keep in mind you might have to resort to a two-by-four to get it through his thick skull."

A deep-timbered voice sounded, and Libby's heart kicked her chest.

"Sounds like Matt's here. Let's get the victuals on," Lenore said. "You slice the roast and I'll get the rest out."

Lenore carried the last of the serving bowls to the dining room as Libby finished carving the meat.

The door opened behind her.

"Lenore, I've finished cutting the roa—" She turned and the words died in her throat. "Matt."

His tawny hair was curled above his shirt's collar band, and the scent of bay rum washed across her. He studied her without revealing his thoughts, but Libby didn't need to know. Her own mind conjured up tempestuous visions from the evening, and she shifted uncomfortably.

"Sadie sure as hell did a job on Dylan," Matt stated with undisguised anger.

Libby blinked and focused on the present. "He looks better than he did yesterday."

A muscle in Matt's jaw flexed. "Dammit! I should've kept him away from her after I knew what she was doing."

"We all thought your threat worked. It's not your fault, Matt."

"I should've known."

"Like you should've known those two men were going to rob the bank?" She shook her head. "Don't torture yourself over things you couldn't have foreseen or prevented, Matt."

She stepped closer to him and his shoulders stiffened.

"I'm paid to know," he stated.

Tentatively, she touched his forearm and flinched at the rigid muscles beneath her hand. "You weren't hired to guess people's intentions."

A tremor passed through his powerful body. "But Dylan could've been killed."

The pain in Matt's expression distressed Libby, and she realized he cared for Dylan as profoundly as she did. Her grasp on his arm tightened. "Then it's my fault as much as yours. I knew what Sadie was capable of, and I didn't take Dylan away from her either. We won't let her near him again, Matt."

"You two bringing the roast or not?" Lenore hollered from the dining room.

"We'll take care of Dylan together," Libby reiterated softly.

She intentionally brushed his scar with her knuckles and ignored his instinctive flinch. "Could you carry the platter in?"

He nodded and picked up the oval plate.

Libby smiled to herself. Her battle to heal his scarred soul had begun with a victorious skirmish.

George Johnson and Virgil Tanner had taken Sunday dinner with friends, so only the five of them gathered around the table. After Lenore said grace, they helped themselves to the abundant food. Matt sat on Libby's right, tilting his head to lessen the jagged line's visibility. She longed to hug him like she did Dylan and whisper that he didn't have to worry.

"Matt, could you pass the gravy?" Libby asked.

He grunted and handed her the bowl. Her fingers lingered on his and Matt snatched his arm back as if he'd been scorched.

"Thank you," she said sweetly.

Matt tried to remain silent during the meal, but Libby wouldn't allow him to withdraw. Unknowingly, Dylan helped in her task.

"Hey, Sheriff, did you see the new colt at the livery?" Dylan asked.

"What?" Matt asked absently.

"The colt at Davis's livery. Did you see him?"

"Nope. I haven't been over there lately. You weren't getting in Harley's way, were you?"

Dylan shook his head. "Nope. He don't like me much, just like Mr. Pearson. But at least he don't come sit with my ma like the old storekeeper does."

Libby shared an understanding glance with Matt.

"I hear Miss O'Hanlon said you could live with her," Matt said.

Dylan grinned and nodded.

"You know, you could stay with me if you wanted to," Matt offered.

Libby shot Matt a frown.

"Why can't all three of us live together like a real family?" Dylan asked excitedly.

"Out of the mouths of babes," Lenore remarked.

Libby glared at the older woman. She turned to Dylan and softened her features. "Only a man and woman who are married can live together."

"Horse apples," Lenore muttered.

Libby ignored the remark. "Mrs. Potts said you could stay with her this week if you'd like. That'll give you time to decide who you'd rather live with, the sheriff or me." Glass shards jabbed Libby's heart at the thought of losing Dylan before she even had him.

Dylan's bruised face appeared troubled, and Libby clasped his small hand in hers. "Don't worry, Dylan. We're all your friends, and no matter who you choose to live with, you'll still be able to visit the sheriff or me whenever you'd like. Everything will work out fine, sweetheart." She forced a smile. "Why don't you and Mrs. Potts and Dr. Clapper go to the parlor? The sheriff and I will clean things up."

Before Matt could protest, Lenore spoke up. "I think that's a fine idea. It'd be nice to have an evening off from doing the blamed dishes. Eli and Dylan and I'll go play some rummy."

Matt scowled but Libby ignored him. She swung through the kitchen door with an armload of bowls, and Matt followed her, his hands laden with dirty plates. Working together, they cleared the table, and Libby poured water from the kettle on the stove into the large wash pan.

"Do you want to wash or dry?" Libby asked.

Matt looked at her as if she'd asked him if he preferred a rattlesnake's bite to a scorpion's sting. "I'll dry."

She nodded tersely and dipped a plate into the hot liquid. "Why did you do it?"

Matt frowned. "Why did I do what?"

Libby's neck bowed and she leaned against the sink. "Why did you tell Dylan he could stay with you?"

"Because he can."

Libby's gaze stabbed him. "But you knew I wanted him with me."

"Maybe I want him with me, too." Matt's well-defined chin thrust forward.

The air vibrated between them.

Libby relented and she sighed. "I hate to see Dylan

have to make such a decision, since I know he cares for both of us."

"Maybe we should do like he said and all of us live together," Matt said.

Libby searched his face for a sign of teasing, but smoldering heat from his eyes scalded her. Her insides melted and flowed like molten lava. She whisked her gaze to a corner of the kitchen and back to the wash water. If only they *could* be a family, man and wife.

"No matter what Lenore thinks, we can't do that without getting married." Her voice carried a breathiness she couldn't disguise. "And marriage is the farthest thing from my mind."

Why the hell had he made the fool-headed suggestion? One wife had been more than enough to sour Matt on the institution of matrimony, yet disappointment dropped like a cannonball in his gut. He crushed the hurt her words wrought and tried to dispel the bitter despair, but nothing quenched the hunger her nearness aroused.

The steam rose, curling the loose tendrils about her face. Matt ached to touch an auburn ringlet and sprinkle kisses across her flushed cheeks. Sternly, he set aside the urges and concentrated on wiping the dishes. He reached for a cup and his fingers brushed hers. Time stopped. Matt stared into Libby's dazzling eyes for a breathless moment, remembering a passion he couldn't ignore. He broke the spell first, but trembled from the heated exchange. The memory of Libby's unveiled breasts and the tentative touch of her soft lips on his challenged his control. He took in deep draughts of air to cool the fire in his blood.

Matt finished drying the dishes, though every moment was a test of his control.

Libby placed the last item in the cupboard and turned to Matt. "You've got something on your face."

"What?"

Libby took the towel from his hands and dipped a corner of the cloth in the rinse water. She raised herself on her toes and lightly dabbed his cheek. Pleasure streaked through Matt like a tornado spinning across a field. She feathered over his scar and he froze. Matt refused to gaze into her eyes as her whisper touch followed the jagged line. If he didn't look, he wouldn't see her disgust and he could pretend it didn't bother her.

A gentle finger raised his chin. "There's no need to be ashamed, Matt."

The words were spoken so softly he thought he imagined them. Swallowing his fear, he focused on Libby's faint freckles and moved upward. No revulsion greeted him. Didn't the scar affect her like it did other women? He searched the golden flecks for a sign of deception, but guilelessness reflected in the green depths. Had she become a master at hiding her emotions?

"I think I got it." Her gentle breath fanned across his jaw.

Her closeness played havoc upon his overtaxed senses, and tempted him to forget he swore he'd never touch Libby again. His tense muscles spasmed with the effort of restraining the impulse to forge a tender trail of kisses from her lush lips down the graceful arch of her pale neck, to the succulent treasures hidden by her demure white blouse.

He stepped back to escape her bewitching spell. His body throbbed and burned, oblivious to his entreaties to ignore her potent allure.

"Here's your towel," she said.

Matt blinked and reached for the cloth. Their hands met, and the contact frayed the last thread of his willpower. He wrapped his arm around her waist and jerked her against his chest. He stared into her startled eyes and nearly lost himself in their wide-eyed innocence.

"Don't tempt me, Libby," he growled. Matt tightened his hold, flattening her soft body against him, and his mouth covered hers with bruising fierceness. She whimpered and a degree of sanity returned to Matt. He released her as swiftly as he'd taken her. "Don't play games with me, or next time you'll have to finish what you start."

Moisture lent a luminescent glow to Libby's eyes, and Matt nearly capitulated to the unexpected tenderness that welled within him. He swore under his breath and spun out of the kitchen like the demons of hell chased him.

Matt continued down the hall, out the front door, and leaned on the porch rail. The cold air irritated his lungs and he coughed raggedly. The pain in his chest replaced the misery of his unsatisfied body. He shivered in winter's embrace, welcoming the numbness that spread through his limbs.

What did Libby hope to accomplish by her sweet gestures? Why did she act as if the scar didn't repel her? He pounded the wood with a fist and swore. Damn her for making him think she cared. He could handle her disdain, even her indifference, but not this seduction by concern.

Matt stood outside until he was certain his emotions were back under control. He heard Dylan's laughter from the parlor and joined the others. Lenore sat in her favorite chair, while Eli and Dylan played checkers by a small table. Libby had settled on the sofa and appeared engrossed in a Godey's lady's book.

"We thought you got lost out there," Lenore said.

"I just stepped out for a breath of fresh air," he replied.

"Come play checkers with me, Sheriff," Dylan called. "I beat Dr. Clapper three times."

Eli stood and stretched. "Good idea. I'm about ready for my Sunday afternoon nap."

Matt took Eli's place across from Dylan, and Eli moved to the other end of the couch and picked up a two-week-old newspaper.

"You want red or black, Sheriff?" Dylan asked.

Matt grinned at the boy's exuberance. "I'll take the red."

Dylan turned the board and Matt made his first move. He studied the boy while they played. Matt's son Joshua would've been a year older than Dylan if he'd survived scarlet fever. He knew Dylan could never replace Joshua, but he filled an emotional void that had remained empty since one-year-old Joshua had died.

Three games later, Dylan remained the checkers champion.

"You're too good for me, partner," Matt said.

"Miss O'Hanlon, why don't you play checkers with the sheriff? I'll watch and make sure he doesn't cheat," Dylan offered.

"The sheriff doesn't like to play games with me," Libby said.

"Why?" the boy asked curiously.

Libby gazed steadily at Matt. "He's afraid he'll lose."

"I thought *you* were scared of losing," Matt said.

Libby stiffened. "I've never backed down from a challenge before, and I'm not about to start now."

Matt arched an eyebrow. "Prove it."

Libby rose from the davenport. Excitedly, Dylan relinquished his chair to her and scrambled onto another one.

"Miss O'Hanlon gets the black pieces. Those are the lucky ones," Dylan exclaimed.

Libby smiled at the boy. "Thank you."

"Traitor," Matt muttered though his tone was tempered with a wink. "Ladies first."

Libby tilted her head in acknowledgment.

She made her first move, then looked at Matt. As

the game progressed, Matt's attention wandered from the board to Libby with increasing regularity. He remembered her satiny heat beneath his fingers, and the taste of her full breasts.

Libby jumped one of his red pieces and her rosy pink lips quirked upward in victory. "Do you still think I'll lose?"

"The game isn't over yet," Matt replied, his gaze on her tempting mouth.

Libby flushed and cast her attention back to the checkerboard.

Matt took his turn. "King me."

Libby scowled.

"I'll do it," Dylan volunteered. He crowned Matt's disk with a captured red piece.

"Ready to surrender?" Matt asked.

Libby shook her head. "I never give up when the cause is worthwhile."

Matt frowned in consternation. What kind of cat and mouse game was she playing? What did she want from him?

His gaze drifted back to her freckle-dusted face and soft alluring eyes. Understanding glimmered in their fathomless depths, and Matt had the impression she'd peeled away the curtains of darkness to see the innermost recesses of his soul. He resisted squirming beneath her scrutiny. Nobody had the right to strip away defenses he'd spent years building. Another look into her gently probing expression melted his resentment. No woman but Libby had ever looked at him with such unassuming acceptance.

"It's your turn, Sheriff," Dylan said impatiently.

Matt shook off his troubling thoughts and brought his attention back to the game. A few moves later, he took her last checker.

"He beat you, Miss O'Hanlon," Dylan said with surprised chagrin. "I thought you'd win with the lucky pieces."

Libby tousled his soft hair. "That's all right, Dylan. The sheriff may have won this round, but there's always another time."

Matt narrowed his eyes. "How many rounds are there?"

"As many as it takes for me to win."

"Libby, dear, there's something I want to show you," Lenore called. She hefted her plump body out of a chair and led Libby out of the parlor.

Matt glanced at Eli. "What's going on?"

Eli shrugged. "Women things, I suppose."

"What are women things?" Dylan asked curiously.

Matt grinned. "Yeah, Eli, what are women things?"

"You know, frippery things women like to jaw about," Eli muttered and turned the page of his newspaper.

Dylan sent Matt a bewildered look.

"Don't ask me, partner. I figure if we ever get to understanding females, we're going to be in a heap of trouble." He stared after Libby and wondered what she and Lenore were up to. With a shake of his head, he set aside his interest in their activities. "How about another game? I'm feeling lucky."

"Let's play poker," Dylan suggested excitedly.

"I don't think Miss O'Hanlon would approve of you gambling." The boy's enthusiasm deflated, and Matt reconsidered. "Why not? If the women can do women things, then us men can do man things. Eli, you want to join us?"

Eli set aside his paper and stood. "Sure. Been awhile since I played, but I figure it'll come back fast enough."

"We can use the checkers for chips," Dylan said.

"Good idea," Eli said and sat down by the table.

Dylan divided the red and black wood pieces into thirds and gave each person his share. He took the cards and dealt with a fluid motion that impressed Matt.

"Who taught you how to handle cards like that?" Matt asked.

"A man I used to know," Dylan replied. "Ante up."

Matt threw in a chip and studied Dylan's serious face. The boy's concentration surprised him, and unease furrowed his brow. They went around the table twice and Matt called. Dylan revealed three of a kind, and Matt and Eli threw their cards down.

"Beginner's luck," Eli murmured.

Matt wasn't so certain. "Did you play poker a lot with this man?"

Dylan raked in his winnings. "Some. He said I was a natural. What did he mean by that?"

"He meant you have a talent for it," Matt replied.

"If the first hand was any indication, he was probably right," Eli said.

Matt's disquiet grew. "Poker is only a game like any other, son, and we don't play it seriously."

Dylan flashed a bright smile. "I know. I think it's fun, especially when I win. I just remember which cards were played."

The enthusiasm in Dylan's expression melted Matt's unease. Dylan's boyish pleasure was a delight to see. He'd endured more than most children, and too often he looked at the world through eyes aged far beyond his years.

Matt dealt the next round and they continued until Eli ran out of chips.

"Looks like I'm flat broke," Eli said.

Dylan giggled. "We weren't playing for real money. You can have some of mine."

"No thanks, Dylan. I'm getting a mite sleepy, and since I haven't had my nap yet, I figure I'd best get to it," Eli said.

He moved to the settee, sank down, and closed his eyes.

Dylan yawned widely.

"Looks like you could use some sleep, too," Matt said.

"I'm not tired."

Matt stood and stretched. "That's too bad, because I think I'll be taking a snooze myself, so you won't have anyone to play poker with."

Matt lowered himself to the couch and propped his feet up on a padded footstool. The wind rattled the shutters, but inside, the comforting fire crackled in the hearth. The homey atmosphere soothed Matt and he closed his eyes.

A few moments later, Dylan planted himself next to Matt. "Maybe I could use a few winks, too."

Matt's lips twitched at his solemn confession.

Dylan pillowed his head against Matt's side and warmth flowed through Matt like a chinook breeze on a frigid winter day. Hesitantly, he wrapped his arm around the boy's skinny shoulders and Dylan snuggled closer, laying his small hand on Matt's chest.

Matt studied the boy and a sense of rightness filled him. The ugly bruise on Dylan's cheek sharply contrasted with his cherubic countenance. Matt's hold tightened protectively around the boy.

And for the first time in years, Matt allowed somebody inside the fortress surrounding his heart.

Chapter 13

Libby and Lenore returned to the cheery parlor to find Dylan and the men sound asleep.

"Looks like Eli wasn't the only one who needed a Sunday afternoon nap," Lenore whispered.

Libby nodded, her attention focused on the man and boy on the sofa. She fought the overwhelming impulse to join them, to sit on Matt's other side and press herself close to his warm, secure body.

"They look like father and son, don't they?" Lenore asked.

The lump in Libby's throat prevented her reply.

"I'm going to make some coffee."

Libby swallowed the fragile emotion. "Do you need some help?"

"You sit down and relax, honey. The day I can't put on a pot of coffee by myself, is the day they lay me in the ground. When it's ready, we can dish up dessert."

Lenore bustled out of the room and left Libby among the napping men. She knelt in front of the fireplace and tucked her skirt around her legs. She added another log and embers popped and sparked, sending a cascade of orange cinders spiraling up the chimney. She breathed deeply of the wood smoke, an aroma rich with memories. She recalled Sunday afternoons she'd spent as a child. Her father would settle into his favorite chair to read the newest medical journal. He'd be asleep within minutes, and Libby and her brother would entertain themselves with a card game or backgammon. Corey had taught her to play mumblety-peg, and they'd often slipped outside to see who could make the blade stick in the ground the most times.

Moisture clouded her gaze and loneliness welled up, erasing the temporary contentment she'd gained in Deer Creek. She had nobody but herself to trust, and Libby grew weary with the constant fear of discovery. Since she'd killed Harrison, she'd lived in the shadow of deceit. She hated to mislead the people she'd come to care for, but if they learned of her horrible crime, her world would again be smashed into a thousand pieces.

The alternative demanded she be punished for her deed, and Libby refused to accept that option. For the four years she'd lived as Harrison's wife, she'd served her sentence. She took a steadying breath and swept an impatient hand across her eyes. Elizabeth Thompson no longer existed, and a new beginning in this Montana wilderness beckoned Libby O'Hanlon. She'd be a fool to ignore the invitation.

She stood, brushed a few gray ashes from her skirt, and eased herself into a wingback chair. Libby intertwined her fingers and laid them in her lap. As she rested her gaze on Matt and Dylan, her heart swelled with fondness. Matt's chin touched Dylan's dark crown, and his arm curled protectively about the boy's too-thin shoulders. The scar angled down Matt's relaxed features, and Libby wished he could remain as unconcerned about the mark while awake.

Her fingernails dug into her palms. Matt deserved better than he gave himself credit for, and she was determined to help him overcome his pointless self-deprecation.

She hadn't intended on becoming ensnared in her

own plan. With every gentle touch, her pulse skittered out of control. With every glance into his whiskey-colored eyes, she became intoxicated by the smooth burn of desire in their depths. With every soft, reassuring word, she longed to press her mouth to his and taste the passion hidden beneath.

Libby had to tread carefully and safeguard her feelings, or she would repeat the mistake of the night before. The line between compassion and passion was a fine one, and she prayed she wouldn't step over the divider again. A doctor did not become emotionally involved with her patient, and Matt had to be healed of the misplaced shame his scar engendered. But the memory of his tender caresses and inflaming kisses tempted her to forget her duty and drown in his passionate possession.

Matt's eyelids flickered open, and Libby steeled herself against his potency. She pressed a finger to her lips and whispered, "Dylan's asleep."

Matt nodded and his smoldering gaze roamed across her, leaving a scorched trail in its wake.

She forced herself not to squirm beneath his steamy inspection. "Lenore's making some coffee to have with dessert."

"Are we going to do the dishes again?"

Libby's cheeks warmed, but she raised her chin defiantly. "If you'd like to."

Lenore entered the room carrying a tray covered with plates of pie. "Libby, could you help me with the cups?"

Relieved to escape Matt's scrutiny, Libby followed Lenore to the kitchen. They returned a few minutes later and found everyone eating pie.

Lenore chuckled. "Nothing like pecan pie to wake a body up."

After Libby finished the last of her coffee, she set the empty cup on her dessert plate. She glanced out the window into the late afternoon's dim light. "The days are so short."

"Before you know it, they'll start stretching out again," Eli assured.

"It won't be soon enough." Uncharacteristic lethargy filled Libby, and she stood. "I'd better get back to the schoolhouse and make sure I'm ready for tomorrow's classes."

Dylan hopped to his feet. "I'll go with you."

Libby knelt in front of him and clasped his thin arms. "You'll be staying here with Mrs. Potts, remember?"

Dylan slid his small hands into his overall pockets and stared at the floor. "Oh yeah."

"Don't worry. You'll see me tomorrow at school."

His chin lifted. "I'll be all right."

Libby pulled him close and smelled the faint scent of carbolic acid in his downy hair. "I know you will, sweetheart, but I'm going to miss you. I want you to be good for Mrs. Potts. Before you know it, I'll be moving back here."

"What if my ma comes looking for me?" Dylan asked.

Fear skittered through Libby and she glanced at Matt.

"You stay right here with Mrs. Potts," he answered. "I don't want you to go anywhere with your mother. Do you understand?"

"Do you think she's sorry she hit me?"

Libby's eyes glazed with unshed tears.

Matt squatted down in front of Dylan and laid his large, gentle hands on his shoulders. "I don't think so, son. You see, your mother has a sickness that makes her do bad things to you, and she won't ever get better. But you got me and Miss O'Hanlon and Mrs. Potts and Dr. Clapper. We all care for you, and want to make sure you don't get hurt again."

Dylan frowned worriedly. "Am I bad because I don't ever want to see her again?"

"Not at all, sweetheart," Libby reassured.

Dylan appeared relieved and he looked at Matt with beseeching eyes. "Will I see you tomorrow?"

"You can count on it," Matt said. He held out his hand and Dylan shook it. "You do as Mrs. Potts says."

"I will," he promised solemnly.

Matt straightened. "I'd best be heading home, too."

"You escort Libby to the schoolhouse first," Lenore commanded. "It's not safe for a young woman to be out walking alone."

"But I've walked alo—" Libby began.

"Matt will take you home, honey," Lenore interrupted.

Libby glanced at Eli and found his attention focused on a piece of lint on his jacket. Her gaze caught Matt, but she was unable to read his shuttered expression.

"Let's get going," he said gruffly.

In the hallway, they tugged on their warm coats and thanked Lenore for dinner. Dylan hugged Libby, then Lenore put her arm around the boy and they waved goodbye.

Libby stepped outside. The chilly wind whisked her breath away. Beside her, Matt coughed raggedly. "Are you all right?"

Matt nodded and gasped for air. He steered her in the direction of the school and they walked in silence.

"Your lungs still hurt, don't they?" Libby asked.

"Some."

"Have you been using the camphor?"

"Yep."

His curt answers stung Libby and she studied him with a sidelong glance. His canvas coat fell to his ankles and emphasized the width of his shoulders and his slim hips. The worn brown Stetson sat low on his forehead, giving his hooded eyes a sinister look, but

Libby recognized the defensive tactic. She knew him too well to be scared off by the harsh expression.

"I feel terrible leaving Dylan with Lenore," Libby confessed.

"He'll be fine."

"Do you think Sadie will go after him?"

The angles of his face seemed carved in granite. "I'll make sure she doesn't."

Libby grabbed his arm and halted their progress. "You aren't going to do anything drastic, are you?"

"Like give Sadie a taste of what she done to Dylan?"

She shuddered at his glacial tone, but answered with equal coldness. "Matching violence with violence never solved anything."

He smiled without humor. "Maybe not, but it'd make me feel a whole lot better."

Anxiety furled in her stomach. "Matt."

"Don't worry. I don't do everything I'd like to." Matt's eyes glittered and his sultry gaze settled on her mouth.

Libby recognized his desire, and she swept her tongue across her dry lips. Her heart kicked like a mule, her chest constricting painfully. A tendril of hair whipped across her face and she impatiently tucked the strand under her fur hat. She ignored winter's bracing bite, centering her attention on the man beside her.

Suddenly a gun exploded and Matt knocked Libby to the ground. More gunfire, and a bullet thudded into the wall behind them. She struggled to breathe under Matt's weight.

"Stay down," he hissed in her ear.

His solid body disappeared from her back, and cold air rushed into her lungs. Matt ran in a half-crouch across the street and ducked behind the livery. Three more shots brought Libby's head up sharply and her heart skipped a beat. What if Matt had been led into a trap? Trembling, Libby raised herself to a kneeling position. She searched the town for a sign of movement, but only curious people peeked out from doorways and windows.

Ominous silence tested Libby's patience and she straightened behind a support pole to peek around the rough wood surface, her concern for Matt outweighing the fear for her own safety. The deadly calm frightened Libby more than the rapid-fire ambush had, and she cautiously moved down the boardwalk's steps to the frozen ground below.

"I thought I told you to stay put," Matt said with irritated concern, and Libby's heart tripped over itself.

He stood in the livery doorway and she hurried to his side, but his stiff posture stopped her from hugging him. She clenched her hands in front of her body. "Are you all right?"

"He got away."

"Did you see who it was?"

Matt shook his head and lifted his revolver to dump the spent cartridges. He replaced the empty cylinders with bullets from his gun belt. "It had to be somebody out to get me. No one would want to shoot you."

What if the attacker had been a bounty hunter who held a paper on her? Her stomach pitched and her mind reeled. She could have been the cause of Matt's death.

"Libby, you look like you seen a ghost." Matt's disembodied voice floated around her.

"I'm not used to getting shot at." *At least that was the truth.*

Matt cursed. "I'm sorry, Libby. Let's get you home so you can warm up."

He took her arm and led her away from the barn. His strength bolstered Libby, and she pulled away from him.

"I'll be all right, Matt." She avoided his gaze to

hide her guilt. "Don't worry. I'm not the fainting type."

He didn't appear convinced and walked close beside her. Matt entered the schoolhouse first. "It's empty. I'll get a fire going."

She followed him to the back room and wrapped her arms around her waist. The area seemed smaller with Matt's towering presence, and Libby shivered with more than cold. Matt lit a kerosene lamp, and she perched on the edge of a hard chair.

With an economy of motion, Matt filled the stove with wood and sparked the dry pieces of kindling he laid around the bottom. The flames' heat radiated outward to chase away the brisk chill.

"Do you want some coffee?" Libby asked.

"Sure."

Libby readied the pot, placed it atop the stove, and leaned back against the crude counter. Matt stood beside a window and carefully peered out. Boiling water and the occasional sputter of liquid on the hot surface accented the tense silence in the room.

Libby's nerves stretched taut and her head pounded. Had the ambush been for her or Matt? If the attacker had been a bounty hunter, wouldn't he simply go to the sheriff's office and tell Matt who he was after? There would be no reason for him to hide his intentions.

She poured coffee into two cups and handed one to Matt.

"Is anybody out there?" Libby asked.

Matt's hawkish gaze scanned through the glass pane. "It's getting too dark to tell."

Libby tightened her fingers into a fist. "What if he was after me?"

Matt swung his startled gaze to her. "Why would anyone want to kill you?"

Libby shrugged weakly. "There are people in this town who disapprove of me."

Matt snorted. "Mrs. Beidler isn't going to have you shot because she doesn't like you."

Despite the coolness of the room, a few beads of sweat formed on Libby's brow. "Why would someone come after you?"

His bleak look captured Libby. "I've done a lot of things in my time, including killing people."

"But that was the war."

He shook his head. "I used to be a Texas Ranger before the war, and I killed my share while riding with them. I've had to shoot a few folks since I pinned on this sheriff's badge, too. All those dead people had friends and family. There's no telling who might be after me."

Libby shuddered. What if Matt *had* been the intended target? Her stomach knotted and she tightened her arms around her middle.

The doctors in the east took a dim view of shootings in the uncivilized frontier, berating the blatant disregard for life. But Libby lived in that world, where guns were a common commodity. She'd seen firsthand how good people sometimes had no choice but to use violence to attain peace, and though she couldn't completely condone the practice of swift justice, she understood the reasons.

Matt misread her silent reverie. "I'm sorry if I offended your tender sensibilities."

Libby ignored his biting sarcasm. "You didn't. Sometimes people have to do things they don't want to when the only option is their own death."

Matt studied her, his face expressionless. "Why don't you act like other women?"

"I'm not other women."

He cupped her cheek in his gloved hand. "No, you're not. No other woman's ever wound me tighter than a watch spring."

His velvety tone wrapped around Libby and she leaned into his caress. She gazed into his veiled eyes, and her insides twisted with now-familiar desire. The need to feel his hard body against her nearly obliterated all coherent thought. With her last thread of willpower, Libby turned away.

Disappointment flared in Matt's features. He masked the emotion with an expression as cold as marble. "I'd better get going and take another look around the town."

He paused in the door leading to the classroom. "You'll be all right. He wasn't after you."

She trembled with fear, but not for her own safety. "Watch your back."

From beneath his hat brim, Matt studied Libby. "I will. You keep that little derringer close by."

"I thought you said he was after you."

"He was, but there's no reason to be taking chances. Stay in and lock the doors like you should've done last night."

"To protect Dylan from Sadie?" Libby narrowed her eyes. "Or to protect me from you?"

"Do it," Matt ordered and spun away.

He stomped across the puncheon floor and the door slammed behind him.

Without Matt, the school seemed unusually quiet. She slipped into the larger room, retrieved the small gun from the desk drawer, and slid the weapon into her side skirt pocket. After collecting some books, she moved back into her living area. She pressed the iron bolt into place and made sure the back door was similarly secured.

The fire's warmth enveloped her, and she removed her coat. After refilling her coffee cup, she tried to concentrate on the work spread out on the table. A branch scraped against a window, startling her. Her heart thrummed a fast cadence. Libby's hand crept into her pocket, her fingers wrapping around the comforting steel. After a few minutes of silence, she relaxed and resumed her lessons.

Throughout the evening, she jumped at the slightest noise. Her clamoring conscience demanded attention, and her mind jumped from one possibility to another. Logic told her the ambusher couldn't have been a bounty hunter, but the conclusion didn't bring her peace of mind. She couldn't bear the thought of Matt being wounded or killed. She deserved her punishment. Matt had done nothing that warranted a death sentence.

She stood and added another stick of wood to the stove. Shivering, Libby wrapped her wool shawl around her shoulders and held her hands out to the fire's heat. The wind howled, echoing the barren loneliness deep inside her. She missed Dylan more than she thought possible. She recalled his sweet smile and trusting eyes, and wished she hadn't left him at Lenore's.

Her heart bucked and she missed a breath. What would happen to Dylan if her past was revealed and she was taken back to Nebraska? Or worse, what if he got in the crossfire between herself and someone bound to collect the reward on her? Dread filled Libby. What had she done? She'd laid aside her prudence and hadn't given a thought to those lives she'd affect by her decision to stay in Deer Creek. Dylan depended on her, and she'd only break his heart if the past collided with her new identity. She had no right endangering his life.

She bit her lower lip. The pain didn't diminish the ache in her chest.

Matt dipped his pen into the ink stand and painstakingly signed his name to a paper. He sighed and tossed the quill on the scratched desktop. "I hope that's all the blamed paperwork for today."

Eli glanced at a few more sheets and set them aside. "Those'll wait until tomorrow."

Matt looked over his shoulder and tried to read some of the words. "What are they?"

"Telegrams from other lawmen. Doesn't look like anything important."

Matt stood and stretched, loosening muscles that had stiffened while he'd labored over reports and licenses. "Things were a lot simpler when I was with the Rangers."

"That was over ten years ago, Matt. Times change."

Matt grabbed a cloth that hung from the damper on the stove and wrapped the material around the coffee-pot's handle. He poured some of the black liquid into a cup. "You want some?"

Eli shook his head. "I'd better get going. I promised Annie Fowler I'd stop by and see how young Sam's doing."

"He still got the croup?"

"Yep. I want to make sure it doesn't turn into anything worse. And while I'm out in that area, I'll check on Herman Callendar's foot. I sure hope he doesn't lose it."

"He should've hired some young feller to chop his wood. Old fool, cutting himself with the axe like that."

"Doesn't surprise me. Herman squeezes his pennies so tight they scream for mercy." Eli stood. "Do you want me to come by tomorrow so we can finish the rest of the paperwork?"

Matt nodded and rubbed his jaw. "Did I tell you Libby volunteered to teach me to read and write?"

Eli brightened with interest. "You'd best take her up on that offer."

"I don't know. I'm supposed to go over there this evening for my first lesson."

Eli frowned. "You're going, aren't you?"

Matt shifted uncomfortably. "I wouldn't want to hurt her reputation any more than I've already done."

"Hell, Matt, if she was worried about that, she wouldn't have suggested tutoring you. You've always wanted to learn, and I don't have the time or the patience to do it. You'd be a fool to let this opportunity pass by."

"Maybe she didn't mean it."

Eli narrowed his shrewd eyes. "Or maybe you're plain scared. If I was a betting man, I'd say she was interested in you, and I'd say the feeling was mutual."

Matt's gaze pierced Eli. "You don't know what you're talking about."

The warning in his tone didn't intimidate the doctor. "If you didn't wear that scar like a shield, you'd see it, too."

Fragments of time when Libby had traced the jagged line with a tender fingertip branded his thoughts. Her soft husky voice echoed in his mind.

There's no need to be ashamed, Matt.

I'm not other women.

The memory of her words coaxed his surrender and her body tempted his control, but distrust ran too deeply to throw aside his wariness. He knew firsthand how love could change to hate, and he'd barely survived the aftermath of the nightmare. He didn't think he could endure another agonizing loss.

"Even if you're right, she doesn't want to get married," Matt stated.

"She tell you that?" Eli asked.

Matt nodded.

Eli shook his head. "She doesn't know what she wants. She's got a few demons chasing her, too."

Matt lifted his head sharply. "What?"

"Don't tell me you haven't seen past them pretty eyes to see the ghosts? She's scared of something, as sure as you and me are standing here, but I'll be blasted if I can figure it out. She hasn't told Lenore anything either. Whatever the problem is, it goes deep. Damned deep."

Concern pressed upon Matt's shoulders. He didn't want to care about another woman. "I suppose she'll tell someone when she's good and ready."

Eli sighed heavily. "Suit yourself. Did you ever figure out who shot at you and Libby last night?"

Matt shook his head. "There were too many tracks."

"While I'm out, I'll ask if anyone's seen any strangers hanging around the area."

"I'd be obliged."

The doctor buttoned his overcoat and picked up his worn black bag. "See you later."

Eli shuffled out and cold air eddied across the floor, bringing a shiver to Matt. He refilled his cup and went to the front window. He planted one booted foot on a chair, resting his elbow on his thigh. Sipping his coffee, he surveyed his town. He recognized everyone who hurried along the boardwalks.

He yawned widely. He'd circled the town much of the night and ensured Libby remained safe from the unknown gunman. He was convinced he was the target, but the slight chance Libby could have been had kept him alert for danger. And Eli's suspicions about Libby's past now didn't ease his mind.

He'd had some doubts himself when Libby arrived in Deer Creek, but he'd cast them aside. He thought back to the first evening at Lenore's and how he'd helped her clean up a broken plate. Matt had brushed her ankle, and she'd reacted instinctively and violently. He'd believed the incident a misunderstanding and forgotten about it. What if there had been more involved?

Unbidden, a memory sprang to mind. During his time with the Texas Rangers, he'd made an illegal foray into Mexico to track down a band of killers. They'd stopped in a tiny pueblo and rested their tired horses. Matt had asked one of the villagers where they could get some food, but the man hadn't understood.

Matt had raised his hand to help illustrate his words and the Mexican had fallen to his knees, cowering before him. Later, Matt had learned the peasant had been beaten so often by the soldiers, the reaction had become reflexive.

He thought about the time Libby had panicked in the root cellar, and his gut clenched. What if she'd been mistreated? He frowned. The man in Mexico had been submissive, unable to look Matt in the eye. Libby didn't have that problem. She'd stood up to Mrs. Beidler without flinching. He'd also been the recipient of her righteous indignation a time or two.

Matt swallowed his uneasiness. Libby's problems had nothing to do with him, and there was no reason to become involved. Impatiently, he moved away from the window and set his empty cup on the paper-littered desk. He strode to the door, jammed his hat on his head, and escaped the stuffy confines of the office.

Outside, he waited for his lungs to adjust to the frigid air, and the image of Libby's concerned face when she'd cared for him at his cabin floated in his mind. She'd saved his life without regard to the hornet's nest she'd stirred up.

He jerked on his cowskin gloves, angry at her for the debt she'd given him.

But he was angrier with himself for wanting to help her.

"How is the lesson coming, Dylan?" Libby asked.

He looked up from the McGuffey's reader and his eyes sparkled like sapphires. "I just finished. I liked this story. It was about a boy and a dog."

"I knew you would." Libby forced a smile. "You know, if you and I live at Mrs. Potts, there won't be a place to keep a dog."

Dylan's expression fell.

Libby eased into a desk beside him. "But if you

lived with the sheriff, he's got enough room to have one."

"I thought you wanted me to live with you."

The hurt in Dylan's expression nearly shattered Libby's resolve, and she clasped his hands in hers. "I do, but I wouldn't mind if you lived with the sheriff. I'd still see you every day, and I know he cares for you as much as I do."

"Would you live with Mrs. Potts?"

Libby nodded.

"Then I guess you wouldn't be alone either."

Libby swallowed tears. "That's right."

She could barely force herself to influence his decision, but Libby would never forgive herself if he chose to live with her and her crime became known. The torment would be even more devastating for herself and the innocent boy.

With forced cheerfulness, she spoke. "You'd better head on back to Mrs. Potts's before it gets dark."

Dylan slid from his seat and stood in front of Libby. "You sure you won't be mad if I lived with the sheriff?"

Libby squeezed his shoulders reassuringly. "Of course not, honey. I'll be happy no matter who you live with."

He heaved a sigh of relief. "Mrs. Potts said she'd make me some gingersnaps today."

Libby ruffled his dark hair. "Then you better get on to the house before Mr. Tanner and Mr. Johnson eat them all."

In the cloakroom, Libby helped him into his jacket.

"You want to come with me?" Dylan asked hopefully.

Though she desperately wanted to, Libby shook her head. "I can't. I have a lot of work to do."

Confusion clouded Dylan's expression. He nodded. "See you tomorrow morning."

He scampered out of the schoolhouse and dashed

across the snow-covered path to town. Libby's sight blurred as she leaned her forehead against the door-jamb. She was a murderer. She had no right to keep Dylan with her. Someday she would have to face the consequences of her deed, and she wouldn't be able to bear the loving boy's disillusionment. She had to convince him to choose Matt, but the knowledge didn't stop the yearning in her heart.

The ache dulled and remained with her through the remainder of the afternoon and into the evening. Libby turned up the lamp's wick and the kerosene fumes stung her eyes. She rubbed at the grainy mois-ture, but the burning sensation diminished only slightly.

The door hinges creaked, alerting Libby to a visitor. She looked up to see Matt shadowed in the entrance. Her pulse raced. "What are you doing here?"

"You did say six, didn't you?" he asked.

Libby blinked. "I'm sorry. I must've been wool-gathering."

Matt fingered the brim of his hat and stepped back. "That's all right. I won't stay."

Libby stood. "No, don't go. I mean, you're here, so we may as well begin. Come and sit down."

He strode to the front of the room and removed his coat. An outdoors scent blanketed him, and her heartbeat stumbled through her veins. She struggled to batten down her defenses, and appraised him with a cool look.

As Libby lowered herself into her chair, Matt eased into the recitation bench in front of the large desk. She clasped her hands together to hide their trembling and concentrated on her task. "Tell me how much schooling you've had."

"Where I grew up there weren't any schools around. My ma tried to teach me numbers and some letters, but we had to keep the ranch together."

"Where was your father?"

"He died at the Alamo. I was only four or five, so I don't remember much about him."

"And your mother?"

"Comancheros killed her when I was fourteen."

Grief squeezed Libby's heart. "I'm sorry."

Matt shrugged. "That was a long time ago."

"What did you do then?"

"I learned how to use a gun and went after them. It took me five years to track down the killers, but I did."

"What happened to them?"

"I killed them," he replied grimly.

A cold shiver raced up Libby's spine. She understood his feelings more than she could admit. "Did you ever go back to your ranch?"

Matt nodded. "Ten years later I tried to make a go of it."

"And?"

Matt's icy glance froze her. "What's that got to do with my lessons?"

Libby refused to be intimidated by his fierce look. "Nothing. I was only curious."

"My turn."

His expression thawed, but Libby couldn't read his thoughts beneath the shuttered expression.

"Where were you born?" he asked.

Startled, she studied his impenetrable look. "Ohio. My mother died giving birth to me, and my father passed on about seven years ago."

"And your brother was killed in the war," Matt added.

Libby nodded. "I told you about him."

"How did your father die?"

Libby shrugged. "They said a heart attack. I was away at school at the time."

Matt speared her with a gaze. "I thought you said you cared for your father before he died."

Libby bit her tongue. The first thread of lies unraveled. "I just told you that so you wouldn't be embarrassed. Actually, I helped my father with many of his patients, and there isn't much I haven't seen."

This time she spoke the truth, but Matt didn't accept her explanation without reservation. "Are you sure he was even a doctor?"

Libby's temper notched upward. "Both he and my brother were doctors. Why are you cross-examining me?"

Matt leaned back in a deceptively relaxed manner. "Is there a reason I should be?"

Libby's heart thudded erratically. "No."

She stood and faced the blackboard. "Let's start by reviewing the alphabet."

Libby's neck muscles throbbed as she wrote out the alphabet. Did he know? Had she done something to cause his suspicions?

Matt carefully printed the letters on his slate as Libby searched her mind for something she might have done or said to give herself away. Other than the slip about her father, she couldn't think of anything.

After Matt finished writing the alphabet, Libby expanded his lesson to sounding out longer words. A couple hours later, Matt grinned triumphantly. "This ai—isn't as hard as I figured it would be."

His enthusiasm warmed Libby. "You're a fast learner, Matt. It won't be long before you'll be reading dime novels to Dylan."

Guardedness crept back into Matt's expression and he nodded. He stood and his broad-shouldered figure dwarfed Libby. She pushed back her chair and rose.

"Thanks," he said. "Six o'clock again?"

"That'll be fine."

Matt shrugged into his coat and placed his hat on his lantern-gilded hair. He angled the brim over the side of his scar and sent Libby a nod. "Good night."

"Good night," she echoed.

He walked to the back of the classroom and turned.

"I haven't caught the person who shot at us last night, so keep your gun handy."

"Do you really think he's still around?"

"It depends on what he was here for. If his purpose was to scare us, he's long gone."

"And if that wasn't his purpose?"

"That's why I want you to be careful."

Libby drank in his concern, and a sunburst of emotions exploded within her. He might have some doubts about her, but the flame between them hadn't dimmed. Libby's gaze caressed his rugged face and the fires burned hotter. She wanted to feel his arms around her, be crushed against his solid chest, and pretend nothing stood between them.

"Don't look at me like that." Matt's hoarse voice revealed his agitation.

In the dim halo of the lantern's glow, Libby recognized desire mingled with bitterness. "But—"

"Stay away." Harshness colored his tone.

"Is that you or your scar speaking?" she asked softly.

Matt's lips thinned and his eyes darkened. He raised his head, drawing the blemished side of his face out of the shadows, and he clenched and unclenched his jaw muscle. "It doesn't matter. You don't want anything to do with me."

His sentiments reflected her own doubts, but the potent attraction dulled the thought like laudanum eased pain. She stared at the tortured anguish in his face, and the longing changed to something more complex. She wanted to comfort him and erase the desolation that darkened his eyes.

Matt's shoulders slumped and the door slammed behind his fleeing figure.

Libby collapsed into her chair.

She struggled between what was best for Matt and Dylan, and her own selfish needs. The tug-of-war buffeted her emotions and wounded her more than anything since her family's death. She had to convince Dylan to live with Matt. They would have each other, and she would content herself with that outcome.

The decision did little to heal the gaping hole in her heart.

Chapter 14

As Matt left the schoolhouse three days later, the brisk northwest wind scurried down his back, cooling his heated skin. His fourth lesson with Libby had not been a test of his reading skills, but a trial of restraint. She hadn't done anything to encourage him. Her nearness was enough to trigger his appetite.

Matt stuck his hands in his pockets and drew the coat together to hide the evidence of his throbbing arousal. He acted more like a young kid ready to sow his oats rather than a man on the wrong side of thirty. Matt swore. He prided himself on his self-control, and unknowingly, Libby O'Hanlon had badly damaged his fortress with her warm-hearted compassion. She was right. He used his scar as a shield to protect himself from risky entanglements. He'd learned the hard way what happened when he bared his soul to a woman.

He glanced up at the blinking stars in the night sky and debated whether to continue his private lessons with Libby. His desire to learn burned nearly as bright as his attraction to her. Her innocent allure seduced him, and he had to use every ounce of willpower to concentrate on her instruction.

Matt entered the town and lantern light from windows spilled across the boardwalk to illuminate his path. He paused in front of the Golden Slipper. Subdued voices sounded from within and he continued on. The red glow from Sadie's house caught his attention, and he crossed the street. He hadn't seen nor heard from the madam since Dylan had gone to Libby. After his confrontation with Sadie Saturday night, he wasn't surprised. Still, he needed to ensure she wouldn't demand Dylan be returned to her.

He cut over to the fancy establishment and stepped inside. The smell of cheap perfume and heavy cigar smoke assailed his lungs and he coughed, wincing at the discomfort. No one met him in the foyer and he wandered into the parlor. He remained half-hidden at the entrance, observing the fondling between the customers and the prostitutes. Ignoring the lewd activity, he searched the room for Sadie. He spotted her sitting on the lap of a handsome well-dressed man Matt had never seen before. He approached her, ignoring the startled glances from the room's revelers.

Sadie eyed him coldly. "You're not welcome here, Sheriff."

"And here I thought you ran a nice, friendly business," Matt said mockingly.

Sadie's face flushed with rage and she disentangled herself from her customer. "Excuse me. I'll be back as soon as I take care of an ugly problem."

The client's lust-filled gray eyes smoldered with impatience.

Matt grinned, tipped his hat to the man, and followed Sadie's rigid back to her office.

She settled into her throne behind the shiny rosewood desk and fixed Matt with a baleful gaze. "You got the bastard. What else do you want?"

Matt remained standing in the center of the opulent room. "I want to make sure you know you won't ever get Dylan back."

The lighted chandelier deepened the circles beneath Sadie's fishlike eyes. "That's up to Judge Benson, isn't it?"

"Once he hears what you done to Dylan, he won't let you near him."

Sadie pressed her fingertips together and studied her long red nails. "Howard Benson's one of my best, shall I say, friends."

Shaken, Matt struggled to maintain his air of confidence. "When I'm through telling him what you done to Dylan, that friendship isn't going to be worth a damn."

Sadie sneered. "You're going to be the one who won't be worth a damn. After I tell the judge what you were before you pinned on that badge, he's going to give the bastard back to me with his blessing. No judge would give a boy to a worthless drunk."

Contempt hazed Matt's vision. "I haven't touched a drop of liquor in three years, and even when I was drunk, I wouldn't have beat an innocent boy."

Sadie pushed a strand of stringy blond hair off her painted face. "But there's always a chance you'd fall back in the bottle, and who knows what you're capable of doing?"

Matt struggled to preserve his composure, but a cold sweat broke out on his forehead. "We're not talking about me, we're talking about Dylan and what kind of life he'd have with you."

Sadie rose and flattened her palms on the desktop. Her breasts heaved and threatened to escape the plunging neckline of her shiny blue dress. "Do you know who Dylan's father was?"

Matt shook his head. "I really don't give a damn."

"Jonas and me, we had some good times moving from town to town, selling bottles of miracle elixir made from rotgut whiskey and sorghum. We done a fine business off folks stupid enough to believe all the lies we told'em." Sadie's laugh chilled him. "Then I got a little careless and got pregnant. When I told Jonas about it, he went crazy and started beating the hell out of me. He left me for dead. Took me nearly a month to recover, and by that time I was showing so I couldn't get rid of the bastard.

"I spent five months there, working like a damn slave for my room and board until he was born. Dylan was the spitting image of his goddamn father, and I swore then and there the bastard would pay for ruining my life."

Matt recoiled from the cloud of crazed hatred surrounding Sadie. "You ruined your own life when you paired up with this Jonas. Let Dylan be."

Coldly, Sadie smiled, revealing yellowed teeth. "I'll get him back because he's mine."

Matt's thread of control threatened to unravel. "Libby O'Hanlon isn't going to let you take Dylan. Even Judge Benson can see a schoolteacher would be a better mother than a whore."

"We'll see about that." Sadie looked like a cat who drank a bowl of cream.

Matt's stomach turned. "As long as I'm alive, you'll never get Dylan back."

Sadie's kohl-blackened eyelashes fluttered. "That can be taken care of, too."

"Go ahead and try it, lady. It'd be my pleasure to toss you in jail until hell freezes over," Matt stated. He spun around and left the lion's den. Sadie's shrill curses followed him out.

He jerked open the door and stepped outside. His breath wisped like fog and disappeared with the bitter wind. With every foot away from the house, his fear increased. If he fought for Dylan, his sordid past would be revealed. Libby would see him without blinders, and she'd turn away. He imagined her disgust, and emptiness yawned wide within him. Was Dylan worth the loss of Libby's respect? Could he live with himself if he didn't fight for Dylan? Or could he compromise?

He'd help Libby gain custody of Dylan. The solution seemed perfect. Dylan would be protected by Libby and himself. There'd be no reason to debate his drinking history if she adopted the boy.

Still, anxiety swept through Matt. Sadie had seemed too confident when he'd mentioned Libby's interest in Dylan.

What did she know that he didn't?

Matt pulled a tarnished watch out of his vest and popped the cover open. Half past four. He closed the lid and slipped the timepiece back in his pocket.

Leaning back in his chair, he contemplated his next meeting with Libby. He would tell her about his visit to Sadie's, omitting his drunken past. In order to keep Dylan from being returned to his mother, he and Libby needed a plan. Judge Benson arrived in town the following week, and Dylan's future would be decided then.

Matt would be damned if he'd allow Sadie to continue using Dylan as a whipping boy for the man who'd sired him. If the verdict went in Sadie's favor, Matt would steal him away before she claimed him.

The door flew open and Dylan whirled inside. "You want to come help me build a snowman?"

Snowflakes powdered Dylan's head and shoulders and garnished his long dark eyelashes. Matt grinned. "Looks like you're already a snowman."

"I mean a real one with a button nose and sticks for arms, and maybe Dr. Clapper will give us one of his pipes so he can be a smoking snowman." Dylan dissolved into giggles.

Matt's chest tightened at the boyish pleasure on Dylan's red-cheeked face. Seeing him having genuine fun brought a burst of warmth in Matt's heart. How could he not accept Dylan's invitation? His smile widened. "I doubt if Eli would care much for that idea, but I bet you and I can still put together a pretty good snowman."

Dylan grabbed Matt's hand and pulled him out of his chair. "Let's go. Time's a'wasting."

Matt chuckled and donned his coat and gloves. He wrapped a scarf around his lower face.

Dylan raised his own scarf over his mouth. "You and I could be a couple train robbers."

Matt glanced at him and noticed only a slight discoloration around Dylan's eye remained from his mother's beating. "Then I'd have to arrest us."

Matt steered him out with a guiding hand on his shoulder. Dylan led them away from town and toward the schoolhouse. Once Deer Creek disappeared behind them, Matt glanced about. What would people think if they saw their sheriff playing in the snow? He chuckled.

"What're you laughing about, Sheriff?" Dylan asked with a muffled voice.

"I think I'm in trouble if the mayor catches me making a snowman." Matt tossed a snowball at Dylan and it splatted on his chest. The boy giggled and pelted Matt with a handful of snow, then he ran.

Libby tilted her head. Was that laughter? She rose from behind her desk and crossed the room to look out the window. She scratched the frost from the glass and blinked. Matt and Dylan were tossing snowballs at each other. Shock gave way to amusement as the mock battle ended with each combatant blanketed in white from head to toe.

This carefree Matt captivated Libby. He appeared even more handsome without reticence guarding his motions. She wanted to hear Matt laugh unabashedly, and share in Dylan's lighthearted fun. The temptation overcame her caution and she tossed aside propriety. She'd taught her last class and had nothing to lose.

Libby dashed to her room and quickly changed into

long underwear and a pair of pants. She pulled on a heavy wool shirt, then tugged her boots over warm socks. After braiding her long hair, she stuffed the thick plait under a fur hat. Buttoning her coat, she had a moment of uncertainty. But the sound of laughter floated in the wind, and her doubts vanished.

Bundled against the cold, Libby plunged into the brisk winter afternoon. As she approached them, Matt glanced up. Surprise shuttered what she could see of his features.

Her quavering heart hammered in her chest. "Mind if I join you?"

"Hi, Miss O'Hanlon," Dylan greeted. "We're making a snowman."

Conscious of Matt's cool gaze, Libby smiled nervously. "I see that. I used to be pretty good at making snowmen. Could you use another helper?"

Dylan looked at Matt. "Is it okay?"

After a moment's hesitation, Matt shrugged. "Why not?"

Libby sensed his tension, and wished he would revert back to the mood he'd been in before she arrived. She forced a perkiness she didn't feel. "What do you want me to do?"

"What do you think, Dylan? This is your project," Matt said.

"You can make the head," he proclaimed.

Libby nodded. "I think I can handle that."

She squatted down and picked up a handful of snow. After palming it into a ball, she rolled it across the white ground.

Matt's gaze flickered to Libby. Trousers molded to her rounded behind and curved around her thighs, leaving nothing to his overactive imagination. Between her pants and the forbidden caresses they'd shared, Matt knew she wasn't nearly as proper as her somber skirts and blouses suggested. The memory of those stolen moments and the enticing picture she made kneeling in the snow brought a rush of heat to Matt's blood.

"What do you think we should use for eyes?" Dylan asked.

"I've got some buttons in my desk," Libby suggested.

"Can I go get them?"

Libby smiled and nodded. "They're in the top middle drawer."

Dylan loped across the snow-littered yard.

"Matt?"

He turned at her tentative call. "What is it?"

"I didn't mean to interfere. You and Dylan sounded like you were having so much fun, and I thought maybe I could join in." She stood and brushed her knees free of snow. "If you don't want me here, I'll go back to the school." Libby cast her gaze downward.

He realized he didn't want her to go. "No, that's all right. Dylan likes having you here."

She glanced at him. "But if you don't want me here . . ."

Her sad eyes twisted his gut and made him feel like a lowdown skunk.

"No, it's not that. You surprised me is all," he said. He pointed at her legs. "Not many women I know wear trousers."

Her lips twitched with a wry smile. "I'm sorry if I've offended your tender sensibilities."

Matt threw back his head and roared with laughter. "The way you look in those pants makes only one thing tender, and it isn't my sensibilities."

The top of Libby's cheeks flushed a deep red, but her eyes twinkled. "You know, there's only one cure for that."

"And what's that?"

Libby grabbed a handful of snow and stuffed the cold wetness down his back. Matt yelped in surprise at her attack, then he looped his arm around her waist and pulled her down on the ground with him. She landed on top of him and he deftly flipped her on to her back, straddling her with his knees to keep her in place.

He scooped powdery flakes into his palm. "Your turn."

Libby laughed and grabbed his arm. "I give up."

"Will you accept my terms of surrender?"

"What are your terms?"

Matt's awareness of her warm, slender body between his thighs pierced him with an arrow of desire. The playfulness in Libby's expression softened and she gazed at him with unconcealed interest. He fought the demanding need in his groin. "One kiss and you can go free."

Libby's eyes widened. "I accept."

Matt dropped the snow in his hand and removed his leather glove. He gently eased her scarf down. A tender smile sculpted her full red lips, and her cheeks glowed with a rosy shine. He wondered how much of her pretty flush the cold painted, and how much was due to her awakening passion. He feathered back a strand of copper hair from her temple. She settled her gloved hands on his shoulders and he shuddered. He traced her smoothly curved jaw with his finger.

"Are you going to kiss me or not?" Libby asked huskily.

"Kisses are a lot like whiskey. If you drink it before its time, it'll burn all the way down. But if you wait for a little while and let it simmer, it goes down a whole lot smoother."

"I hate to tell you this, but I'm already a bit warm." Her eyes twinkled.

Matt smiled. "Then I'd best get to it before it spoils."

He bent his head and covered her mouth gently. He caressed her honeyed lips, paying them homage with his own form of adoration. She twined her fingers through his hair. His pulse pounded in his head, and lightning coiled in his stomach. Groaning, he drew away before he lost control.

Libby studied him with a heavy-lidded gaze, then reached up with a questing hand. She trailed a gloved finger down his scar and he started. Libby laid her palm against his cheek. "I think your kisses are better than all right."

A weight seemed to disappear from Matt's shoulders, and his lips quirked upward. "Didn't anyone ever tell you not to tempt a man?"

She giggled. "You make me sound like Eve in the garden of Eden."

With a lightness he hadn't experienced in years, Matt chuckled. "We'd better get up before we melt a hole in the snow."

Matt stood, extending his hand to Libby. Without hesitation, she accepted his assistance and Matt pulled her to her feet. She didn't withdraw from his grasp, and he squeezed her fingers gently. Libby's warm smile sent a ray of sunshine to the depths of his soul.

Dylan rejoined them and opened his fist, revealing two blue buttons. "Can I use these?"

"They're perfect," Libby said. "Aren't they Matt?"

He smiled and nodded, his gaze on her. "Perfect. If Miss O'Hanlon is done with the head, we can get your snowman put together."

Libby pointed to the ball she'd made. "How's that?"

"It's perfect," Dylan echoed. "C'mon and help me, Sheriff."

Matt winked at Libby, and he and Dylan placed the ball of snow on top of the two larger ones. Matt lifted the boy and Dylan pressed the eyes into the packed snow.

Libby angled her head and studied the creation. "I think it needs a nose and a mouth."

A scavenger hunt ensued, and fifteen minutes later, the snowman was completed.

"What're you going to name him, Dylan?" Libby asked.

The boy thought for a long moment. "He looks just like the bartender at the Golden Slipper."

Matt chuckled. "He does look a mite like Albert, all right."

"Then that's his name," Dylan proclaimed.

Libby smiled. "What do you say the sheriff and I walk you back to Mrs. Potts'?"

Dylan nodded. He reached for Matt's hand and grasped Libby's with his other one.

Matt glanced at Libby and she sent him a smile that traveled clear to his unprotected heart.

They could be a family.

A sense of belonging enveloped him. He cared for Libby and Dylan with a depth he hadn't believed he'd ever feel again. Matt's throat tightened at the thought of Dylan calling him Pa. The boy's true parentage didn't bother Matt. He'd be proud to call Dylan his own, and he'd raise him to know right from wrong.

He imagined Libby as his wife. Her compassion would soothe his wounds, and she'd share his bed at night. They would love one another until the early hours of morning, and fall asleep in each other's arms. Her unwavering acceptance of him would banish the demons that chased him in his slumber. She would never deceive him like Rachel had done.

They stopped in front of the boardinghouse.

"Go on in and change into some dry clothes before you catch a cold," Libby advised Dylan.

"Are you and the sheriff going to come in?" Dylan asked.

"I'd better get back to the schoolhouse and change, too," Libby replied. "And I think the sheriff should do the same. He might get real sick again if he doesn't."

She squatted down. "Do I get a hug?"

Dylan moved into her embrace and he wrapped his arms around her.

"Are you going to move into Mrs. Potts's tomorrow?" he asked.

"Not until Sunday."

Dylan nodded and turned to Matt. "I decided to come live with you, Sheriff."

Surprise shot through Matt. "I thought for sure you'd want to live with Miss O'Hanlon."

He shook his head. "She'll have Mrs. Potts, but you won't have anybody. Besides, Miss O'Hanlon said I could get a dog if I lived with you."

Matt turned to Libby. "Is that so?"

"You don't mind, do you?" she asked.

How could he tell her the judge would make the final decision about Dylan, and he wasn't about to award custody of a young boy to a former drunk? He looked at Dylan's apprehensive face. "I don't mind at all. This way I can make sure you don't steal any more apples from Mr. Pearson."

Matt tempered his words with a wink.

Dylan sighed in relief. "When do you want me to move in?"

"Why don't we wait until after Christmas? I don't even have a tree in my cabin, and Mrs. Potts always puts a real nice one up in the parlor."

"Are you and Miss O'Hanlon going to help?"

"I'll be there," Matt assured.

"I've got to help get the schoolhouse decorated for the party," Libby said. "When we finish with that, I'll be over. Now scoot inside before you freeze."

Dylan waved and dashed in the house.

"I meant what I said. You could get a relapse of pneumonia if you don't get some dry clothes on," Libby warned.

A smile twitched Matt's lips. "Yes, ma'am. But I plan on walking you home first."

Libby opened her mouth to argue.

"And no arguments," Matt spoke up.

He reached for her hand and they walked side by side in the evening dusk.

"Why did you do it?" he asked.

"Do what?"

"Convince Dylan he should live with me."

Libby stared into the gloom. "Don't be ridiculous. Dylan made his own decision."

"So, your telling him he could have a dog if he lived with me isn't what you'd call influencing him?"

"I might have mentioned it, since I knew how much he wanted a dog. I also knew he couldn't keep one at Lenore's."

"You don't seem all that upset he picked me and not you."

Libby shrugged. "A boy needs a man he can look up to, and you'd make a wonderful father."

"What if the judge doesn't agree with you?"

Libby looked up at him. "Why wouldn't he allow Dylan to stay with you? You're a sheriff, for heaven's sake. He'd be crazy to put him back with Sadie."

"I talked to Sadie last night. She told me Judge Benson is a regular customer. She thinks she'll get Dylan back without a problem."

Libby's face paled. "You don't believe that, do you?"

"I don't know." Matt sought the courage to confess his drinking problem. He took a deep, steadying breath. "She's going to tell him about the time I spent more time drunk than sober."

Libby shook her head impatiently. "But that was years ago. You don't drink anymore."

Matt stumbled to a standstill and stared at Libby. "You knew?"

"A couple of people told me about it. If we can convince the judge you've been sober for a few years and the chances of you returning to your old drinking habits are almost nonexistent, he'll have to give you custody of Dylan."

Relief washed through him like a swelling wave. She'd known all along, and still she cared for him. "I was afraid you'd hate me if you knew."

Disappointment clouded Libby's face. "You really thought that little of me? Matt, I don't care what you've done in the past. You're a generous and kindhearted man. Haven't I been able to get that through your thick skull?"

Wonder filled him and he gazed at Libby, seeing her in a different light. "You really don't care, do you?"

Libby groaned. "Lenore said I should've used a two-by-four. Maybe she was right."

Matt pressed his lips to the back of her hand. "I don't think that's necessary. I think I finally got the message. In fact, I think I got all of them."

Matt shivered on the outside, but inside, warmth infused him. They walked the remaining distance in comfortable silence.

"Are you too tired to tutor me this evening?" Matt asked.

Libby shook her head. "Come back after you change, and I'll have some supper for us—then we'll continue your reading lesson."

Lightly, he trailed his finger down the side of her flushed face. He studied her ripe mouth, and slanted his lips across hers. Libby's arms circled his neck, pulling him closer. His body met her soft curves and he moaned deep in his throat. His heart beat in time with Libby's, his breath merging with hers. Finally, Matt retreated, though he continued to hold her against him.

"You'd better go change, Matt," Libby whispered.

He nodded and reluctantly released her. "I'll be back."

Matt slipped away in the cover of darkness, and Libby ached to have him back beside her. She climbed the wooden steps into the schoolhouse, then hurried back to her room.

Her somber attire back in place, Libby fried potatoes and added chunks of ham to the skillet. She hummed a spirited tune that matched her cheerful mood. She had seen the transformation on Matt's face. The change came like the sun to chase away the dark clouds. She'd sensed his startled relief that someone could accept him with all his scars.

She paused and frowned. What now? Where did she and Matt go from this point? He had branded her with gentle kisses that had the power to arouse her and make her forget who she'd been and what she ran from. Did he want more from her, now that he understood he had nothing to be ashamed of? And if he did, could she love him, knowing the risk of discovery hung around her neck like a tightening noose? Was she even capable of love, after what she'd endured at Harrison's sadistic hands?

Troubled thoughts swirled through Libby's mind. A door hinge creaked. "Matt, is that you?" she called.

Eerie silence answered.

Libby moved the pan off the stove and picked up the lantern. The pale yellow glow lit her path into the classroom. "Matt?"

Though unable to see anybody, Libby's hair prickled at the nape of her neck. "Who's there?"

Click.

Libby whirled and spied a rough-looking man with a revolver aimed directly at her. She gasped and pressed her palm to her mouth. Her heart raced uncontrollably.

"What do you want?" Libby managed to ask.

Two long strides placed the grizzled stranger directly in front of her. He leered, showing stained teeth between his thin lips. "Put the lamp on the desk."

With a trembling hand, she did as he commanded.

"Sit down," he ordered.

Libby stared into muddy brown eyes under shaggy dark brows. "What do you want?"

He grabbed her arm with bruising fingers and flung her into the chair. Libby slammed against the wooden slats, and tears clouded her eyes.

"Get your hands behind your back."

"What're you going to do?"

"Shut up. Do like I said."

She leaned forward and clasped her shaking hands behind her. "Who are you?"

He moved around her and lashed her wrists together. The rope bit into her skin, slowing the circulation and numbing her fingertips. He yanked her braid, forcing her gaze up at him.

"You're going to help me kill the sheriff."

His fetid breath rolled across Libby and her stomach pitched. She could barely speak past the terror lodged in her throat. "Why?"

He tightened his hold on her hair, and the pain brought a new flood of tears blurring her vision.

"He murdered my brother and the Bible says 'an eye for an eye,'" the outlaw stated venomously.

Fear sleeted down Libby's spine. "But he must have done something. Matt wouldn't kill anybody without justification."

The man's close-set eyes narrowed and he released Libby. He paced, his boot heels ominous in the evening's stillness. "Ain't nothing Jimmy done was bad enough to be shot down."

"What did he do?" If she could keep him talking, maybe Matt would be alerted to the man's presence.

He untied the grimy bandanna from his neck and approached her. "You just relax, and maybe I'll let you live."

He looped the filthy scarf across her mouth and Libby gagged from the salty taste of stale sweat embedded in the material. "That'll keep you quiet."

The would-be murderer's lecherous gaze raked

Libby, and she shivered. He lowered his gun, and used the barrel to trace across her shoulder and down across the rise and fall of her breast. "Been a long time since I had a woman." He rubbed his crotch with a dirt-encrusted hand. "Maybe after I take care of the sheriff, you and I can have a little fun. You got a bed back there?"

Panic threatened to strangle Libby. Her heart hammered in her chest and sweat coated her palms.

The faint strains of whistling strayed into the room. Her captor straightened. Libby recognized the tune as "Dixie" and dread froze her. Matt.

"Looks like I got my second chance."

Libby swiveled her startled gaze to the stranger. *He* was the one who'd shot at them last Sunday. He'd missed then, but this time he wouldn't. She pushed out of the chair, but a rough shove forced her back down. He pressed the gun's cold steel against the side of her head. Libby struggled for air, and she feared she would suffocate. Red dots skimmed across her vision.

The door in the cloakroom opened.

"I hope you made a lot for supper. I'm starved," Matt called. He entered the classroom and stopped short.

"Howdy, Sheriff. We got some unfinished business."

Fury swept through Matt's eyes. With visible effort he drew a blank curtain across his features, but Libby noticed the tic in his jaw and the tension in his broad shoulders. She stared at Matt, willing him to leave before the vengeful man killed him.

"I figured you'd be long gone with all that money you and your brother stole," Matt stated.

"Not until you're dead just like Jimmy. Get your hands up, away from your gun."

Matt raised his arms. "Let her go. It's me you want."

He shook his head. "She's my insurance that you won't try nothin'."

Matt glanced at Libby and he sent her a steady, reassuring look. He turned back to the thief. "How'd you know I'd be here?"

"I been watchin'," he said proudly. "You been comin' here every night about this time. I figured I'd slip in and get the drop on you."

"You done a good job of it."

Libby's breathing slowed, and she kept a watchful eye on Matt—he had an idea. She wished she could read his mind. His coat was open and his ever-present holster lay against his thigh. If he could reach his gun before the outlaw shot him, he'd have a chance. But with the barrel against her temple, Matt wouldn't try anything. He'd have to wait until the man moved his weapon.

"Jimmy was my only kin," he said. "Now I got no one. You have any idea what that's like?"

Matt nodded. "More'n I care to admit. You aren't the only one to have lost family."

Regret flickered across his granite features and Libby's vision blurred. She recognized his pain and the realization he may not have time to amend his past.

The thief shifted and Libby sidled a glance at him. His nostrils flared and his face contorted with rage.

"But Jimmy's dead because of you."

He raised the gun and Libby reacted. She pushed out of her chair, her shoulder striking his arm. An explosion sounded close to her ear and he flung her aside like an old saddle. She collided with the wall, her head cracking against the wood. As darkness danced in her peripheral vision, she slumped to the floor. Vaguely aware that gunshots echoed in the close confines, Libby's fear for Matt overwhelmed all other thoughts. She struggled to stand, but her legs refused to obey her command.

"Libby, are you all right?"

She focused on Matt's familiar face and blinked. Was he real? Or had her heartsickening fear conjured him up? He eased her forward and she leaned against his solid, reassuring chest as he removed the nauseating gag.

"Matt?" Libby didn't recognize her weak voice. He freed her hands and she touched Matt's angular jaw. "Thank God you're all right. I thought . . ."

Tenderly, he curved his large palm around her cheek and gazed down into her eyes. "I thought his first shot hit you."

"And I thought he killed you." Libby's reserve crumpled, and she wrapped her arms around him. Burrowing her face into the crook of his neck, Libby trembled uncontrollably. She tightened her hold, afraid to release him and find she'd only imagined him. The scent of bay rum and wool surrounded her, and Matt's secure embrace slowly dissipated her paralyzing panic.

"Shhh, everything will be all right," Matt crooned softly.

His muscular body sent waves of awareness coursing through Libby's veins. She tilted her head back, her gaze colliding with eyes the color of sunlit whiskey.

He brushed an auburn curl behind her ear. "I'm sorry, Libby. I almost got you killed."

Did she tell him the situation could have easily been reversed? She shook her head and flattened her hand against his buttoned vest. "You can't blame yourself for what happened, Matt."

He trembled beneath her touch. "I don't know what I would've done if he'd shot you."

Desperation clouded his rugged features, and he crushed her to him. Capturing her lips with his, Matt branded her with a searing kiss. Libby clung to him. Exhilaration filled her and fed the banked fire within her. Her blood thundered in her veins, obliterating everything but the feel of him. The taste of him. The sight of him. The need of him.

Heedlessly, she'd stumbled into the tender trap.

She loved him.

Chapter 15

$\sim$ ⎯⎯ $\odot$ ⎯⎯ $\sim$

Matt released her and drew a shaky breath. "I'll clean this mess up."

Libby shuddered. "Is he dead?"

"I think so."

"We should make sure."

Matt stood and pulled Libby to her feet. "I'll check."

She shook her head and smiled wanly. "I'm the daughter of a doctor. It won't bother me."

He studied her a moment and nodded. Taking her hand, he led her to the figure lying in front of the desk. Blood pooled beneath the outlaw's head. Matt squatted down beside the outlaw's still form.

Libby stared at the darkening stain. In her mind, the wood floor became marble and the rivulet scarlet.

Dear God, what if Harrison had been alive? She was a doctor, and she hadn't even examined Harrison! Libby refused to consider the possibility. She'd struck him a powerful blow. She'd killed him accidentally, and she hoped he hadn't suffered before dying.

Matt straightened stiffly. "He's gone. Go back to your room and stay there. I'll take care of him."

Libby clung to Matt. "You're coming back, aren't you?"

He kissed her forehead softly. "I'll be back."

Libby stumbled into her small quarters and sank into a chair. She ached to have Matt's steadying presence beside her.

She'd thought she loved Harrison during his romantic courtship, but the depth of her feelings for Matt showed her how shallow the emotion had been. Dear, strong, honest Matt had captured her soul, giving her life where desolation had resided.

He'd cured her just as she'd healed him.

Would she be capable of physically loving him? She stood and crossed the short distance to the stove. She poured warm water from the kettle into a tin basin. Using her cupped hands, she sluiced water over her warm cheeks.

What if she froze like she'd done in the cellar? What if she remained frigid, unable to make love because of Harrison's legacy? She'd disappoint Matt, and he'd shoulder the blame for her lack of passion. But what if the memories didn't haunt her? She'd already allowed Matt liberties she never believed herself capable of giving, and his touches had enflamed her, carrying her to the threshold of heaven.

Could she afford to take the chance?

Could she afford not to?

"I'm back."

Matt announced his return and Libby hastily dried her face and finger-combed her tangled hair.

He paused in the doorway and his worried gaze scrutinized her. "Are you all right? You're awfully pale."

Libby smiled. "Now that you're back, I'll be fine. Why don't you take off your hat and coat while I warm up supper?"

Matt hung his duster from a wooden peg beside Libby's cloak and, after a moment's hesitation, removed his Stetson. Libby placed the skillet of potatoes and ham on the hot stove.

"Who was he, Matt?" she asked.

Matt crossed the room and stood by Libby. "He and his brother were the ones who robbed the bank before Thanksgiving. This one's horse print matched the one I'd trailed. I found the stolen money in the saddlebag."

"Mr. Pinkney will be happy. I'm just glad it's all over," Libby said with a shudder. "If you don't mind setting the table, there's plates and cups in the cupboard and silverware in the drawer."

Matt found the dishes and placed them on the rough wood surface.

Libby's gaze swept over Matt, noting the breadth of his shoulders beneath the brown vest and collar-band shirt. His pants hugged his hips and thighs and Libby swallowed nervously. While he'd had pneumonia, she'd seen every inch of his glorious male body, but she'd studied it through clinical eyes. Now the thought of his nakedness brought liquid heat to the juncture of her thighs. She could barely stand to look at him without touching him.

"You keep staring at me like that and I won't be held responsible for my actions," Matt commented huskily.

Libby's cheeks burned with embarrassment. Flustered, she returned her attention to the pan. The potatoes and ham had burned at the bottom of the skillet, and she groaned.

"I know how those charred potatoes feel," Matt whispered close to her ear.

His breath fanned across her neck and sent wonderful tingles shimmying down her spine. He encircled her waist, pulling her against his chest snugly. Libby's heartbeat tripped erratically.

"Aren't you hungry?" Libby asked breathlessly.

"Ravenous." He nibbled her earlobe.

Libby shivered under the sensual assault. "Supper's ready."

"Good." He trailed a scorching path down her neck and ended the quest with a lingering kiss in the hollow of her collarbone.

His hard arousal pressed against her buttocks, and Libby closed her eyes at the intimate contact. Dizzy from Matt's onslaught of her senses, Libby floundered in the rising tide of passion.

Matt drew back and he breathed heavily. "I suppose we'd better eat."

Still caught in the web of desire, Libby wondered which appetite he referred to. She hungered for more of the wonderful sensations he conjured with his light caresses. He stepped away, and reality intruded.

"Yes, I suppose we should," she said faintly.

Trancelike, Libby set the skillet on the table and sat in the chair Matt held for her. He lowered himself in the seat beside her and grimaced.

"What's wrong?" Libby asked with concern.

Matt grinned self-consciously. "Nothing a dip in a freezing stream won't cure."

Libby lowered her gaze. He wasn't the only one who needed cooling off. She had no desire for food and used her fork to push the blackened supper about on her plate. Through lowered lashes, she noticed Matt didn't do justice to his meal either.

Tension as thick as molasses seeped between them. She noticed Matt's every movement. She imagined his calloused, gentle fingers tracing her face instead of holding a fork; his sensuous lips feeding on her breasts, instead of on well-done potatoes. The knowledge that she loved him only enhanced the yearning to be held within his secure arms.

"Did I ever tell you what I thought when I first saw you step off the stagecoach?" Matt asked softly.

Libby shook her head.

"I thought you had the prettiest eyes I'd ever seen. As green as new grass in the springtime." He chuckled. "But you were so proper. I figured you must've thought you landed in hell with the devil to greet you."

"Not the devil. Only a cousin," Libby teased.

He swept the back of his hand down her arm and Libby's nipples hardened against the fabric of her chemise. "I still find it hard to believe a beautiful woman like you risked her reputation to care for someone like me."

Libby clasped his forearm, and the heated skin beneath his linsey-woolsey shirt warmed her palm. "You shouldn't. I never thought twice about the decision I made. You're worth more than a hundred reputations."

Matt's eyes smoldered and he trailed his finger along her smooth jaw. "You always think of others before yourself. That's one of the things I like about you."

"Besides my green eyes?"

He smiled crookedly. "Your green eyes, your flaming hair, your stubborn independence, your compassion. I like everything about you." He tipped her head up and kissed the slight dimple in the center of her chin. His expression sobered. "When I thought you'd been shot, all I could think of was that I'd never be able to see your beautiful face light up with a smile, or hold you in my arms. I don't think I would've forgiven myself if you'd been killed because of me."

"But I wasn't," Libby reminded firmly. "One of the first things I noticed about you is that you blame yourself for things beyond your control. You have broad shoulders, but you can't take the responsibility of the whole world on them."

"Not the world. Only you and Dylan."

She blinked back unexpected tears at Matt's words. She'd had no one to watch over her since her father and brother died. She cleared her throat before she could speak. "I'll wash up the dishes, then we can get started on your lessons."

She stood. Matt joined her, looping his arm around her waist. "I have a better idea. Why don't I give the lessons tonight?"

Her stomach fluttered. "What kind of lessons?"

"Lessons like *n* as in nose." He kissed the tip of hers.

A smile twitched Libby's lips. "You're a fast learner."

She raised herself on her tiptoes and tickled his earlobe with her tongue.

"H for beautiful copper hair." He untied the bow, and her curls tumbled down her back. He buried his hands in the flowing silk and gently tilted her face upward. "And *m* for sweet, tempting mouth."

He brushed his lips across hers.

Libby sighed, drugged by the tender persuasiveness of Matt's caress. Her entire universe centered on the magic Matt performed, turning her insides to thick syrup.

"And *c* for chest," she said in a low, throaty voice. Using clumsy fingers, she unbuttoned his vest and swept an impatient hand inside his shirt.

Matt groaned and halted her exploration. "I'm only a man, Libby."

She paused and looked up at him breathlessly. "I've never asked you to be more."

"Yes you have. You want me to be a saint, but I can't. I want you, Libby." His beseeching gaze searched her eyes.

Unbearable yearning blossomed within Libby. She had never believed she could feel such quaking desire for a man, not after living with Harrison's perversions. "Love me, Matt."

"Are you sure?"

"I've never been more certain of anything in my life," she stated solemnly.

Matt reached past her and turned down the kerosene lamp, bathing the room in dim shadows. Removing his holster, he draped the gun belt over a chair. Then he led her to the narrow bed, framed her face in his large hands, and slanted his mouth across hers.

Libby shivered with delight. She wondered if her heart would be able to endure the heavenly pleasure of Matt's caresses. He skimmed his palm down her side, pausing on the fullness of her breast. Libby gasped and new waves of passion inundated her. His feathery touch followed her waist and curved downward over her buttocks. He pulled her against his arousal, and Libby instinctively rotated her hips across the hard flesh.

Matt grasped her rounded derriere and clenched his teeth. "Stop."

Libby stilled immediately. Had she made him angry? "Did I hurt you?"

Matt chuckled hoarsely. "In a manner of speaking. You keep doing that, and I'm afraid this evening will end much earlier than I want it to."

He wasn't mad. Yet Libby felt woefully inadequate at the pleasures she'd recently discovered between a man and a woman, and her cheeks burned with humiliation. "Tell me what to do. I don't want to do anything wrong."

"You're doing just fine, darlin'. It's me. I don't want to disappoint you."

He didn't want to let her down! Her heart sang. "You could never do that, Matt."

She wanted to confess her newfound love but felt the time wasn't right. She slid her fingers through the curly mat on his chest and reveled in the joy of merely touching him.

He burrowed his hands beneath Libby's hair and found the top button of her blouse. With trembling fingers, he unbuttoned the back of the shirtwaist and peeled the material forward. Libby withdrew her arms from the long sleeves, and the top hung from her waist. Matt weighed her breasts in his palms and

Libby shuddered. He lowered his head and laved her pebbled nipples, moistening the thin chemise covering her bosom.

Keeping her fullness cupped in his hands, he whispered in her ear, "Take off your clothes, Libby."

Remove your clothes, Elizabeth.

Harrison's commanding voice echoed in her mind, and she froze.

The heat of desire disappeared, replaced by the barrenness of winter. In her mind, her tyrant husband strolled around her, cruelly pinching a breast, then a buttock. He'd violated her womanhood with vicious fingers. She'd clamped her lips together and refused to cry out. He brought out the narrow leather belt and wielded the strap across her unprotected back until she could no longer stifle her sobs.

Libby pushed Matt away. "Oh God!"

She jerked her blouse on and awkwardly fastened a few of the buttons.

Confused, he stared into her haunted eyes. "You're bound to be scared, but I swear, I'd never hurt you."

Fear paled Libby's face, and Matt wanted to comfort her. He reached for her, but she stepped back. His own raging needs had made him forget she was a virgin. He cared too much for her to force himself upon her. Matt wanted her first time to be a special gift from him.

"It's all right, Libby. We can just sit on the bed and I'll hold you. I'll ask nothing else of you," Matt soothed.

Her apprehension faded but didn't disappear completely. "You promise?"

Matt nodded. "I promise."

He lowered himself to the narrow bed and leaned against the wall. Libby eyed him nervously and perched on the edge of the straw mattress.

"I won't bite," he teased gently.

The words, meant to be lighthearted, only reminded Libby again of the ugliness of her past experiences. Apprehensively, she eased back, but kept her spine ramrod straight. "I'm sorry, Matt. I thought I could go through with it."

"I understand. It's your first time and all."

She glanced down at her clenched hands in her lap. "No—I was raped."

Matt's breath caught in his throat, and deadly rage filled him. "When?"

"Before I came to Deer Creek."

He pondered her shocking confession, remembering the instances when she'd reacted violently to his touch. He hadn't even considered the ugly possibility. He covered her fists with his hand. "I'm sorry. I wish you would've told me earlier."

"It's not something I like to talk about."

He whispered a kiss across her knuckles. "I don't blame you. While I was a Ranger, a woman came to me and told me she'd been assaulted by a man. I believed her, but nobody else did. Most folks figured the lady asked for it."

Libby nodded. "That's why I've never told anyone before. I truly believed I could forget about it."

Matt wanted to find the man responsible for the shadows in her desolate eyes, and tear him apart limb by limb. He kept his voice steady. "It's not that easy, is it?"

"No," she whispered. She studied him with glistening eyes. "I thought you could chase the awful memories away."

Matt's throat tightened. He wrapped an arm around her shoulders and hugged her. Libby's soft curves played havoc upon his self-restraint. He buried his nose in her burnished ringlets and closed his eyes, inhaling the sweet fragrance of Libby and lilacs. Despite what she'd been through, Libby remained a loving, compassionate woman. She'd had the strength to take in a boy who nobody else wanted, and she'd taken on the demons that tormented him. She deserved to know the truth about him, too.

"Did you know I was married before?" he asked.

Libby pulled back and looked up at him. "No."

He cupped her head in his hand and eased her cheek down to rest on his chest. "I left the Rangers in fifty-eight to go back to the place where I'd been raised by my ma. I fixed up the house and corrals and bought a few horses. I met Rachel at an auction. She was there with her father. She was the most beautiful woman I'd ever laid eyes on, with white gold hair and clear blue eyes. We were married six months later, and had a son less than a year after that. I figured I was the luckiest man alive, with a lovely wife and a boy to carry on my name."

"What happened?"

"We only had Joshua about a year when he came down with a fever and died."

Libby's arm crept around his waist and she squeezed him. "I'm so sorry, Matt."

The sting of the memory didn't seem as sharp as before, and he continued. "I was, too. I don't think Rachel ever got over it. I joined the Confederate army a few months after that and left her with her parents. When I came back nearly three years later, I found she wasn't the same woman I'd married. But then, I guess I wasn't the same man either. I'd been scarred by a saber, and I'd seen more death than a man should ever have to."

"What did your wife do?"

The pain of Rachel's betrayal brought a long pause. "She took one look at me and swore I'd never touch her again. She let every other man bed her, but not her lawful husband."

"Oh, Matt, how horrible." Empathy radiated from her sensitive features.

He shook his head bitterly. "That wasn't the worst of it. She got pregnant by one of her lovers. The baby was born dead, and Rachel bled to death. I left Texas the night after they were buried and I never went back."

Libby raised her tear-filled gaze and laid her palm along the side of his face. "No wonder you thought a woman couldn't love you. Rachel used your scar as an excuse. If she had really cared for you, she'd never have done such a terrible thing."

Matt blinked back the moisture blurring his sight. "Eli told me the same thing, but I didn't believe him."

"If you hadn't been scarred, she would've justified her affairs some other way. It wasn't you, Matt, it was her." Gently, she pressed her lips to the jagged line.

Her light kiss sent a shaft of longing through Matt. Her plump breasts flattened against him, scorching him with their tempting softness. His body tightened with a desire so strong he wanted to tear off her cumbersome skirt and bury himself in her moist heat.

She'd been raped, and he lusted after her like a damned bull. Ashamed by his physical response, Matt forced himself to breathe deeply and ease the painful ache in his groin. He remained tense, afraid to touch her, yet desperately wanting to. He closed his eyes, but visions of her pearlescent breasts and the memory of her satiny thighs sent his costly control straight to hell. He grew thick with need.

"Libby, I can't stay here," Matt whispered hoarsely. "If I do, you may end up hating me."

Libby's rapid pulse fluttered in her slender neck. "No, don't go."

Matt grasped her upper arms tightly, angry with her for not understanding, and furious with himself for not being able to restrain his base instincts. "I might hurt you, and I'd never be able to live with myself if I did."

Her eyes pleaded with him to stay. "You could never do that, Matt. Besides, we haven't finished the lessons yet."

She brushed the tip of her pink tongue across her lower lip. *"L* is for I love you, Matt."

Libby's breathy declaration dispelled Matt's remaining demons, and he threw off the last chain of distrust surrounding his soul.

"I love you more than life itself, Libby," he said prayerfully.

Libby drew away from Matt and stood. He stared at her, confused. Didn't she want his love in return?

A tremulous smile curved her lips and she reached behind her. A moment later, her blouse fell to the floor. She unbuttoned her skirt, and the material pooled beside her shirtwaist.

Her erect nipples strained against the thin white fabric. The cotton drawers stretched over her shapely thighs. Matt's heart thundered like a herd of wild horses, and blood surged to his loins. Libby enfolded him within her welcoming arms, laying her cheek on his crown. Her womanly scent wafted up, and Matt savored the passionate fragrance.

With trembling fingers, he tugged the satin ribbon holding her chemise together and the material fell open, exposing her taut breasts. He pressed his lips to a soft slope and trailed a line of kisses to the summit.

He gently flicked his tongue across the hard nubbin, and Libby groaned from the exquisite torment. His tawny hair brushed and tickled her chest. His mouth branded her with hot dew. He seared a moist path to her waist, and untied the drawstring of her drawers. He slipped his hands into the band, easing the garment down to her ankles. Libby stepped out of the material. Cool air whispered across her skin, and goosebumps arose on her arms and legs.

Matt's breath caught in his throat. Clothed only in the lantern's golden glow, she resembled a wispy dream, as ethereal as an angel.

"You're even more beautiful than I imagined,"

Matt whispered huskily. He ran his hand over her hip. Her skin was cool, but her heated gaze appeared both excited and wary. He looped an arm around her waist and gently urged her to the mattress. "Lie down, angel eyes."

She eased down on the narrow bed, and Matt stretched out beside her stiff body. "Relax, Libby. I won't do anything you don't want me to."

Matt sketched a delicate line from the dusky tip of Libby's breast down her ribcage, and followed the concave curve of her waist. He laid his hand on her silken belly, and teased the auburn curls at the juncture of her thighs. Her muscles rippled beneath his touch and she grabbed his arm.

"What are you doing?" she demanded breathlessly.

"Do you want me to stop?"

"Yes. No. I don't know."

He brushed his lips across hers, bridling her stampeding fear and easing the tension from her willowy body. "I promise I'll be gentle."

Matt skimmed his palms down her slender legs and returned to the apex of her thighs. He found her hot slickness with his searching fingers, and his thumb stroked her bud of desire.

Libby's breath skipped and she whimpered. "Oh, Matt, I'm going to burst."

Matt strained for control of his ascending passion. "It gets even better."

"How?"

Despite the precarious hold on his fragile restraint, Matt chuckled. "You'll see."

He continued to manipulate the sensitive nub and her moisture drenched his fingers. Gently, Matt probed deeper in her narrow passage.

Libby dug her heels into the mattress and lifted her hips to meet Matt's intimate invasion. She captured Matt's face between her hand, and his whiskers rasped erotically across her palms. As Libby nipped his lower lip, the whirling vortex Matt created in the center of her passion spiraled out of control. The explosion caught her unprepared, and she shattered into a thousand splinters of light.

Her body remained weightless and slowly floated back to earth. She opened her eyes, and Matt's beloved face hovered above her.

"I never knew," Libby whispered in wonder.

"We're not done yet."

Disbelief filled her.

He rose from the bed and removed his clothing. Libby stared unabashedly at his muscular buttocks and the evidence of his own arousal. Fear tiptoed into her mind. Would he hurt her now, just as Harrison had done? Would everything he'd made beautiful be destroyed? She wouldn't be able to bear it. The disappointment would destroy her heart, wounding her more critically than the physical pain Harrison had inflicted, because she loved Matt.

He rejoined her, his arousal brushing her thigh. She remembered the suffering Harrison's hard flesh had brought her, and she shuddered.

"Are you cold?" Matt asked solicitously.

She shook her head and admitted her misgivings. "I'm afraid, Matt. You might hurt me like he did."

Matt trembled. "Only because he forced himself on you. When two people love each other, the joining is pleasurable for both. Just let nature take its course, angel eyes."

He brushed her nipples with his fingertips and hot liquid again pooled in her belly. His hands, so large yet so gentle, followed the dip and hollow of her waist. His manhood throbbed against her, and curiosity impelled her to trace her forefinger across his rigidness.

Matt moaned and she drew back as if burned.

"No, that's all right. It's been some time. I don't know how much longer I can wait," Matt said.

"I want you to show me how it can be between a man and a woman in love."

Her innocent request severed Matt's thread of control. He rolled on top of her and positioned himself between her long, graceful legs. He shifted and brought the tip of his desire to her dewy entrance.

"Remember, Libby. I love you," Matt whispered.

He swooped down to capture her mouth with his, and she locked her arms around his neck. As he inched into her tightness, she grew still beneath him. Her breathing shallowed, and her face paled.

"Matt, I—"

"It's all right. I'll go slow and let you get used to the feel of me," he reassured.

He prayed he'd have the strength to curb the demands of his fevered desire.

He kissed her eyelids and his muscles trembled with impatience. Sweat beaded his forehead. He nibbled her velvety earlobe, and she yielded to the pleasure of his caresses. Her tension eased, and Matt slid another inch into her heavenly warmth. She tightened around him, her fingernails raking his back. He hardly noticed the pain. His entire concentration focused on holding himself immobile within her moist sheathe, to allow her to grow accustomed to his firm length.

He'd never needed a woman as much as he needed sweet, loving Libby.

She trembled, and the echoing tremors broke Matt's resolve. He penetrated her completely, her snug heat encompassing his throbbing hardness. All coherent thought escaped Matt as he rocked back and forth within her. His existence revolved around the woman below him and the perfect joining of their bodies.

Libby's fear evaporated, and awe filled her eyes. She met him stroke for stroke. He grasped her hips and buried himself deeply into her moistness.

"Matt," Libby whimpered.

Unbearable tension tightened in Matt's stomach, and the rising swell of his passion approached its pinnacle. His release arrived like the pounding of an ocean wave, and he poured his life into her deepest recesses.

Afterward, Matt rolled to Libby's side and gathered her close. She laid her damp head on his shoulder, a contented smile curving her swollen lips. Her tripping heartbeat matched the tempo of his.

"I didn't think anything could feel so wonderful. So right," Libby whispered.

"I didn't either," Matt admitted.

Libby's puzzled gaze flickered across his face. "But you were married."

Matt swallowed. "Rachel said she never enjoyed it."

"Now I know she truly didn't love you," Libby said. She brushed a lock of tawny hair from his sweat-slicked forehead and grinned impishly. "I'll have to tell Lenore she was right."

He frowned, puzzled. "About what?"

"She told me you could probably show a woman a fine time in bed."

Startled embarrassment warmed his face. "She did, did she?"

Libby dropped a light kiss on his jaw. "She also said if she was thirty years younger, she'd be setting her bonnet for you."

With a deft motion, Matt lifted Libby atop him and trapped her within his arms, flattening her round breasts against his chest. Her body was soft and smooth. "I'm afraid she would've been disappointed. I've already found a bonnet that suits me just fine."

He rotated his hips sensually and Libby's mischevious smirk disappeared, replaced by a new awareness. She wanted him again. Her cheeks flamed. Harrison had said her desire was sinful, an evil to be beaten out of her. She had taken shameless pleasure in Matt's arms, but he had seemed to enjoy her unabandoned response.

His arousal grazed her leg and she gasped in surprise.

"I didn't think a man could be ready again so . . ." Her voice trailed off and she glanced away, embarrassed.

He feathered his thumbs across her winged brows. "He can if he loves the woman as much as I love you. I'll always want you."

She twined her fingers through the springy curls at the base of his throat and studied the slight cleft in his masculine chin. Trepidation threatened to rob her voice. "Is it wrong for a woman to enjoy it?"

Matt's low-timbered chuckle resonated through Libby. "I'll take that as a compliment." He sobered and shook his head. "No, it's not wrong. I figure God planned it that way, making men and women like He did. Love isn't anything to be ashamed of, Libby."

"Really?"

He nodded. "I swear it."

She wondered if he'd still want her if he knew the truth of her repeated rapes. Her eyelids fluttered closed and her tears remained hidden, as did the ugly memories. Desperately, Libby wished Matt would love her again and vanquish the past to a place where even she couldn't find it.

She opened her eyes to see concern etched in Matt's rough-hewn features. He had stolen her love and given it back a hundredfold. She owed him her life, her sanity, and the truth, but the confession remained lodged in her throat.

"I want you again, Matt," she asked with a trembling voice.

Matt caught her face between his calloused yet

gentle hands. He shook his head and a devilish grin captured his lips. "Good, because I planned on staying the rest of the night."

He brought her face downward to meet his mouth. With infinite tenderness, he banished Libby's dark misgivings, and she lost herself in the ecstasy of Matt's caresses.

The invasion of cold air roused Libby and she blinked in the early morning coral glow that painted the small room. She spotted Matt tucking his shirttails into his pants, and the lethargy of her body gave way to shyness. She tugged the quilt to her chin and observed Matt. Despite the many times they'd made love throughout the too-short night, Libby's desire was again aroused by his broad shoulders and muscular thighs. Her newfound knowledge of the pleasures of passion served to stoke the glowing embers.

"Good morning, angel eyes."

Matt's deep rugged voice sent a delicious shiver of delight through Libby. "Good morning."

He lowered himself to the edge of the bed and kissed her forehead. "I'm sorry for waking you. I don't want anyone to catch me here. Your reputation is already in trouble because of me. Besides, you looked tired."

Libby noticed the circles beneath his eyes. "So do you. Why don't you come back to bed?"

His rich laughter brought a tingle to Libby's core. "If I come back to bed, we won't be going back to sleep."

Libby smiled. "That's all right, too."

He swept a few strands of hair from her face and tucked them behind her ear. "You should rest. Today's going to be a long one, with all the decorating and the dance tonight. We'll have the rest of our lives together."

Libby stilled. What did he mean?

Matt's gaze flickered down to his bronzed hand, which rested on the colorful quilt. His uncharacteristic nervousness sent anxiety racing through Libby.

"When you first came here you said you weren't interested in getting hitched," Matt began, "but I'm hoping you changed your mind. I mean, I know I haven't had much learning, and a sheriff doesn't have much to offer a woman besides a lot of worry."

Libby captured his apprehensive face between her palms. "What is it you're trying to say, Matt?"

He took a deep breath and raised his gaze to her. "I've admired you ever since you stepped off the stagecoach, and I been too stubborn to admit it until now. I'd be proud to call you my wife, if you'll have me. Libby, will you marry me?"

Her heart skipped a beat. Did she have the right to capture the happiness she'd never thought she'd possess even for a night? Could she forget the horrors Harrison had inflicted upon her and convince herself she wasn't a murderer? She could pretend her life started the day she stepped off the stagecoach in Deer Creek. The four-year marriage would cease to exist in her memory, and Matt would become her first and only true husband. She'd found in him a best friend, a considerate lover, and a compassionate man. He was the white knight she'd dreamed of as a young girl.

But what of her other dream? Would Matt allow her to work with Dr. Clapper? She'd forsaken her medical practice as Mrs. Harrison Thompson, and she'd learned she couldn't ignore the healer within her. She loved Matt, but she also possessed a gift to share.

She lowered her hands and clasped the blanket. "Before I give you my answer, I have to know one thing, Matt. Would you let me work with Dr. Clapper?"

"Why wouldn't I? He says you'd be a good nurse, and I know from personal experience he's right. I'd be proud to have my wife help with the doctoring."

The anvil weight lifted from Libby's shoulders. She believed him.

Dare she take the chance and become his wife?

The answer came like a breeze whispering through the trees.

Libby hugged him close. "Yes, I'll marry you."

Matt's strong arms tightened around her shoulders and the quilt slipped to her waist, revealing her firm breasts. Temptation enticed him to love her one more time before leaving, but he covered the alluring sight with the blanket. She had agreed to marry him, and the next time they shared a bed, she would be his in name also.

"I didn't think I'd ever get married again, but then I never expected to find anyone like you either," Matt said. "I'd like to set the date as soon as possible."

Libby smiled. "How about tomorrow?"

"Christmas day?"

"Is that too soon?"

Matt chuckled. "You're even more impatient than me. I was thinking of the first of the new year."

"We have to wait a week?"

The dismay in Libby's tone warmed Matt. "Lenore would shoot both of us if she didn't have time to get things organized."

Libby laughter shimmered like light through a prism. "You're right. January first it is."

"If you don't mind, I'd like to make the announcement tonight at the dance," Matt said hesitantly.

She frowned. "Why should I mind?"

Matt shrugged a shoulder. "Folks'll try to talk you out of getting yourself hooked up with someone like me."

"There's nothing anyone can say that'll convince me not to marry you. You've given me more than anyone could possibly imagine. I'm the luckiest woman in the world. I can't believe you truly love me."

"Believe it, angel eyes." He skimmed his hand

down her back, and paused. With light fingers, he discovered narrow bands of raised skin. Libby's body stiffened beneath his touch. His pulse thudded in his ears. If those marks were what he suspected. . . .

"Turn around, Libby," he said quietly.

"Why?"

"I want to see your back."

Libby's white face revealed her agitation. She attempted to smile, but the result resembled a grimace. "It's nothing, Matt. Just an accident I had a long time ago."

Empathy twisted his gut into knots. "You don't have to lie to me, Libby. Let me see."

She stared at him, her eyes sparkling like morning dew on a blade of grass. Reluctantly, she twisted her upper body and allowed Matt to view what he'd felt beneath his fingers.

Belt marks crisscrossed her back in four places. Matt's blood thundered in his veins. Who would hurt beautiful, gentle-hearted Libby? "Who did this?"

She remained silent.

Helpless anger clawed at his insides. "Dammit, Libby, who hurt you?"

Her neck bowed and her shoulders shuddered. Carefully, as if she were fragile china, he grasped her arms and straightened her. Tears tracked down her ivory cheeks, and protectiveness overwhelmed Matt. He embraced her, burying his face in her tangled auburn curls.

Suspicion rippled a new wave of rage through Matt. "Did the man who forced you do this?"

Libby nodded against him.

Matt swore and tightened his hold on her. "Is there anything else you haven't told me?"

"I don't want to talk about it. What happened is in the past. Can't we leave it there?" she replied in a muffled voice.

He understood her unwillingness to talk about the

attack, but Matt wanted to make someone pay for hurting her. The need for vengeance against the man who brutalized her boiled in his blood. He took a deep breath and pressed his lips to her hair.

"You don't have to be scared anymore, Libby," Matt vowed. "I'll protect you."

He stretched out on top of the quilt beside her, keeping her cushioned in his arms. She'd been scarred, too, but Matt worried more about the damage to her inner self than the marks on the outside. She'd sensed his hidden pain and healed him of his tortured memories. He wished he could do the same for her.

He knew only one way to achieve his goal, and he already possessed the tool he needed: he'd love her every day for the rest of his life.

Chapter 16

Libby awakened for the second time that morning and found herself alone. The sunshine through a frosted pane of glass made her realize it was nearly midmorning. Soon people would arrive to prepare the schoolhouse for the evening's festivities.

She bounced out of bed, groaning at the stiffness of her thighs. The recollection of the intimacies she'd shared with Matt brought a glow to her insides that minimized the discomfort. She'd finally discovered why most married people were so happy. And why they missed their companion so terribly. She loved Matt even more for merely holding her in his arms until she'd fallen asleep in the early morning.

Quickly, Libby washed up and dressed in a blue calico dress, forsaking her usual drab wear. Her light mood refused to allow somber clothing to camouflage her newfound joy. She braided her hair into one thick plait that hung to her waist. Pinching her cheeks, she wondered if anyone would see a difference in her. She laughed softly. Lenore would. And the older woman would bask in smug satisfaction at the upcoming nuptials.

Libby thought of Dylan, and how excited he'd be to learn the three of them could live together as a family.

A ready-made family. Contentment swelled within

Libby. She was grateful Harrison hadn't gotten her pregnant, yet she sometimes wondered if the fault had been hers. Her monthly had always arrived on schedule, but perhaps something in her prevented conception. Despite her knowledge of the human body, she didn't know if she'd ever be able to give Matt children.

The possibility terrified Libby. She didn't think she was strong enough to release the love she'd just found. She refused to ponder the situation any further. It was Christmas Eve, and she had a busy day ahead of her.

The sound of voices announced the arrival of those who'd volunteered to help decorate. She wiped her palms against her skirt pleats and went to meet them.

The morning passed swiftly, and by noon the work was completed and everyone had left. The classroom was adorned with a ten-foot pine tree, decorated with homemade ornaments and strings of popcorn and wild berries. The desks had been pushed against the walls, and a nativity scene was set up in a front corner. As Libby rehearsed the children's program in her mind, her stomach fluttered with anxiety. She hadn't been so nervous since she'd taken her final medical exam.

"Sure don't look like a schoolroom anymore."

Libby turned at the sound of Matt's voice. She tilted her head back and gazed up at his handsome face. The memory of the night heated her face, and her heart constricted with newfound love. He held his hat in his gloved hands, his eyes twinkling. He appeared more relaxed than she'd ever seen him.

"Hello, Matt," she greeted shyly.

"Is that any kind of welcome for a man—from his soon-to-be wife?"

He opened his arms, and Libby entered their welcoming embrace. She inhaled his familiar scent. He raised her chin with his forefinger and kissed her lips lightly. "How did the morning go?"

Libby smiled and motioned to the room with her hand. "Everyone pitched in and got it done in no time at all." She gazed up at his eyes, feeling she could lose herself in their adoring depths. "I missed you."

"I missed you, too. Dylan and I went out to find a tree for Lenore, and we put it up in her parlor. She sent me over here to fetch you for dinner."

"Sounds wonderful."

She hurried to the back room to retrieve her hooded cloak, and they stepped out into the crisp cold. When Matt took her hand, she wrapped her fingers around his secure hold.

He guided her around a pile of horse droppings in the street. "What do you think of us adopting Dylan after we're married?"

She smiled. "I was hoping you'd want to."

Matt grinned. "So you'd already thought about it?"

Libby nodded. "He needs a stable home, and we already love him. I hope his mother doesn't make things too difficult."

"If I know Sadie, she will. We have to be prepared to fight for him."

Libby moved closer to Matt. "We'll do it together."

Comfortable silence surrounded her, and she absorbed Matt's loving attentiveness like a bee drinking a flower's nectar. He opened the door to the boarding-house, and the fragrance of pine and apples brought happy memories tumbling out of their hiding places.

Dylan skidded to a stop in front of them. "Hi, Miss O'Hanlon."

Libby squatted down and hugged the boy. "Hello, Dylan. I hear you and the sheriff have been busy this morning."

"We went out in the woods and chopped down a tree. Mrs. Potts said we could decorate it this afternoon. I've never decorated a Christmas tree before."

"You'll enjoy it, sweetheart."

Lenore bustled into the entry. "Come on in and

hang your wraps up. I kept lunch warm. How did the decking-out go, over at the school? Did you get the place all spruced up? I was going to come over, but I been baking all morning, getting goodies ready for tonight."

Matt chuckled. "Calm down Lenore, or your tongue's going to lasso your lips and you won't be able to do any jawing tonight. Course, that way someone else might be able to get a word in edgewise."

Playfully, Lenore slapped Matt's arm. "What's got you in such a chipper mood?"

Matt shrugged innocently, his hair brushing his collar. "It's Christmas Eve. Isn't that a good enough reason?"

He winked at Libby.

Lenore wagged a finger at him. "I can smell a skunk in the coop. What's going on?"

Dylan sniffed. "I don't smell a skunk, Mrs. Potts."

Laughter rang in the foyer and the boy looked at them, puzzled.

Lenore placed a chubby hand on Dylan's shoulder. "It's just a saying, honey. What do you say we have some chicken and dumplings?"

"As long as there isn't no skunk in it," Dylan said solemnly.

Matt smothered his amusement. "I'm not partial to skunks myself, partner."

Lenore linked her arm through Libby's crooked elbow. "Come on, dear. Those two'll come when they get hungry enough."

After eating, they moved into the parlor. Boxes containing ornaments littered the floor. With little encouragement, Libby, Matt, and Dylan set to work trimming the tree.

An hour later, Libby stepped back to admire their handiwork and her attention focused on Dylan, perched on Matt's broad shoulders. In Dylan's small hand was an angel fashioned from white yarn and pieces of silk and velvet. He reached forward and placed the cherub on the evergreen's top spire.

Libby clapped. "Good job, Dylan."

Matt bent down and Libby swung Dylan to the floor. Matt wrapped his arm around Libby's waist and she leaned against his solidness, her hand resting on Dylan's back. She hadn't celebrated Christmas since she'd married Harrison, and had avoided the resurrection of joy-filled childhood memories. Icy fingers of desolation had circled her heart the past four years, but now sunshine lit up her soul. Matt had given her the best present she could have wished for: the renewed belief in miracles.

Lenore entered the room with a tray of gingerbread cookies and set the platter on the small table. She planted her fists on her ample hips. "Now, there's a right nice sight. Dylan, why don't you run into the kitchen and get yourself some milk to have with these cookies?"

Dylan nodded and trotted out of the parlor.

"So when's the wedding day?" Lenore asked without preamble.

Libby's mouth gaped. "How did you know?"

"It's as obvious as the nose on your face." Her round face split with a wide smile. "Why, I told Eli the other night, I'd eat my petticoats if you two didn't get hitched by spring. Course, he didn't believe me. He told me to stop meddling, but that'd be like asking a bear not to scratch. Besides, I knew you two would be good for each other."

"We're planning on the first," Matt said.

"When you two make a decision, you sure don't lollygag about. Next week! Heavens to Betsy, I'll never have enough time to get everything organized. I've got to make a cake, send out the word and get folks to bring something for the dinner afterward, make sure the musicians get there. Goodness, and we can't forget about a wedding dress!"

"Calm down, Lenore. We don't plan on having a large wedding. Right, Matt?" Libby glanced at him.

His lips twitched. "As long as you're there, it's big enough for me."

"But the whole town will want to come see the sheriff and the schoolteacher get hitched. I bet you even Adelaide Beidler will want to come. Lord knows, she wouldn't want to miss a chance to spread some gossip." Lenore enfolded Libby in a motherly embrace. "Congratulations, honey. You're getting the second-best man in all of Deer Creek."

She released her and Libby grinned. "We're hoping to adopt Dylan once we're married."

"Of course you would." Lenore plucked a linen handkerchief from the valley between her bountiful breasts and dabbed her eyes. "I'm so happy for you."

Dylan came into the room. "What's wrong, Mrs. Potts? Why are you crying?"

"Because I got some wonderful news."

Matt went to Dylan and squatted down in front of him. "Remember when we talked about the three of us living together?"

The boy nodded. "You said we couldn't because you two weren't married."

"That's right, but we've changed our minds. Miss O'Hanlon and I are going to get married—then you can live with both of us."

"You mean like a real family?" Dylan asked.

Libby joined them. "Would that be all right with you?"

"Yippee!" He wrapped one skinny arm around Libby's neck and the other around Matt, pulling them into a tight circle. "I'll be just like the other kids." Dylan drew back and his thin face sobered. "What about my ma? Won't she be mad?"

Matt nodded. "She won't be happy about you living with us and she might try to fight it, but we're going to make it all legal so she can't ever take you back."

Anguish shadowed his eyes, and his lower lip trembled. "Will she hit me?"

Libby empathized with his anxiety. She'd gained her freedom because she'd been driven to murder, but Sadie's presence would be a continual reminder of Dylan's past. "She's still your mother and you'll see her around town. If you want to talk to her, make sure the sheriff or I are with you. We won't let her hurt you again."

Dylan glanced at Matt.

"Don't look so worried, partner," Matt reassured. "Things'll work out."

The unease slid from the boy's features. "When can we be a family?"

Libby smiled up at Matt. "One more week."

"Not nearly enough time," Lenore muttered. "Come sit and have some gingerbread, and we can start making plans."

The schoolhouse rang with voices and laughter from the milling crowd. The holiday fragrances of cinnamon and pine were underscored by a potpourri of perfumed water and hair tonic. Colorful dresses added rainbow splashes to the gaily decorated room. It appeared most of the townspeople had come out to celebrate Christmas Eve.

Standing beside a table laden with food, Libby ran a nervous hand down her close-fitting jade silk basque and smoothed the matching skirt over her hips. Wearing a red dress that gave her the appearance of a ripe tomato, Lenore approached Libby.

"I knew that dress would look beautiful on you. You don't need any of those fancy flounces or bows with that figure of yours," Lenore remarked.

"Thank you, but I shouldn't have accepted it. It must have cost dearly."

Lenore flapped a pudgy hand. "It's your Christmas

present, and you would've hurt my feelings if you hadn't taken it."

Libby gave Lenore a quick hug. "Thank you."

"You're welcome for the hundredth time. Now relax and enjoy yourself. Matt should be here anytime now."

Libby sighed. "He said he'd be here at seven-thirty. I wish he could have come earlier."

"Eli said Matt had a few things to do at the jailhouse."

Libby grinned wryly. "I'm acting like a silly school-girl."

Lenore shook her head. "Nope, like a woman in love with her man."

The buzz of voices dwindled to a few murmurs and Libby glanced up. Matt had arrived. Everyone in the room faded into obscurity as her attention focused on the powerfully built man. A black broadcloth coat spanned his wide shoulders, and matching trousers hugged his muscular legs. His rugged face appeared hesitant, and Libby sensed his discomfort. His veiled gaze searched the room and lit upon her. His features relaxed.

Lenore gave Libby a gentle shove. "Well, go on over to him and really give Mrs. Beidler something to talk about."

Although the noise in the room increased, Libby knew she was the focus of attention.

"Good evening, Sheriff," she greeted formally.

"Howdy, Miss O'Hanlon," Matt said with a Texas drawl. His admiring gaze traveled down her figure and settled on her face. "Mighty fine-looking duds you're wearing tonight."

"Thank you. You look pretty dapper yourself. Why don't you take off your hat?"

Matt plucked the brown Stetson from his head and hung it on a nearby peg. A tawny curl spilled across his weathered forehead, and Libby resisted the impulse to brush back the unruly lock. His eyes glittered, as if he could read her mind.

He laid a firm hand against her spine and ushered her through the throng; a swath opened for them to pass.

"Howdy Matt," a deep voice greeted.

Matt paused and shook the blacksmith's monstrous hand. "Merry Christmas, Harley." He turned to the petite woman beside him. "Mrs. Davis."

"Hello Sheriff, Miss O'Hanlon," Janie Davis said, a twinkle in her hazel eyes. She turned to Libby. "You know, Harley always threatened to haul the sheriff to these shindigs, but looks like things might be different now."

Matt shrugged. "There might be a change or two in the air."

Harley grinned broadly and slapped Matt's back. "Glad to hear it."

Mrs. Davis turned to Libby. "Are you still interested in one of Beauty's puppies?"

She nodded.

"They should be old enough in a couple weeks to leave their mother."

"Could I bring Dylan by tomorrow to pick one out?" Libby asked.

"That'd be fine," Mrs. Davis assured. "He'll get first choice."

"Thank you."

Matt and Libby moved past the Davises.

"What's this about a pup?" Matt asked, his lips close to Libby's ear.

His warm breath fanned across her neck and a delightful shiver rippled through her. "When I heard their dog had puppies, I asked Mrs. Davis if I could have one for Dylan as a Christmas present."

"You're going to make him one happy little boy."

"I hope so. He deserves some happiness."

They joined Eli. "I hear congratulations are in

order," he said, and shook Matt's hand. "Lenore was near busting with the news by the time I got back to town this evening. It's about killing her to keep quiet until you make the announcement."

"Thanks, Eli. She'll have to hold the secret a little longer," Matt said. "Where'd you go today?"

"Out to Flanagans'. Their youngest boy fell through the ice on the pond."

Libby glanced at Matt and back at Eli. "Another case of pneumonia?"

The doctor shook his head. "There's no congestion in his lungs, and only a slight fever."

"That's good. Had his body temperature fallen?"

"Some, but by the time I left it was normal. I told them to keep him warm and quiet for a day."

"If you're busy this week, I can go out and check on him," Libby volunteered.

Eli smiled. "That'd be fine." He peered at Matt. "You going to mind Libby coming and going to help with the sick folks?"

Matt smiled, a hint of pride in his rugged face. "Nope. I think she'll make a right fine nurse."

Would he be so supportive if he knew she was a doctor? Instinctively, Libby knew he would approve. She wanted to hug him. The people surrounding them restrained her impulse. She made a silent promise to properly thank him later.

"When does the program start?" Eli asked.

"In twenty minutes. I'd better go see how the children are doing." She took a deep breath. "Wish me luck."

Matt feathered a light kiss across her cheek. "Good luck, angel eyes."

Heat suffused Libby's face and she hurried away.

Half an hour later, Libby stood at the front of the classroom, watching the nativity scene played out by her students. Her stomach knotted and she forced herself to unclench her fists.

Jacob Olson, as Joseph, stuck a foot out to trip Seth, but the wise man stepped over the outstretched ankle and shot Jacob a dirty glare. Emily Windham's angel halo slipped to the side, and hung at a ninety-degree angle for most of the play. Six-year-old Micah Sattler tripped on his robe, nearly flattening baby Jesus in the cradle. Dylan, however, performed his role as a shepherd perfectly, keeping his expression somber to match the reverence of the event.

The program ended with the children singing "Silent Night," and applause filled the classroom. As the students bowed in unison, pride flooded Libby. Her eyes misted. She would miss teaching; the realization surprised her.

She glanced at Matt and caught his wink. She smiled back, contentment replacing her momentary sadness. She would have Matt and Dylan, and maybe God would see His way to bless them with their own children.

As parents crowded around Libby, she accepted their congratulations with heartfelt happiness. Then, excusing herself from the middle of the group, she hurried to Matt's side. Dylan stood close to the sheriff.

A lank of hair fell across the boy's forehead and Libby finger-combed the strands back. "You were wonderful, Dylan."

His blue eyes sparkling, he said, "It was fun pretending to be somebody else. I'm going to go eat with Lester." He dashed away to join the blacksmith's son.

"I'm a little hungry myself," Matt admitted.

"Now that the program's over, I'm starving."

Matt guided Libby to the tables heaped with food. They filled their plates and found a corner to sit. Libby basked in the warmth of Matt's presence, her nerves vibrating with awareness of his masculinity. She gazed at his mouth, remembering how his lips had devoured hers, and her own insatiable appetite.

"Maybe we should get married tonight," Matt commented.

Libby blinked. "What?"

Matt's roguish smile crinkled the corners of his twinkling eyes. "The way you're looking at me, I don't know if I can wait a full week."

Understanding dawned on Libby and her mouth quirked upward. "Who says we have to wait until we have a piece of paper?"

Matt shook his head firmly. "We'll wait until we're wed proper-like."

His resistance to her offer professed his love and respect for her. She wrapped her fingers around Matt's strong hand and squeezed it gently. "You're right."

She finished her meal and glanced up to see Mrs. Beidler headed their way.

"We've got trouble coming," she said softly to Matt.

He looked up and swore.

Mrs. Beidler stalked toward them, her crimson hat bobbing on her bird-nest coiffure. Libby braced herself for the storm.

"I thought you'd at least have the decency to stay away from Miss O'Hanlon after all the talk, Sheriff," the bandy-legged biddy hissed.

"The only talk there was came from you, Mrs. Beidler," Matt said.

The stuffy woman's red face matched her pretentious bonnet. "I never . . ."

"That's right, you haven't, Mrs. Beidler. If I choose to court Miss O'Hanlon and she agrees, I don't think that's any business of yours." Matt drew Libby close to his side.

Libby encircled his waist with her arm. "I'm flattered to have Matt take an interest in me."

Mrs. Beidler's adam's apple bobbed. "Now I know

you have lost all sense, Miss O'Hanlon. I will speak to my husband about your dismissal."

Libby smiled sweetly. "No need, Mrs. Beidler. I quit."

The older woman's mouth dropped open, making her resemble a frog catching flies. "But you can't!"

"Why not?"

"Because—because I was going to fire you."

Libby shrugged. "I'm sorry I spoiled your fun."

Matt's body shook with repressed laughter. "I'm not sorry."

Mrs. Beidler clamped her mouth shut and spun away.

"I almost feel sorry for her," Libby said.

Matt snorted. "Don't. She's never spared a drop of compassion for anyone."

The musicians started up a toe-tapping tune.

"May I have the pleasure of this dance, Miss O'Hanlon?" Matt asked gallantly.

"I'd be honored, Sheriff Brandon."

Matt led Libby to the middle of the room, where they joined the other couples. He danced with an ease that surprised Libby. Secure in his strong grasp, she followed his lead and relaxed. The music flowed through her, and Matt's hand warmed her waist through the silk and petticoats. Enveloped in the cocoon of his protective arms, Libby forgot about everyone but her future husband.

She lost count of the times she and Matt danced. When the small band took a break, Matt escorted her to a chair. "I'll get us some punch," he said.

Libby brushed back a spiraled tress that had escaped the loose chignon at the base of her neck. She'd always hated the corkscrew curls of her fiery hair, but Matt didn't seem to mind.

A few minutes later Matt returned with two cups of punch. Handing one to Libby, he sipped the other.

"I see the men are gathered around the other punch bowl. Did you want to join them?" she asked.

Matt shook his head. "I haven't touched a drop of liquor in three years. I don't see any reason to start now. Besides, I think it's time we made our announcement."

Libby's stomach did a somersault, and she trembled with excitement. She stood, placing her hand on his forearm. The firm muscles beneath her fingers telegraphed strength, and she smiled up at him. "I'm more than ready."

Matt led her to the musicians' slight platform.

"Excuse me. Can I get everyone's attention? I have an announcement to make," he called out.

The room hushed, and curious gazes fell upon them. Libby struggled to remain still and not squirm like a child in church.

"I'm proud to announce, Miss O'Hanlon has agreed to become my wife," he stated. He grasped Libby's hand. "We're to be married next Sunday."

Deer Creek's citizens surged forward to congratulate them, and Libby accepted their good wishes with a warm smile. As she glanced over the crowd, she noticed a figure shadowed in the doorway. An icy sliver of foreboding slithered down her back. The man stepped into the lanterns' light, and Libby's heart jerked. Shock froze the scream in her throat.

The ghost of Harrison Thompson glided toward her.

Chapter 17

❦

A s Libby tensed, Matt followed her unblinking gaze. The stranger he'd seen at Sadie's approached. Libby's freckles were stark against her white face.

"What's wrong?" Matt asked in a low voice.

She continued to stare at the newcomer as if he were the devil himself.

"What is it?"

Libby didn't appear to hear his question. He took hold of her arms and forced her to look at him. "Do you know him?"

Libby struggled to escape. "It can't be. He's dead!"

The townspeople closest to Matt and Libby stared in avid curiosity.

"What're you talking about?" Matt demanded.

The expensively suited man broke through the throng of well-wishers. "I think she's talking about me."

Matt scowled at the tenderfoot. "Who the hell are you?"

"My name is Harrison Thompson, and you, sir, are holding my wife."

Disbelieving anger infused Matt, but outwardly he remained unruffled. "All right folks, go on back to what you were doing. I'll handle this."

He led the too-silent Libby from the platform, motioning for the band to start up. The fiddler complied, and music masked the uncomfortable silence. Matt guided Libby and Thompson to the back room. He settled Libby in a straightback chair and turned to Thompson. "I hate to tell you this mister, but this here is Miss Libby O'Hanlon, my betrothed, not your wife."

Thompson chuckled. "Come, come Mister—"

"Sheriff Brandon."

"A sheriff this time." Thompson stared down at Libby with a pitying look. "Poor woman, quite insane."

Unease rippled down Matt's spine. "What're you talking about?"

"She has a somewhat sensitive problem, which I do hate to reveal, but I suppose I must." He took a deep breath. "Elizabeth cannot be satisfied by one man."

Libby gasped and shook her head. "That's not true."

Her outburst captured Matt's attention, and he watched her as Thompson continued.

"She has taken many lovers since I married her four years ago. The latest incident was when I caught her with my foreman. I locked her in her room, hoping confinement would cure her. Four months ago she escaped and tried to kill me. While I lay unconscious, she ran away."

Matt glanced away from Libby's pale face. "You're the one who's crazy. Libby ain't married. Now get the hell out of here, before I throw you in jail for disturbing the peace."

"If you must toss someone into a cell, perhaps it should be your 'Miss O'Hanlon' for attempted murder." Thompson's voice cut like a razor's edge.

"Libby couldn't harm a fly, much less kill a man. I don't know who you are, mister, but you sure as hell ain't her husband."

"Why don't you ask Elizabeth?"

"No reason to. I know you're lying."

"Ask her."

Matt looked at Libby. She stared at the man who proclaimed to be her husband with wide, fear-filled eyes. He took a step closer to her side to protect her from Thompson's ravings. "Look Thompson or whoever the hell you are, I want you out of here. Now."

"Are you afraid of the answer, Sheriff?"

Matt clenched his teeth and stared at Thompson a full minute. He leaned over Libby. "Libby. Libby, do you hear me?"

She blinked and turned to gaze at Matt. "I'm sorry. I ruined everything."

Doubt flitted through him, but he thrust the emotion aside. Libby wouldn't have lied to him. She wasn't Rachel. He covered her trembling hand with his, and spoke softly. "There's nothing for you to be sorry about. I'll get rid of him."

Her slender fingers curled around his wrist.

Matt turned his anger back on Thompson. "Get the hell out of here before I break you in two."

The fancy-dressed man reached into his coat and withdrew a folded piece of paper. This is our marriage certificate. We were wed on September second, eighteen sixty-six in Ohio."

Ohio. Libby had said she'd come from Ohio. Matt's gaze swept across the paper, wishing Eli were there to read the words to him. He squinted at the cursive and recognized the word marriage. Uncertainty returned, but the need to believe Libby was too strong. "You could've picked this up anywhere."

"But I didn't," Thompson said impatiently. "That woman is Elizabeth Thompson, and she is my lawful wife."

Matt's mind raced. Who would've created such an elaborate sham?

Sadie. She had staged the hoax to get back at him

and Libby for taking Dylan. "What were you doing at Sadie's place the other night?"

The man blinked, off balance for the first time since he'd appeared. He regained his equilibrium and feigned a smile. "I had just arrived in town after a long tedious journey, and my needs were more than I wished to inflict upon Elizabeth. Surely you can understand that, Sheriff."

Matt shook his head. "No, I don't. Especially since you consider your so-called wife a whore."

Thompson's expression froze. "Despite her condition, I continue to treat her as a lady. She is the woman I married."

"Why'd you wait two days to claim her?"

"I wasn't certain she was here in this town. I just learned today she would be here this evening."

"Folks usually come check with me if they're looking for someone. Why didn't you?"

Thompson's face reddened and he seemed to struggle with his temper. "You are stalling, Sheriff. That woman is my wife, and I demand that you hand her over to me this instant."

He moved toward Libby and Matt stepped between them. "Stay away from her," he warned.

"I'm merely going to ask the question which you seem unable to." He turned to Libby. "Are you Elizabeth Thompson?"

Libby's haunted gaze moved to Matt and sidled away, unable to meet his eyes. Two tears rolled down her wan cheeks.

Her silence damned her more than any words she could've spoken. Matt's fingers clenched into a fist, and he slammed the tabletop. Ignoring the pain that raced up his arm, he stooped over Libby, his face an inch from hers. "Why?"

Her eyelids flickered open. "I thought I'd killed him." Libby jumped out of her chair and reached for

Matt. "I was—am—his wife, but the other things . . . I swear, they're not true!"

He wanted to trust her. With trembling hands, he clasped her shoulders. "Tell me the truth, Libby. If you want to stay here with me and Dylan, we'll find a way."

Thompson grabbed Matt's arm. "Take your filthy hands off my wife."

Matt glared at the suited man. "You want to lose that hand, Thompson?"

As Matt's unflinching gaze speared Thompson, the wealthy man released him.

Thompson turned to Libby. "You are mine, Elizabeth. And you're coming with me."

Libby recognized the barely controlled rage in his voice, and the familiar insanity glowing in his eyes. Terror shivered down her spine. Harrison would have no qualms killing Matt if he stood in his way.

"Do you love him?" Matt's question drew her attention.

I hate him with every breath I take.

She loved Matt as much as she despised Harrison, and for that reason she couldn't risk his life—but she couldn't deceive him any further. Though her knees trembled, her gaze held steady to Matt's probing scrutiny. "I have to leave Deer Creek because of love, Matt."

He flinched, and the angles in his craggy face sharpened. He stared at her for a long moment, then disgust filled his features. "I hope you have many happy years together."

Harrison's smile oozed. "Don't feel too badly, Sheriff. You're not the first one she's fooled."

Matt spun around and barreled out of the small room like the hounds of hades were at his heels.

"You did very well, Elizabeth. You should have been an actress, superbly performing the role of loving wife," Harrison said.

Libby could barely stand to look at him. "I hate you."

Dylan appeared in the doorway, his step hesitant and his thin face pinched. "Miss O'Hanlon?"

Libby forced a smile to her stiff lips. "What is it, sweetheart?"

"What's wrong? Why'd the sheriff leave?"

Libby glanced at Harrison, hiding the revulsion his appearance produced. "I'd like to speak to Dylan alone."

Harrison eyed the boy with distaste. "I don't see—"

"Please." She hated to plead, but she had no choice.

"All right, but only for a minute. I wish to get back to *our* hotel room."

He strutted out, leaving Libby swallowing the bitter gall his words wrought. She drew Dylan further into the room and knelt in front of him, taking his small hands in hers. "That man, he's my husband. He's come to take me back with him."

Dylan frowned. "But you and the sheriff are going to get married, and we're going to be a family."

Libby shook her head, fighting tears. "I'm sorry, Dylan. I didn't know he was still alive. If I had known, I wouldn't have come to Deer Creek. You have to understand that if I could, I'd stay here with you and the sheriff, but I can't."

"Why can't you tell that man to go back home and you stay here with us?"

"I wish it were that simple, but he's my husband. I have to go with him."

"What if the sheriff was your husband instead?"

"Then I'd stay here forever and ever." Libby swept a few strands of hair from Dylan's forehead. "But as much as we wish it, I can't ever marry the sheriff as long as I'm already married." She managed another smile. "But you still get to live with the sheriff, and the two of you will be a family. He loves you."

Tears filled the boy's eyes. "But I don't want you to go! Please, Miss O'Hanlon, stay with us."

Libby hugged Dylan and he wrapped his arms around her neck. "I can't." Her voice was thick with tears. "I'm going to miss you very much, sweetheart."

"Isn't this a charming picture?" Harrison's droll tone angered Libby, but she held her temper for Dylan's sake.

She eased the boy out of her embrace. "You be good for Lenore."

He nodded, drawing his forearm across his eyes. "I love you, Miss O'Hanlon."

Before Libby could reply to his unexpected declaration, he was gone.

Harrison's thin lips twisted into a sneer. "Isn't that the whore's son?"

Unable to speak past the lump in her throat, Libby ignored his question and stood. She clutched the folds of her gown and raised her chin.

"It's time we depart, Elizabeth." Harrison guided Libby out into the classroom.

Conversations ceased and gazes swiveled in her direction, but she refused to meet the curious stares. Through a haze of misery, she donned her heavy cape.

"Is it true, honey? Is that stiff-necked dandy your husband?" Lenore asked.

Libby couldn't ignore her trusted friend. "Yes."

"Why?"

She clasped Lenore's hands, tears burning in her eyes. "I thought he was dead."

Harrison wrapped his arm around Libby's shoulders, forcing her away from Lenore. "Come, Elizabeth."

"We'll talk later, honey," Lenore said.

Nodding, Libby allowed Harrison to lead her out of the schoolhouse.

* * *

Dylan shrugged into his coat, not bothering to button it up. He slipped out the back door and followed Miss O'Hanlon and her husband. Dylan didn't like the gussied-up man; he had mean snake eyes. He couldn't understand why Miss O'Hanlon had married someone like him.

He stayed far enough behind them that he wouldn't be caught spying. Miss O'Hanlon's husband shoved her roughly onto the boardwalk, and Dylan nearly ran over to help her. But the man grabbed her arm and pulled her into the fancy hotel. Dylan stood outside the building for a moment, wondering how he could sneak in. Cracking open the door, he noticed the clerk had his back to him, and Dylan shot inside and up the stairs.

A door closed at the end of the hall, and he tiptoed toward it. Miss O'Hanlon's voice inside confirmed that it was the right room. He pressed his ear against the wood and listened.

"Can you believe this is the best room in this sorry excuse for a hotel?" her husband said.

"How did you find me?" Miss O'Hanlon's voice sounded scared.

"Pinkerton's. You made it so simple by using your mother's maiden name. I almost hated to pay them for such an easy task. Remove your wrap, Elizabeth."

"No."

Dylan could hear the man's sigh. "It looks like I will have to remind you of your position as my wife."

"You lay one hand on me and I'll scream."

Dylan's fingers curled into tight fists. If the man hurt Miss O'Hanlon . . .

"I've waited four months. I can wait another few days," her husband stated.

"I'm going to file for a divorce."

The man's laugh sounded as hateful as Dylan's mother's, and he shivered with terror.

"Don't be silly, Elizabeth." Her husband's voice

was mean. "I'll never let you go. You'll pay for what you did to me the rest of your life. However long—or short—that will be."

"You won't get away with it. I'll tell the sheriff and he'll help me."

"I doubt that. Your Sheriff Brandon won't believe anything you tell him now. Still, perhaps you need a bit of an incentive, my dear. Perhaps—the life of the whore's bastard?"

"You wouldn't!"

"I would do anything to keep you, my dear. Remember this, Elizabeth: if I'm forced to kill him, his death will be on your conscience. And for good measure, I would also shoot your boorish sheriff."

Dylan gasped and pressed his knuckles against his mouth. If the man would kill them, he would hurt Miss O'Hanlon, too.

What could he do? He had to help her.

The sheriff—he would know what to do.

Dylan scurried down the hall, his heart pounding in his chest.

"You bastard," Libby hissed.

Harrison grabbed a handful of hair and yanked downward, forcing Libby's head back. "I can see we'll have to work on your manners."

His oily gaze slid down her body, and with his free hand he opened her cape. Staring at her décolletage, his nostrils flared. He cupped her breast in his palm, twisting the nipple through the silky material.

"Let me go!" Libby cried.

He ignored her plea. "I want to know what happened between you and Sheriff Brandon."

"Nothing you'd understand."

Harrison raised his hand to strike her.

"Go ahead, hit me," Libby dared. "Then try to explain the bruises on my face."

His jaw tightened. "Damn you, Elizabeth. Once we're away from this place, I shall mete out your punishment accordingly."

Calm acceptance flowed through Libby. Not even a ripple of the familiar fear accompanied Harrison's threats. She'd been scared for so long, but she'd endured and was stronger for it.

Harrison eyed her coldly. "Consider the fate of the whore's bastard and your erstwhile lover before you say anything further, Elizabeth. Whether they live or die depends on you."

Icy fear slid through her. She'd been so wrong. She still had too much to lose.

"Remove your clothing, Elizabeth, or I will remove them for you."

Libby fumbled with the buttons, and Harrison impatiently slapped her hands aside. He ripped her blouse open and she drew her arms free of the sleeves. Her skirt whispered down her hips, pooling at her feet. After taking off her shoes, she remained motionless, feeling his seething gaze slither across her body.

His fingers moved to his belt, and he removed it with deliberate motions. An involuntary shudder passed through Libby.

"Get on the bed." He punctuated the command with the snap of the leather strap against her thighs.

Libby flinched but didn't cry out. She did as he ordered. He could only violate her body, not the soul hidden beneath the flesh.

"Open your eyes, Elizabeth. I want you to watch."

Ensconced in her safe haven, his strident voice merely rippled over her. He grabbed her shoulders and shook her. He slapped her face, the crack resounding in the small room. Head thrust to the side, Libby tasted coppery blood. He backhanded her other cheek. She wouldn't fight him. He wouldn't win this time.

"Damn you, Elizabeth! Why aren't you scared?"

He would be disappointed. She'd endured many forms of torment; there was little he hadn't done before.

He panted above her, and Libby could sense his frustration. Without her usually terrified participation, he couldn't satisfy his perversion.

He moved off the bed and she opened her eyes. A moment later, he rolled her to her side and drew her hands together. Using two silk neckties, Harrison tied her wrists behind her back and bound her ankles. Adrenaline surged, and Libby's taut nerves screamed in resistance. Her instincts warned her to escape the madman, but that was what he craved. Forcing herself to breathe evenly, she gazed over Harrison's shoulder and concentrated on a dark stain on the wall.

He gagged her with a white handkerchief, then dug in his traveling bag once more and withdrew a bottle of expensive brandy. He unrolled a piece of clothing and a snifter appeared. "A person of good breeding never drinks liquor from the bottle."

Libby stared at him. He'd always been insistent on maintaining the highest level of decorum, except when they were alone. Now he seemed obsessed with his twisted version of gentility. Had the blow she'd dealt him worsened his madness?

Harrison splashed some brandy into the delicate glass, swirled the liquid, and drank the contents in one gulp. He repeated the procedure again and again.

"You've ruined everything," he accused with a hint of a slur.

A bubble of hysteria arose in Libby, and she fought the sobbing laughter in her throat. He was the one who had ruined everything, including her life.

He aimed an unsteady finger at Libby. "You know how much I dislike it when you disobey me."

Libby clamped her teeth down on the gag. She knew

from experience how Harrison's viciousness increased a hundredfold when he drank.

He lit a cigar. The tobacco's acrid odor stung Libby's nose, and the smell bridged the gap between past and present. The old terror broke free of its chains. She whimpered and the sound startled her.

Harrison stood and stumbled to Libby's side. He clenched her chin between his thumb and forefinger, and moved the orange end of the cigar toward the slope of one of her breasts.

"You disappoint me, Elizabeth," he said, spewing his foul breath across her. He lowered the glowing ember to her chest, and Libby jerked beneath the piercing burn. Horrified by the new torment, she screamed, but the cloth muffled her cry.

Harrison studied the brand he'd imprinted on her. "As I lay in my bed recovering from your bungled attempt to kill me, I plotted ways to make you pay for your inexcusable behavior." He sighed. "Of course, I must wait until we've returned home, where we won't be disturbed." His lips twisted with an evil smile, and his glassy gaze settled on Libby. "I've become quite creative."

He squeezed her nipple between his cruel fingers and Libby retreated inside herself. Her eyelids closed, and she concentrated on blank peacefulness. Libby thought of Matt and imagined his touch, his scent, the sound of his gruff voice softened by love. The pain faded to oblivion and her husband ceased to exist. If she didn't acknowledge him, he couldn't hurt her.

As if through a long tunnel, Libby heard a hinge creak and Harrison's voice penetrated her inner sanctuary. "I have an appointment to keep, my dear. After that, perhaps I will give your uncouth sheriff his Christmas present."

The door clicked and blessed silence surrounded Libby. Relief flowed through her aching body. Her muscles relaxed and she drifted back into her world with Matt.

Matt.

My God, Harrison is going to kill Matt! Renewed terror surged through her, and she sat up and swung her feet to the cold floor. After the feeling returned to her lower limbs, she stood and hopped across the room. She turned with her back to the door, using her bound hands to twist the doorknob, but Harrison had locked her in. Tears of frustration blurred her vision.

She thrust her shoulder against the solid wood. She couldn't even pound loud enough for someone to hear her. Libby sat on the floor and kicked, but without her shoes she made little noise.

Hopelessness engulfed her. She had to warn Matt so he wouldn't be caught unaware by a bullet in the back, and she had to convince him Dylan was in danger, too. Matt may hate her, but she trusted him to protect the boy they both loved.

Libby pushed herself to a sitting position and leaned back against the wall beside the door. Dressed only in her undergarments, she shivered in the cold room and prayed someone would come down the hall before she froze to death.

Adding another log to the fireplace, Matt tried to keep his mind blank, but images of Libby invaded his thoughts. He pushed himself upright, and his gaze searched the silent corners of his cabin. He'd imagined Libby turning the house into a home, bringing laughter to chase away the emptiness. He had thought his painful loneliness had ended, and that he'd have children to carry on his name. His fingers curled into a tight fist, and he ached for a shot of whiskey to deaden the bitter taste of betrayal.

Wandering into his bedroom, he spotted the tiny

box on the nightstand and lifted the lid. Set in a gold band, a small emerald winked at him. The ring would have been Libby's Christmas gift.

Married. Jealousy boiled in Matt. The thought of Libby lying with her husband brought an overwhelming desire to strangle Thompson. Matt struggled to regain control of his murderous urge.

He dropped the square package on his disheveled bed, and cursed himself for a fool. The fool he was; the fool he'd always been.

Pounding at the door startled him, and he strode through the cabin. Throwing open the door, he was surprised to see Dylan, red-faced and panting. He quickly ushered the boy into the warmth.

"What're you doing out this late?" Concern roughened Matt's voice.

Dylan grabbed his arm. "I been looking all over for you. You gotta help her!"

"Who?"

"Miss O'Hanlon. That man's got her."

Matt hunkered down in front of the boy and took hold of his shoulders. "That man's her husband, Dylan. I can't take her away from him."

The boy appeared on the verge of tears. "But you have to. He's mean and he's gonna hurt her."

"How do you know that?"

"I followed them to the hotel and listened outside their room. I heard him say he'd kill you and me if Miss O'Hanlon tried to get away from him. And I think he was going to hurt her, like my ma hurt me."

Matt remembered the night he and Libby had made love. Her terror, and the scars on her back, had been real. Sickness churned in his gut. It was her own husband who'd beaten and raped her! Matt had promised to protect her, then he'd sent her straight into the arms of the monster who'd brutalized her.

I have to leave Deer Creek because of love.
The true meaning of her words struck him.
    She loved him, not Harrison—and she'd placed his life ahead of her own well-being.

Chapter 18

✦❞❝✦

"I want you to go to Lenore's and stay there, Dylan," Matt ordered.

"But I want to help Miss O'Hanlon."

"You already have. I'll bring her back to you, I promise."

Dylan studied him with solemn eyes, then nodded. "Okay."

He ushered the boy out of the cabin and sent him off toward Lenore's. Matt ran down the street, his boots slipping in the snow. He'd let Libby down; he prayed he wasn't too late to remedy his mistake. He barreled into the hotel and stopped at the clerk's desk. "Which room is Thompson in?"

The young man pressed his spectacles up on his pointed nose. "Mr. Thompson doesn't want anyone to disturb his wife. Especially not you, Sheriff."

Matt grabbed his shirt front and hauled him across the counter. "What number, Orville?"

The pasty-faced clerk pointed up the stairs with a shaking finger. "T-twelve."

Matt released him and raced up the staircase two steps at a time. He found the room, tried the knob and pounded on the door. "Open up or I'll kick it down!"

Listening for a moment, he heard a small whimper.

352

Matt drew his gun, raised his booted foot and kicked. The door frame splintered beneath the force of the blow, and he burst into the room. He spied Libby on the floor, his gaze taking in the dark bruise on her cheek, and an angry red mark the size of a silver dollar above her left breast.

He'd failed her.

"Libby." His heart pounded in his throat and his hand shook when he slid his revolver into the holster. Matt knelt beside her, removed the gag, and pulled her into his arms. "I'm sorry, God, I'm so sorry."

He cut the material from her raw wrists. A cold sweat chilled him, and he carefully sliced the rope holding her ankles. She'd pleaded with him to stay with her, to believe her; but he'd cast her aside.

He yanked off his coat and wrapped it around Libby with the warm inner lining against her clammy skin. "You feel like an ice block."

Libby's teeth chattered, but she shrugged aside his jacket. She flattened her hands against Matt's chest, desperation in her face. "He's going to k-kill you, b-both you and Dylan. You have to hide s-someplace where Harrison will never find you."

He pulled the top blanket off the bed and dragged it to the chair. He sat down, Libby in his lap, and covered her with the quilt. "Shhh, it's all right. A lot of folks have tried to get rid of me, but I'm still here."

"But Dylan—"

"I'll make sure he stays safe, too."

She wound her arms around his neck and sobbed, laying her head against his shoulder. "No matter how much you hated me, I knew you would take care of Dylan."

Matt pressed his lips tenderly against her forehead. "I couldn't hate you, sweetheart. Fact is, I could never stop loving you."

She sagged with relief, and rested her cheek against his chest. The heat from her battered face seared Matt through the layers of clothing. He damned himself for not believing in her. If he'd listened, he would have heard the abject fear in Libby's voice and seen the terror in her eyes.

"Why didn't you tell me?" he asked, his tone thick with concern.

She stiffened. "Tell you what?"

"That Thompson was the one who'd beaten you."

"Please, Matt, I don't want to talk about it."

He felt her breath fan across his neck. "Did he rape you again, Libby?"

"Harrison is my husband," she whispered hoarsely.

Gently, Matt framed her bruised face with his hands and raised her head. "Even husbands can violate their wives. No more lies between us, Libby. Did he rape you?"

Her eyes filled with moisture and she shook her head. "I wouldn't fight him, and he needs that before he can . . ." She swallowed. "Before he takes me."

Briefly, Matt closed his eyes in relief. At least she'd been spared that. "Where'd he go?"

"I don't know. He said he had an appointment to keep, but who would he know in Deer Creek?"

Matt swore. "Sadie. I saw Thompson with her the other night, though I didn't know who he was at the time."

A silvery tear slipped down her cheek. "I thought I killed him, Matt. I hit him over the head, and there was so much blood. I panicked. I didn't even check to see if he was still alive. I just got away as fast as I could."

Matt thumbed away the moisture trailing down her swollen face. "You were scared, sweetheart. There's no need for you to feel guilty. Listen to me—you had every right to protect yourself."

Footsteps pounded up the stairs, and Libby looked up, frightened.

"It's all right," Matt reassured. He shifted to pull

his gun out of its holster. He thumbed back the hammer, ready to defend Libby from the bastard he swore would never touch her again.

"Matt, Libby, where are you?" Lenore's voice sounded.

He slipped the revolver back into its place against his hip. "In here."

Lenore and Eli burst into the room. Lenore stopped to stare at Libby, and her hand flew to her mouth. "Oh, honey!"

"That son-of-a-bitch husband of hers did it," Matt said grimly.

"We know. Dylan told us," Eli spoke.

"Where is he?" Libby asked.

"At the boardinghouse," Lenore replied. "The same place you're going."

Matt stood with Libby cradled against his chest and gently set her in the chair. "You go with Lenore and get some rest. I'm going after Thompson."

Libby grabbed his arm. "Don't!"

"I have to, angel eyes." He leaned over and kissed her cool lips, then turned to Lenore. "Make sure she doesn't get away from you."

"I'll make sure she stays put, even if I have to sit on her," Lenore assured.

Matt glanced at Libby. Her pinched face brought a stab of self-recrimination. He sent Libby a terse nod and left.

A blaze of lights lit the interior of Sadie's house. He shoved open the door, pulling out his gun in one smooth motion. Upstairs, a man shouted and a woman screamed an obscenity.

A movement caught Matt's attention and he turned to see Becky, the young prostitute who'd helped Dylan, peek out from behind the kitchen door. He pressed his forefinger to his lips and crossed the distance between them.

"You seen a man called Thompson?" he asked.

Becky's blue eyes widened in terror. "You got to help Sadie, Sheriff. He's gonna kill her."

"Thompson?"

Becky nodded. "He dresses real fancy and acts like he's a king, but he's plain mean."

Even young Becky had seen the truth—why hadn't he?

"Where are the other girls?" Matt asked.

"In their rooms. They're scared to come out."

"Stay down here, out of the way."

"All right." Becky shrank back into the kitchen.

Matt slipped to the winding stairs and peered up from behind the baluster. He couldn't see anything, but the shrieks grew louder. He crept up the stairs, then froze at the top. The sounds of a struggle drew him toward a closed door. Keeping his back against the wall, Matt held his revolver in one hand and cautiously turned the knob, easing the door open a few inches.

Harrison Thompson grabbed Sadie by her hair and slapped her viciously. Matt had no liking for the madam, but the blood on her face and the front of her camisole brought a fleeting moment of pity. Thompson raised his fist and struck Sadie, who stumbled back. Her head cracked against the windowsill and she slumped to the floor, her neck at an odd angle.

Matt shoved the door open and stood framed in the entrance. "Hold it, Thompson. You're under arrest."

The man's surprise quickly turned to disdain. "Really, Sheriff, she's only a whore."

"Is that how you think of Libby, too, as 'only a whore'?" Matt's voice vibrated with fury.

Thompson drew his shoulders back. "Elizabeth is my *wife.*"

"Then why do you beat her? Aren't you man enough to love her the way a husband is supposed to love his wife?" Matt taunted.

Thompson's face flushed. "Our relationship is none of your concern, Brandon."

"You're dead wrong on that one, Thompson. I just came from the hotel. I found Libby freezing to death, tied up like some helpless lamb ready for slaughter. She told me everything."

Thompson's hands clenched at his sides. "I've told you she is a sick woman. She doesn't know the difference between the truth and a lie."

Matt shook his head in disgust. "You're the one who's sick. A man who can't be a man unless he beats the hell out of a woman."

"Ma!" Dylan's young voice rang out.

The boy dashed past a surprised Matt and fell to his knees beside his mother's still body. "Ma? Ma, wake up!" He looked up at Matt, his face grief-stricken. "You gotta help her. She's not breathing."

Matt wanted to pull the boy into his arms and comfort him, but he couldn't. Not with Thompson in the room. "She's dead, Dylan," he said as gently as he could.

A tear slid down the boy's cheek and he turned to Thompson. His sorrow changed to anger. "You killed her!"

Dylan attacked Thompson, but the man caught him, wrapping an arm around his neck. Dylan kicked ineffectually, and a tightening against his throat stilled his struggle. "Put down the gun, Sheriff, or I'll break the little bastard's neck."

Cold dread swept through Matt. He lowered his gun to the floor and raised his hands. "Let the boy go. He can't hurt you."

Thompson's smile, devoid of any warmth, chilled Matt. "Perhaps not, but his death would hurt Elizabeth."

Matt's lips curled into a snarl. "You hurt that boy and I'll track you to the ends of the earth."

"Not if you're dead, too." Thompson reached into his coat pocket and withdrew a nickel-plated derringer. He gestured Matt to move out of the way. "Back up."

Reluctantly, Matt took a few steps into the hall.

Thompson dragged a white-faced Dylan out of the room and to the top of the staircase, keeping his double-barreled gun trained on Matt. He cocked the hammer, and the ominous click echoed off the gaudy walls. "I'll give Elizabeth your regards, Brandon."

Dylan opened his mouth and bit down hard on the arm around his neck. Thompson swore, and shoved him away. Dylan struggled to maintain his balance, but lost the battle and toppled down the long flight of stairs.

Libby lowered her head against the onslaught of wind-driven snowflakes, and buried her hands in her coat pockets. Her bruised face was protected from the cold and hidden from curious gazes with a woolen scarf. She hunched her shoulders in an effort to keep her camisole from rubbing the raw burn above her breast.

After Lenore had escorted her to the boarding-house, Libby sought out Dylan. But the boy had disappeared, and she, Lenore, and Eli had begun to search for him.

Sadie's house loomed before her. Anxiety chipped away at Libby's courage, but the possibility of Dylan being inside chased away her apprehension.

A gunshot exploded from within and she jumped. Her heart thudding, she rushed into the house.

At the bottom of the stairs lay Dylan, his body too still, and his left leg twisted awkwardly. A dark wetness stained the lower leg of his trousers, and scarlet dyed the white rug beneath him. In her mind, she returned to Nebraska and stood with an iron poker in hand, staring down at Harrison's body. Her breath roared in her ears and she wrestled with the image from the past, forcing it to the black recesses of her memories.

She sank down beside the boy. "Dear Lord, no!" Not Dylan. Fear made her lightheaded and guilt washed over her.

Libby fumbled to remove her gloves and scarf. With shaking fingers, she searched for Dylan's pulse, but gave up and leaned over to lay her ear against his narrow chest. His heart pounded steadily and she breathed a sigh of relief.

Where was Matt? He'd promised to protect Dylan. The frightening thought triggered horrific images of Matt shot in the back, and icy tentacles of dread tightened around her soul.

"So nice of you to join the party, Elizabeth."

Libby's breath jammed in her throat, and she looked up to see Harrison at the top of the stairs. She followed his weapon's aim and gasped. Matt held his hand over his left arm; blood seeped between his fingers. The gunshot she'd heard had been for Matt, not Dylan.

"Is he still alive?" Matt's husky voice called down.

She nodded and ran her hand over Dylan's leg. A bone protruded from the skin. A shiver skidded down her back, and she rubbed her damp palms across her skirt. "He needs help. Are you all right?"

Matt grimaced. "It's only a flesh wound."

Libby looked at Harrison. "I have to get Dylan over to Dr. Clapper's office."

Harrison sneered. "You're a doctor. Why don't you help him?"

Surprise showed on Matt's face. "A doctor?"

Libby nodded but didn't explain. Harrison's callous indifference sparked her fury. "You pushed him down the stairs."

Harrison shrugged. "When an insect bites me, I get rid of the pest."

Libby scrambled to her feet and stood over Dylan protectively. "You're insane!"

"How many times have I told you not to be so emotional?"

Helplessness inundated Libby and she clenched her hands at her sides. She knew he wouldn't listen, yet she had to try. "Please, their injuries need to be treated."

Harrison laughed. "Don't be ridiculous. Once your sheriff and the whelp are dead, you'll be at my mercy. The way it used to be."

Libby shook her head. "No. I'm not going back with you. And if you kill them, I'll make sure you hang."

"You will return with me, whether you wish to or not."

"It's over, Harrison. You can't hurt me anymore," she asserted.

A muscle in Harrison's jaw jerked. "You can't escape me, Elizabeth. I own you."

"I'll never belong to you. If you kill Matt and Dylan, I'll find a way to get away from you."

"You're bluffing." Harrison's face contorted with anger.

"No, I'm making you a promise." Without Matt or Dylan, she would have no reason to live.

"I won't let you go. I *own* you. Nobody else would have you except me, and I gave you everything you wanted."

"You gave me nothing." She gazed up at Matt and his steady eyes met hers. The power of his love flowed through her, giving her strength. "Matt and Dylan are all I need."

"No! You're my wife, Mrs. Harrison Thompson. These people are nothing. Do you hear me? Nothing!"

Libby shook her head. "It's over, Harrison."

He turned and Libby became his target. "You owe

me for everything I've given you these past four years: my name, my wealth, my protection."

She stared up at the revolver aimed at her chest. She searched for a sign of fear within herself, but only regret tempered her acceptance of death. If only she and Matt had had more time. Libby took a deep breath. "You gave me nothing I wanted or needed, Harrison, and it was only you I needed protection from. Go ahead and shoot. I only ask that you spare Matt and Dylan. With me dead, there's no reason to harm them."

"I don't see any reason to leave witnesses, my dear," Harrison said. He thumbed back the hammer.

Libby's gaze wavered from the gun barrel, and she focused on Matt's cherished face. She wanted to weep for the pain she'd given him in exchange for his love, but there was no time left for apologies.

"Get down, Libby!" Matt shouted.

He streaked into motion and Harrison whirled toward him. Libby stared in horror as he aimed at Matt, but Matt's solid shoulder crashed into him, slamming Harrison against the wall. The smaller man tried to knee Matt in the groin, but missed and jabbed his thigh. Matt stumbled back, his heels dangerously close to the stairs. Libby gasped, her heart leaping into her throat. She started up the steps but stopped, torn between Matt and Dylan.

Matt gripped Harrison's wrist, keeping the weapon pointed to the side. Harrison squirmed and struck Matt a glancing blow to the jaw with his free hand. Matt's head snapped back and he grunted, but re-turned the punch. Harrison's slighter frame gave him more agility and he dodged Matt's knuckles. Unable to break free of Matt's hold, Harrison butted his head against Matt's chin and grabbed his upper arm, pressing his fingers into Matt's bullet wound. Matt groaned and drew back until the balustrade stopped him.

Libby shuddered, cold sweat covering her brow. One push and Matt would plunge to his death.

Using the heel of his hand, Matt forced Harrison's chin upward and the man retreated. Matt took advantage of his combatant's withdrawal to move away from the railing. Libby closed her eyes briefly and wiped her damp forehead with an unsteady hand.

Then Harrison attacked, ramming Matt back against the bannister. The wood cracked beneath his weight, and Matt exhaled noisily. Libby's fear tottered toward terror. Harrison pushed his forearm against Matt's neck, and Matt's back arched over the rail, emptiness gaping below him. Libby bit her lower lip. Matt's face reddened with the effort to gain freedom, and he grunted, exerting all his strength. His muscles, hardened by years of labor, gave him the advantage, and he pressed Harrison back. Abruptly lunging, Matt knocked Harrison to the floor and landed on top of him. As Harrison tried again to shoot him, Matt grappled for the weapon and it disappeared between their bodies. A muffled gunshot ended the scuffle—and the two men lay motionless.

"Matt!" Libby clutched her skirt and raced up the staircase, then dropped to her knees beside them. "No, Matt, you can't be dead! Dear God, please!"

Matt stirred beneath Harrison's limp form. He shoved Harrison's body aside, and Libby hastily helped him to sit upright. Sweat trailed down his face, and his chest was stained crimson. Libby touched the wet stickiness with shaking fingers. "Matt?" she quavered.

He shook his head. "It's his."

Libby glanced at Harrison. Scarlet liquid bubbled from a ragged hole in the left side of her husband's chest.

Libby threw herself against Matt, wrapping her arms around his shoulders. "I thought . . ."

He hugged her close. "Shhh. Everything's going to be all right now."

His warm caress and strong embrace assured Libby he was truly alive. She glanced at Harrison and placed a tentative hand on his neck. No pulse. She drew away and shuddered. "This time he really is dead."

Matt looked at the blood-covered body. "He can't hurt you again, Libby. Ever. How badly hurt is Dylan?"

Libby scrambled to her feet and helped Matt up. Her relief fled, and fear for Dylan's life engulfed her. "I need to examine him, but . . ." She paused. "I think he's got a compound fracture."

"What's that?"

Libby clasped Matt's calloused hand. "The leg bone has broken through the skin."

Matt's face lost much of its ruddiness. "In the war, they cut off the leg if the bone broke through. It was either that or die from infection."

Libby nodded. "I know. My brother told me about the horrible things he had to do in the tent hospitals." She squeezed his fingers. "But this isn't the war."

She hurried down the stairs ahead of Matt and knelt close to the boy. The detachment she usually possessed didn't emerge. Dylan wasn't merely a broken body, but a boy whom she loved like the child she'd never had.

"I have to splint the leg to make sure it doesn't rip the skin open even further." Her voice trembled.

A thin girl approached them. "Is he . . ."

"He's still alive, Becky," Matt said.

Libby looked at the timid young woman. "Becky?"

Her frightened doelike gaze settled on Libby. "Yes?"

"Could you find me a couple sticks about a foot long? And bring back a piece of cloth to tear into strips."

Becky scurried away.

Libby concentrated on removing the material from around Dylan's injury while Matt observed over her shoulder. "Where's Sadie?" she asked.

"Thompson broke her neck."

Libby pressed her lips together. She hadn't cared for Sadie, but no one deserved to die at Harrison's deranged hand.

Becky brought back two pieces of wood and gave them to Libby. She held up a bedsheet. "Will this do?"

"That'll be fine," Libby answered. "Rip it into strips."

Becky rent the cloth into the needed pieces.

Worry shaded Matt's eyes. "What can I do?"

"Hold the sticks on either side of his leg while I tie them in place," Libby replied. She concentrated on the task instead of Dylan's pale face. There would be time enough later for tears and guilt. She tied the lengths of cloth around the crude splint, and her fingers brushed Matt's hand.

"You can save him, Libby," he said softly.

She didn't deserve his faith. Because of her deception, two people had been killed, and Dylan might lose his leg.

"What happened here?"

She glanced up to see Eli dressed in his heavy wool coat.

"He fell down the stairs. He's got a broken leg and he's unconscious," she replied.

Eli squatted down and studied the red stain growing across the material holding the splint. His somber gray eyes narrowed. "It's a bad one."

"I know."

Eli glanced around. "Where's Thompson?"

"Dead," Matt replied flatly. "Sadie, too."

A whimper escaped Becky, who stood a few feet away.

"I see," Eli said simply. "By the looks of it, you didn't get off scot free either."

"This ain't nothing. We need to get Dylan over to your office."

"Is there something we can use to carry him?" Libby asked. "His leg has to remain straight."

Eli removed his long jacket and spread it on the floor beside Dylan. "Let's lay him on my coat and carry him over on that."

Libby stood and stepped back. Carefully, Eli and Matt transferred Dylan from the blood-soaked rug to the center of the overcoat. The ragged stuffed dog rolled out of Dylan's jacket to the floor, and Libby picked up the toy, hugging it close. Dylan's scent washed across her, and the barrier restraining her tears cracked. Why couldn't she have been the one at the bottom of the stairs, instead of Dylan?

"Are you all right?" Matt asked.

She nodded, unable to speak past the grief lodged in her throat.

Matt curved his fingers around her hand. "He'll be fine. He's got the two best doctors in the whole territory looking after him."

Libby looked up at the familiar contours of Matt's rugged face. She'd let him down, after all he'd given her.

"Give me a hand, Matt," Eli said.

Working in tandem, Eli and Matt lifted the coat with Dylan cradled in the middle.

Libby paused beside Becky and squeezed her hand. "Thank you."

"I'll send a couple of men over to take the bodies to Howard's," Matt said. He and Eli went through the doorway with their precious charge.

Libby hurried to the schoolhouse for her bag and met them at Eli's office, where Dylan lay on an examination table. His dark hair spilled across his pale face, and he moaned. Tears pooled in Libby's eyes, but she dashed them away with an impatient hand. Dylan needed her.

She edged between Matt and Eli. "Get me a pan of warm water." She glanced at Eli's puzzled expression. "I'm a doctor."

One corner of his lips quirked upward. "By God, I knew there was something special about you."

Matt hastened out of the room. Libby removed the crude splint and cut the trousers away from the injury. A pearly white bone jutted out below his knee, and blood continued to flow out of the open wound.

"I don't know, Libby," Eli said over her shoulder. "I've never been one to wait until the leg turns black before getting rid of it."

Libby stared at the more experienced doctor. "You think we should remove the leg immediately?"

"In all my years of practicing medicine, I only seen one person with a break like this keep his leg. The rest either lose it or die," Eli said grimly. He swore under his breath. "I don't want to do it, but we'll just be putting Dylan through a lot of needless pain if we wait."

"Ain't there some other way?" Matt demanded from the doorway, clutching a metal pan. He set the container of water on the counter and approached the unconscious boy. Matt laid a large hand on Dylan's still shoulder. "If you take Dylan's leg, he ain't going to be able to run or play ever again. He probably won't ever be able to set a horse either. A man needs both his legs if he's going to make anything of himself."

The anger and misery in Matt's tone echoed Libby's own feelings. How would she live with the guilt? And what would Dylan think if she removed his leg? Would he hate her?

Sternly, Libby halted her wayward thoughts. Her heart pounded in her breast and sweat coated her palms. "I think I can save the leg and Dylan's life."

Both men looked at her.

"We can clean the wound with carbolic acid, then we'll set the bone. As long as we keep the area free of dirt and dust, he'll have a chance," Libby explained.

"I read about that carbolic acid in one of the journals I got. You figure it'll work?" Eli asked.

"It's been used with success back east. I've got some in my bag." She opened the black case and removed a bottle of clear liquid. "We'll need to dilute it with some water."

"Eli, you in here?" Lenore called from the front of the office.

Libby didn't think she could maintain her composure if Lenore disrupted her. "Matt, could you keep Lenore company?"

Matt gazed at Libby, noting the dark circles beneath her eyes and the shaky posture of her shoulders. "All right."

He glanced once more at Dylan's too-still body and moved out of the room, closing the door behind him.

"Land sakes, Matt, I hope that blood isn't all yours," Lenore exclaimed.

He shook his head. "Most of it is Thompson's."

"Is he dead?"

Matt nodded. "He was going to kill Libby. Sadie's dead, too. Thompson got a little rough with her."

"What goes around, comes around, I say. Sadie done enough beating on poor little Dylan; she had a lot to answer for. It was bound to catch up with her sooner or later. Same with that husband of Libby's. I don't think I ever saw a slipperier character. I don't know how Libby ever got hooked up with the scoundrel. So what's going on in there? Libby didn't get hurt, did she?"

"No, not Libby. It's Dylan." Matt explained what happened. He swallowed hard. "Libby thinks she can save his leg."

Lenore's gaze drifted to the door barring them from

Dylan. "We have to hope for the best, Matt. There's no use in worrying about things beforehand. What's going to happen will happen, and you and I don't have much say in the matter." She removed her coat and rolled up her sleeves. "By the looks of it, some of that blood is yours."

Grudgingly, Matt removed his coat. By the glow of two lanterns, Lenore cleaned the flesh wound on his upper arm.

"One good thing's come out of this. You and Libby can get hitched, if you've still a mind to," Lenore said.

Matt shrugged and an arrow of pain shafted through his wounded arm. He grimaced. "I don't know if she'll have me."

"And why wouldn't she? She loves you, you thick-headed Texan!"

"I didn't believe her, Lenore. She told me Thompson lied, but I walked out on her, and look what happened. He damn near killed her, and Dylan might be a cripple because of me."

"Horse apples. All the bad that's been done is nobody's fault but Harrison Thompson's. *He* brought misery to good folks like you and Libby and Dylan. There's no use blaming yourself, when the real culprit will by lying in a pine box soon enough."

"That's easy enough to say, Lenore." If he'd trusted Libby, he could have prevented the damage Thompson had dealt out since he'd arrived. How could she ever forgive him for doubting her?

Despite Matt's protests, Lenore arranged a sling for his injured arm.

"There, that should take care of you," she said. "What do you say we have some coffee?"

Half an hour later, Matt poured himself a third cup of the bracing liquid and returned to his chair to continue his vigil. Lenore sat quietly, her hands folded in her lap, and Matt suspected she was praying.

Matt did some of that himself, hoping God hadn't forgotten who he was.

Finally, the door to the examination room opened and Eli appeared.

Matt stood. "How is he?"

Worry etched Eli's creased face and he shrugged his thin shoulders. "We cleaned the wound out like Libby said, and set the bone. She's got real steady hands. The next twenty-four hours will tell if he keeps the leg or not."

Matt's heart thudded in his chest. "But he'll live?"

The doctor's frown eased slightly, and he nodded. "He's a strong lad. I think he'll pull through."

"Can I see him?"

"Go on in. Libby won't leave his side."

Matt entered the examination room, where Dylan lay small and pale beneath several blankets. Libby stood over him, holding his hand. The front of her dress was stained with blood, and pride surged through him for the courageous woman he'd nearly lost.

"Eli says you done a good job," Matt said in a hushed voice.

Libby turned, and her face appeared drawn and haggard, as if she'd fought on the losing side of a battle. "I'm not sure if it's good enough." She blinked and the mask lifted for a moment to reveal her torment. She glanced back down at the boy . . . their boy. A few strands of auburn hair fell across her shoulders. "We'll have to wait to see if infection sets in."

Matt curled his fingers into a tight fist. "This never should have happened."

Libby paled, and tears filled her eyes. "I should be lying there, not Dylan. Harrison came here because he was after me. I knew what he was capable of doing. If I hadn't come to Deer Creek, none of this would've happened. Sadie wouldn't be dead, and Dylan wouldn't be lying there."

Her anguish twisted Matt's stomach into a knot, and he took a step toward her, but stopped short of touching her. "If you hadn't come to Deer Creek, Sadie might've killed him without anyone caring. You gave that boy love and a place to live where he didn't have to be afraid. *You* done that."

She blinked and rubbed the back of her hand across her eyes. *Had* she saved Dylan from a fate worse than he suffered now?

Matt cupped her chin in his palm and raised her face. "If you hadn't shown up here, I would've gone on lonely and bitter. You gave me and Dylan hope for a life filled with happiness." His voice gentled. "Don't you take that away from us, Libby."

She wanted to believe Matt's words. She wanted to believe his and Dylan's lives were better because she'd come to Deer Creek. She wanted to believe they had a future together.

Matt caressed her cheek tenderly. "When my wife died, I thought I was free of her, but deep down inside Rachel was still there. She kept saying no woman could ever love a man like me. And when Thompson first arrived, I thought you'd used me." He took a deep unsteady breath. "I doubted you, Libby. If I hadn't, I could've protected you and Dylan. Can you forgive me?"

Confusion mingled with disbelief. "But none of this was your fault."

Matt stepped back and ran his blunt fingers through his thick hair, gazing at her with grief-filled eyes. "Even after everything you gave me, I didn't trust you."

She swayed toward him, reaching out to lay her hand against his chest. "It's me who doesn't deserve your forgiveness, Matt."

Matt shook his head. "But I was the one who let you down."

From behind the wooden door, Eli's voice cut into their conversation. "Good God. Why don't you both just apologize?"

Libby gazed at Matt. Her fear lifted, and a smile twitched her lips. "I'm sorry for all the lies, Matt."

"I'm sorry for running away when you needed me most, Libby. I'll never leave you again. I promise." Gently, Matt traced the line of her jaw. His gossamer touch sent a shiver of longing coursing through her.

"Our demons can finally rest in peace," he whispered.

Libby nodded, unable to speak. The scents of bay rum and Matt enveloped her in a cloak of belonging.

"Miss O'Hanlon?" Dylan's voice was so weak Libby could barely hear him.

She moved to his side and laid her hand on his warm forehead, brushing his hair back. "Hello, sweetheart. How are you feeling?"

Dylan's nose wrinkled. "I feel like I been kicked by a mule."

Libby laughed gently and tears gathered in her eyes. "Not quite. Do you remember what happened?"

She watched him grope for the memories, and sadness touched his boyish face. "Ma's dead, isn't she?"

Libby opened her mouth, but the words wouldn't come.

Matt moved around to the other side of Dylan. "I'm afraid so, partner."

"What about Miss O'Hanlon's husband?"

"He's dead, too," Libby replied.

Silence permeated the room for a full minute, and Libby thought Dylan had fallen back to sleep.

"I know I should be sorry they're dead, but I'm not. They were mean," Dylan said hoarsely.

Helplessly, Libby looked to Matt. She didn't know how to respond to the boy's confession.

"It's not right to be wishing anybody's death," Matt said. "But at least they can't hurt you or Miss O'Hanlon anymore."

Dylan nodded somberly and moaned. "My leg hurts something awful."

"When you fell down the stairs, you broke it."

A hint of fear appeared on his pale face. "Will it be all right?"

"I think you'll be just fine," Libby assured him. She turned and picked up Dylan's ragged stuffed dog from a counter. She tucked it under the blankets, beside the boy. "Now you have to rest and get your strength back, so I can give you your Christmas present. You get to pick out your very own puppy."

Dylan's eyes widened. "Really?"

Libby smiled. "Really. But for now, your old puppy will have to keep you company."

He clutched the toy close to his chest and his eyelids drooped. "A real dog and a real family."

He fell asleep with a smile curving his innocent lips.

"He will be all right, won't he?" Matt asked.

Libby pulled the blankets snugly around Dylan and came around the bed to stand close to Matt. "We'll have to watch his leg closely for a while longer, but I have a feeling everything's going to work out fine. "

She cupped her hand around his whiskered jaw. He turned his face into her palm, and pressed his lips to the sensitive skin. "Thank you," he said, his tender tone caressing her.

Libby's heart pounded against her ribs.

"For what?" she asked breathlessly.

"For saving his life." He raised his head and whispered a tender kiss across her cheek. "And for saving my life. Don't you ever leave me, Libby O'Hanlon."

She looked up. Brandy-colored eyes glistened with a love so powerful it swept her breath away.

"Never," she vowed, and sealed the promise with a kiss filled with all of her tomorrows.

Epilogue

Montana
May, 1871

"**L**ooks like winter's last blow ended with a whimper," Lenore commented, with a glance out the cabin window. "Kind of like Adelaide's objections to the newest schoolteacher leaving."

Libby shook her head and smiled tolerantly. "How many teachers does that make since the first of the year?"

"Last count was five. George Johnson sure didn't waste any time courting Miss Meara. Two weeks of stepping out, and now they're hitched."

Libby placed the last of the disinfected medical tools in her black bag and shook her head. "Poor Mr. Pearson. He was so sure he'd get her to the altar. I feel kind of sorry for him."

"I thought you didn't like him. You said he was a lecherous old man," Lenore said with a puzzled look.

Libby shrugged, a mischievous smile on her lips. "Ever since I lanced that boil on his backside, he's treated me with the utmost respect."

Lenore laughed and slapped her round thigh. "I knew you'd settle right in after all the fuss blew over."

"By the way, you never did tell me how you got Mrs. Beidler to stop her gossip about Matt and me."

"Let's just say that we reached an understanding," Lenore said enigmatically.

Libby quirked an eyebrow upward, but recognized this was one piece of information Lenore wasn't about to impart. "Has Mr. Tanner moved to his ranch yet?"

"A couple more days and his cabin will be done. The boardinghouse is going to be a mite lonely."

Libby removed her white pinafore. "Not for long. Eli will be moving in next week."

Lenore reddened, but a saucy grin lit her face. "I figured if you could be a doctor and a wife, I could own a boardinghouse and be a wife, too."

The door opened and Matt strode in. Seeing Lenore, he stopped abruptly. "Afternoon, ·Lenore. What brings you out here?"

"Spring fever." She eyed the sheepishness in Matt's face. "Looks like the same thing brought you here." She leaned close to Libby and whispered, "Come on by the house tomorrow and I'll do those alterations for you." She winked. "Now's the perfect time to celebrate."

The twinkle in the older woman's eyes warmed Libby's face, but one look at Matt and her embarrassment fled. After five months of marriage, she still couldn't hide the pleasure his mere presence instilled in her. The door closed behind Lenore, and Libby crossed the room to be captured in Matt's strong arms. He tossed his hat at a wooden peg, but missed. He kissed her, and though they'd shared hundreds of caresses, she still lost herself in his embrace.

"Where's Dylan?" Matt asked.

"He and George Washington are out chasing squirrels," Libby murmured.

Matt grinned. "I wonder what old George would

say if he knew a mangy hound dog had been named after him."

Libby laughed softly. "You were the one who said he could name him anything he wanted, and it so happened he'd been studying the presidents. I'm just glad he didn't name him Royal Flush."

Matt sobered. "He did get to be quite a poker player those weeks he spent in bed, didn't he? Do you think he'll ever get over his limp?"

Libby shook her head. "It's hard to say. At least he didn't lose his leg."

Matt sighed. "You're right. Sometimes I look at him and wish . . ."

She squeezed his hand. "We can't change the past, Matt. We can only look forward."

He hugged her snug against his chest and Libby closed her eyes, listening to the steady heartbeat below his shirt. She wondered what he'd say when she told him. She'd been so afraid she wouldn't be able to conceive after . . . No, she wouldn't allow the memory of Harrison Thompson to spoil the joy of her surprise.

"I have something to tell you, Matt," she said shyly.

"You won't be home tonight because you have to help Eli deliver another baby?" Matt guessed with a hint of exasperation in his voice.

"Not exactly." She stepped back, took his hand in hers, and placed it on the curve of her stomach. "Eli will have to deliver this one alone."

Matt stared at Libby, his mouth agape. Regaining his senses, he whooped loud enough to raise the cabin's rafters. He picked Libby up and swung her around. Suddenly he stopped and set her down, his face filled with concern. "Are you all right?"

Libby laughed. "Don't worry, I'm not going to break. Women have babies all the time."

"Not mine." Wonder filled Matt's handsome face. "When?"

"Around Thanksgiving."

"A year after you came to Deer Creek and drew me back among the living," Matt commented softly. His tone turned solicitous. "Are you tired? Maybe you should lie down and take a nap."

"I have a better idea." She raised an eyebrow suggestively.

Matt chuckled. The low, deep sound turned Libby's insides to hot, thick syrup. "You're insatiable, Libby Brandon."

"You have no one to blame but yourself." Tenderness welled within her. "You've made me the woman I am today."

Matt nuzzled her neck and trailed his lips down her bodice. "I'll never get tired of loving you, angel eyes."

He clasped her hand and led her into the bedroom.

An hour later, Libby lay in the crook of Matt's arm. Contentment swelled within her. She'd found her knight in shining armor, hidden beneath a scarred soul. She'd rescued him. And he'd found the woman beneath the fear, and saved her from a life of cold emptiness.

Spring had blossomed in their winter hearts.

Avon Romances—
the best in exceptional authors and unforgettable novels!

Avon Romantic Treasures

Unforgettable, enthralling love stories,
sparkling with passion and adventure
from Romance's bestselling authors

SUNDANCER'S WOMAN *by Judith E. French*
77706-1/$5.99 US/$7.99 Can

JUST ONE KISS *by Samantha James*
77549-2/$5.99 US/$7.99 Can

HEARTS RUN WILD *by Shelly Thacker*
78119-0/$5.99 US/$7.99 Can

DREAM CATCHER *by Kathleen Harrington*
77835-1/$5.99 US/$7.99 Can

THE MACKINNON'S BRIDE *by Tanya Anne Crosby*
77682-0/$5.99 US/$7.99 Can

PHANTOM IN TIME *by Eugenia Riley*
77158-6/$5.99 US/$7.99 Can

RUNAWAY MAGIC *by Deborah Gordon*
78452-1/$5.99 US/$7.99 Can

YOU AND NO OTHER *by Cathy Maxwell*
78716-4/$5.99 US/$7.99 Can